各類
英文考試
適用

Grammar for Tests.
英文文法概念 總整理

柳澤尚 著　彭尊聖／鄭玉瑋 譯

修訂二版

2 weeks ago

It was a frog.

3 months later

It will be a prince.

now

英文真的很難嗎？

如果要用英文來說明中文的「書」這個字，你會怎麼說呢？你應該不會說：「『書』就是依一定的目的、文體所寫出的內容，然後將它抄寫下來或印刷出來，結集成冊的東西。」因為，英文中就有對應的 book 這個字了，所以只要簡單地說「『書』就是 book」就可以了。

那麼，如果要解釋「泡菜」，可以簡單地找到英文對應的字嗎？不行。因為英文中沒有對應泡菜的字。所以若要解釋泡菜，你就必須說：「泡菜就是一種用鹽來醃白菜、蘿蔔、海帶等，然後使其發酵而製成的一種食品。」因此要將泡菜的來龍去脈作「概念」式的解釋，而且裡面還有「醃」、「發酵」這些字，就必須要再對這些字多作說明了。

反過來說，如果要用中文去解釋英文單字，我們該如何說呢？我們會說：「book 就是『書』。」所以，只要套用中文所對應的字去解釋就可以了。在中文裡如果沒有相對應的字，你就必須要用「概念」來解釋。在英語裡，以 until 和 by 這兩個意思相似的介系詞為例，until 相當於中文「直到」的意思，所以解釋時可以說：「until 就是『直到』的意思。」；可是在中文裡找不到 by 的對應字，我們就只能解釋它的概念了。

要從頭了解一個生疏的概念，不是一件容易的事。英文裡還蠻多像 by 這樣的字，所以，學習英文時，除了要了解很多單字的概念外，還要了解現在完成式、不定詞、關係代名詞、假設語法等文法概念；英文句子和中文句子的表現方式也完全不相同，都要從頭了解。所以，每當我們遇到這些生疏的概念時，我們就將它們原原本本地記起來就對了。如果認為它們很難理解而不去記，或者只一昧地要從沒有對應的英文字裡，找出對應的中文意思，那麼，英文對我們而言，就是一種難學的語言了。

本書特色

本書主要說明「文法概念」。所謂的概念,對說明的人來說,不是一件容易的事;對想要理解的人來說,也不是一件容易的事。不過,爬再高的山也要從山腳開始爬起。將基本概念弄清楚,就是學英文最聰明的方法了。在英文文法中出現的被動詞、助動詞、關係詞、子句、不定詞和介系詞等,在中文裡是很陌生的概念,而且找不到對應的字,這是因為英文和中文這兩種語言在根本上就不同。因此,在學習英文的時候,與其在中文裡找尋對應的字詞,不如徹底理解英文最基本的概念,才是有效學習之道。

本書和坊間的文法書不同。本書在說明單元的重要概念之後,還附加了「圖表」再說明　次。也就是說,相同的內容先用中文解釋一遍,再用圖表幫讀者作整理和複習。將概念製成圖表,能讓人一目了然。

另外,每一章節後的「單元綜合問題」所收錄的題目,都是從多益、托福、國家考試等試題中所挑選出來的。除了讓讀者理解正確的英文文法概念,加以活用之外,同時還能準備考試。在「單元綜合問題」中,有一些較長的題目,因為這些題目兼顧了「句法」和「語意」這兩個層面。很多人都以為只要知道文法的句法、會解題,就可以應付考試,卻忽略了去理解句子含意的重要性。在目前各類考試的英文文法考題中,除了句法類的題目之外,語意類的題目也有一定的比重;而出現在本書「單元綜合問題」中比較長的題目,就同時兼顧了句法和語意。

本書是「基礎書」,也是「應考必備書」。在英文文法的所有概念中,本書只挑選最核心的、最基礎的部分來說明。

另外,在「單元綜合問題」中所收錄的題目,都是從眾多考試的考題中,考慮其難易度、正確性和出題頻率後,精心挑選出來的題目。無論你正準備什麼考試,或者是為了什麼目的而學英文,相信本文法書對你都會有極佳的幫助!

本書結構

◎用例句來說明英文文法概念

英文文法中出現的被動詞、助動詞、關係詞、子句、不定詞和介系詞等，在中文裡是很陌生的概念，而本書透過例句來說明這些概念，以增進讀者的理解。

◎用概念習題來確認學習

透過例句和圖表學習各單元的文法概念後，一定要做每頁下面的練習題。這能夠幫你確認自己是否真正理解各個單元的文法重點。

◎用圖表來作整理

各單元的文法概念說明之後，都附加「圖表」再說明一次。相同的內容先用中文解釋一遍，再用一目了然的圖表，幫讀者作整理和複習。

◎單元綜合問題

單元綜合問題所收錄的題目，都是從多益、托福、國家考試等考題裡嚴選出來的。所以本書除了可當作學習英文文法的「基礎書」之外，還可當作準備考試的「應考必備書」。

即使眼前還看不到未來，也確信它會實現——這就是一種「信念」。

每個人的心中都有夢想，但確信該夢想會實現的人卻不多。

本書就是獻給那些確信夢想會實現，並能在現實的浪濤中奮戰的年輕人！

CHAPTER 10

70 名詞關係子句：What

A
> The shop didn't have the thing **that** I wanted. 那間店沒有我想要的東西。
> The shop didn't have **what** I wanted. 那間店沒有我想要的東西。

B
> The shop didn't have **what** I wanted. 那間店沒有我想要的東西。
> I wanted to know **what** happened to Mike.
> 我想知道麥克發生了什麼事。

A 關係詞中，what 和 who、which、that 的層次完全不同。what 的特點是它裡面包含了先行詞。這兩個例句的意思完全一樣，所以可以看出「先行詞（the thing）＋ that ＝ what」的關係。what 裡面包含了 the thing。

因此，what 子句的「功能」也和其他關係子句不同，它時常是被當作「名詞」來使用。例句一，「that I wanted」是用來修飾前面的 the thing，具有「形容詞」的功能；例句一，「what I wanted」則是前面的動詞 have 的受詞，具有「名詞」的功能。要翻譯 what 子句時，前面被省略的先行詞也要翻譯出來，即「……的東西（名詞）」。

B what 子句的「形式」也和其他關係子句一樣。只要將「the thing that I wanted」中的 the thing 刪除，剩下的「that I wanted」，就跟「what I wanted」形式一樣了。that 是 wanted 的受詞，what 也是 wanted 的受詞。也就是說，what 是關係子句中的一個名詞，關係詞子句有它才是完全子句。

what 具有主詞和受詞的功能。例句一「what I wanted」中的 what 是 wanted 的受詞；例句二「what happened to Mike」中的 what，則是 happened 的主詞。

概念習題

1-8 空格中填入 that、which、what 其中之一，以符合句意。

1 I tried to understand _____ the foreigner was saying, but I couldn't.
2 I tried to understand the words _____ the foreigner was saying, but I couldn't.
3 Susan gives her children everything _____ they want.
4 _____ you have to think about is your profit.
5 Nirvana is the word _____ Hindus use to describe a sense of inner peace.
6 Water and petroleum are two liquids _____ occur in large quantities in nature.
7 An individual is presumed to be like _____ our society expects him to be.
8 From these beans, Europeans experienced their first taste of _____ seemed a very exotic beverage.

例句

以豐富的例句，導引出單元文法重點，並透過例句說明文法概念，幫助讀者活用文法。

概念習題

透過例句和圖表了解單元文法重點後，讀者可立即練習本習題，確認是否已真正理解單元文法重點。

	先行詞	關係代名詞	
特點	the thing	+ that	I wanted

what I wanted

	名詞功能		形容詞功能
功能	what I wanted	≠	that I wanted

完全子句

形式	what	I	wanted	what	happened to Mike	
	受詞	主詞	及物動詞	主詞	不及物動詞	個動詞片語

1. You must not believe all that you see. 不要盡信所見之事。
2. You must not believe what you see. 你不要相信你所看見的。
3. What Thomas is looking for is a job in advertising. 湯瑪士正在找廣告業的工作。
4. ~~That/Which~~ Thomas is looking for is a job in advertising.〔錯誤用法〕
5. I managed to get all the CDs that my son asked for. 我設法弄到我兒子要的 CD。
6. I managed to get all the ~~CDs what~~ my son asked for.〔錯誤用法〕
7. No one knows what will happen next. 沒有人知道接下來會發生什麼事。
8. No one knows ~~what it~~ will happen next.〔錯誤用法〕

9-11 選出一個最適合填入空格中的答案。

9 _____ is only a hot bowl of soup.
① That you need
② What is needed
③ That is needed
④ What you need it

10 This new style of painting needs our understanding of _____ painting should be.
① that
② any
③ the
④ what

11 Left hand does not know _____ .
① what is the right hand doing
② what is doing the right hand something
③ what the right hand is doing
④ what the right hand is doing something

圖表整理

以簡明的圖表解構文法概念或重要句型,單元文法概念先以中文解說,再以圖表說明一次,幫助讀者整理並加深印象。

● **單元綜合問題**

每章之後都有單元綜合問題,讀者可立即複習各章節文法概念,倍增學習效果;亦可作為考前模擬試題。

目錄

CHAPTER 1 動詞和時態 (Verbs & Tense)

CHAPTER 2 句子的結構和動詞 (Sentence Structure & Verbs)

CHAPTER 3 助動詞 (Auxiliary Verbs)

CHAPTER 4 主動與被動語態 (Active/Passive Voice)

CHAPTER 5 名詞和冠詞 (Nouns & Articles)

CHAPTER 6 代名詞 (Pronouns)

CHAPTER 7 形容詞和副詞 (Adjectives / Adverbs)

CHAPTER 8 介系詞 (Prepositions)

目錄

CHAPTER 1

動詞和時態
Verbs &Tense

1 動詞的功能和變化

A
John **speaks** Spanish fluently.〔正確用法〕約翰能說一口流利的西班牙語。
John ~~speech~~ Spanish fluently.〔錯誤用法〕

B
John **spoke** Spanish fluently. 約翰（那時）說了很流利的西班牙語。
John is **speaking** Spanish fluently. 約翰正在說著一口流利的西班牙語。
John has **spoken** Spanish fluently. 約翰已經說了一口流利的西班牙語。

C
play - play**ed** - play**ed** / play**ing**〔規則變化〕
speak - sp**oke** - sp**oken** / speak**ing**〔不規則變化〕

A 「動詞」是組成一個句子的關鍵要素。動詞位在句子主詞之後的第一個位置上，扮演連結句子的關鍵角色。在句子的動詞位置，若不放動詞，而放其他詞類，就是錯誤的句子。例句中的 speaks 是動詞，但 speech 是名詞。

B 動詞在句子中被使用時，會有許多形式的變化。「spoke」、「speaking」、「spoken」都是動詞 speak 的變化形，這樣的變化形再搭配 be / have，會形成十二種變化形式。這十二種動詞變化形式，稱作「動詞的十二種時態」。

C 除助動詞外，所有動詞都有「原型－過去式－過去分詞」和「現在分詞」，這些也就是十二種時態的基本。「現在分詞」就是「動詞原型＋ ing」，所有動詞都一樣。「playing」和「speaking」是 play 和 speak 的現在分詞。動詞的過去變化有兩種，一種是像 play 這樣「原型動詞＋ ed 的規則變化」（played, played），另一種是像 speak 這樣的「不規則變化」（spoke, spoken）。played/spoke 是過去式，played/spoken 是過去分詞。

 概念習題

1 在下表空格處，填上正確的字。

原型動詞	過去式	過去分詞	原型動詞	過去式	過去分詞	原型動詞	過去式	過去分詞
1 read			9		broken	17	cost	
2	caught		10	got		18		stolen
3		left	11		eaten	19 cut		
4	said		12	sent		20		took
5 laugh			13 buy			21		met
6		thought	14		lost	22 give		
7 bring			15 do			23		rose
8	went		16 know			24		heard

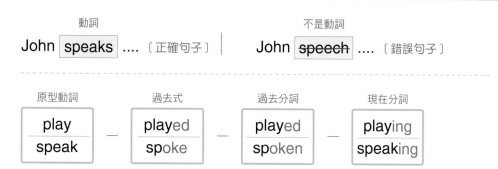

動詞
John speaks .... 〔正確句子〕

不是動詞
John speech .... 〔錯誤句子〕

原型動詞	過去式	過去分詞	現在分詞
play / speak	played / spoke	played / spoken	playing / speaking

▲ speak 的十二種時態

1. He speaks.   〔現在式〕
2. He spoke.   〔過去式〕
3. He will speak.   〔未來式〕
4. He has spoken.   〔現在完成式〕
5. He had spoken.   〔過去完成式〕
6. He will have spoken.   〔未來完成〕
7. He is speaking.   〔現在進行式〕
8. He was speaking.   〔過去進行式〕
9. He will be speaking.   〔未來進行式〕
10. He has been speaking.   〔現在完成進行式〕
11. He had been speaking.   〔過去完成進行式〕
12. He will have been speaking.   〔未來完成進行〕

▲ 不規則動詞舉例

原型	過去式	過去分詞	字義
cut	cut	cut	切；剪
hit	hit	hit	打（擊）
spread	spread	spread	使伸展
buy	bought	bought	買

原型	過去式	過去分詞	字義
begin	began	begun	開始
run	ran	run	跑
sing	sang	sung	唱（歌）
break	broke	broken	打破

2-6 選出括弧中最符合上下文者。

2 Pablo and Paula (giving, given, are giving) information to people at the job fair.

3 The look on his face (harded, hardened, hardnessed) suddenly.

4 The incidence of illness (differs, differences) greatly between men and women.

5 At least 300 staff will (lose, lost, loss) their jobs if the company closes.

6 New companies (experience, experiment) a lot of difficulty in their first few years.

·動詞和時態

2 現在式

A
Jim and Tom **take** a shower every morning. 吉姆和湯姆每天早上沖澡。

Tom **takes** a shower every morning. 湯姆每天早上沖澡。

B
The sun rises in the east. 〔真理〕太陽從東邊升起。

The adult mosquito usually **lives** for about thirty days.
〔一般事實〕成蚊通常有 30 天的壽命。

My father usually **goes** to work by bus. 〔重覆行為〕我爸爸通常搭公車上班。

Isabel works at the sports shop. 〔職業〕伊莎貝爾在體育用品店上班。

A 現在式的形式，就是直接用動詞「原型」即可。不過這時的原型不再叫做原型，而應該叫做**現在式**。而且，如果主詞是第三人稱單數，現在式必須變成「原型＋(e)s」。Jim and Tom 兩個人，是複數，所以用 take；Tom 是單數，而且是第三人稱，所以用 takes。「現在式」表現的內容是什麼呢？現在式並不是表現現在當前的情形，而是表現連接現在、過去、未來，持續、重覆的「普遍事實」。「Jim and Tom take a shower . . .」，並不是 Jim 和 Tom 現在正在沖澡，而是每天早上都會重複做沖澡這個動作的意思。

B 所謂現在式表現「普遍的事實」，具體地說，就是表現「真理、諺語、格言」、「一般事實」、「重覆的行為與習慣」、「職業」等。例句一「太陽從東邊升起。」不只適用於現在的事實，而是過去、現在、未來全都適用的普遍真理。例句二說明一般的事實，例句三說明重覆的行為，例句四說明職業。

概念習題

1-3 請依括弧內提示的動詞，填入適當的現在式。

1 He _____ (do) not make a lot of money, but he _____ (like) his job.

2 An eagle _____ (fly). It _____ (have) long, strong wings.

3 My sister _____ (be) a good singer, and I _____ (be) a good singer, too. My sister and I _____ (be) good singers.

4-5 選出一個最適合填入空格中的答案。

4 Neptune _____ about thirty times as far from the Sun as the Earth is.
① is   ② are   ③ was   ④ were

	不是第三人稱單數　現在式＝原型		第三人稱單數　現在式＝「原型＋s」	
形式	Jim and Tom	take	Tom	takes

含義	take a shower	「現在、過去、未來」每天沖澡

過去　現在　未來

		真理、諺語、格言	一般事實
用法	現在式	重覆的行為與習慣	職業

▲ be 動詞的現在式和縮寫

he is → he's　　she is → she's　　it is → it's　　Mary is → Mary's
I am → I'm　　there is → there's　　there are → there're　　you are → you're
they are → they're

1. The earth goes round the sun. 地球繞著太陽運轉。
2. Sue always gets to work early. 蘇總是很早去上班。
3. I usually drive to work, but sometimes walk.
   我通常開車上班,但有時會走路上班。
4. Sam is good at mathematics. He solves every problem.
   山姆數學很好,他解答了每個問題。
5. May and Dan are in the TV studio. 梅和丹正在電視攝影棚裡。
   * 在現在式中,經常會用到 always、usually、never、every day、every morning 等副詞。

5 In general, dogs and bees _____ unless offended.
　① are not bite　② did not bit　③ does not bite　④ will not biting　⑤ do not bite

6-9 下列句子若有錯誤,請改正。

6 Most factories in Korea today was safe.

7 Pablo're a teacher at the elementary school.

8 He goes on ski trips every winter with his friends when he lived in Canada.

9 Through history we all know parents always worried about their children.

3 現在進行式

A
> Jim and Tom **are taking** a shower right now. 吉姆和湯姆正在洗澡。
>
> Tom **is taking** a shower right now. 湯姆正在洗澡。

B
> He ~~is having~~ plenty of money but no style. 〔錯誤用法〕
>
> He **has** plenty of money but no style. 〔正確用法〕他很有錢，卻不體面。
>
> They **are having** prawn fried rice now. 他們正在吃蝦仁炒飯。

A 現在進行式的形式是「be 動詞＋動詞 -ing」，其中 be 動詞要用哪一個（is/am/are），由主詞來決定。「（right）now」常和現在進行式一起使用。現在進行式表示「現在正在做什麼」，是「現在這個時間點」正在發生的事。例句中，「are taking」和「is taking」是 take 的現在進行式，表示「現在正在沖澡」的意思。

B 動詞中表示「狀態」的動詞，不能以進行式表示。例如 have，是「擁有什麼」的意思，為最具代表性的「狀態動詞」，所以不能是進行式。但是如果狀態動詞不表示狀態，是表示「某一動作開始動作」時，就可以用進行式了；所以當 have 表示「吃」這個動作時，就可以用進行式。
英文的動詞，依其含義，可分作「動態動詞」和「狀態動詞」。這兩種動詞比較起來，**動態動詞較多表現動作的「一時性」**；狀態動詞則較多表現狀態的「永續性」。「進行式」表現的是**一時性**，不是永續性，所以進行式只能和動態動詞一起使用。

概念習題

1-4 選出括弧中最符合上下文者。

1 Scott (is, are, Ø) collects ancient coins.

2 Scott (is, are, Ø) collecting ancient coins.

3 Isabel (does, is) not work at her father's store.

4 Lots of young boys and girls (are dance, dances, are dancing) at the party.

5-6 選出一個最適合填入空格中的答案。

5 My little girl always wonders why the sun _____ in the east.

① rose   ② rises   ③ is rising   ④ will rise   ⑤ has risen

	複數	現在進行式	第三人稱單數	現在進行式
形式	Jim and Tom	are taking	Tom	is taking

含義	are taking a shower	「現在」正在沖澡

過去 ← 現在 → 未來

動作動詞

Tom │ is taking │ …. 〔正確句子〕

狀態動詞

He │ is having │ …. 〔錯誤句子〕

▲ 狀態動詞舉例（不可以用進行式）

be (成為)	**appear/look/seem** (看起來好像)	**believe** (相信)
know (知道)	**understand** (了解)	**like/love** (喜歡／愛) **hate** (恨)
have/own (有／擁有)	**hear** (聽)	**see** (看) **want** (想要)

1. Please be quiet. I am working. 請安靜。我正在工作。
2. The children are playing in the park. 孩子們正在公園裡玩耍。
3. The student is studying at school right now. 那名學生現在正在學校唸書。
4. The student studies at school every day. 那名學生每天都會去學校唸書。
5. I am reading my grammar book right now. 我現在正在讀我的文法書。
6. I usually read the newspaper in the morning. 我早上通常會看報紙。
7. I know Ms. White. 我認識懷特太太。
8. I am knowing Ms. White. 〔錯誤句子〕

6 Alice and Steve _____ to each other. I can't hear them.
① whispered ② whisper ③ are whisper ④ have whispering
⑤ are whispering

7-11 將括弧中提示的動詞，依照句意，換成現在式或現在進行式，填入空格中。

7 A: Where is Simon? B: He _____(cook) the dinner.

8 Ann _____(stay/always) home in the evening.

9 Alice _____(be) hungry right now. She _____(want) a sandwich.

10 At the market Nancy _____(look) at the pears. They _____(look) fresh now.

11 The students _____(talk) in French together for practice every day. Right now they _____(talk) in Chinese.

動詞和時態

4 未來式

(A) Susan **will/is going to** leave at 8:00 tomorrow. 蘇珊明天八點將會離開。

(B)
House prices **will** rise again next year.〔預測〕房價明年會再上漲。
They**'re going to** have a baby in the spring.〔預測〕他們將在春天生下寶寶。
I've asked her but she **will** not come.〔意志〕我問過她了，但她不會來。
I**'m going to** be a famous pop singer.〔意志〕我將成為知名的流行歌手。

(C)
I'll call you **when** I **get** home from work. 我下班回到家後會打電話給你。
I'll call you **when** I ~~will get~~ home from work.〔錯誤用法〕

A 「未來式的形式」為助動詞 will 和 be going to 後面接原型動詞，形成「will ＋原型動詞」或「be going to ＋原型動詞」。未來式是表現「未來」發生的事，所以在本質上就有「不確定性」。

B will 和 be going to 都有表示「預測」和「意志」的意思，但兩者本質卻有些差異。表示「預測」時，will 是指「普通」的預測；be going to 則指「確實」的預測。例句一，「房價會上漲」是普通的預測；例句二，「會生下寶寶」則是很有把握的準確預測。另外，表示「意志／意圖」時，will 是在「說話的這個時間點」決定的；be going to 則是在「說話這個時間點之前」就決定了。例句三，「她不會來」，是在說話的這個時間點，她所決定的；例句四，「我將成為知名的流行歌手」，則是在說此話之前就已經決定好了。

C 雖然是指「未來的事」，但以 when 為句首的條件副詞子句，不能用未來式，要用「現在式」代替。雖然 will call 是未來式，但後面的 will get 因位在 when 副詞子句中，所以要用 get。除了 when 以外，還有 if、before、after 等副詞子句，都要用現在式代替未來式。

1-3 選出一個最適合填入空格中的答案。

1 In the near future, the investors _____ him to get useful information.
① contact ② contacted ③ are contact ④ will contact

2 Mary: What have you bought these vegetables for, Peter?
Peter: I _____ make a large salad for dinner this evening.
① will ② will be going ③ am going ④ am going to

3 When I _____ Mr. Alvarez next week, I'll invite him to my party.
① will call ② am calling ③ called ④ call

表示未來的助動詞　　動詞原型

| 形式 | Susan | will / is going to | leave | ... |

預測	will: 普通的預測
	be going to: 確實的預測
意志	will: 說話這個時間點決定的
	be going to: 說話這個時間點之前決定的

未來式　　　雖然是未來的事，但用「現在式」表現

I | 'll call | you | when I get home from work.

▲ 不能使用未來式的連接詞

時間	**when** (當…時), **before** (…之前), **after** (…之後), **until** (直到…), **while** (當…時), **as soon as** (一…就…), **by the time** (到…的時候)
條件	**if** (如果…), **unless** (除非…)

1. The weather tomorrow will be warm and sunny. 明天天氣將是溫暖、有陽光的。
2. Today is Annie's birthday. I'll send her a card.
   今天是安妮的生日，我將寄張卡片給她。
3. Anita is going to sell her car. 艾妮塔將賣掉她的車。
4. Oh dear! The bus is leaving. I'm going to be late.
   哎呀！公車要開走了。我要遲到了。
5. I'll come as soon as I finish. 我辦完事就來。
6. Wait here until I come back. 在這裡等我，直到我回來。
7. I'll go to the party if you go too. 如果你也參加派對，那我就去。

4-10 選出括弧中最符合上下文者。

4　I (will fly, fly, flew) to Canada and have a rest in three years.

5　If it (rains, will rain) tomorrow, I'm going to go to a movie.

6　There isn't a cloud in the sky. It (is going to, will) be a lovely day.

7　I'll give you my answer when I (saw, see, will see) you Sunday afternoon.

8　Vicky: Do you have a ticket for the play?

　　Daniel: Yes, I (will, am going to) see it on Tuesday.

9　When I retire in two years, I (have worked, will have worked) for 30 years.

10　They won't get to the theater on time unless they (leave, will leave) at seven.

5 過去／過去進行／未來進行

A Tom **finished** college three years ago. 〔過去〕
湯姆三年前就已經完成大學學業了。

At night we **used to** go out with our friends. 過去每晚我們都會和朋友出去。

B David **was eating** breakfast yesterday at seven o'clock. 〔過去進行〕
大衛昨天早上七點鐘正在吃早餐。

C David **will be eating** breakfast tomorrow at seven o'clock. 〔未來進行〕
大衛明天早上七點鐘將會吃早餐。

A ⋯⋯「過去式」就是用**動詞的過去式**，表示和現在無關的「過去事實」。過去式常會出現表示過去時間點的字詞。如果用「used to ＋原型動詞」這個形式，表示更加強調已經過去了的意思。used to go 比起 went 更強調已經過去，以例句來說，就是「以前去，現在已經不去了」的意思。

B ⋯⋯「過去進行式」的形式是「was/were ＋ V-ing」，表示在「過去某一時間點」正在進行的事。主詞若為複數動詞用 were，主詞為單數用 was。

C ⋯⋯「未來進行式」的形式是「will be ＋ V-ing」，表示在「未來某一時間點」正在進行的事。過去進行、未來進行和現在進行一樣，都是動作正在進行，只不過發生的「時間點」不同。is eating 的過去式為 was eating，未來進行式則為 will be eating。

概念習題

1-3 選出一個最適合填入空格中的答案。

1 While Tony _____ his car, he discovered a dent in the door.
① washed ② was washing ③ is washing ④ washes

2 When you visit New York, _____.
① it is snowing ② it snows ③ it will be snowing ④ it will snowing

3 Born in Massachusetts in 1852, Albert Farbanks _____ to make banjos in Boston.
① begins ② began ③ is beginning ④ will be beginning

過去式的形式

過去式

Tom | finished | college three years ago.

We | used to go | out with our friends.

used to ＋原型動詞

過去式的含義

沒有任何關聯

finished

過去　　　　斷絕　　　　現在

進行式 形式／含義

過去的某一時間點　　現在　　未來的某一時間點

was eating　　is eating　　will be eating

1. Two students were absent last Friday. 這兩名學生上週五沒來上課。
2. The dinosaurs died out 65 million years ago. 恐龍在六千五百萬年前就滅亡了。
3. The Wright brothers were the inventors of the airplane. 萊特兄弟發明飛機。
4. It is 10 o'clock now. He is working.〔現在進行式〕現在是十點鐘，他正在工作。
5. At 10 o'clock yesterday he was working.〔過去進行式〕
   昨天十點鐘時他正在工作。
6. At 10 o'lock tomorrow he will be working.〔未來進行式〕
   明天十點鐘時他將在工作。
7. While two of the boys were changing the tire, the others stopped other cars on the road. 當這兩個男孩換輪胎時，其他人把車停在路上。
8. I was watching television when Chris called me.
   克莉絲叫我的時候，我正在看電視。

4-11 將括弧中提示的動詞，換成正確的時態填入空格中。

4 Janet _____(quit) smoking six months ago, and she looks much better.

5 Tom burnt his hand when he _____(cook) the dinner.

6 No, don't come between 7 and 8. I _____(have) dinner then.

7 My father _____(walk) to work every morning, but _____(take) a taxi yesterday.

8 Elizabeth used to _____(go) out every Friday night.

9 Now it _____(rain). I see Paul holding his umbrella.

10 While I _____(wash) dishes last night, I _____(drop) a plate.

11 I'll meet you at the airport this evening. After you _____(go) through customs, you can see me. I _____(stand) just outside the gate.

動詞和時態

6 現在完成式

A

Mom: Can I cook something for you? 媽媽：要我煮些東西給你吃嗎？

Son: I **'ve** just **eaten** lunch. I'm not hungry. 〔現在完成〕

兒子：我已經吃過午餐了。我不餓。

Mom: When did you eat? 媽媽：你什麼時候吃的？

Son: I **ate** half an hour ago. 〔過去〕兒子：我半個小時前吃過了。

B

I **have lost** my grammar book. 〔結果〕我把文法書弄丟了。

We **have lived** here for ten years. 〔持續〕我們已經住在這裡十年了。

Anne **has** already **gone** to bed. 〔完成〕安已經上床睡覺了。

I **have** never **been** to Mexico City. 〔經驗〕我從沒去過墨西哥市。

A 「現在完成式」的形式是「have / has ＋動詞的過去分詞」。eat 的現在完成式為「have/has eaten」。當「過去發生的事」和「現在」仍有關聯時；也就是說，過去發生的事，它的影響或動作會一直持續到現在，就用「現在完成式」。

何時該用現在完成式，何時該用過去式呢？過去的事，只局限在過去的時間，就用「過去式」；過去的事，不局限在過去的時間，仍和現在有關聯時，就用「現在完成式」。現在完成式中，不能出現表示過去時間點的字詞。以例句來說明，「have eaten」和「ate」都表示在「過去」完成了「吃」的這個行為。如果過去這個吃的行為，和「現在」仍有關聯，即「所以現在肚子不餓」，就要用「現在完成式」。如果將過去這個吃的行為「局限在過去」，即「半個小時前吃過」，就要用過去式。

B 若要更具體地說明和「現在的關聯」，就是：

（1）過去的事實，現在仍受它的影響。〔結果〕

（2）過去的事實，現在仍在持續。〔持續〕

（3）不管什麼時候發生，現在之前或過去，只看現在動作已經完成。〔完成〕

（4）表示到目前為止曾經做過或沒做過某事。〔經驗〕

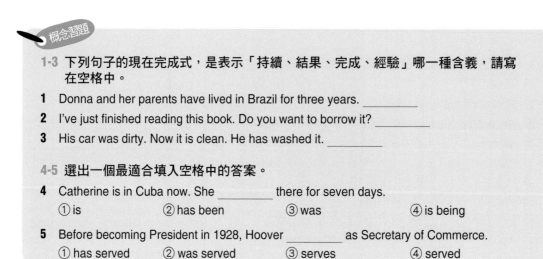

概念習題

1-3 下列句子的現在完成式，是表示「持續、結果、完成、經驗」哪一種含義，請寫在空格中。

1 Donna and her parents have lived in Brazil for three years. _____

2 I've just finished reading this book. Do you want to borrow it? _____

3 His car was dirty. Now it is clean. He has washed it. _____

4-5 選出一個最適合填入空格中的答案。

4 Catherine is in Cuba now. She _____ there for seven days.

① is　　②has been　　③was　　④is being

5 Before becoming President in 1928, Hoover _____ as Secretary of Commerce.

① has served　　② was served　　③ serves　　④ served

形式	I have eaten → have + 動詞過去分詞

含義	在過去吃了午餐 ——因此→ 到現在肚子不餓

用法	① 結果 — 過去發生的事，到現在仍受「影響」
	② 持續 — 某件事，從過去一直「持續」到現在
	③ 完成 — 現在之前發生的事，只看現在動作已經「完成」
	④ 經驗 — 從過去到現在的期間中，曾經或不曾「經驗」過

和過去式一起使用，表示「過去」的字	和現在完成式一起使用，表示「現在」的字
last, ago, in, yesterday	since, for, so far, recently

1. We've eaten all the eggs. 〔結果〕我們已經把蛋全都吃完了。
2. They've known each other since they were at school.
   〔持續〕他們在學校的時候，就已經認識彼此了。
3. We've just come back from our holiday. 〔完成〕我們剛度假回來。
4. Have you ever eaten caviar?〔經驗〕你吃過魚子醬嗎？
5. Jennifer has been in Mexico for two days. 珍妮佛已經在墨西哥兩天了。
6. We haven't had any problems so far. 我們目前沒有任何疑問。
7. Julia saw the Statue of Liberty last week. 茱麗亞上週看到了自由女神。
8. Jennifer arrived in Mexico two days ago. 珍妮佛兩天前抵達墨西哥。

6-9 將括弧中的動詞，換成正確的時態填入空格中。

6 The child _____(have) a fever all night, but he's better now.

7 The child _____(have) a fever since midnight. I'll take him to the doctor.

8 My son Robert _____(be/not) above the ground since his birth.

9 Ivan _____(bring) up four children to adulthood. Now they are all successful.

10-11 選出括弧中最符合上下文者。

10 His wife, Sylvia, has not smoked (for, since) a year now.

11 In the U.S., NASA has sent astronomers to space (in, since) the early 1960s.

7 過去完成式

A When I arrived at the party, Tom **had gone** home already.
當我們抵達舞會時，湯姆已經回家了。
Before he came here, John **had made** a lot of friends.
約翰在來這裡之前，就已經交到許多朋友了。

A 「過去完成式」的形式是「had ＋動詞過去分詞」，即把現在完成式中的 have / has 換成過去式「had」。
例句：「go」和「make」的過去完成式為「had gone」和「had made」。

英文文法中的時間點大致分成**未來**、**現在**、**過去**、**更過去**。「更過去」指「比過去還要之前」發生的事，
用「過去完成式」來表現。

例句一：「我抵達舞會」的時間是過去，動詞用「過去式 arrived」；而「Tom 回家」的時間比「我抵達」
還要更早發生，動詞用「過去完成式」had gone。

例句二：「John 來到這裡」的時間是過去，動詞用「過去式 came」；而「他交了很多朋友」的時間比
「來到這裡」還要更早發生，所以動詞用「過去完成式 had made」。

概念習題

1-4 選出一個最適合填入空格中的答案。

1 When I met him yesterday, he told me that his uncle _____ two weeks before.
　　① has died　　　② died　　　　③ had died　　　④ dies

2 I don't know Matt. In fact, I _____ him before.
　　① didn't meet　　② have never met　③ do not meet　　④ had never met

3 George didn't come to the cinema with us because he _____ the film twice.
　　① saw　　　　　② has seen　　　③ had seen　　　④ sees

4 Dylan looks younger and healthier than he did when I _____ with him in 1997.
　　① speak　　　　② spoke　　　　③ has spoken　　　④ had spoken

had + 動詞過去分詞

形式　Tom had gone home already.
　　　John had made a lot of friends.

含義

更過去　　　　　　　　　　　　過去

湯姆回家　約翰交許多朋友　　我抵達宴會　約翰來這裡
過去完成式　　　　　　　　　　過去式

▲ 過去完成式 = 現在完成式的過去式

My bag isn't here. I've left it behind. 我的袋子現在不在這裡，我把它留在原處了。
My bag wasn't there. I'd left it behind. 我的袋子不在那裡，我把它留在原處了。
Joe is not hungry. He has already eaten. 喬現在不餓，他已經吃過了。
Joe was not hungry. He had already eaten. 喬不餓，他吃過了。

1. It was twenty to six. Most of the shops had just closed.
   當時是 5 點 40 分，大部分的商店都已關門了。
2. I went to the box office at lunch-time, but they had already sold all the tickets.
   我午餐時間去售票處，但是票已全部售出。
3. I didn't go to the movie because I had seen it before.
   我沒去看電影，因為我以前已經看過那部電影了。
4. I felt really tired yesterday because Teresa and I had been to a party the evening before. 因為前天傍晚和泰瑞莎去參加一場派對，所以我昨天好累。
5. I was about twenty. I had been studying computer science for several years.
   我快二十歲時，就已經鑽研電腦科學好幾年了。

5-13 將括弧中提示的動詞，依照句意，換成過去式、現在完成式或過去完成式其中之一，填入空格中。

5　Jake went to Jill's house, but she wasn't there. She _____(go) out.
6　Jake went to Jill's house and talked for some time. Later she _____(go) out.
7　The man looked familiar. I _____(see) him somewhere before.
8　The man looks familiar. I _____(see) him somewhere before.
9　Somebody _____(break) into the house during the night.
10 When I got home, I found that someone _____(steal) my fur coat.
11 It isn't raining now. It _____(stop) at last.
12 Mr. Thomas _____(die) about ten years ago.
13 When Michael got to the party, Eric _____(already go) home.

動詞和時態

8 未來完成式

A

John **will have worked** here for a year next October.
約翰明年十月就在這裡工作一年了。

[John has worked here for eleven months. 約翰已經在這裡工作了十一個月。]

John **will have finished** his homework by 10 o'clock.
約翰將在十點前完成他的家庭作業。

[John has finished his homework now. 約翰已經完成他的家庭作業。]

B

John **will have finished** his homework by 10 o'clock.

John **will finish** his homework soon. 約翰就快完成他的家庭作業了。

A ···「未來完成式」的形式是「will have ＋動詞過去分詞」。「will have worked」是 work 的未來完成式，「will have finished」是 finish 的未來完成式。**完成式**含有「完成、完了」的意思。在完成式中，現在完成式的基準點是**現在**，過去完成式的基準點是**過去**，而未來完成式的基準點就是**未來**。未來完成式，以未來的某個時間點為基準，「到那個時候事情已經完成，或事情一直持續到那個時候」的意思。例句一：「John will have worked . . .」，以未來時間「next October」為基準，意思是「約翰一直持續工作到明年十月，就工作一年了」。例句三：「John will have finished . . .」，也是以未來時間「10 o'clock」為基準，是「到 10 點時，家庭作業就完成了」的意思。簡單地說，未來完成式就如同把現在完成式的時間改成未來一樣。

B ···「未來完成式」和「未來式」兩者要區分清楚。**未來式**是以「現在」的時間點，預言未來會發生的事；**未來完成式**則是以「未來」的時間點，預言未來會發生的事。在未來完成式中常會搭配使用 by . . .（到……時候）。例句二：「John will finish . . .」，表示在現在這個時間點預測未來會發生的事。例句一：「John will have finished . . .」，則是表示在未來的時間──到十點的時候，會發生的事；也就是說話者站在未來的時間點──十點所作的假設。

📝 概念習題

1-3 選出一個最適合填入空格中的答案。

1 Computers _____ over many of the jobs now.
　① took　　　　　② have taken　　　③ will take　　　　④ will have taken

2 After Ali returns to his country next month, he _____ working at the Ministry of Agriculture.
　① starts　　　　② has started　　　③ will start　　　　④ will have started

3 By 2100, the world's population _____ to around 30,000 million.
　① increases　　　　　　　　② has increased
　③ will be increasing　　　　　④ will have increased

will have + 動詞過去分詞

形式　　John　will have worked ...

含義

現在完成 → 現在

未來完成 → 未來

現在 ─預言→ 未來　未來式

未來完成式 ←預言─ 未來

1. The painting will have been finished by 4:15PM.
   下午 4 點 15 分之前將會完成油漆工作。
2. A: Will you have read this book by tomorrow? B: Yes, I'll have finished it by then.
   A: 你明天之前會讀完這本書嗎？ B: 是的，我明天前會讀完。
3. When they get there, the film will have already started.
   當他們抵達時，電影將已經開始放映了。
4. I hope I'll have won lots of prizes before I'm twenty.
   我希望在二十歲之前贏得很多獎項。
5. I'll have worked here for a year next September.
   明年九月，我就在這裡工作一年了。
6. Trevor and Laura will have lived here for four years next April.
   明年四月，特瑞福和羅拉就在這裡居住四年了。
   * 未來完成式常和 by、for 搭配使用。

4-11 將括弧中的動詞，換成正確的時態填入空格中。

4 Daly and Jim _____(know) each other for nineteen years now.

5 Next year Daly and Jim _____(know) each other for twenty years.

6 A: Honey, where are all the children? B: They _____(go) to bed already.

7 When Tom arrived home, the house was quiet. All the children _____(go) to bed.

8 Jim always goes to bed at 11 o'clock. Mary is going to visit him at 11:30 this evening. When Mary arrives, Jim _____(go) to bed.

9 According to the weather forecast, the rain _____(clear) by tomorrow evening.

10 The sun _____(rise) at 5:45 a.m tomorrow.

11 Chang came to the US from China nearly three years ago. Next Monday he _____(be) here exactly for three years.

1-10 選出一個最適合填入空格中的答案。

1 The Hawaiian alphabet _____ five vowels and only seven consonants.
① consist of
② consisting of
③ consistent of
④ consists of

2 The major cause of ocean tides _____ the pull of the Moon on the Earth.
① are
② is
③ have been
④ was

3 We are having a great time on our trip! I'll tell you all about it when I _____.
① get home
② will get home
③ get to home
④ will get to home

4 My son bought this bike two years ago and he _____ it every day since then.
① used
② am using
③ has used
④ use

5 The Chicago branch of the company _____ three years ago today.
① opens
② has opened
③ was opening
④ opened

6 By the year 2018, the information superhighway _____ accessible to all.
① will become
② will be becoming
③ will have become
④ will became

7 The ex-president _____ from cancer for years before he died last night.
① suffers
② is suffering
③ has been suffering
④ had been suffering

8 John and Mary are cleaning the house because they _____ a party.
① have
② are going to have
③ had had
④ will have

9 Give me back the book when you _____ it.
① have finished reading
② will have read
③ will finish
④ will have finished reading

10 By the time Steve and Alice had their first baby, they _____ for 5 years.
① were married
② will got married
③ have been married
④ had been married

11-16 閱讀下段文字，回答問題。

11 空格中分別填入動詞 bite 的正確形式。
（若有其他必要的字，也請填入。）

When my turtle _____ my older brother John, he ran around the house. And he fell screaming to the ground. So I whispered to my turtle, "I'd like to be your friend if you promise you will _____ my brother again."

12 下段文字中有一個錯字。請找出來，並且更正。

Ants use smell to mark a path to food.

Female butterflies attract male butterflies with a smell. And worker bees responded to the smell of the queen bee.

13 將括弧中提示的動詞，依照正確的時態填入空格中。

These days, almost everyone keeps at least one pet at home. But in most cases, carrying around a pet can be very troublesome. Don't worry anymore! An American company _____ (invent) a new product called Puppy Purse. It is a purse for your dog.

14 依據劃線部分「聽到後面跟著某人的腳步聲，就急忙地回家了」的意思，符合文意，將動詞 hurry 改成正確時態後，填入空格中。

It was a late summer night, and I (　　) home when I heard someone's footsteps following me. I walked very fast, but the sound of the footsteps was getting closer and closer.

15 選出劃線部分文法錯誤者。

I ① always enjoyed your class for the past two years. When I first ② came to you and ③ told you about my difficulties in your class, you ④ gave me words of encouragement I ⑤ will never forget.

16 將括弧中提示的動詞，依照正確的時態填入空格中。

In 1984, Bud and Michele finally _____ (establish) Global Volunteers, an organization that helps people throughout the world. Since then, they _____ (send) almost 13,000 volunteers to 25 countries.

① established – sent
② establish – have sent
③ have established – have sent
④ established – have sent
⑤ have established – sent

17-24 選出劃線部分文法錯誤者。

17 The professor ① with ② her assistants ③ having made some important ④ discoveries.

18 ① Have you ② study English verb tenses ③ when you ④ were in high school?

19 ① The discovery of "jumping ② genes" ③ has been made some thirty ④ years ago.

20 ① As he ② watched the TV program, Stephen ③ suddenly realized that he ④ saw it before.

21 When I ① will eat ② at that restaurant, I ③ 'm going to ④ have a big bowl of clam chowder.

22 ① John's grandfather ② has fallen ill, but he ③ is ④ much better now.

23 ① Despite many ② arguments, John ③ is still believing that men ④ are superior to women.

24 One of ① the greatest wishes of humans today is that we ② have discovered a cure ③ for cancer in the ④ next few years.

CHAPTER 2

句子的結構和動詞
Sentence Structure & Verbs

9 第一類句型 不及物動詞

A　Jane plays the piano beautifully. 珍彈奏美妙的鋼琴音樂。

B
John arrived. 約翰到了。
John arrived there. 約翰到那裡了。
John arrived at the party. 約翰到舞會會場了。

A 英文的句子是由**主詞、動詞、受詞、補語、修飾詞**五個構成句子的元素所組成。有些長句具備這五個元素，也有只具備其中某幾個元素的短句。這五個構成句子的元素，組成句子時，排列方式有一定的規則。

這五個元素在所有句子的排列順序，最先都是「主詞＋動詞」，之後有的接「受詞」，有的接「補語」，而「修飾詞」則是看狀況插在中間。主詞、動詞、受詞、補語是句子的必需部分，它們決定了「句子的結構」。尤其受詞和補語的組合，是決定句子結構的關鍵性因素，而它們又受到前面動詞的影響，所以句子的結構是依「動詞的種類」來決定的。

例句一最前面的「Jane」是**主詞**，位在第二位的是**動詞**「plays」，動詞後面的名詞「the piano」是**受詞**，句子最後的副詞「beautifully」，是修飾動詞的**修飾詞**。

B 動詞最重要、最基本的兩大類為「不及物動詞」和「及物動詞」。arrive 是「到達」的意思，意思很完整，所以其後不接名詞，像這樣的動詞稱作**不及物動詞**。

只需主詞和不及物動詞就可完成的句型，稱為「第一類句型」。第一類句型的基本結構是「主詞＋動詞」。構成第一類句型的必需要素只有**主詞**和**動詞**，後面不接受詞或補語，也就是說，不接任何名詞或形容詞。不過表時間或地點的「副詞」或「介系詞＋名詞」，可依情況使用，例句中的「there」和「at the party」就是表地點的副詞。

要注意的是，不及物動詞後面可以接「介系詞＋名詞」，但絕對不能直接接「名詞」。

1-8 選出括弧中最符合上下文者。

1 A terrible earthquake occurred (in, Ø) Turkey.

2 Everyone in the office sat (on, Ø) the floor.

3 He apologized (to, Ø) his girlfriend.

4 Mr. Brooke came (to, Ø) the airport to meet (with, Ø) Mrs. Castle.

5 I want to lie (on, Ø) the beach in the sun.

6 I walked (to, Ø) a street corner and waited (for, Ø) the school bus.

7 Anthropologists research (about, Ø) the habits of people living in the past.

8 The author wrote (about, Ø) many books. He wrote (about, Ø) poor people living in the suburbs.

	主詞	動詞	受詞	修飾詞
句子	Jane	plays	the piano	beautifully
	位在句子最前面	位在句子第二位	動詞後的名詞	句子最後的副詞

主詞	不及物動詞		
Jane	arrived	Ø.	沒有名詞／形容詞
		there.	副詞
		at the party.	介系詞＋名詞

1. Your views do not matter. 你的看法不重要。
2. Nothing happened. 什麼事都沒發生。
3. He lay down on the sofa. 他躺在沙發上。
4. Headaches usually occur at night. 頭痛通常發生在夜晚。
5. A woman appeared at the far end of the street. 一個女人出現在遠遠的街尾。

▲ 不及物動詞舉例

apologize (道歉)	appear (出現)	arrive (到達)	come (來)
die (死去)	disappear (消失)	fall (掉落)	go (去)
graduate (畢業)	happen (發生)	hesitate (遲疑)	lie (說謊/躺)
listen (聽)	live (住)	matter (有關係)	object (反對)
occur (發生)	participate (參加)	remain (維持)	sleep (睡覺)
rise (上升)	wait (等待)		

9-11 選出一個最適合填入空格中的答案。

9 The red balloon _____ gently into the air.
　① rise　　　　② rose　　　　③ raise　　　　④ raised

10 Every student in the class is going to participate _____ in these discussions.
　① active　　　② activity　　　③ actively　　　④ act

11 Lorma _____ medical school last year.
　① graduates　　② graduated　　③ graduation of　　④ graduated from

10 第二類句型 不完全不及物動詞和「There ＋ be ＋名詞」句型

A
- Sam **is** angry. 山姆生氣了。
- Sam **is** a chairman. 山姆是會長。
- Sam is ~~angrily~~. Sam is ~~anger~~.〔錯誤用法〕

B
- **There is** a picture **in my room.** 我房間裡有一幅畫。
- **There are** five pictures **in the classroom.** 教室裡有五幅畫。
- ~~A picture is~~ **in my room.**〔錯誤用法〕

A **be** 動詞是「是什麼」、「是如何」的意思，所以它後面一定要接「什麼」、「如何」，這樣句子才完整，而「什麼」、「如何」稱作補語。需補語補充說明的動詞叫做「不完全不及物動詞」，由**不完全不及物動詞**構成的句子叫做「**第二類句型**」。

第二類句型的基本結構是「主詞＋動詞＋補語」。補語的位置大致上放「名詞」或「形容詞」，除非有特殊情況，一般來說不能接「副詞」。形容詞和名詞用來補充說明主詞，動詞則連接主詞和補語。不完全不及物動詞也稱作「連綴動詞（linking verb）」。

例句中的形容詞「angry」和名詞「a chairman」用來補充說明主詞「Sam」；而「angrily」是副詞，所以不能放在補語的位置。

補語用名詞還是形容詞，要區分清楚。例句一：「Sam is angry.」是正確的表現方式；若變成「Sam is anger.」就錯了，因為如果用名詞「anger」，就表示 Sam ＝ anger（山姆是憤怒），顯然不合理。

B 當要表現「那裡有什麼或存在什麼」時，即「無生命的有」，就要用「there ＋ be ＋名詞（主詞）」的句型。這種句型的特點是主詞放在 be 動詞之後，所以主詞決定 be 動詞。以例句來說明，「a picture」是單數，所以 be 動詞用「is」；「five pictures」是複數，所以 be 動詞用「are」。

「there is . . .」這樣的形式，一定要放在主詞 a picture 的前面，也就是放在句子的最前面；如果把 a picture 放在最前面，變成「A picture is in my room.」是錯誤用法。

概念習題

1-10 選出括弧中最符合上下文者。

1 He appeared (sudden, suddenly) in the doorway.

2 Life appears (joyless, joylessly).

3 Sandstone cuts (easy, easily).

4 Mary looks (beautiful, beautifully, beauty) in her dress.

5 There (remain, remains) considerable doubt over the program.

6 It may sound (like strange, strange, strangely).

7 The new washing machine works (smooth, smoothly).

8 There (seem, seems) to be some difficulty in fixing a date for the meeting.

主詞 ‧ 不完全不及物動詞 ‧ 補語

Sam | is | angry. (形容詞)
a chairman. (名詞)

補充

Sam | is | ~~angrily.~~ 副詞
Sam | is | ~~anger.~~ 抽象名詞

決定

There
There | is
are | be 動詞 | a picture
five pictures | 主詞

決定

▲ 不完全不及物動詞舉例

be (是)	appear/seem (出現/似乎)
become/grow (變成/成長)	feel (感覺到)
look (看)	keep/remain (保持/維持)
smell (聞起來)	sound (聽起來)

1. These are my favorite pictures. 這些是我最喜愛的照片。
2. The boys seem happy. 男孩們似乎很開心。
3. The metal felt smooth and cold. 這塊金屬感覺很光滑、冰涼。
4. That sounds arrogant, doesn't it? 那聽起來很自大，不是嗎？
5. There is an elevator in the building. 這棟大樓裡有座電梯。
6. Look! There has been a rainbow in the sky. 看！天空出現彩虹。
7. There remains one matter still to be discussed. 還有件重要的事仍要討論。
8. There appears to be a lack of communication. 看來是缺乏溝通。
   * there 後的 be 動詞，也可以換成 remain、appear、seem 等動詞。

9 An employee may feel (discomfort, uncomfortable) because of his or her gender.

10 (There, It) is a red car outside the house. / (There's / It's) mine.

11-12 選出一個最適合填入空格中的答案。

11 The president kept _____ during the conference.
① silently   ② silence   ③ in silence   ④ silent

12 There _____ many people at the party last Saturday.
① are   ② seem   ③ were   ④ have been

句子的結構和動詞

11 第三類句型 及物動詞

A ─[I **caught** a big fish. 我抓到一隻大魚。

B ─[I waited **for** the reply. 我等待回覆。
We discussed ~~about~~ the matter.〔錯誤用法〕

A ─ catch 是「抓住……」的意思，後面一定要接名詞，才能表示抓住某東西。這個完全受到動詞影響的名詞稱作動詞的「受詞」，而這樣的動詞則稱作「及物動詞」。用及物動詞組成的句子形式，稱為「第三類句型」，它的基本結構是「主詞＋動詞＋受詞」。

B ─ 前面解說不及物動詞時，提到不及物動詞可接「介系詞＋名詞」，但及物動詞後只可接名詞，也就是只能用名詞當它的受詞。包含不及物動詞的句型為「不及物動詞＋介系詞＋名詞」；包含及物動詞的句型為「及物動詞＋受詞」。例句中的「waited」是不及物動詞，所以後面要接介系詞「for」；而「discuss」是及物動詞，所以後面不能接介系詞 about。

因為關係到介系詞的有無，所以區分清楚動詞是及物動詞，還是不及物動詞，這點是很重要的。「不及物動詞＋介系詞」的例句，請參考 Unit 14「動詞＋介系詞」。

 概念習題

1-3 選出一個最適合填入空格中的答案。

1 We finally _____ London on Tuesday morning.
 ① reached in ② arrived in ③ got ④ reached at

2 A number of foreign workers _____ the country without permission.
 ① enters ② enter into ③ entered ④ enters to

3 Harold _____ down on the sofa and raised his feet for an hour or more.
 ① lie ② lay ③ lies ④ lays

及物動詞	受詞：名詞 / 代名詞
I caught	+ a big fish .

不及物動詞	介系詞		及物動詞	介系詞	
I waited	for	the reply	discussed	~~about~~	the matter.

▲ 及物動詞舉例

afford (買得起), allow (允許), blame (責備), bring (帶), catch (抓住), deny (否定), enjoy (享受), examine (檢查), excuse (原諒), fix (修理), greet (問候), have (有), hit (打), inform (通知), interest (使……產生興趣), invite (邀請), lay (置放), like (喜歡), make (做), mean (意指), need(需要), raise (舉起), rob (搶劫), seat (使……就座), surround (圍繞), thank (謝謝)

1. Children like cookies. 小朋友喜歡餅乾。
2. He desperately needed money. 他急需錢。
3. John is holding a pen in his hand. 約翰手上正拿著一支筆。
4. Egypt has hot summers and mild winters. 埃及夏天很炎熱，冬天很暖和。
5. I'm looking at these photos. They're really good. 我正在看這些照片，拍得很好。
6. Listen to this music. It's great! 聽聽這音樂，很棒呢！
7. Jane answered ~~to~~ the question. 珍回答了這個問題。
8. He entered ~~into~~ the room briskly. 他迅速地進入房間。
9. He reached ~~at~~ the door. 他抵達門口。

▲ 不能寫成「及物動詞＋介系詞」的例子

accompany ~~with~~ (陪同……), answer ~~to~~ (回答……), attend ~~to~~ (出席……), enter ~~into~~ (進入……), marry ~~with~~ (和……結婚), mention ~~about~~ (提及…..), reach ~~at~~ (抵達……), resemble ~~with~~ (類似……)

4 選出文法錯誤的句子。

① The twins had a dreadful quarrel. They won't even talk to each other.
② Clive disappeared from a room by himself.
③ I called you earlier, but nobody answered to the phone.
④ No matter how he tried, Kelvin couldn't think of her name.

5-7 劃線部分正確寫 T，錯誤寫 F。

5 My sister wants to <u>marry with</u> a rich man.

6 She must <u>invite</u> Susan and Tom for dinner.

7 Elementary school students generally <u>attend to</u> special art and music classes.

12 第四類句型 授與動詞

A ─ He **gave** Melanie some flowers. 他給了梅蘭妮一些花。

B ─
He **gave** some flowers **to** Melanie. 他給了梅蘭妮一些花。
He **bought** some flowers **for** Melanie. 他買了一些花給梅蘭妮。
He **asked** a question **of** another person. 他問了另一個人一個問題。

A give 這個動詞有「給某對象什麼東西」的意思,所以後面應該要有給的「對象」和給的「東西」兩個受詞。例句中第一個接的受詞,是給的「對象」,指的是受惠者「Melanie」,主要是指人的名詞,稱作**間接受詞**;第二個接的受詞,是給的「東西」,指直接給出去的東西「some flowers」,主要是指事物的名詞,稱作**直接受詞**。後面要接兩個受詞的動詞稱作「授與動詞」。由授與動詞所組成的句型是「第四類句型」,它的基本結構是「主詞+動詞+間接受詞+直接受詞」。

B 第四類句型的特點是「間接受詞前加**介系詞**」。可使用的介系詞有 to、for、of,該使用哪一個介系詞,完全由**動詞**決定。例如:「give + to」、「buy + for」、「ask + of」。

概念習題

1 選出不能填入空格中的答案。

I'll _____ my brother the picture.
① send　　　　② give　　　　③ remind　　　　④ show

2-3 選出一個最適合填入空格中的答案。

2 The teacher _____ the student the answer to the problem.
① said　　　② told　　　③ talked　　　④ mentioned

3 We bought ice cream _____ all the children.
① to　　　② of　　　③ for　　　④ with

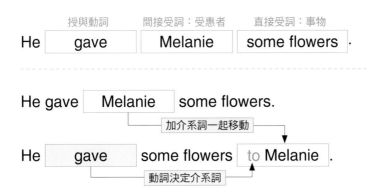

▲ 授與動詞舉例

間接受詞 加「to」一起移動	bring (帶), give (給), lend(借), offer (提供), sell (賣), send (寄), show (展示), teach (教), tell (告訴)
加「for」一起移動	buy (買), make (做), spare (讓出)
加「of」一起移動	ask (問)

1. I showed the man my ticket. 我給那個人看我的票。
2. I showed my ticket to the man at the door. 我給在門口的那個人看我的票。
3. John offered Mary some help. 約翰提供了瑪莉一些幫助。
4. John offered some help to Mary. 約翰提供了瑪莉一些幫助。
5. Will you make me a cup of coffee? 你要煮杯咖啡給我嗎？
6. Will you make a cup of coffee for me? 你要煮杯咖啡給我嗎？

4 選出文法正確的句子。
① Could you make some coffee to us?
② Well, actually, my parents lent to me the money.
③ You should ask a question of another person.
④ I created my daughter a doll's house.
⑤ Fine, someone has offered a job for me.

5-7 下列句子若有錯誤，請改正。
5 John explained me the rule of the game.
6 I showed to the officer my driver's license.
7 I had to describe the doctor my symptoms.

13 第五類句型 不完全及物動詞

A
> They **made** Bob angry. 他們惹鮑伯生氣。
>
> They made Bob ~~angrily~~. 〔錯誤用法〕
>
> They've always **called** him Johnny. 他們總是叫他強尼。

B
> They made Bob **angry**. 〔第五類句型〕他們惹鮑伯生氣。
>
> He read the letter **angrily**. 〔第三類句型〕他看那封信看得很火大。

A make 是「使……變成……狀態」的意思,所以動詞後面要接「使什麼」變成「什麼狀態」兩個部分。**受詞**和**受詞補語**兩者都需要的動詞叫做「不完全及物動詞」。由不完全及物動詞所組成的句型,是「第五類句型」。

第五類句型的基本結構是「主詞+動詞+受詞+受詞補語」。這裡的**受詞補語**和第二類句型(不完全不及物動詞)的主詞補語一樣,可以是**名詞或形容詞**;除非有特殊情況,一般來說不能為**副詞**。

受詞補語的功能為補充說明受詞。例句「…Bob is angry」的「angry」補充說明「Bob」;「...him Johnny」「Johnny」補充說明「him」,這樣的關係就像第二類句型的「主詞+主詞補語」一樣。

B 第五類句型和第三類句型(及物動詞)的差別在補語的詞類不同,第三類句型的補語是**副詞**,用來修飾動詞;而第五類句型的補語是**形容詞或名詞**,用來補充說明受詞。兩句的含義完全不同。angry 是指「讓鮑伯變成生氣的」,angrily 是指「他生氣地……」。

概念習題

1-2 辨明兩句的差異,並將句子翻譯成中文。

1　① Finally I found the book easy.　_____

　　② Finally I found the book easily.　_____

2　① She made her daughter a new dress.　_____

　　② She made her daughter a doctor.　_____

3-4 選出一個最適合填入空格中的答案。

3　They also organize their day-to-day life _____.

　　① careful　　　② care　　　③ carefully　　　④ carefulness

▲ 不完全及物動詞舉例

| appoint (指派), | call (叫), | consider (考慮), | elect (選舉), |
| find (發現⋯⋯處於某種狀態), | keep (保持), | leave (離開), | make (做) |

1. Flowers make our rooms cheerful. 鮮花讓我們的房間生氣盎然。

2. The noise kept him awake. 噪音讓他保持清醒。

3. You'll find it exciting. 你將會發現它很刺激。

4. They called him foolish / a fool. 他們叫他傻瓜。

5. The country elected a woman (as) its new president.
   這個國家選了一位女性為新任總統。

4 The sedative makes people _____.
① sleep   ② sleepily   ③ sleeplessness   ④ sleepy

5-9 下列句子若有錯誤，請改正。

5 My boyfriend called me a fat slob.

6 I had always considered myself as a strong woman.

7 At the federal court they found him guilty of murder.

8 He made the platform strongly enough to hold ten men.

9 The new law has left many people poor.

句子的結構和動詞

14 「動詞＋介系詞」和「動詞＋介系詞型副詞」

A The plane **touched down** ten minutes ago. 〔不及物動詞＋副詞〕
這架飛機十分鐘前降落了。

B She **looked after** the baby. 〔不及物動詞＋介系詞〕她照顧寶寶。

C They **turned on** the light. 〔及物動詞＋副詞〕他們開燈。
They **turned** the light **on**.

D The police **accused** him **of** murder. 〔及物動詞＋介系詞〕警方指控他謀殺。

觀察句子中的動詞型態，你會發現，很多時候只有一個動詞而已，不過「動詞＋介系詞」或「動詞＋介系詞型副詞」的情形也不少。所謂的「介系詞型副詞」，就是介系詞後面不接受詞，就一個**介系詞**而已，這時不能稱它為介系詞，要叫介系詞型副詞，屬於**副詞**。也就是說，一個介系詞的後面不接「受詞」，就是**介系詞副詞**；反之，接「受詞」，就是介系詞。

動詞加介系詞或介系詞型副詞之後，又衍生出許多含義。舉例來說，動詞 give 的基本意思是「給」，give in 卻是「提出、讓步」的意思；give up 是「放棄」的意思；give off 是「發散」的意思。

A touch down 是「不及物動詞＋副詞」的形式，不能接「受詞」，所以「ten minutes ago」是**副詞**。簡單的說，就是把「不及物動詞＋副詞」視為一個整體，當**不及物動**詞用。

B look after 是「不及物動詞＋介系詞」的形式，要接「受詞」，所以「the baby」是**受詞**，把「不及物動詞＋介系詞」視為一個整體，當**及物動**詞用。這部分可參閱 Unit 11 的「第三類句型」說明。

C turn on 是「及物動詞＋副詞」的形式，要接「受詞」，所以「the light」是**受詞**，把「及物動詞＋副詞」視為一個整體，當**及物動**詞用。這時 the light 不是「on」的受詞，而是「turn」的受詞，所以也可以把 the light 寫在 turn 和 on 之間。

D accuse . . . of . . . 是「及物動詞＋受詞＋介系詞＋受詞」的形式，及物動詞和介系詞後面都要接「受詞」。要注意的是，「及物動詞＋介系詞」，被當作慣用語用。

1-8 在提示的介系詞中，挑選一個最合適的填入空格中。（不能重複使用）

of	off	to	out	up	as	with	in

1 You must not complain _____ your food. （抱怨）

2 We're listening _____ a play on the radio. （聽）

3 All the students should hand their essays _____. （提交）

4 Compare this busy road _____ ours. （比較）

5 I couldn't make the symbol _____ at all. （理解）

6 I have to put _____ the exam. （延後）

7 I regard creativity _____ a gift. （視為）

8 The detective did not give _____ the chase. （放棄）

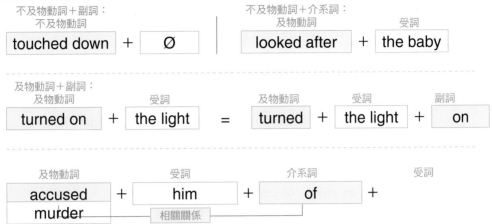

不及物動詞＋副詞： 不及物動詞			不及物動詞＋介系詞： 及物動詞			受詞

不及物動詞＋副詞： 不及物動詞 `touched down` ＋ `∅`

不及物動詞＋介系詞： 及物動詞 `looked after` 受詞 ＋ `the baby`

及物動詞＋副詞： 及物動詞 `turned on` 受詞 ＋ `the light` ＝ 及物動詞 `turned` 受詞 ＋ `the light` 副詞 ＋ `on`

及物動詞 `accused` 受詞 ＋ `him` 介系詞 ＋ `of` 受詞 ＋ `murder` 相關關係

1. I usually get up late on Sundays. 我每逢週日都晚起。
2. Sue was very late because her car broke down. 蘇的車子拋錨，所以嚴重遲到。
3. We're just talking about Jack's new job. 我們正在談論傑克的新工作。
4. You can always depend on Simon in a crisis. 遇到危急時，你可以信賴賽門。
5. Melanie took off her coat. = Melanie took her coat off. 馬蘭妮脫掉大衣。
6. The fire fighters put out the fire. = The fire fighters put the fire out.
   救火員滅了大火。
7. Jim didn't borrow any money from the bank. 吉姆沒向銀行借錢。
8. The lawyer explained the new law to the people. 這位律師向大家解釋新法律。

▲ 在 C 類型中，受詞是代名詞時，受詞一定要置於動詞和副詞之間。

√ They turned it on.	X They turned on it.
√ The fire fighters put it out.	X The fire fighters put out it.

9-12 選出一個最適合填入空格中的答案。

9 How did they dispose _____ the body?
① with ② in ③ to ④ of

10 They accused the watchman _____ negligence.
① for ② with ③ of ④ on

11 Some miners called for a strike, but the union _____ at the last minute.
① called off it ② called off them ③ called it off ④ called them off

12 The factory replaced most of its workers _____ robots.
① with ② at ③ to ④ of

圖表整理

「動詞＋介系詞」&「動詞＋介系詞型副詞」舉例

A 類型	break down (失敗), break out (爆發), come about (發生), come in (到達), eat out (到餐廳吃飯), die out (逐漸消失), drop in (順便拜訪), fall down (失敗), get along (和睦相處), get/wake up (起床／醒來), go on (繼續), grow up (長大), hang up (掛斷電話), look/watch out (小心), settle down (安頓下來), show up (出現), stand out (堅持), stay up (熬夜), take off (脫下), touch down (著陸)
B 類型	apply for (申請……), believe in (信仰；信任), belong to (屬於……), care for (照顧……), come from (來自……), complain of (抱怨……), concentrate on (全神貫注於……), consist of (由……構成), deal with (應付……), depend on (依賴……), dispose of (解決……), insist on (堅持……), laugh at (嘲笑……), live on (以……為生), listen to (聽……), look at (注視……), look into (深入調查……), object to (對……反對), reply to (回覆……), search for (尋找……), wait for (等待)
C 類型	bring about (引起), bring back (帶回), bring up (養育), call back (收回), call off (取消), carry out (完成), find out (找出), give back (恢復), give up (放棄), hand in (提出), lay off (解雇), make out (辨別出), put off (延遲), put on (穿上), put out (熄滅), switch / turn on (打開), take off (脫下), think over (仔細考慮), try on (試穿), turn down/up (拒絕／出現), work out (解決)
D 類型	attribute A to B (認為 A 是 B 所有), compare A with/to B (拿 A 和 B 比較), deprive/rob A of B (從 A 奪走 B), explain A to B (解釋 A 給 B 知道), provide A with B (提供 B 給 A), prevent/keep A from B (讓 A 遠離 B), regard A as B (把 A 認作 B), remind A of B (提醒 A B), replace A with/by B (用 B 取代 A), spend A on B (把 A 花在 B 上), suggest A to B (使 B 聯想到 A)

在空格中填上合適的字，以符合中文的意思。

1 work _____（解決）

2 apply _____（申請）

3 consist _____（構成）

4 explain _____（解釋）

5 call _____（取消）

6 belong _____（屬於）

7 spend _____（花……在……上面）

8 deprive _____（奪走）

9 break _____（爆發）

10 show _____（出現）

11 deal _____（應付）

12 attribute _____（認為……是某人所有）

13 bring _____（引起）

14 provide _____（提供）

15 insist _____（堅持）

16 depened _____（依賴）

17 prevent _____（阻止）

18 bring _____（養育）

19 object _____（反對）

20 remind _____（提醒）

1-11 選出一個最適合填入空格中的答案。

1 A jazz song might _____ each time it is played.
① sounds different
② sound differently
③ sounds differently
④ sound different

2 We believe that you can cope _____ particular problems very well.
① on ② for ③ with ④ in

3 In New England _____ beautiful fishing villages and manufacturing towns.
① has ② many
③ about ④ there are

4 It never _____ them that he is a victim to their greed.
① came ② happened
③ brought to ④ occurred to

5 My boss _____ a favor of me.
① told ② spoke
③ asked ④ talked

6 Many people go to college straight from high school. Some of them _____ college in order to get a well-paid job.
① attend to ② attended
③ attends at ④ attend

7 Modern industrial methods made blacksmiths, stone carvers and cobblers _____.
① extinct ② coming
③ to enter ④ extinction

8 I had a problem with my tooth. The doctor _____.
① pulled it out ② pulled out it
③ pulled them out ④ pulled out them

9 He won't object _____ him by his first name.
① to your calling ② you call
③ about your calling ④ for calling

10 Ms. Morea _____ her students that they can do anything.
① requests ② says
③ listens ④ teaches

11 A: What is Mr. Porter doing in the class?
B: He is _____ a problem to the students.
① asking ② speaking
③ responding ④ explaining

12-13 選出文法正確的句子。

12 ① Joan made a birthday cake to her boyfriend.
② Susan married with a wealthy businessman.
③ I counted on him but I was disappointed at his work.
④ The baby is asleep. Don't wake up him.

13 ① As usual, she complained the rainy weather.
② There is at least 200 separate Indian languages in North America.
③ Society must regard the person as the habitual criminal.

④ The doctor explained his family the condition of the patient.

14 選出文法錯誤的句子。

① Can you lend me $15 until tomorrow?
② As Mary approached to the garden, her mood lightened.
③ Why don't you lie down on the sofa for a while?
④ As the days shortened, the work week lengthened.

15 哪一句是下列中文最正確的翻譯？

我們今天談論了許多主題。

① We have talked millions of stories today.
② We have shared with a lot of subjects today.
③ We have covered a wide range of subjects today.
④ We have discussed about a variety of subjects today.

16-21 閱讀下列文字，並回答問題。

16 於下列劃有底線的動詞中，選出不符合句意者，並更正。

George ① was special in so many ways. His special sense of humor and passion for life ② brought so much pleasure to others. I'll always ③ forget and cherish the happy times we had together. I will ④ call you after the funeral to see if I can come by to see you. In the meantime, I ⑤ send you my love and sympathy.

17 選出括弧中最符合上下文者。

The Titanic, one of the largest ships ever made, is famous for its tragedy. On the night of April 14, 1912, it was going from Southampton to New York. On the way, it (hit, hit with) a large iceberg. This (did, made) a hole on the side of the huge ship. Water (entered, entered into) the ship through the hole, and it began to sink.

18 找出下列文字中文法錯誤的字，並且更正。

Long ago, people who lived in caves made fires. They used fires to keep warmly. At night they used them for light and found that they could see better with fires on.

19 填入符合文意的字。

Every four years, the world turns its attention to the World Cup. The most successful teams in the soccer tournament have traditionally come from South America and Europe. However, over the years, there _____ been a number of surprising results.

20 填入符合文意的介系詞。

A music teacher wanted to explain _____ his students the difference between music and noise. He brought a set of different sized blocks of wood _____ the class. The students were surprised to see him throw the blocks randomly at the wall. Everyone agreed it was noise.

21 將括弧中提示的字，換成正確的形式，填入空格中。

Hollywood stars have little privacy. Everyone can see everything they do. We can read all about their private lives in newspapers and magazines. Many film stars find it _____ (difficulty) to lead a normal life.

22-28 選出劃線部分文法錯誤者。

22 ① In the United States, ② naturalism became ③ popularity in the ④ plays of Eugene O'neill.

23 ① Hold the big picture below ② your nose. Pretend you ③ are looking through it. Then ④ move away it slowly.

24 ① Throughout my boyhood I ② enjoyed a ③ voluntary exercise. I called it ④ as writing histories.

25 Often when the weather is ① terribly hot, people ② have very thirsty ③ but are not ④ extremely hungry.

26 Kate looked ① so ② ill that we decided ③ to bring her ④ to the hospital.

27 Billy ① resembles after his brother ② so slosely that I ③ mistook him ④ for Andy.

28 Spain ① is a European country. It ② lay east of Portugal and north of Africa. It ③ has coasts on ④ the Atlantic Ocean.

CHAPTER 3

助動詞
Auxiliary Verbs

15 助動詞的位置、功能和特點

A ┌ It **must** have rained last night. 昨晚一定有下雨。
    └ Paul **could** not read when he was three. 保羅三歲的時候還不會看書。

B ┌ Jeff **has** told the truth. 傑夫已經說實話了。
    └ Jeff **should** have told the truth. 傑夫早應該說實話的。

C ┌ She can ~~speaks~~ Chinese. 〔錯誤用法〕
    │ She ~~cans~~ speak Chinese. 〔錯誤用法〕
    └ She hopes ~~to can~~ speak Chinese. 〔錯誤用法〕

所謂的**助動詞**，顧名思義就是「輔助主要動詞的字詞」。主要動詞就是指 go、seem、catch、give、make 等「一般動詞」，也就是決定句子形式的關鍵。助動詞分為「一般助動詞」和「情境助動詞」。一般助動詞是「do」、「does」、「did」等，幫助一般動詞形成問句和否定句；情境助動詞是「will」、「can」、「may」等，又分為「純粹助動詞」和「準助動詞」。

A ‥ 助動詞的「位置」，一般都是在**主要動詞**之前。即使是像「have rained」這樣的動詞片語，助動詞也是要在主要動詞前面；如果動詞片語中有否定詞 not，助動詞仍然一樣要在 not 前面。

B ‥ 助動詞的「功能」為在主要動詞中再附加上「允諾、建議、邀請、提議、推測」等含義。附加上的含義，不是主詞的意思，而是將說話者的心態反映在句子裡。例句一：「Jeff has told」是「傑夫已經說了」的意思；例句二：「Jeff should have told」是「傑夫早應該說的」之意，其中的「應該」即傳達出了「說話者的想法」。

C ‥ 助動詞後面的動詞要用「原型動詞」。以 speak 為例，助動詞後只能接原型動詞 speak，如果接現在式 speaks、過去式 spoke、分詞 speaking/spoken 等都是錯誤的用法。另外，因為助動詞本身只有「現在式」和「過去式」兩種形式，所以 can 只會是「can」或「could」，絕對不會出現 cans 或 is canning 或 to can 等形式。

概念習題

1-2 選出一個最適合填入空格中的答案。

1 It was an easy test and he _____ passed, but he didn't.
① had better ② must ③ may to have ④ ought to have

2 The owl _____ well in the dark, but it hunts on moonlit nights.
① cannot to see ② not can see ③ can not see ④ can saw not

3-6 加入括弧中提示的助動詞後，重組句子。

3 with / his partner / working / Daniel / be (will)

4 his own / not / Johnny / business / start (might)

5 something / said / about me / have / you / to Jeff (must)

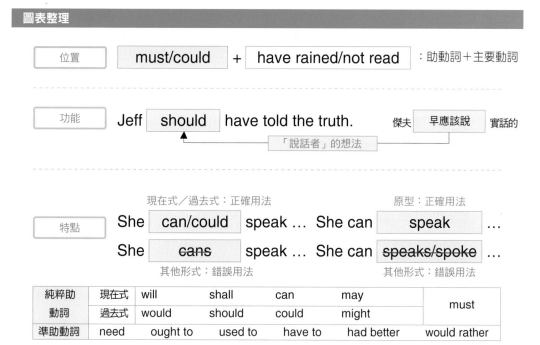

1. My pants are dirty. I should wash them. 我的褲子髒了，我應該要清洗的。
2. Emma can write programs. 愛瑪會寫程式。
3. Melanie might help us. 瑪蘭妮也許會幫我們。
4. It may rain tomorrow. 明天可能會下雨。
5. She isn't answering the phone. She must be out. 她沒接電話，八成是出門了。
6. Mike will go there. 麥克將會去那裡。

6 not / Julie / have / that she planned / him / to remain single / told   (should)

7-10 下列句子若有錯誤，請改正。

7 We haven't decided yet. We may gone back to Canada.

8 A regular walking program can effectively combatting many symptoms of arthritis.

9 You had better to take the patient to the Emergency Room right now.

10 Ron may not call us this weekend because he might not have a phone yet. But he promises he will calls us soon.

16 Will/Would

A [Mike **will** arrive **around six** tomorrow. 〔純粹未來〕麥克將於明天六點左右抵達。

B [You'**ll** feel better after you have something to eat. 〔預測〕
吃一些東西後，你將會感到舒服些。

C
I'**ll** buy you a bike for your birthday. 〔意志〕你生日時，我將會買部腳踏車給你。

My brother said he **would** stop smoking. 我哥哥說他會戒菸。

The key went into the lock, but it **would**n't turn.
鑰匙插進鑰匙孔裡，但是打不開。

D
Olga is very kind. She'**ll** always help people. 〔重覆、習慣〕
歐嘉很好心，她總是幫助別人。

Sunday mornings my mother **would** bake. 週日早上我媽媽會烤東西。

「will」基本上大致分成兩種功能，即表示**未來時態**和**助動詞**的功能。雖然這兩種功能時常混合使用，但原則上是可以被區分的。

A 所謂表「未來時態」的功能，就是在未來式中直接使用 will，來表現出「純粹未來」的含義。以 arrive 為例，現在式是 arrive、過去式是 arrived、未來式是 will arrive，其中未來式 will arrive，只表示「時間上的未來」。〔參考 Unit 4 未來式〕

B 所謂「助動詞」的功能，即 will 是 can、must 等情境助動詞其中之一，拿來當作助動詞使用。will 當作助動詞使用時，它的前提是純粹未來；而在這純粹未來之上，還會附加一些新的含義，叫做「混合未來」。所謂新的含義，第一個是表示一般的「預測」。例句「You'll feel . . .」基本上是未來的事，但其中也包含了說話者的「預測」。

C 第二個新的含義是反映主詞的「意志」。具體來說，就是：保證「I'll buy . . .」、意圖「he would stop . . .」、堅持「it wouldn't . . .」等。

D 第三個新的含義是表現某件事重覆發生的「重覆、習慣」，包含了「確信」的意味；因為某件事持續反覆地發生，所以那件事是可以確實預測的。在例句「She'll always help people.」中，除了表示直至目前時常幫助別人的「重覆」含義之外，也包含了未來仍會持續幫助別人的「確信」含義。

概念習題

1-2 選出一個最適合填入空格中的答案。

1 A fortune teller predicted I _____ a lot of money before the end of the year.
① inherited　② shall inherit　③ will inherit　④ would inherit

2 She _____ on washing her hair just when I want to have a bath.
① insist　② will insisted　③ is going to insist　④ will insist

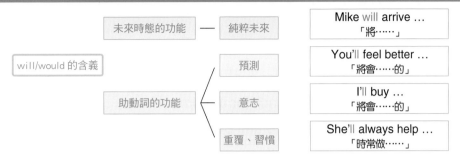

1. I was told Mike would arrive around six. 我被告知麥克會在六點左右抵達。

2. I will/shall leave at five on Monday evening.
   〔純粹未來〕我將在週一傍晚五點離開。
   * 在「純粹未來」中，主詞是第一人稱（we/I）時，英式用法會以 shall 代替 will。

3. I will be a good husband to you.〔意志〕我將會做你的好丈夫。

4. We won't stay longer than three hours. 我們將不會停留超過三小時。

5. Ask her again. Perhaps she'll change her mind.
   〔預測〕再問她一次，也許她會改變心意。

6. Accidents will happen. 意外會發生。

7. People will always say the things you want to hear.
   別人總會跟你說你想聽的事。

3-4 選出和提示句中的 will 功能相同者。

3 The concert will start in a minute.

① A: Mom, can I go to a party on Friday night? B: Well, where will it be?
② A: Please come to my party. B: I promise I'll be there.
③ The product with better-known brand name will always sell better.
④ Will the Olympic Games take place in my country?

4 I will say no more on these matters, important though they are.

① You'll feel better when you take this medicine.
② Mary will be here at six tomorrow.
③ Steve loves music. He'll sit for hours listening to his stereo.
④ A: I've got so many invitations to write. B: I'll write some for you.

17 Can/Could 和 May/Might

A

Bob **can** play the piano.〔能力〕鮑伯會彈鋼琴。

Bob **is able to** play the piano. 鮑伯會彈鋼琴。

Can/Could I use your pencil for a moment?〔允諾〕我可以借用你的鉛筆一會兒嗎？

The couple **could** travel to any part of the island they wanted.
這對夫妻可以隨心所欲地遍遊全島。

The couple **were allowed to** travel … 這對夫妻可以去……旅行。

We **can/could** go to a movie.〔推測〕我們可以去看電影。

B

You **may** have a cookie after dinner.〔允諾〕晚餐後你可以吃一塊餅乾。

It **may/might** rain tomorrow.〔推測〕明天也許會下雨。

A──助動詞 can 表示「能做……」，有**能力**的含義。表示能力的 can 也可以換成 be able to，不過一般還是用 can 比較多。can 的過去式是 could。

can 也表示「做……也可以」的**允諾**含義。在疑問句中 could 比 can 含有更莊重的意味；而在直述句中 could 就是 can 的過去式。表示允諾的 can 也可以換成「be allowed to」。例句中的「the couple could . . .」表示對過去的允諾。

can 也表示「也可能會……」，有**推測**的含義。這個推測是表示事情發生的可能性，和能力不同。例句「We can go to a movie.」是「我們也可能會去看電影」的意思，而非「我們有能力去看電影」，所以在表示推測的含義中，could 不是 can 的過去式，而是同義的另一個助動詞。

B──may 表「做……也可以」**允諾**的含義。在疑問句中，may 和 might 意思相似；不過在直述句中，might 是 may 的過去式。表示允諾的 may 和 can，意思幾乎是一樣的；不過，正式場合或要表現正式的說法時，會用 can 而不用 may，may 主要是對個人的允諾。

may 也表示「不知道是不是、可能是」的**推測**含義。在表示推測的含義中，might 不是過去式，所以可以和 tomorrow 在同一句中出現。表示推測的 may 和 might，以及 can 和 could 的意思幾乎一樣。

 概念習題

1-2 選出一個最適合填入空格中的答案。

1 _____ my children go into the amusement park before it is officially open?

① Could   ② Might   ③ Can   ④ Will

2 It is no doubt that some native languages _____ die out in the near future.

① may   ② might   ③ could   ④ are able to

3-5 填入適當的字，使兩句意思相同。

3 Monkeys can't speak human language.

Monkeys _____ not _____ _____ speak human language.

圖表整理

can 的含義	能力	Bob can play the piano. （能做……） = Bob is able to play the piano.
can/may 的含義	允諾	The couple could travel ... （可以……） You may have a cookie after dinner. *can = may = be allowed to*
	推測	We can/could go to a movie. It may/might rain tomorrow. （可能會……）

1. A bird can sing. = A bird is able to sing. 〔能力〕鳥會唱歌。

2. He couldn't walk when he was six months old. 他六個月大時，還不會走路。

3. You may stay up until 2 a.m. 〔允諾〕你可以熬夜到兩點再去睡覺。

4. In those days only men could vote in elections.
   在過去，只有男人可以投票選舉。

5. Professors can take a year away from university. 教授可以離開大學一年。

6. Alicia could be at the mall. 〔推測〕艾莉西亞可能在購物中心。

7. John may not be at the meeting tomorrow. 約翰明天也許不會參加開會。

8. I can / could / may / might be home late tonight. 我今晚可能晚點才會在家。

4 Students cannot use calculators in exams.

Students _____ not _____ _____ use calculators in exams.

5 Perhaps you are right.

You _____ _____ right.

6 選出和提示句中的 could 用法相同者。

> That could be one reason for the disaster.

① When he was a child, my son could run very fast.

② You can't park here — it's a no parking zone.

③ This summer we could visit some interesting places in the U.S.

助動詞

18 Must/Have to

A
> People **must** drink water.〔必要〕人必須喝水。
> People **have to** drink water. 人必須喝水。

B
> Jack **has to/had to** study for his test. 傑克為了考試必須讀書。
> Jack ~~musts/musted~~ study for his test.〔錯誤用法〕

C
> You must **not** bite your nails. 你不可以咬你的指甲。
> You **don't** have to study tonight.[~~have not to~~] 你今晚不必讀書。

D
> Bill has been driving all day — he **must** be tired.〔強烈推測〕
> Bill has been driving all day — he ~~has to~~ be tired.〔錯誤用法〕
> 比爾已經開車開了一整天,他一定累了。

A must 和 have to 表示「必須要……」,有強烈的含義。不過 must 含有說話者的「權威」,have to 則沒有此含義。

B 因為 must 是「助動詞」,所以只能有 must 這個形式,musts 或 musted 等都是錯誤用法。相反的,have to 是「一般動詞」,所以主詞若是第三人稱單數,就要用「has to」;如果是過去式,就要用「had to」;否定句或疑問句時,就要加 do/does/did 等助動詞來幫忙。

C must 的否定句和 have to 的否定句,兩者意思是不同的。must not 是「做……是不行的、不行做……」的意思,don't have to 是「沒有做……的必要」的意思。例句:「I don't have to study.」是「沒有去讀書的必要」,也就是「即使不讀書也可以」的意思,而非「去讀書是不行的」之意。

D must 含有「邏輯上的必然」的「強烈推測」之意,翻譯成「一定是……準沒錯」;相反的,have to 則沒有強烈推測。以例句來說明,因為 Bill 開車開了一整天,所以就邏輯上來說他一定是疲累的,和 must 含義相反的是 cannot,中文意思是「絕對不能」。

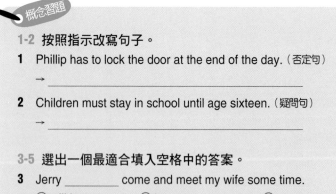

概念習題

1-2 按照指示改寫句子。

1 Phillip has to lock the door at the end of the day.（否定句)
→ _____

2 Children must stay in school until age sixteen.（疑問句)
→ _____

3-5 選出一個最適合填入空格中的答案。

3 Jerry _____ come and meet my wife some time.
① will have to   ② have to   ③ musts   ④ will must

must/have to 的含義	—	必要	People must drink water.（必須要……） *must = have to*

must：助動詞	~~musts / musted(X)~~		must not	做……是不行的
have to：一般動詞	has to / had to		don't have to	沒有做……的必要

must 的第二個含義	—	強烈推測	He must be tired.（一定是……） *must ≠ have to*

1. Must you do shopping now? 你現在一定要買東西嗎？

2. This book must not be removed from the library.
   這本書不可攜帶至圖書館外。

3. I had to do shopping yesterday. 我昨天一定得購物。
   *I ~~must/musted~~ do shopping yesterday.〔錯誤用法— must / musted 不能用過去式〕

4. Do you have to do shopping now? 你現在一定要買東西嗎？

5. I don't have to drive to work. 我不用開車上班。

6. The Smiths must have a lot of money. 史密斯家一定很有錢。

7. There must be something wrong with the engine. 這部引擎一定哪裡出問題了。

4 You _____ strike a match. The room is full of gas.

   ① must not   ② don't have to   ③ have to not   ④ must have to

5 Frederick has a weak heart. He _____ have a heart attack.

   ① musts   ② must   ③ has to   ④ must have to

6-9（6-7）填入 must not 或 don't/doesn't have to。
     （8-9）選出括弧中最符合上下文者。

6 During class, students _____ leave the room without teacher's permission.

7 Mario _____ make hotel reservations because he can stay at his uncle's.

8 I (had to, must, musted) be at the hospital at 4 o'clock yesterday.

9 You've just eaten your lunch! You (can't, must, have to) be hungry.

19 Should/Ought to/Had better

A
Your eyes are poor. You **should** wear glasses. 〔建議〕

Your eyes are poor. You **ought to** wear glasses.

Your eyes are poor. You **had better** wear glasses.
你的視力不好，最好戴眼鏡。

B
The lakes **should** be visible from here. 〔推測〕

The lakes **ought to** be visible from here. 從這裡應該可以看到那些湖。

C
You ought **not** to lock the door. 〔否定〕你不應該鎖門。

You had better **not** lock the door. 你最好不要鎖門。

A ··· should / ought to / had better 含有「做……會比較好」的建議之意。比起 must / have to，強度較弱，有對主詞提出「規勸、提議、忠告」的含義。「should」和「ought to」強度一樣，而「had better」強度比它們再稍強烈一些。

B ··· should / ought to 也含有「推測」的含義。should 的推測又叫做「試驗性的推測」，表示雖然對自己說的話沒有十足的把握，卻是依據「到目前為止知道的事實」所作的推測。以例句來說明，「The lakes should . . . here.」雖然不是很有把握，但仍具有某種程度的可能性。另外，「had better」則沒有推測的含義。

C ··· 「should not」、「ought not to」、「had better not」這些都是助動詞的否定用法。

1 空格中填入適當的字，使三句意思相同。

① It's going to rain. You _____ take an umbrella.

② It's going to rain. You _____ to take an umbrella.

③ It's going to rain. You _____ better take an umbrella.

2 選出一個最適合填入空格中的答案。

You _____ your visa extended before it expires.

① had better to get   ② had to get better

③ had better get   ④ had better got

1. Students should/ought to come to class every day. 學生們應該每天都要來上課。
2. The government should/ought to do something about the economy.
   政府應該要為經濟做些努力。
3. Sally should/ought to be at work by now. She's normally there at this time.
   莎莉應該在工作，通常這個時間她都在公司。
4. Should we invite Sue to the party? 我們應該邀請蘇來參加派對嗎？
5. Ought we to invite Sue to the party? 我們應該邀請蘇來參加派對嗎？
6. A: We'd better leave soon. B: Yes, we had. / we'd better.
   A: 我們最好快點離開。
   B: 是的，我們最好如此。

3 選出和提示句中的 ought to 意思相同者。

Helen doesn't feel well. She ought to see a doctor.

① We're going to France for our summer holiday. It should be really interesting.
② Andrew ought to pass his driving test easily. He's a very good driver.
③ People shouldn't talk on their cell phones while driving a car.
④ There shouldn't be any problem with my computer. It's brand-new.

4-6 選出括弧中最符合上下文者。

4 You (must, should) not smoke in a non-smoking area.

5 You (had better not, had not better) ask Alice out again if you don't want to.

6 Ron, you (ought not to, ought to not, not ought to) pull the cat's tail!

20 Need/Used to 和 Would rather

A
Peter **needn't** worry about the test. 〔助動詞〕彼得不需要擔心這個考試。
Peter **doesn't need to** worry about the test. 〔一般動詞〕
Steve **needs to** lose a little of weight. 史蒂夫需要減重。
Steve ~~need lose~~ a little of weight. 〔錯誤用法〕

B
Nell **used to** smoke, but she doesn't anymore. 〔動態〕
妮兒過去曾抽菸，但是她現在已經戒菸了。

My brother **used to** be interested in bird-watching. 〔狀態〕
我弟弟過去曾對賞鳥感興趣。

C
I **would rather** not say anything. 我寧可什麼都不說。

A need 在否定句和疑問句中，可當作「助動詞」，也可當作「一般動詞」；但在肯定句中，就只能當作「一般動詞」。need 當助動詞使用時，要用「need＋原型動詞」的形式；當一般動詞使用時，要用「need＋to＋原型動詞」的形式。例句「needn't worry」的 need 是助動詞，「doesn't need to worry」的 need 是一般動詞。如果在肯定句中，將 need 當成助動詞使用，變成 need lose，就是錯誤用法。
need 含有「需要去做……」的必要性之意；和 must 意思相似。否定句中的「needn't」或「don't need to」，和「don't have to」意思完全一樣，是「不需要去做……」的意思。

B used to 是強調「已經過去」的助動詞。「Nell used to smoke」比起「Nell smoked」更強調已經過去了，強調「現在已經不抽菸了」的含義。「used to」後面如果接像 smoke 這樣的一般動詞，含有「過去規律的習慣」的意思，「used to」就可以換成「would」，兩者意思相同；不過，如果 used to 後面接「be 動詞」這樣的狀態動詞，「used to」就不能換成「would be」了。「used to」的否定形式是「didn't use to」或「used not to」（英式用法）。

C would rather 是「寧願……」的意思，有「偏好」的含義。

概念習題

1 選出正確的句子。
　① Jason needs not know I'm here.
　② He doesn't need speak about what happened.
　③ Tom need do some shopping on his way home from work.
　④ Does Alice need to make all that noise?

2-3 下列句子若有錯誤，請找出並更正。
2 Sally was used to love Jim, but he didn't love her.
3 He'd rather die than making me think he needed help.

1. Tom doesn't need to work so late, does he? 湯姆不需要工作到這麼晚，不是嗎？

2. Tom needn't work so late, need he? 湯姆不需要工作到這麼晚，他需要嗎？

3. Tom doesn't have to work so late, does he? 湯姆不需要工作到這麼晚，不是嗎？

4. A: Does Tom need to work so late? B: Yes, he does.
   A: 湯姆需要工作到這麼晚嗎？ B: 是的，他需要。

5. A: Need Tom work so late? B: Yes, he must.
   A: 湯姆需要工作到這麼晚嗎？ B: 是的，他必須。

6. I used to live with my grandparents. 我曾經和祖父母住。

7. We didn't use to go out much in the winter months.
   我們在冬天的那幾個月裡不常出門。

8. I'd rather go on holiday in July. 我寧願七月去度假。

9. I'd rather take a taxi to the station than go by bus.
   我寧願搭計程車去車站，也不要搭公車去。
   *would rather 後面若有 than，than 的後面也要接原型動詞。

4-6 選出一個最適合填入空格中的答案。

4 People in ancient civilization _____ goods rather than use money.

① used to trade   ② was used trade   ③ use to trade   ④ had used trade

5 A good reader _____ everything he or she reads.

① needs not to understand   ② does not need understand

③ don't have to understand   ④ need not understand

6 Thomas would _____ finish the work tomorrow.

① not rather   ② rather not to   ③ not finishing   ④ rather not

21 邀請 / 勸誘 / 限制

A
Will/Would/Can/Could you switch on the light, please?
你可以幫我開燈嗎？

Would you like a sandwich? / **Will** you have a sandwich?
你要來個三明治嗎？

B
Can/Could/May I borrow your eraser? 我可以借用你的橡皮擦嗎？

Can/Could I help you with the heavy box? 我可以幫你搬這個重箱子嗎？

C
Shall I open the window for you? 我幫你開窗好嗎？

Shall we go out for dinner tonight? 我們今晚出去吃晚餐好嗎？

D
Would you like some cake? — Yes, please. / No, thanks.
你要來些蛋糕嗎？一好，謝謝你。／不用了，謝謝。

Do you like cake? — Yes, I do. / No, I don't.
你喜歡蛋糕嗎？一是的，我喜歡。／不，我不喜歡。

「助動詞」在疑問句中，主要表示「邀請、勸誘、限制、允諾」等含義。因為是疑問句，所以主詞一定是對方「you」，或說話的「I」。同一個助動詞的過去式（例如 would）要比現在式（例如 will）更莊重。

A will、would、can、could 出現在主詞是「第二人稱 you」的疑問句中時，主要是表示「邀請」對方。

B can、could、may 出現在主詞是「第一人稱 I」的疑問句中時，主要是表示「允諾、邀請」。might 不常使用。can、could 表示「提議」的意思，中文的意思是「這樣做可以嗎？／為你做……可以嗎？」

C shall 和主詞為第一人稱的「I」和「we」一起使用時，表示「提議」，是「做……好嗎？／做……如何？」之意

D would like 是 want 的禮貌說法，「想要……」的意思。若沒有 would 只有 like，是「一般的喜歡……」的意思。「would like」不只用在疑問句，直述句也可以使用。

概念習題

1 選出不能填入空格中的答案。

A: _____ use your telephone?　　　B: Certainly.

① May I　　　② Can I　　　③ Will I　　　④ Could I

2-3 選出一個最適合填入空格中的答案。

2 A: _____ answer the phone for me, please?　　　B: Yes, of course.

① Would he　　　② Would she　　　③ Would you　　　④ Would they

3 _____ to come to my party on Saturday?

① Do you like　　　② Would you like　　　③ Will you like　　　④ Shall you like

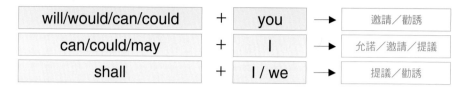

1. Could you open the door? 你可以開門嗎？
2. Would you mail this letter for me? 你可以幫我寄這封信嗎？
3. May I use your phone? 我可以用你的電話嗎？
4. Could I borrow your dictionary? 你可以借我字典嗎？
5. I wonder if you could look after my dog for a while.
   我在想，你是否可以幫我照顧小狗一會兒？
6. Shall we talk about something more important now?
   我們現在可以談些比較重要的事嗎？
7. She would like another apple. 她想要另一顆蘋果的。
8. I would like to ask you one question. 我想問你一個問題。

4-7 選出括弧中最符合上下文者。

4 Jennifer, I'm out of razor blades. (Could, May, Shall) you please buy some for me?

5 It's beautiful today. (Would, May, Shall) we go on a picnic?

6 I'm hungry. (I like, I'd like) steak and chips.

7 He (likes, would like) to spend his evenings in front of the television.

8 空格中填入適當的字，使兩句意思相同。

　　Would you like me to mail these letters for you?

　　= _____ I mail these letters for you?

22 助動詞的發生可能性

A ─〔 Eric **may/might** leave tomorrow. 艾瑞克也許明天會離開。

B

Is David in his room? 大衛在他的房間裡嗎？

— I'm not sure. He **may/might/could** be. 我不確定，他也許在裡面。

— Yes, he **must** be. I heard him come in.

是的，他一定在裡面。我聽到他進來。

— No, he **can't** be. There's no light in his room.

不，他不可能在，他房間的燈沒亮。

That **will/would** be the postman. 那可能是郵差。

A 過去式的「might」可以和表示未來時間的「tomorrow」一起出現在同一個句子中嗎？

八個純粹助動詞（除 shall 外），都具有「首要功能」和「次要功能」。所謂的**首要功能**，就像 can 表示能力、**must** 表示義務一樣，就是每一個助動詞它原本所具有的含義。所謂的**次要功能**，就是追加的含義，也就是每個助動詞都共同具有「發生可能性」的含義。所謂的發生可能性，就是指某事可能會發生、會成真的一種「推測」。

助動詞有發生可能性的意思時，可以用**現在式**和**過去式**，但這裡的「過去式」和一般所謂的過去式含義不同，為「發生可能性比現在更低」的意思；所以過去式 might 如果表示發生的可能性，就可以和 tomorrow 一起出現在句子裡。

B 在助動詞中「發生可能性」最高的就是「must」了，因為其他的助動詞只是靠「推測」來判斷，而 must 是依據「證據」來判斷；和 must 相反，發生可能性最低的是「can't」。「will/would」是對未來綜合性的預測，發生可能性排在 must 之後；should/ought to 是依據到目前為止的知識作預測，可能性排第三高，can/could 和 may/might 發生可能性一樣，排在可能性最低的 can't 之前。「can」主要是用在**疑問句**和**否定句**中。例句中，「he may/might/could be」沒有明顯的根據；而「he must be」和「he can't be」則是根據「聽見他進去的聲音」和「沒有燈光」所作的推測。

1-2 空格中填入適當的字，使兩句意思相同。

1 I'm not sure. Maybe you are right.

= You _____ be right.

2 It's certain that he's Jennifer's husband.

= He _____ be Jennifer's husband.

3-4 選出一個最適合填入空格中的答案。

3 The dog looks very clean. The owner _____ take care of him.

① must ② ought to ③ cannot ④ may

① must	一定是……
② will / would	很可能是……
③ should / ought to	大概是……
④ may / might / can / could	也可能是……、不知道是不是……
⑤ can't	絕不是……、不可能是……

助動詞的發生可能性順序

助動詞當作發生可能性的含義使用時

過去式　　　　未來

Eric **might** leave **tomorrow**.

正確表現

1. Simon must be in the living room. 賽門一定在客廳。
2. Debbie can hardly be at home yet. It's only 5. 黛比不太可能在家，現在才五點。
3. A woman may/might/could be looking for a man that will be kind to her.
一個女人可能會找一個對她好的男人。
4. If it's raining tomorrow, the sports can take place indoors.
如果明天下雨，體育競賽可改在室內舉行。
5. There might be some complaints. 也許會有些抱怨。
6. An increasing number of people will be using the Internet to find potential
mates. 將會有愈來愈多人藉由網路來尋找可能的伴侶人選。
7. Try phoning Robert — he should be home by now.
打給羅伯特看看，他現在應該在家。

4 If litmus paper is dipped in acid, it _____ turn red.
① may ② can ③ should ④ will

5-10 選出括弧中最符合上下文者。

5 I saw Jim going out. He (can't, will not) be at home.

6 Sylvia certainly (will, might) not understand if you don't explain the problem.

7 If you begin now, the job (should, ought) to be finished by next Tuesday.

8 Bill (might, shall) visit you in Canada next year, if he can save enough money.

9 Even expert drivers (might not, will, can) make mistakes.

10 A computer (might, must) connect you with others that you (may, must) not meet otherwise.

助動詞

23 助動詞＋完成式 (have ＋動詞過去分詞)

A
> They must **be** right.〔現在〕他們一定是對的。
> = I'm sure that they **are** right.
> They must **have been** right.〔過去〕他們當時一定是對的。
> = I'm sure that they **were** right.

B
> He **may/might/could** have missed the train. 他也許已錯過火車。
> The guests **will/would** have arrived by that time.
> 客人將在那個時間前抵達。
> He **must** have left his umbrella on the bus. 他一定是把雨傘遺忘在公車上了。
> You **should/ought to** have finished the work. 你早該完成工作。

C
> I **needn't have** gone to the office yesterday. 我昨天不需要去辦公室的。
> I **didn't need** to go to the office yesterday. 我昨天不需要去辦公室。

A 助動詞若表示「發生可能性」時，就能用過去式來表示過去，要在助動詞後面接「完成式（have ＋動詞過去分詞）」；所以就不適用「助動詞＋原型動詞」這條規則。「they must be right」推測他們「現在是對的」，「they must have been right」推測他們「過去是對的」。原型的 be 表示「現在」，完成式的 have been 表示「過去」。

B 「助動詞＋ have ＋動詞過去分詞」的形式表示「過去」。前面學過的「may、might、could」是一半一半的推測，「will、would」是有根據的推測，「must」是必然，全都是表示**發生可能性**。但是「will have ＋動詞過去分詞」是發生可能性和未來完成式混用的情形，並不常用。「should have ＋動詞過去分詞」是「應該要做了……的才對」的意思，表示有些可惜或勸告。

C 例句「needn't have gone」是「沒有必要去，但還是去了」的意思；「didn't need to go」是「沒有必要去，所以就沒有去了」的意思。

 概念習題

1-11 選出括弧中最符合上下文者。

1 Is Sam sick? / He may (have been, be).
2 Was Sam sick? / He may (have been, be).
3 There is no food left in the fridge. Tom must (have eaten, eat) it all.
4 Tom has eaten all the food. There must (have been, be) none in the fridge.
5 I may (have left, leave) the key at the office last night.
6 There is no answer to the doorbell. John must (have left, leave) home.
7 My son got lost again last night; I should not (have let, let) him go by himself.
8 When I woke up this morning, the heat was on. I (must, should, might) have forgotten to turn it off.

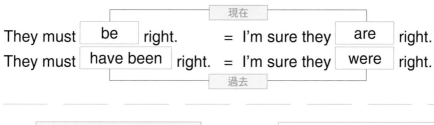

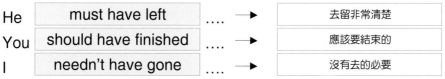

1. He may/might/could have left the room without permission.
   他可能沒經過允許就離開這房間了。
2. Elizabeth may/might/could not have heard the news special last night.
   伊莉莎白也許昨晚沒聽說這則新聞特輯。
3. Nancy must have found a job. 南希一定已經找到工作了。
4. She can't/couldn't have been swimming all day. 她不可能游泳游一整天。
5. You shouldn't have left Peter. 你不應該離開彼得。
6. Jake should have started his job on Monday. 傑克週一應該已經開始工作了。
7. You needn't have told them about my plan.
   你不需要告訴他們我的計畫（但你為什麼說了呢？）。
8. I didn't need/have to tell them about my plan. 我不需要告訴他們我的計畫。

9 You (needn't have washed, didn't need to wash) all those clothes — it's going to rain.

10 A: Has he received my email? B: I'm not sure. He (might, must, should) have received.

11 A: Did you ask Ann for help?
   B: No, I (needn't have, didn't need to) — I managed perfectly well on my own.

12-13 選出一個最適合填入空格中的答案。

12 It _____ last night, for the ground is wet.
   ① must rain   ② must rained   ③ must have rained   ④ must had rained

13 Hello, Ann. The party last night was great. You _____ have come. Why didn't you?
   ① must   ② should   ③ might   ④ needn't

助動詞

1-12 選出一個最適合填入空格中的答案。

1 Mary asked me if he could help her and I replied, "Yes, he _____."
① can ② cans
③ could ④ did can

2 _____ I use your phone? / Of course. Go right ahead.
① May ② Will
③ Must ④ Should

3. During my schooldays, I _____ go to the library after class.
① would ② should
③ ought to ④ have to

4 That's nonsense. I _____ believe it. / Me, either.
① must ② can
③ can't ④ may not

5 I tried to dissuade him from his plan, but he _____ not hear my advice.
① will ② would ③ shall ④ should

6 During the potato famine of the 1850s, they _____ go to America to find food and work.
① had to ② have had to
③ ought to ④ must

7 I have known many who could not when they _____, for they had not done it when they could.
① did ② would ③ might ④ could

8 He told me that _____ live with his roommate again next year.
① he'll rather not ② he'd rather not
③ he won't rather ④ he'd rather didn't

9 I've lost one of my gloves. I _____ it somewhere.
① have been dropped
② should have dropped
③ must have dropped
④ could be dropped

10 They _____ have enjoyed their holiday. The weather was terrible.
① could not ② may
③ should ④ would

11 She was too nervous to reply, but fortunately she _____ anything.
① didn't need to say
② needn't to say
③ needed not say
④ needn't have said

12 She thought that they should _____ the supervisor at the previous meeting.
① reward ② have rewarded
③ be rewarded ④ had rewarded

13-16 閱讀下列文字，並回答問題。

13 請找出下段文字中文法錯誤的字，並更正。

I just want to have a cup of coffee at a coffee stand. I say: "I like a large cup of coffee."

14 選出括弧中最符合上下文者。

That kind of simple response does not score any points. To score good points a man (need to respond, needs to respond, needs respond) the same way a woman would, by giving details.

15 選出一個最適合填入空格中的答案。

Life isn't always easy. We all need this when we start something new. Think of a time when you were nervous about trying to do something new and it was difficult as well, but in the end, you succeeded. Was there someone who helped you to keep going, so you didn't give up? He or she _____ a parent, a friend, or someone else.

① might be   ② might have
③ might was   ④ might have been
⑤ might had been

16 選出一個最適合填入空格中的答案。

No two people in the world have exactly the same opinion. Do you think it's difficult to get along with them? No. People with different views and opinions can respect each other and live happily together. You _____ like the same food, sports, or music as your friends.

① have to   ② don't have to
③ must not   ④ must have

17-24 選出劃線部分文法錯誤者。

17 You ① will need ② finish your work completely before you ③ decide to go to ④ a movie.

18 On ① the other hand, your approach ② is able to ③ be a drawback when things ④ change.

19 You must ① complete all of the ② tax forms and ③ submitting them ④ by tomorrow.

20 You ① shouldn't help him; ever since you ② offered him help, he has started ③ to depend on others ④ for his homework.

21 We ① have the party in the garden if the weather ② is good tomorrow. If not, ③ it'll ④ have to be inside.

22 You ① 'd better ② leaving now before ③ you cause ④ any more trouble.

23 He ① said softly that he would rather ② starve than ③ stealing to get what he ④ needed.

24 If ① the universe ② is expanding, then in the past it ③ must ④ be smaller than it is now.

CHAPTER 4

主動與被動語態
Active/Paassive Voice

24 主動語態和被動語態

A
Gustave Eiffel **built** the Eiffel Tower.〔主動語態〕
賈斯特夫・艾菲爾建造巴黎鐵塔。
The Eiffel Tower **was built** by Gustave Eiffel.〔被動語態〕
巴黎鐵塔是賈斯特夫・艾菲爾所建造。

A 英文中同個句子有「主動語態」和「被動語態」兩種表現方法,就「某個相同的內容」用英文來表示時,兩者都可以。例如「艾菲爾建造了巴黎鐵塔」這句話,用英文來表示時,主詞可以是艾菲爾,也可以是巴黎鐵塔。以「行為者」(A) 為主詞來造句時,就是「A……B」的**主動**表示法,稱作「主動語態」;若以「B……by A」(B) 為主詞來造句時,就是「B 被 A……」的**被動**表示法,稱作「被動語態」表示法。無論是用主動語態或是用被動語態,所表達的都是相同的內容,所以這兩種表達方式之間時常都具有「相互間的特殊關係」:

① 主動語態的受詞和被動語態的主詞是一樣的。「the Eiffel Tower」是主動語態的受詞,也是被動語態的主詞。

② 主動語態要改成被動語態,只要改成「be +動詞過去分詞」即可。動詞「built」是主動語態,它的被動語態就是「be built」。動詞的型態是區分句子是主動語態,還是被動語態的關鍵要素。

③ 主動語態的主詞和被動語態的「by +受詞」中的受詞一致。以例句來說,主動語態的主詞 Gustave Eiffel 和被動語態中的受詞一樣。另外,被動語態中的「by +受詞」如不需特別指名主使者是誰,經常被省略。

概念習題

1-3 空格中填入適當的字,使兩句意思相同。

1 They planted several trees a few days ago.

= Several _____ _____ _____ a few days ago.

2 People play baseball in most countries of the world.

= _____ is _____ in most countries of the world.

3 The cat ate the cheese.

= _____ _____ was _____ _____ the cat.

4-7 選出一個最適合填入空格中的答案。

4 Some epidemics were caused (by bacteria and viruses, bacteria and viruses).

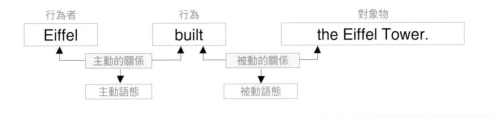

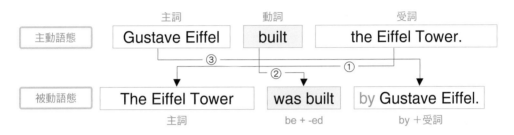

1. The hotel supplies towels.〔主動態：towels 是受詞〕這間旅館提供毛巾。
2. Towels are supplied by the hotel.〔被動態：Towels 是主詞〕這間旅館提供毛巾。
3. People speak English all over the world.〔主動態：speak 是動詞〕
   全世界都有人說英文。
4. English is spoken all over the world.〔被動態：is spoken 是動詞〕
   英語通行全世界。
5. The man ate the fish.〔主動態：The man 是主詞〕這個人吃了這條魚。
6. The fish was eaten by the man.〔被動態：by＋受詞 the man〕
   這條魚被這個人吃了。

5 We (saw, were seen) a huge elephant at the circus.

6 The criminals (caught, were caught) by the security guards yesterday.

7 Ms. Hopkins (received, was received) an award at the contest.

8-9 選出一個最適合填入空格中的答案。

8 Our class _____ Mr. Adams last week.
   ① was taught   ② taught   ③ was taught by   ④ taught by

9 A student _____ my old computer.
   ① bought by   ② was bought   ③ was bought by   ④ bought

主動與被動語態

75

25 被動語態的時態

A The best movie **is chosen** by the committee. 〔現在〕
The committee chooses the best movie. 委員會選出最佳影片。

B The best movie **will be chosen** by the committee. 〔未來〕
The committee will choose the best movie. 委員會將選出最佳影片。

C The best movie **is being chosen** by the committee. 〔現在進行〕
The committee is choosing the best movie. 委員會正在選出最佳影片。

D The best movie **has been chosen** by the committee. 〔現在完成〕
The committee has chosen the best movie. 委員會已選出最佳影片。

主動語態有十二個時態，被動語態只有八個時態。「被動語態」沒有未來進行式、現在完成進行式、過去完成進行式、未來完成進行式等四個時態。被動語態的時態，幾乎都是以「過去分詞」來結尾。

A 主動語態是「現在式」，換成被動語態，就是「be 動詞＋動詞過去分詞」。主動語態的動詞 chooses，在被動語態中變成 is chosen，主詞是第三人稱單數，所以 be 動詞用 is；be 動詞若是 was/were，那就是過去式。

B 主動語態是「未來式」，換成被動語態，就是「will be ＋動詞過去分詞」。will choose 改為「will be chosen」。

C 主動語態是「現在進行式」，換成被動語態，就是「be 動詞＋ being ＋動詞過去分詞」。將例句中的 is choosing 改成「is being chosen」。be 動詞改成 was/were，就是過去進行式。

D 主動語態是「現在完成式」，換成被動語態，就是「has / have ＋ been ＋動詞過去分詞」。將主動語態的 has chosen 改成「has been chosen」。has/have 改成 had，就變成過去完成式。未來完成式的被動語態是「will have been ＋動詞過去分詞」。

概念習題

1-4 將下列句子換成被動語態。

1 In football, the quarterback throw the ball.

→ _____.

2 Sportswriters honored the athlete last year.

→ _____.

3 The outfielder is catching the ball.

→ _____.

4 I have not finished my homework yet.

→ _____.

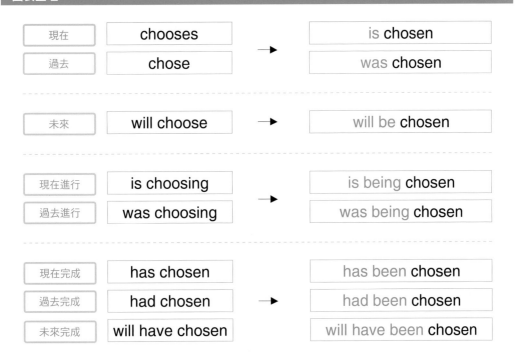

現在	chooses	→	is chosen	
過去	chose		was chosen	
未來	will choose	→	will be chosen	
現在進行	is choosing	→	is being chosen	
過去進行	was choosing		was being chosen	
現在完成	has chosen	→	has been chosen	
過去完成	had chosen		had been chosen	
未來完成	will have chosen		will have been chosen	

1. In hotels, the sheets on the bed are changed every day. 旅館裡的床單每日更換。
2. The dishes will be washed by Steve. 史蒂夫將清洗這些盤子。
3. This package must be sent immediately.〔must 和 will 的用法相同〕
   這個包裹必須馬上寄出。
4. The bridge is being reconstructed. 這座橋正在重建中。
5. The jewels were being protected by a guard. 這些珠寶受到保全的保護。
6. The bridge has been reconstructed. 這座橋已經被重建。
7. The letters had been typed by Ms. Anderson. 安德森小姐已繕打了這些信件。

5-6 選出一個最適合填入空格中的答案。

5 The conference _____ due to lack of interest.
　① has postponing　　　　　　② has been postponing
　③ has been postponed　　　　④ is being postponing

6 The baseball game _____ in Cleveland.
　① was playing　　② was being played　　③ was been playing　　④ be played

7-9 選出括弧中最符合上下文者。

7 The money (should be spent, should been spent) on a sports and leisure complex.

8 I have (been, being, Ø) paid for my service by my boss.

9 The contract will (have, have been, have being) signed by Bob by tomorrow.

26 主動語態和被動語態的特點

A
All the **money** was stolen last night. 昨晚全部的錢都被偷了。
All the money ~~stole~~ last night. 〔錯誤用法〕

B
My question was **answered** by Mrs. Bell. 比爾太太解答了我的疑問。
The sailors ~~were disappeared~~ in the storm. 〔錯誤用法〕
這些航海水手在暴風雨中失蹤了。

C
Lola invited **Tom** to the party. 羅拉邀請湯姆來參加宴會。
Tom was invited Ø to the party. 湯姆被邀請來宴會。

A 有些句子只要知道主詞的意思，就知道要用主動語態還是被動語態。主詞是 money，動詞是 steal，錢一定是「被偷」的，所以 steal 在這裡只能用被動語態。

B 如果無法從主詞判定用主動語態，還是被動語態時，就必須用其他標準了。第一，「不及物動詞」不管在任何情況下，都沒有被動語態。因為要變成被動語態，一定要有主動語態的受詞（這個受詞要被拿來當作被動語態的主詞）；有受詞，動詞就一定是及物動詞，所以只有「及物動詞」才能變成被動語態。

C 第二，及物動詞後若有受詞就是主動語態，及物動詞後若沒有受詞就是被動語態。因為主動語態的受詞變成了被動語態的主詞；所以在被動語態裡，動詞的後面沒有受詞。動詞 invite 是「邀請」的意思，是及物動詞，它後面有受詞 Tom，表示是主動語態：如果沒有受詞，就表示受詞當主詞了，成為被動語態。

 概念習題

1-8 選出括弧中最符合上下文者。

1 We (met, were met) at the airport by our uncle.
2 We (met, were met) our uncle at the airport.
3 The people were invited (their friends, by their friends) to the party.
4 The people invited (their friends, by their friends) to the party.
5 An accident (has occurred, has been occurred) in the East-Bound Lane.
6 The Oscar ceremony (is seen by, sees by, sees) millions of viewers.
7 The first scientific textbook on human anatomy (published, was published) in 1673.
8 Soccer (originally played, was originally played) by amateurs in Britain, but now it (dominates, is dominated) by professionals worldwide.

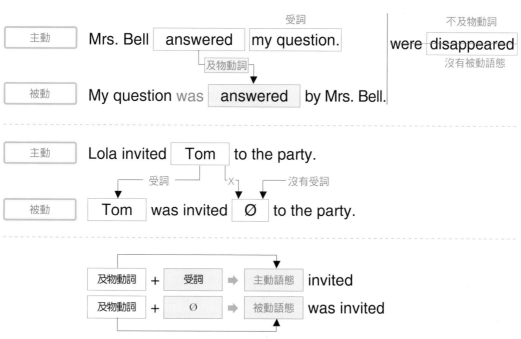

1. Many accidents are caused by careless people. 許多意外的都是粗心的人所造成。
2. A new theater has been built near my house at this time.
   現在在我家附近已建好一家電影院。
3. Fog is ~~occured~~ in valleys frequently.〔錯誤用法：occur 是不及物動詞〕
   山谷裡經常起霧。
4. The train was ~~arrived~~ at three.〔錯誤用法：arrive 是不及物動詞〕火車三點抵達。
5. The match was won by the best chess player. 這場比賽由棋藝頂尖高手獲勝。

▲ 被動語態用法的口訣

（１）不管什麼情況，不及物動詞都沒有被動語態。
（２）如果及物動詞後面有受詞，就是主動語態。
（３）如果及物動詞後面沒有受詞，卻有「by ...」，就是被動語態。

9-11 選出一個最適合填入空格中的答案。

9 Millions of years ago, the entire world _____ by dinosaurs.
　① has ruled　　② has been ruled　　③ was ruled　　④ was ruling

10 Many exciting events _____ in the amusement park.
　① happen　　② are happened　　③ has happened　　④ have happening

11 The meeting was called and _____ the serial murder in the village.
　① discussed about　　　　② was discussed about
　③ discussed　　　　　　④ was discussed

主動與被動語態

79

27 深入了解被動語態

A
Somebody gave **Bob the money**. 有人給鮑伯錢。

Bob was given the money. 鮑伯拿到錢。

The money was given to Bob. 這些錢給了鮑伯。

B
The movie made him **a star/popular**. 這部電影讓他成為明星／受到歡迎。

He was made **a star/popular** by the movie.

他因為這部電影而成為明星／受到歡迎。

C
She **got** hired for the job. 她獲得這份工作。

A 「第四類句型：授與動詞（參閱 Unit12）」是有**兩個受詞**的句型。因為有兩個受詞，所以被動語態就有兩種表現方式了。Bob 是間接受詞，the money 是直接受詞。如果 Bob 是主詞，那被動語態動詞「was given」後面就直接接 the money；而如果 the money 是主詞，被動語態動詞後面要先接介系詞 to，再接 Bob。這個介系詞和第四類句型改為第三類句型時，所添加的介系詞相同。

B 「第五類句型：不完全及物動詞（參閱 Unit13）」是有**受詞**和**受詞補語**的句型。受詞當作主詞，變成被動語態後，受詞補語留在原位即可。例句中，「a star」和「popular」就是受詞補語。

A-B 第四類句型和第五類句型的被動語態有一個共同點，就是兩者的被動語態動詞「was given 和 was made」的後面，都可以接名詞「the money 和 a star」。一般的被動語態句子，其動詞後面不能接名詞；不過第四類句型和第五類句型為例外，可以接名詞。

C 「be ＋動詞過去分詞」有時也可以換成「get ＋動詞過去分詞」，不過這種型態，含有偶然的、出乎意料發生的意思，或只在日常口語中；要特別注意，此型態不能改成「by ＋受詞」的句型。

概念習題

1-3 將下列句子按照提示的主詞改成被動態。

1 Someone told me that George was ill.

→ I _____.

2 Someone has offered Mike the opportunity to study abroad.

→ Mike _____.

3 They made Newton President of the Royal Society.

→ Newton _____.

4-8 選出括弧中最符合上下文者。

4 My sister (gave, was given) a flower by her friend.

間接受詞　　直接受詞

Somebody gave | Bob | the money.

Bob | was given | the money. 　The money | was given | to Bob.

受詞補語

第五類句型被動語態　He | was made | + | a star / popular.

第四類句型被動態　　　　　名詞

Bob | was given | + | the money.

第四類句型／第五類句型
被動語態的特點

第五類句型被動態　　　　　名詞

He | was made | + | a star.

1. Somebody told the students the answers. 有人告訴這些學生答案。
   → The students were told the answers. / → The answers were told to the students.
2. Someone will send you an invitation. 有人將會寄邀請函給你。
   → You will be sent an invitation. / → An invitation will be sent to you.
3. This will keep the children amused. 這將會讓孩子們一直開心著。
   → The children will be kept amused by this.
4. We'll call the baby Jean. 我們會把寶寶取名叫珍。
   → The baby will be called Jean. 這個寶寶的名字會叫珍。
5. Some people get shot in action movies. 有些人在動作片中被射傷。

5 My sister (gave, was given) a flower to her friend.

6 Jane (sent, was sent) her brother a telegram.

7 The truth was considered (evident, evidently).

8 The little girl told a lie, but she (didn't punish, is not punished, didn't get punished).

9-10 選出一個最適合填入空格中的答案。

9 His name was James, but he _____ Jim by the boys.
   ① called　　② was called　　③ was called as　　④ called as

10 I _____ that the meeting was cancelled.
   ① had told　　② told　　③ was told him　　④ was told

1-8 選出一個最適合填入空格中的答案。

1 A mass of data _____ in the computer.
① can store
② can is stored
③ can be stored
④ can to be stored

2 Most of Antarctica _____ ice and snow. Less than one percent of the land is ice-free.
① covers
② is covered with
③ covers with
④ is covered

3 I distinctly remember leaving the bag by the window. Now it _____.
① disappearing
② was disappeared
③ has been disappeared
④ has disappeared

4 Lead _____ as a material for sculpture since the time of the early Greeks.
① has used
② had used
③ used
④ has been used

5 A government minister _____ guilty of fraud yesterday.
① was found
② has been found
③ found
④ has found

6 The healthful properties of fiber have _____ for years.
① knew
② known
③ be knowing
④ been known

7 De Vincenzo _____ that she was a liar.
She _____ him that her child was seriously ill and near death.
① told — told
② told — was told
③ was told — told
④ was told — was told

8 Only a madman would _____ that the time will soon come.
① dream
② dreamed
③ be dreamed
④ had dreamed

9 選出有文法錯誤的句子，並更正。
① Where were you born? / In London.
② We were woken up by a loud noise during the night.
③ The school that most of the children attended was called Telpochcalli.
④ A thick blanket of fog was covered the town.
⑤ After the petals were opened, there was no beautiful rose.

10-13 閱讀下列文字，並回答問題。

10 選出括弧中最符合上下文者。

Tourism is not good news for the environment. First of all, millions of tourists (pollute, are polluted) the air and the seas. Secondly, as more hotels (build, are built), some of the world's most beautiful places (destroy, are destroyed) forever. And finally, water is running short as people (use, are used) more water.

11 選出劃線部分時態錯誤者，並更正。

Recycling helps protect the environment. For example, fifty kilograms of recycled paper ① saves one tree. Some cities ② have trained their citizens to separate garbage. People have to ③ put cans and plastic bottles in different garbage bags. Paper also ④ is kept separate. The plastic, metal, and paper ⑤ take to special centers for recycling.

12 選出一個最適合填入空格中的答案。

Sign language for the deaf _____ to the United States in 1816. Now it is the fourth most used language in the United States today. In most respects, sign language is just like any spoken languages. The only difference is that in sign language, information _____ through the eyes rather than the ears.
① brought — processed
② was brought — is processed
③ is brought — is processed
④ has brought — processes
⑤ was brought — processed

13 請在空格中填入動詞 give 的適當形式。

Love isn't the only reason people give flowers. Flowers are often presented for a celebration such as birthdays and _____ to mothers on Mother's Day by children.

14-21 選出劃線部分文法錯誤者。

14 ① Of the over 1,300 volcanoes in the world, ② only about 600 can ③ classify as ④ active.

15 The ① homeless man ② arrested and charged ③ with ④ pickpocketing the commuters.

16 Carnivorous ① plants ② are generally eaten ③ insects to ④ obtain nitrogen.

17 Typhoons ① are commonly occurred ② in Asian countries especially in ③ coastal countries ④ during the fall and spring.

18 She ① brought up in the belief that pleasures ② were sinful. ③ As a result, she now ④ leads an ascetic life.

19 The U.S. military ① says that the prison now ② is held about 395 men ③ on suspicion of ④ links to Al-Qaida.

20 ① The crime rate has ② gone down in the United States ③ while the prison population ④ has been risen.

21 The ability ① to reproduce has long ② regarded as a ③ special property ④ of living things.

CHAPTER 5

名詞和冠詞
Nouns & Articles

28 名詞的特點、形式、功能

A [**My** mother **bought some** cake at **the** bakery.
我媽媽在麵包店裡買了一些蛋糕。

B [**Education** is central to a country's economic develop**ment**.
教育是一個國家經濟發展的核心。

C [**Carol** is **a student**. she is reading **a book** about **butterflies**.
凱羅是一個學生。她正在閱讀一本關於蝴蝶的書。

A 當名詞放在句子中時,就單單一個名詞直接放入的情形非常少,幾乎都要搭配「其他詞類」來使用。這是名詞和其他詞類最不同的地方。mother、cake、bakery 都是名詞,它們分別和所有格(my)、不定代名詞(some)、冠詞(the)一起搭配使用。此外和名詞搭配使用的,還有指示代名詞和形容詞。名詞由於搭配了這些詞類,就變得複雜許多,所以有必要一項一項地去了解它。

B 名詞大多都是單一個字,和其他詞類一樣,所以不容易從字形上分辨出是不是名詞。不過,有一些名詞是由其他詞類衍生出來的,稱作「衍生名詞」,這種衍生名詞都有特定的語尾,所以可以從字面上分辨得出來。education 的「tion」和 development 的「ment」就是最具代表性的衍生語尾了。

C 名詞可以當作主詞、補語、及物動詞的受詞、介系詞的受詞等。以例句來說,Carol 是主詞、a student 是補語、a book 是及物動詞 read 的受詞、butterflies 是介系詞 about 的受詞。

概念習題

1-2 找出下列句中「其他詞類+名詞」的形式,並說明它在句中的功能。

1 Some people are eating cotton candy on a stick.

2 The successful flights of the early balloons entertained many people.

3-8 劃線部分的字如果詞類有錯,請更正。

3 <u>Develop</u> is gradual <u>grow</u>.

4 She had the <u>able</u> to explain things clearly and concisely.

5 That salmon dish was a grand <u>succeed</u>, wasn't it?

6 The information revolution has changed people's <u>perceive</u> of wealth.

7 <u>Mean</u>, <u>pronounce</u> and grammar come together.

▲ 衍生名詞舉例

payment (付款)	examination (檢查)	decision (決定)	kindness (仁慈)
belief (相信)	ability (能力)	arrival (到達)	teacher (教師)
scientist (科學家)	freedom (自由)	intelligence (智慧)	

1. I like my classmates. 我喜歡我的同學。
2. She has a few problems. 她有一些問題。
3. Most tourists don't visit this part of the town. 大多數遊客不參觀鎮上的這一區。
4. The kids are riding the Ferris wheel at the fair.
   孩子們正在乘坐遊樂場上的摩天輪。
5. What's the difference between an ape and a monkey? 猿和猴有什麼區別？
6. Birth order strongly affects personality, intelligence and achievement.
   出生順序影響人格、智力和成就甚鉅。

8 There is a <u>different</u> between normally coded messages and engineered messages.

9-10 劃線單字若為名詞寫 N，若為動詞寫 V。

9 Ralph and his colleagues <u>study</u> the health and life styles of 16,932 Harvard men.

10 Moreover, <u>studies</u> show that energetic activity could reduce hypertension.

11-12 選出一個最適合填入空格中的答案。

11 The _____ of the American Civil War are still being felt in the twentieth century.
　① affects　　② effects　　③ affect　　④ effect

12 Violence and homicide are not always the work of criminals and _____.
　① terrors　　② terrorism　　③ terrorists　　④ terror

29 不可數名詞

(A) [cheese (起司), hope (希望), luggage (行李), Mary (瑪莉)

(B) [**Cheese** is a good source of fat. 起司是脂肪的一項主要來源。

(C) [Would you like **a piece of** cheese to go with your bread?
你想要來片起司配你的麵包嗎？

名詞分為「可數名詞」和「不可數名詞」。**可數名詞**顧名思義就是可以量化的名詞，**不可數名詞**就是無法量化的名詞。這個差別關係到名詞的單複數形、不定冠詞、數和量的不定代名詞等的使用，要特別注意。

A 不可數名詞包含**物質名詞**「cheese」、看不見的**抽象名詞**「hope」、表集合同類的**集合名詞**「luggage」、全世界只有一個的**專有名詞**「Mary」。

B 不可數名詞的特點：第一，前面不可加「不定冠詞」；第二，不能使用「複數形」；第三，經常是「單數形」，搭配單數動詞使用。所以 a cheese/cheeses/cheese are 都是錯誤的表現方式。

C cheese 是不可數名詞，但也會有要表示一塊起司、兩塊起司的時候，這時不能說 a cheese、two cheeses，要說「a piece/slice of cheese」或「two pieces/slices of cheese」。piece/slice 等又稱作「單位量詞（unit of measure）」，可以是複數形。

1 不可數名詞寫 U，可數名詞寫 C。

名詞	U/C	名詞	U/C	名詞	U/C	名詞	U/C
1 advice		8 moon		15 news		22 job	
2 egg		9 jewelry		16 hope		23 flower	
3 dollar		10 island		17 weather		24 ocean	
4 apple		11 traffic		18 work		25 information	
5 accident		12 music		19 toothpaste		26 mail	
6 cake		13 library		20 necklace		27 furniture	
7 money		14 milk		21 water		28 envelope	

不可數名詞的種類	cheese 物質名詞	hope 抽象名詞	luggage 集合名詞	Mary 專有名詞

不可數名詞的特點	A̶ cheese 不能用不定冠詞	Cheeses̶ 不能用複數形	Cheese a̶r̶e̶ 搭配單數動詞

單位量詞	a piece/slice of two pieces/slices of	cheese	a cheese two cheeses	(X)

▲ **不可數名詞舉例**

> ability (能力)　audience (觀眾)　clothing (衣服)　weather (天氣)　paper (紙)
> furniture (傢俱)　gold (黃金)　glass (玻璃)　housework (家事)
> information (資訊)　knowledge (知識)　money (錢)　news (新聞)　traffic (交通)
> vocabulary (字彙)　water (水)　wealth (富有)　work (工作)

1. Blood is red. 血是紅色的。
2. The money is quite safe. 這些錢相當安全。
3. He went to pick out some furniture. 他去挑些傢俱。
4. The news was very depressing. 這個新聞令人心情低落。

　　a glass of water〔一杯水〕/ a carton of milk〔一瓶鮮奶〕/ a cup of coffee〔一杯咖啡〕
　　a piece of advice〔一項建議〕/ a piece of information〔一則資訊〕/ a piece of luck
　　〔一次好運〕/ a piece of paper〔一張紙〕/ a piece of bread〔一片麵包〕/ a piece of
　　furniture〔一件傢俱〕

2-6 選出括弧中最符合上下文者。

2　I usually eat (two piece of, two pieces of, two of) bread.

3　You need (a vitamin, vitamins), too. Do you take (a vitamin pill, vitamin pill)?

4　Josh had (an accident, accident) and spilled (a water, water) all over his work.

5　Some (words, vocabularies) are difficult to spell than others.

6　His retirement came as (a surprise, surprise) to everyone in the department.

7 請選出文法正確的句子。
　　① A furniture is often made of a wood.
　　② There was more news about Britain, and everyone was shocked by them.
　　③ A little knowledge is dangerous thing.
　　④ Quite a few packages have been brought in.

30 可數名詞和複數形

A ─ book（書）, teacher（老師）, accident（意外）

B
It is **a pen**. 它是一枝筆。
They are **pens**. 它們是筆。

C ─
They're building two new **schools** in the town.
他們正在鎮上興建兩間新學校。
Several **children** waited outside the door. 一些孩子在門外等。

A 可數名詞大部分都是「普通名詞」。事物 book 和人 teacher 都是普通名詞。意外事故「accident」雖然不是事物也不是人，但它是普通名詞，因為意外事故是指「現實世界中發生的具體事件」，發生了一件、兩件，是可以量化的。英文中像 accident 這樣的可數名詞很多，請注意。

B 可數名詞最大的特點就是，它一定是「單數形」或「複數形」其中之一。**單數形**的形式是「不定冠詞（或不定代名詞）＋單數名詞」，**複數形**的形式是「名詞＋複數形語尾 s/es/ies」。例句中的「a pen」是單數形，「pens」是複數形。如果主詞是複數，卻只單單出現一個 pen，就不正確了。

C 名詞的複數形變化有「規則變化」和「不規則變化」。在單數形後「直接加 s 或 es 或去 y 加 ies」，就是規則變化；反之，則為不規則變化。shools 是**規則變化**的複數形；children 是**不規則變化**的複數形。

 概念習題

1 將所提示的字的複數形填在空格中。

單數形	複數形	單數形	複數形	單數形	複數形	單數形	複數形
1 bag		5 leaf		9 game		13 fax	
2 woman		6 libary		10 child		14 tomato	
3 mouse		7 church		11 country		15 pen	
4 day		8 goose		12 person		16 foot	

2-3 選出一個最適合填入空格中的答案。

2 It is well-known that our brains possess _____ numbers of cells.

① such a large   ② such large a   ③ such large   ④ a large such

可以量化的 可數名詞	**book** 事物	**teacher** 人	**accident** 具體事件

一不定冠詞

a pen
可數名詞的單數形

複數形的意思

pens
可數名詞的複數形

規則變化的複數形

school	schools
bus	buses
month	months
baby	babies

不規則變化的複數形

child	children
woman	women
foot	feet

▲ 名詞不規則變化舉例

① 不規則變化	man → men（男人）, mouse → mice（老鼠）, tooth → teeth（牙齒）, goose → geese（鵝）
② 單數形＝複數形	sheep（綿羊）, deer（鹿）, fish（魚）, Chinese（中國人）
③ 外來語	datum → data（資料）, bacterium → bacteria（細菌）, crisis → crises（危機）

1. Tom is a doctor. 湯姆是位醫生。
2. Tom's parents are doctors. 湯姆的父母是醫生。
3. A dog is an animal. 狗是一種動物。
4. Helen has got blue eyes. 海倫有雙藍眼睛。
5. There are some eggs in the frigde. 冰箱裡有些蛋。

3 This book gives all sorts of useful _____ on how to repair _____.
　① information — car　　　　　② informations — cars
　③ information — all car　　　　④ information — cars

4-9 下列句子若有錯誤，請找出並更正。

4 Sydney is usually full of tourist.

5 Don't spend all your moneys on the first day of your holiday!

6 In the United States, inches and feets are still used as units of measurement.

7 There are probably dozens of way that this problem can be solved.

8 Seven species of birds of prey has been observed recently.

9 More fish is being raised on farms and fishing boats have been pushed farther.

名詞和冠詞

31 要注意的單數形和複數形

(A) [**Economics is** a difficult subject. 經濟是艱深的科學。

(B) [One million **dollars** is a lot of money. 一百萬是很多錢。

(C) [Many **people** never take any exercise. 許多人從不做運動。

(D) [These **trousers** are very expensive. 這些褲子很貴。

名詞中有「單數形」和「複數形」。單數形和複數形要注意的事項整理如下：

A economics 這個名詞的字尾是 s，但它不是複數名詞，而是單數名詞。在學科名和病名中，很多這樣的字。

B one million dollars 是「一百萬」的意思，是複數，所以用複數形 dollars；但是它後面要接單數動詞，不能接複數動詞，因為不能把它看作是 1 元的一百萬倍，而是要將它視為一個整體。表示時間、距離、重量等的名詞複數形，都要搭配單數動詞。

C people 並沒有添加複數形的字尾，但它要搭配複數動詞使用，因為它的意思是「人們」。

D trousers 是「褲子」的意思，褲子可以數出一條、兩條，所以它是可數名詞。也因為褲子都有兩個褲管，所以是「成對名詞」，固定用複數形，後面也固定接複數動詞。其他還有很多和衣服、用品有關的名詞，都是這類的名詞。

概念習題

1-8 選出括弧中最符合上下文者。

1 People (think, thinks) that you've gone mad.

2 Three billion dollars (was, were) withdrawn from the bank.

3 Rabies (isn't, aren't) a very common disease in Britain.

4 I want to cut this cloth. I need (a scissor, some scissors).

5 Politics (is, are) a constant source of interest to me.

6 My trousers (have, has) got a hole in (it, them).

7 (A police, A policeman) was been shot dead in an ambush.

8 Susan was wearing (a black jeans, black jeans).

複數形	單數動詞		複數形	單數動詞
economics	is		dollars	is

單數形	複數動詞		單數形	複數動詞
people	take		trousers	are

接單數動詞	學科名稱	economics (經濟學) mathematics (數學) physics (物理學) politics (政治學) statistics (統計學)
	疾病名稱	measles (麻疹) diabetes (糖尿病) rabies (狂犬病)
	複數形	five dollars (五元) three weeks (三週) forty miles (四十哩) five pounds (五磅)
接複數動詞	單數形	mankind (人類) police (警察) cattle (牛)
	衣服	pants (褲子) jeans (牛仔褲) shorts (短褲) stockings (長襪)
	用品	shoes (鞋子) scissors (剪刀) chopsticks (筷子)

1. Three weeks is a long time to wait for an answer.
   等一個答案要等三個星期是滿長的時間。
2. The police are also looking for a second car. 警方也在找第二台車。
3. Those are nice jeans. 那些牛仔褲很棒。
4. Measles is an infectious illness. 麻疹是傳染性疾病。
5. Statistics is a branch of mathematics. 統計學是數學的一個分支。
6. Statistics show that 50% of new businesses fail in their first year.
   統計資料顯示，有一半的企業在開業第一年就失敗。

9-10 請找出下列句子的錯誤，並更正。

9 Forty miles are a long way to walk in a day.

10 I can't find my shoes. Do you know where it is?

11-13 選出一個最適合填入空格中的答案。

11 Because my pants were torn by the nail, I'm going to buy a new _____.
  ① pair   ② trousers   ③ one   ④ trouser

12 A: I had to pay fifty dollars for these cups. B: They're probably _____.
  ① worth many   ② worth so   ③ worth it   ④ worth them

13 _____ an accurate advance signal of inflation.
  ① Economic give   ② Economics give   ③ Economics gives   ④ An economic give

名詞和冠詞

32 名詞的所有格

A
You should take the bus. 你應該搭公車的。
The bus has stopped. 這輛公車已經停下來了。

B
This is Lucy's bicycle. 這是露西的腳踏車。
Do you see the plate of the bus? 你看到那部公車的車牌了嗎？

C
a boy's books 一個男孩的書　　boys' books 男孩用書。
men's shirt 男用襯衫

D
This is Lucy's bicycle. 這是露西的腳踏車。
This bicycle is Lucy's. 這輛腳踏車是露西的。

A．名詞被當作「主詞」或「受詞」使用時，它的形式不變。例句的「the bus」是受詞，「The bus」是主詞，無論是當作主詞或當作受詞，名詞 bus 的形式都一樣。

B．名詞被當作「所有格」使用時，它的形式則會變化。如果名詞是「人、動物」，所有格要變成「名詞＋'s」；如果是「事物」，所有格要變成「of ＋名詞」。「Lucy's bicycle」的 Lucy 是人，所以所有格就變成 Lucy's；「the plate of the bus」的 the bus 是事物，所以所有格就變成 of the bus。

C．表示所有格要加 s 時，單數形和複數形不同。「boy's」是單數名詞 boy 的所有格；「boys'」是複數名詞 boys 的所有格。複數名詞的所有格不能加「's」，只要加「'」就可以了。不規則複數形的 men 的所有格是加「's」。

D．一般來說，所有格之後都會接名詞，但也會有不接名詞的情形出現。不接名詞的所有格，稱作「所有格代名詞」，用以和所有格區別。例句中 Lucy's bicycle 是「Lucy 的腳踏車」的意思；而 Lucy's 是「Lucy 的東西」的意思，所有格代名詞是「……是 Lucy 的」的意思，是代名詞，所以算是名詞。（參考 Unit 35）

概念習題

1-4 將括弧中提示的字改成所有格，填入空格中。

1 Mr. Hopkins answered the _____ questions. (student)

2 Mr. Hopkins answered the _____ questions. (students)

3 Mary is a _____ name. (woman)

4 Sarah and Mollie are _____ names. (women)

5-6 選出一個最適合填入空格中的答案。

5 I didn't go to the party last night. Did _____ go to the party?
① John friends　　② John' friends　　③ Johns friends　　④ John's friends

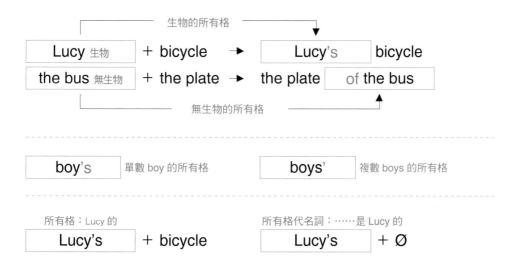

1. a woman's hat 一個女人的帽子
2. the girl's name 這個女孩的名字
3. a women's university 一所女子大學
4. the girls' names 這些女孩的名字
5. my sisters' room 我姊妹們的房間
6. my parents' car 我父母的車
7. the world's population 全球人口
8. John and Jill's car
   約翰和吉兒共有的車
9. the door of the garage 車庫的門
10. the middle of the book 書的中間
11. A: Whose bike is that?
    B: That is Peter's.
    A: 那是誰的腳踏車？
    B: 那是彼得的。

6 The woman, a mother of two boys, agreed on invitation rights for _____ .
① the boys father ② the boy's father ③ the father of the boys ④ the boys' father

7-12 請找出下列句子的錯誤，並更正。

7 A: Are these Becky's keys? B: No, they're Sylvia's.

8 Sara Hale influenced the taste and thought thousands of women.

9 The worker's wages were more important than their working conditions.

10 I think I'll visit the hairdresser's while I'm in town.

11 When I arrived at my uncle's home, I found that my cousins' were not there.

12 Some Asian's diets may contain over 0.5 kilogram of rice every day.

名詞和冠詞

33 a/some/the 和無冠詞

A

A dog is an animal. 狗是動物。

I just bought **a** new hat and **some** new belts.
我剛剛買了一頂新帽子和一些新皮帶。

B

The hat was quite expensive, but **the** belts weren't.
那頂帽子相當貴，但是皮帶不貴。

C

Ø Milk is good for you. 鮮奶有益健康。

I'm afraid of Ø dogs. 我怕狗。

A 不定冠詞有「a」和「an」兩個。由其後所接名詞的字首發音來決定用 a 還是 an，字首是子音，用 a；字首是母音，用 an。dog 的 d 是子音，所以用 a；animal 的 a 是母音，所以用 an。
名詞在句子中第一次出現時，如果是**可數名詞的單數形**，前面就要加「不定冠詞 a 或 an」，這個 a 是表示「不確定的某一個」的意思。但如果是**可數名詞的複數形**或是**不可數名詞**第一次出現，就加「some」，這時的 some 是表示「不確定的幾個或某一些」的意思。例句中的 hat 是單數，所以前面加 a；因為 belts 是複數，所以前面加 some。

B 之前已經提過的名詞**再次出現**時，名詞前面要加「定冠詞 the」，不管名詞是不可數名詞、可數名詞、複數形、單數形，都一樣加 the。這時的 the 是表示「限制、限定」的意思。在 A 項中，hat 和 belts 是第一次出現的名詞，所以加 a 和 some，而到了 B 項，因為 hat 和 belts 已經在 A 項中提過了，所以要加定冠詞 the。

C 不使用冠詞的情形叫做「無冠詞」。當名詞不使用冠詞時，表示該名詞沒有特定的含義，只是一般的含義而已。例如：milk 不是指特定的某些牛奶，而是指一般的牛奶。在這種情形下，如果名詞是可數名詞，該名詞一定要用複數形；例句的 dog 是可數名詞，所以要用 dogs。

1-9 選出括弧中最符合上下文者。

1 (A, Ø) house in San Diego is expensive.

2 (A, Ø) houses in San Diego are expensive.

3 (Ø, The) rice is very expensive in England.

4 We went to a good restaurant last night. (Ø, The) rice was not bad.

5 In the trunk, there's (a, an, some) oil, (a, an, some) spare tire, and (a, an, some) old flashlight.

6 We had (a, the, Ø) fine weather yesterday.

7 Encyclopedias may be used to answer (question, questions) or to solve problems.

8 (A, The, Ø) meat that they sell at that store isn't fresh.

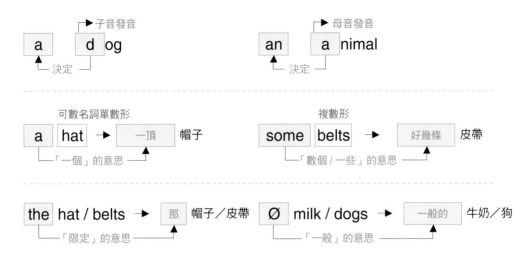

1. I met a girl and a boy. I didn't like the boy much, but the girl was very nice.
我遇見一個女孩和男孩。我不喜歡那男孩，但那女孩人很好。

2. I've bought a car. The car is quite expensive, but very comfortable.
我買了一台車。這台車相當貴，但非常舒適。

3. There's some cake in the kitchen if you'd like it. 如果你想吃蛋糕，廚房裡有一些。

4. We've been having some problems with our TV. 我們的電視出了問題。

5. Wolves hunt in groups known as packs.
狼都是集體，也就是成群結隊地進行獵捕。

6. Look at the wolves in that field. 看看那些在原野中的狼。

7. I enjoy talking to old people. 我很喜愛和老人家說話。

9 We need to buy (a, the, some) tomatoes because (the, some, Ø) tomatoes in the garden are still green.

10-12 選出一個最適合填入空格中的答案。

10 Rachel is wearing _____ necklace. _____ necklace is round her neck.
① a – A　　② a – The　　③ the – A　　④ the – Some

11 Ben should sit on _____ of his father at the dinner table.
① left side　　② a left side　　③ some left side　　④ the left side

12 _____ long been cultivated and bred for their beauty and fragrance.
① Flower has　　② A flower has　　③ The flower has　　④ Flowers have

1-9 選出一個最適合填入空格中的答案。

1 The carpenter measured the _____, width, and height of the cabinet.
① longth   ② length
③ long   ④ longing

2 The walls of this building are _____ thick.
① ninth inches   ② nine inches
③ ninth inch   ④ nine inch

3 For breakfast I usually have some toast, _____.
① cereal and milk   ② cereals and milk
③ cereals and milks ④ cereal and milks

4 There is a _____ university in my neighborhood.
① woman   ② woman's
③ women   ④ women's

5 _____ are good for you.
① Vegetables   ② Vegetable
③ A vegetable   ④ The vegetable

6 The researcher is interested in the social _____ of these actions.
① signify   ② significance
③ significant   ④ significantly

7 As a high school _____, he was supposed to live on about $60 a month.
① mathematic teacher
② mathematics teacher
③ mathematic teachers
④ mathematics teachers

8 Here, let me give you a _____ with that heavy box.
① hope   ② lift   ③ hand   ④ push

9 He endeavored to improve _____ of the society that he lived in.
① democracy
② the democracy
③ a democracy
④ some democracies

10 選出有文法錯誤的句子，並更正。
① My family are all fast learners.
② She refused to give evidence at the trial.
③ Do some research before you buy a house.
④ It is difficult to find job these days.

11-15 閱讀下列文字，並回答問題。

11 選出一個最適合填入空格中的答案。

When we meet someone for the first time, we notice a number of _____ about that person — physical characteristics, clothes, firmness of handshakes, gestures, tones of voice, and the like. We then use these _____ to fit the person into ready-made categories.
① thing — impression
② things — impression
③ thing — impressions
④ things — impressions

12 選出劃線部分文法錯誤者，並更正。

The library in Blue River, Oregon, is one of the most unusual ① library in the world. If you want to borrow ② a book from this little library, you don't need ③ a card. There's no time limit on borrowing, and everything is free. There's not even ④ a librarian around most of the time, and ⑤ the library door is never locked, day and night. The library is on the honor system.

13 請找出錯誤用字，並更正。

Eat healthy food, get plenty of physical activity, get plenty of sleep, avoid bad stuff like cigarettes, alcohol, and drugs, and get a doctors' checkup each year.

14 空格中填入 choose 的正確形式。

Too much _____ in everyday life makes me feel I'm a stranger in my own country.

15 選出劃線部分文法錯誤者。

Sabriye Tenberken is ① extraordinary woman. She runs ② a school for ③ blind children in Tibet. Born in Germany, she lost her sight at 13. But she made ④ a decision to live her life fully.

16-24 選出劃線部分文法錯誤者。

16 People ① say that ② there are three ③ basic ④ type of muscles ⑤ in human beings.

17 ① Soccer is a ball ② games ③ played by two teams, each is made up of ④ 11 players.

18 The news on ① the paper ② are old, since ③ we've already heard it ④ on television.

19 ① Rabbits have large front ② tooth, short tails, ③ hind legs and ④ adapted feet.

20 In coastal and ① inland waters there ② are such ③ sea creature as ④ shrimps and clams.

21 He was ① fired as host of a ② child's television show, and ③ his dream looked ④ dead.

22 Another ① one of our fellow ② brothers and sisters ③ dies of ④ starvations every day.

23 Some ① people are ② allergic to ③ certain type of ④ food, such as ⑤ strawberries and seafood.

24 ① Kepler's laws described ② the positions and motions ③ of the planets with great ④ accurately.

CHAPTER 6

代名詞
Pronouns

34 人稱代名詞的特點和種類

A Henry loves Sara. **He** gave **her** a flower today.
亨利愛莎拉，他今天送她一朵花。

B I picked up the plate and put **it** on the table. 我拾起一個盤子，並且把它放在桌上。
I have two pictures. **They** are beautiful. 我有兩幅畫，它們很美。
I can go with **you**. 我可以和你一起去。

C **We**'re foreign students. Teachers help **us**. 我們是外國學生。老師幫助我們。

A 前面已經提過的名詞，又再次提到它時，這時會用「人稱代名詞」來代替之前提過的那個名詞。人稱代名詞可以代替人，也可以代替事物。

因為人稱代名詞是代替名詞，所以它的功能也和名詞一樣，大多被用來當主詞或受詞。例句一中，代名詞「He」代替 Henry，是主詞；代名詞「her」代替 Sara，是受詞。

B 人稱代名詞會隨著所代替的名詞「種類」而有所不同。如果它所代替的名詞是複數名詞，代名詞就用 they；如果是單數名詞中的男性 Henry，代名詞就用 he；如果是單數名詞中的女性 Sara，代名詞就用 she；如果是單數名詞中的事物 the plate，代名詞就用 it。

I、we、you 不能代替先行詞。I 是「我」、we 是「我們」、you 是「你」或「你們」的意思。

C 名詞當作主詞或受詞，該名詞的形態完全不變。但是代名詞當作主詞和受詞時，兩者的形態就不同了。在主詞的位置，就要用主格；在受詞的位置，就要用受格。以例句來說，we 是主格；移到受詞的位置就變成受格 us。

概念習題

1-6 空格中填入正確的人稱代名詞。

1 Susan and her sister got up late. _____ missed the school bus.

2 Because the window would not budge, we had to leave _____ open.

3 Catherine has a book. _____ bought _____ last week.

4 Peter Hamilton is a new student in our class. _____ is from Georgia. I met _____ yesterday on the street.

5 On the first day of my new math class, the teacher told my classmates and _____, "As a class, _____ need to hand in your homework on time."

6 The fish have ceased to develop eyes because they live in such dark water that they no longer have any use for _____.

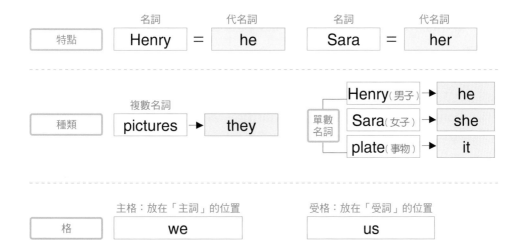

1. The windows are dirty. I must wash them. 窗戶好髒，我必須清洗它們。
2. Mike is in class. He is taking a test. 麥克在課堂上，他正在考試。
3. Sara bought a hat. She loves it very much. 莎拉買了一頂帽子，她非常喜愛它。
4. My husband and I have a new car. We got it last month.
   我先生和我有台新車，是上個月買的。

7-9 選出一個最適合填入空格中的答案。

7 In my country, we never call our teachers by their first names. We call _____ "Professor" or "Teacher."

① it   ② them   ③ him   ④ they

8 King cobras use poison by spitting _____ into the eyes of their prey.

① you   ② they   ③ it   ④ we

9 You can learn more about new computers by actually working with _____ than by merely reading the instruction manual.

① it   ② them   ③ you   ④ one

35 人稱代名詞：所有格、所有格代名詞、反身代名詞

A — [Is this **your** raincoat? / No, it's **yours**. 這是你的雨衣嗎？／不，它是你的。

B

Tom is watching **himself** in the mirror. 〔反身用法〕
湯姆正看著鏡子裡的自己。

Tom is watching him in the mirror.（him 不是 Tom，是別人）
湯姆正看著鏡子裡的他（他不是湯姆，是別人）。

The President **himself** opened the door. 〔強調用法〕總統自己開門。

A 主格和受格時常都以單獨一個字出現，但**所有格**就一定要以「所有格＋名詞」的形式出現。這個「所有格＋名詞」要視為一個整體，當作主詞、受詞、補語使用。

當「所有格＋名詞」被視為一個整體，要用一個代名詞來代替它時，這個代名詞就稱做「所有格代名詞」。「所有格代名詞」時常都是單獨一個字出現的，當作**名詞**使用。例句一中，your raincoat 是「所有格＋名詞」；yours 是所有格代名詞。這兩者的功能，都是 is 的補語。

B 在字尾加上「-self」或「-selves」的代名詞，叫做「反身代名詞」，主要當作**受詞**使用。「反身代名詞」和「人稱代名詞的受格」要區分清楚。當主詞和受詞是同一個人或事物時，就用**反身代名詞**，稱為「反身用法」；如果不是同一人，那就要用該名詞的受格，或該代名詞的受格。例句二中，himself 和 Tom 是同一人；而 him 和 Tom 則不是同一人。

反身代名詞也可以緊接在主詞之後，或放在句子最後，這種用法稱為「強調用法」。例句三中的 himself，就是用來強調主詞 the President。

 概念習題

1-4 選出括弧中最符合上下文者。

1 My friends are on vacation, too. (Their, Theirs) families are here.

2 The statesman dedicated (him, himself) to serving people in the country.

3 We asked (her, herself) to stay with us for dinner.

4 Be careful with that knife or you'll cut (you, yourself, yourselves)!

5-8 請找出劃線部分有文法錯誤者，並更正。

5 What kind of bird is that? / <u>Its</u> a crow.

6 My relatives all live in the States — <u>his</u> are in France.

7 They say it's a beautiful place, but I <u>myself</u> have never been there.

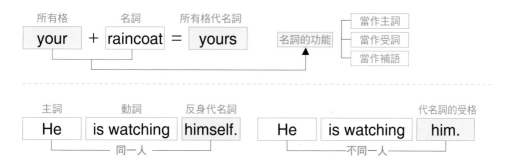

人稱代名詞	I	we	you	he	she	it	they
所有格	my	our	your	his	her	its	their
所有格代名詞	mine	ours	yours	his	hers	Ø	theirs
反身代名詞	myself	ourselves	yourself / yourselves	himself	herself	itself	themselves

* yourself 是「你自己」，為單數；yourselves 是「你們自己」，為複數。it 沒有所有格代名詞。

1. A: Did you eat your ice cream? B: Yes, I ate mine.
   A: 你吃了你的冰淇淋嗎？B: 是的，我吃了我的（冰淇淋）。
2. I spent my vacation in Bali, and they spent theirs in Australia.
   我在峇里島度假；而他們在澳洲度假。
3. Steve lost his umbrella. I'm sure that is his.
   史帝夫的雨傘不見了，我確定那是他的（傘）。
4. It's our own fault. We should blame ourselves.
   那是我們自己的錯，我們應該責怪自己。
5. I'm making myself a sandwich. 我正在為自己做一份三明治。
6. It must be true —he said so himself. 那必定是真的，他自己都這麼說。
7. Sue gave me a book. I don't remember its title.
   蘇給我一本書，我不記得書名了。

8 Ours successes and failures will make us better people.

9-11 選出一個最適合填入空格中的答案。

9 Steve has set up a business. He doesn't have a boss. He works for _____ .
   ① him   ② his   ③ he   ④ himself

10 We compared the scores and found that theirs were higher than _____ .
   ① us   ② our   ③ ours   ④ ourselves

11 The government is defending _____ foreign policies against a lot of criticism.
   ① its   ② it's   ③ it   ④ itself

36 指示代名詞

A
> **This** is a pear; **that** is an apple. 這是一顆梨子；那是一顆蘋果。
>
> **That** is a machine. / **That** room is for the teacher.
>
> 那是一台機器。／那個房間是給那位老師用的。

B
> I don't like **this** coat / **these** coats. 我不喜歡這件大衣／這些大衣。
>
> **That** money is mine. ~~Those money~~ is mine. 那些錢是我的。

C
> Japan's culture is different from **that** of Korea. 日本的文化和韓國的不同。
>
> Asia's cultures are different from **those** of America.
>
> 亞洲的文化和美洲的不同。

A this、that 還有複數形的 these、those 被稱做「指示代名詞」。它們和人稱代名詞不同，不是用來代替先行詞，它們是用來指人或事物是「這個、那個」的代名詞。

this 是指在距離上、在時間上，和說話者較「接近」的那一個東西。that 是指在距離上、在時間上，和說話者較「遠」的那一個東西。例句一中，a pear 距離說話者較近所以用「this」；an apple 距離說話者較遠所以用「that」。

這些指示代名詞都是單獨使用的，也具有名詞的功能；它也可以像形容詞一樣，和名詞一起搭配使用。例句二中，That 是單獨使用的形式；That room 是和名詞搭配使用的形式。

B 因為 this 和 that 是單數，所以要搭配單數名詞使用；these 和 those 是複數，所以要搭配複數名詞使用。另外，this 和 that 也可以接不可數名詞，但 these 和 those 就不可以接不可數名詞了。例句二中，因為 money 是不可數名詞，所以 those money 是錯誤的用法。

C that 和 those 除了有指示代名詞的功能之外，它還有避免前面提過的名詞再重覆出現的代名詞功能。例句一中，that of Korea 中的 that，是代替前面提到的單數名詞 culture；those of America 中的 those，是代替前面提到的複數名詞 cultures。

概念習題

1-5 請將正確的指示代名詞填入空格中。

1 Can you sign _____ form here for me?

2 His own experience was different from _____ of his wife.

3 A: May I speak to Mr. Smith? B: Who is _____?

4 These glasses are mine and _____ are yours.

5 In modern societies the achievements of women don't even approach _____ of men.

6-9 下列句子若有錯誤，請找出並更正。

6 This is cherry trees.

7 A: It's so boring here. B: I know. Nothing happens in that place.

指示代名詞	this / these	在近處	名詞的功能 That
	that / those	在遠處	形容詞的功能 That room

this ＋單數名詞	these ＋複數名詞	those ＋不可數名詞
this coat	these coats	~~those coats~~

代名詞 that —— 代替單數名詞（culture）　　代名詞 those —— 代替複數名詞（cultures）

1. I'm just looking at this picture. 我正在看這張照片。
2. I'm not satisfied with these results. 我不太滿意這些結果。
3. That table is nice, isn't it? 那張桌子很不錯，不是嗎？
4. Hello? This is Laura speaking. Who's this, please?
   喂，我是蘿拉。請問你是哪位？
5. The climate in Seattle is quite different from that in Chicago.
   西雅圖的氣候和芝加哥不一樣。
6. His dress is that of a gentleman, but his speech and behavior are those of a clown. 他的穿著就像一位紳士，但是他的言語和行為卻像個小丑。

8 Have you heard those news about John and Mary?

9 In natural disasters, the number of the injured is much more than this of the dead.

10-12 選出一個最適合填入空格中的答案。

10 _____ of shoes seem to be expensive, but they are relatively comfortable.
① This kinds　② This a kind　③ These kind　④ These kinds

11 Economic development in the West far surpasses _____ in the East.
① those　② those one　③ that ones　④ that

12 People compare the ideas of William Wordsworth with _____ of John Dryden.
① that　② this　③ those　④ these

37 One

A ⌐ **One** of their daughters **has just got married.** 他們其中一個女兒才剛結婚。

B ⌐ They sold their house, **and moved to** a smaller **one**.
他們賣了他們的房子，然後搬到較小的房子。

C ⌐ His family **is** a large **one**. **It** consists of eight members.
他家是大家庭，有八位成員。

Do you have a camera? / No. / You should buy **one**.
你有沒有相機？／沒有。／你應該買一台的。

Do you have my camera? / **It**'s on the desk.
你有沒有拿我的相機？／它在桌上。

A one 能以 one、one book、one of their daughters 等形式來使用。這時的 one 是「一個」的意思，但詞類卻不同，它們分別是**名詞**、**數詞**、**限定詞**。one 不能和不可數名詞搭配使用。

B one 也具有避免前面提過的名詞再重覆出現的「代名詞」功能。例句中，a smaller one 的「one」是代替前面提到的單數名詞 house；要代替的名詞若是**複數**，就要用「**ones**」。因為代名詞 one 只代替名詞，所以它會和形容詞 smaller 或冠詞 a 搭配使用。

C 前面學過的代名詞 it 和這裡的 one 該如何分辨呢？one 只能代替**名詞**，而 it 可取代**名詞**和**所有格代名詞**。例句一中 one 只代替 family，it 取代了 his family。it 和 one 不同，it 不能和冠詞或形容詞一起使用，而且通常都是單獨一個字。

因為 one 只代替名詞，所以不是用來具體地指稱某樣東西；而 it，因為連所有格代名詞都代替，所以可用來具體指稱某樣東西。例句二中的 a camera 是指正在談論「相機」這項物品，並沒有具體地指出是哪一部相機。而相反的，例句三的 my camera 就能具體知道是指「我的相機」。a camera 要用 one 來代替，my camera 要用 it 來代替。

 概念習題

1-3 請指出劃線部分的 one/ones 是指哪一個名詞。

1 My new house is much bigger than my old <u>one</u>.

2 We needed hundreds of hats for the convention, so we bought the cheapest <u>ones</u>.

3 Companionship and social support are, perhaps, one reason why married people tend to live longer than unmarried <u>ones</u>.

4-8 選出括弧中最符合上下文者。

4 If you need a raincoat, I'll lend you (one, it).

5 I've got a few books on Chinese food. You can borrow (one, it) if you want.

6 I sent an e-mail to you yesterday. Have you got (one, it)?

| 數字 | one book（單數名詞） | one of their daughters（of＋複數名詞） |

| 代名詞 | 代替
They sold their [house], and moved to a smaller [one]. |

family：名詞

His family is a large [one].

| one / it |

his hamily：所有格代名詞＋名詞

[It] consists of eight members.

| 非具體指稱的名詞 | | 具體指稱的名詞 | |
| a camera | → one | my camera | → it |

1. This is one of my favorite books. 這本是我最愛的書之一。
2. French croissants are so much better than the English ones.
   法式可頌比英式的還好吃。
3. I need a hat. I think I'd better buy one. 我需要一頂帽子，我想我最好去買一頂。
4. A: Where's my hat? B: It was on the desk a minute ago.
   A: 我的帽子呢？ B: 它一分鐘前還在桌上。
5. A: Have you a watch? B: Yes, I have one. It's Swiss.
   A: 你有沒有手錶？ B: 有，我有一支，它是瑞士製的。
6. The train was so crowded that we decided to catch a later one.
   這班火車擠滿了人，所以我們決定搭下一班。

7 I need a cup of coffee. Would you like (one, it), too?

8 One of the (child was, children were, children was) killed in the crash yesterday.

9-11 9-10 選出一個最適合填入空格中的答案。11 選出劃線部分有錯誤者。

9 I don't have a decent bookcase, so I am going to _____.
　　① have it made　　② have one made　　③ have that made　　④ have it

10 When I buy something, my husband sometimes doesn't like _____.
　　① one　　② ones　　③ that ones　　④ it

11 ① While blue is ② one of the most popular ③ color, it decreases ④ the desire to eat.

代名詞

38 All/Most/Every

A

> **All** children **like playing.** 小朋友都愛玩。
>
> **All** (of) that money **has been spent on books.** 全部的錢都用來買書了。
>
> **Most** children **like playing.** 大部分的小朋友都愛玩。
>
> **Most** of that money **has been spent on books.** 大部分的錢都用來買書了。
>
> **Every** child **likes playing.** 每個孩子都愛玩。

A all、most、every、some、any、many、much、few、little 等不是代替前面提過先行詞的代名詞,它們要像名詞一樣使用,也可以像名詞前面的形容詞一樣使用。它們大部分都含有「數」或「量」的含義,所以也被稱為**數量詞**或**限定詞**。

all 和 every 是「全部」的意思,most 是「大部分」的意思。all 是將焦點放在對象的全部上,而 every 是將焦點放在構成全部的每一個個體上。

all 和 most 可修飾**可數名詞**,也可修飾**不可數名詞**,every 只可修飾**可數名詞**。要注意的是,every 後的可數名詞一定要是「單數形」的,而且也只能搭配「單數動詞」使用。例句二和四中,all 和 most 修飾的 money 是不可數名詞;例句一和三中,children 是可數名詞的複數形,而例句五的 every 修飾的是 child,是可數名詞的單數形。

all 搭配名詞使用時,可以用「all children」(all +名詞)和「all of the children」(all + of + the +名詞)兩種形式表現。all children 是指一般的全部,all of the children 是指特定的全部。「all + of + the +名詞」中的 the,可以換成所有格或指示代名詞。most 也和 all 一樣,有這兩種形式。all 後面的 of 也可以省略,變成 all the children。every 不可以用 every of the children 這種形式,只能用 every child。

1-8 選出括弧中最符合上下文者。

1 When we play, I lose every (game, games).

2 When we play, I lose all the (game, games).

3 (All, Most, Every) city in Japan has a good transportation system.

4 (Most, Every) of the students in this class like mathematics.

5 (Every, Most) luggage must be checked at an airport.

6 All of my (homework is, homeworks are) finished.

7 The boys played video games (all, every) day last week.

8 Yesterday the boys played video games (all, every) day.

all / most + 複數可數名詞 children / money 不可數名詞

every + 單數可數名詞 child

all ＋名詞
all children　　世上所有的孩子（一般的全部）

all of the children　　那些孩子的全部（特定的全部）
all ＋ of ＋ the ＋名詞

〔錯誤用法〕
~~every of the children~~

1. The police interviewed every employee about the theft.
   這位警察和每位職員都談過這件偷竊案。
2. The police interviewed all the employees about the theft.
   警方和所有的職員都談過這件偷竊案。
3. Most people take their holidays in the summer. 大部分的人都在夏天度假。
4. Most of the people were pleased to hear the news.
   大部分的人都很開心聽到這個消息。
5. Everybody / everyone stopped talking. 每個人都停止談話。
6. I work hard every day. 我每天都努力工作。
7. The buses run every ten minutes. 這部公車每十分鐘發車一次。

   *every 也可以當作「每⋯⋯」的意思使用。

9 下列各句哪一句文法完全正確。
① Most of Koreans work on Saturday.
② We looked carefully at every cars that drove fast.
③ Most research in this field have been carried out by Russians.
④ There were traffic lights every ten yards.

10-11 選出一個最適合填入空格中的答案。

10 _____ the coal that we now mine was formed about 300 million years ago.
① Most　　② The most of　　③ Most of　　④ Most of the

11 _____ village or tribe of the Indian confederacy had its annual green corn dance.
① All　　② Every　　③ Most　　④ The all

39 Many/Few、Much/Little、A lot of

A
Alice has **many** books.〔數〕愛麗絲有很多書。
Alice has **a few** books. 愛麗絲有一些書。

B
Mary doesn't have **much** money.〔量〕瑪麗沒有很多錢。
Mary has **a little** money. 瑪麗有一點錢。

C
Alice has **a lot of** books/money.〔數／量〕愛麗絲有好多書／錢。

D
We've made **a little/quite a little** progress.〔肯定〕我們已經有點／相當進步了。
We've made **little/very little** progress.〔否定〕我們只有一點點的／很少的進步。

A-C　many/a few 是表示「數」，要搭配**複數動詞**使用，後面要接**可數名詞**的**複數形**。例句中的「books」
就是可數名詞的複數形。
much/a little 是表示「量」，要搭配**單數動詞**使用，後面要接**不可數名詞**。例句中的「money」就是
不可數名詞。
a lot of/lots of/plenty of 表示「**數和量**」都可以，後接**可數名詞**或**不可數名詞**都可以。後接可數名詞
時，表示**數**，搭配**複數動詞**使用；後接不可數名詞時，表示量，搭配單數動詞使用。例句中的「a
lot of books」是複數，「a lot of money」是單數。a lot of 換成 lots of 或 plenty of 都可以。

D　使用 few 和 little 時，要正確區分肯定還是否定。a little 是「有一點點」的意思，是**肯定**的含義；little
是「很少、幾乎沒有」的意思，是**否定**的含義。quite a little 是「相當多」的意思，是**肯定**的含義；
very little 是比 little 還少的意思，是**強烈否定**。few 和 little 的用法完全相同。例句中，a little progress
和 quite a little progress 是「有一些進展」和「有許多進展」的意思，都是肯定的含義。little progress
和 very little progress 是「幾乎沒什麼發展」的意思，都是否定的含義。

概念習題

1-2 空格中請填入適當的字，使兩句意思相同。(也可能填入兩個字以上)

1 Lucy has received a lot of mail because she is very popular.

= Lucy has received _____ mail because she is very popular.

2 Did you visit many places in America?

= Did you visit _____ few places in America?

3-6 空格中填入 a little / very little / a few / very few 其中之一，以符合句意。

3 They have _____ money. They have been unemployed for ages.

4 We may get _____ rain today. We'd better take umbrellas with us.

5 We have _____ problems with the new computer. It often fails to work.

複數可數名詞		不可數名詞	
many / a few	+ books	much / a little	+ money

	複數可數名詞
a lot of	+ books
	+ money 不可數名詞

肯定	強烈肯定	否定	強烈否定
a few a little	quite a few quite a little	few little	very few very little

1. I want to visit many cities in Australia. 我想遊覽澳洲的許多城市。
2. How much sugar would you like in your coffee? 你的咖啡要加多少糖？
3. It rained a lot last week. The garden needs little water.
   上週下了好多雨，花園只需要一些些水份。
4. There are a few cakes left over from the party. 有一些蛋糕是派對剩下的。
5. There are few cakes left over from the party. 有一點點蛋糕是派對剩下的。
6. Very few people can afford those prices. 很少人可以付得起那些價格。
7. I know quite a few people there. 我在那裡認識不少人。
8. Eggs have lots of cholesterol. 蛋含有很多膽固醇。(lots of = a lot of)

---

6 There are lots of men in the club, but _____ women.

7-8 選出一個最適合填入空格中的答案。

7 They were able to give him _____ information, so he needed more.
  ① little   ② a few   ③ a little   ④ few

8 There is a need for _____ vending machines in the student lounge.
  ① a little   ② many a   ③ a few   ④ much

9 選出不能填入空格中的答案。
  The city is regaining _____ of its former splendor.
  ① some   ② a little   ③ much   ④ many

40 Some/Any 和 No/None

A
Mom has left **some** food/apples for me. 媽媽留了一些吃的東西／蘋果給我。

Mom has**n't** left **any** food/apples for me. 媽媽沒留任何吃的東西／蘋果給我。

B
There aren't **any** letters for you. 沒有任何一封信是給你的。

I haven't read **any of** the letters. 我還沒看過任何一封信。

C
There are **no** letters for you. 沒有一封信是給你的。

I have read **none of** the letters. 我還沒看過任何一封信。

D
Any student can answer the question. 每位學生都可以回答這個問題。

A some 和 any 是表示「數」或「量」，而且是不具體的「不確定」的數或量，翻譯成「一些、任何」。some 和 any 後面接可數名詞或不可數名詞都可以。例句的 food 是不可數名詞，apples 是可數名詞的複數形。
　「some」一定要用在肯定句中，「any」一定要用在否定句和疑問句中。

B any 和名詞搭配使用時，有「any + letters」和「any + of + the + letters」兩種形式；這和前面提到的 all/most 的情形一樣。而 some 也和 any 一樣，也有這兩種形式。

C any 用在否定句中，和 not 一起搭配使用。**not** 和 **any** 合用時，也可以換成 **no** 或 **none** 的形式。用 no 時，要像例句的 no letters 一樣，後面一定要接名詞；用 none 時，要像例句的 none of the letters 一樣，none 一定要像名詞一樣單獨使用。

D any 除了表示數或量以外，也可以當作「任何人、任何事物」的意思使用（和 all 的意思相似）。當作人或事物的意思使用時，後面接可數名詞或不可數名詞都可以；而且除了可以用在否定句，也可以用在肯定句。any 當「任一、每一」使用時，不能用複數形，而是要用**單數形**，這點要注意。例句中 student 就是可數名詞的單數。any 當「若干」、「一些」、「一點」、「絲毫」等使用時，後接不可數名詞與複數形的可數名詞，一般用於疑問句、否定句、if 子句中。

1-4 空格中填入 some、any、no、none 其中之一，以符合句意。

1 Alice has received _____ information. It's very useful to her.

2 Alice has not received _____ information.

3 Tom's parents take good care of him. He has _____ problems.

4 I sent invitations to all the people, but _____ of them came to the party.

5-10 選出括弧中最符合上下文者。

5 I have (something, anything) in my trouser pocket.

6 I've hurt my right arm, so I can draw (no, none, any) pictures.

7 The baby doesn't need (a, some, any) help. He can walk by himself.

8 I don't have (a, some, any) letter.

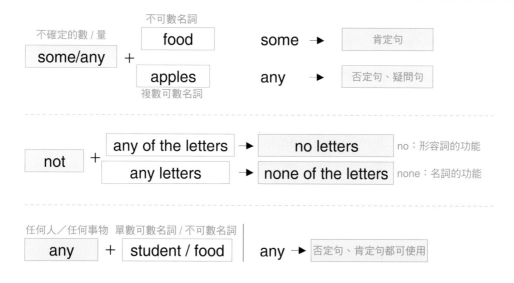

1. We have already received some of the information. 我們已經收到部分訊息。
2. There are some beautiful plants in your garden. 你的花園裡有些美麗的植物。
3. You don't know any of my friends. 你不認識我的任何一位朋友。
4. Can I have some of your cake? 我可以吃一些你的蛋糕嗎？
   *「形式」是疑問句，但實際「內容」是直述句。
5. There were no potatoes left. 馬鈴薯都沒了。
6. None of my children have/has blonde hair. 我的孩子沒有任何一個是金髮。
7. Any food would be better than nothing at all. 有得吃就好，總比什麼都沒有好。

9 Could you give me (some, any) examples of this disease?

10 A: What kind of container do you need? B: (Some, Any) container will do.

11-13 選出一個最適合填入空格中的答案。

11 Not all teachers left early this afternoon; _____ stayed late and finished it.
   ① no   ② any   ③ some   ④ none

12 When I was young, I saw _____ big bear in the forest.
   ① a   ② some   ③ any   ④ none

13 Despite her illness, Maria had lost _____ of her enthusiasm for life.
   ① no   ② none   ③ any   ④ many

代名詞

115

41 Both/Neither/Either

A

John held his melon in **both** hands. 約翰雙手都拿著甜瓜。

At first, **neither** man could speak. 一開始，兩位男士當中沒有人可以說話。

Do you see **either** end of the tunnel? 你看到隧道的任一端盡頭了嗎？

B

Denis and Jerry were friends. **Neither** was successful.
丹尼斯和傑瑞是朋友，他們沒一個人成功。

Neither man was successful. 兩位男士當中沒有人成功。

Neither of the men was successful. 兩位男士當中沒有任一個人成功。

C

They have two children. **Both** live abroad.
他們有兩個孩子，兩位都居住在國外。

We should listen to **both sides** of the argument.
我們應該聽聽雙方的論點。

Both (of) the books were very instructive. 這兩本書都很有啟發性。

A 對象是兩個的時候，才能用 both、neither、either 這些字。both 指「兩個都是」；neither 指「兩個都不是」；either 指「兩個中的某一個是」。neither 等於「either ＋ not」。
「both」時常搭配**複數動詞**使用，後面接**複數名詞**。neither 和 either 時常搭配**單數動詞**使用，後面接**單數名詞**。例句中，both hands 是「兩隻手都是」的意思，是肯定的含義。neither man 是「兩個人都不是」的意思，是完全否定的含義。either end 是「兩端其中的一端」的意思。

B 「neither」放在句中使用時，有三種形式：「單獨用 neither」、「neither ＋單數名詞」、「neither of ＋複數名詞／代名詞」。三種形式都要搭配**單數動詞**使用。而「either」也和 neither 一樣，有這三種形式。

C both 基本上和 neither 一樣，也有這三種形式。不同的是 both 後面要接複數名詞，而且要搭配複數動詞使用。both 後面的 of 可以省略。

概念習題

1-5 空格中填入 both、either、neither 其中之一，以符合句意。

1 I have bought two books. I haven't yet read _____ book.

2 I didn't keep _____ hands on the steering wheel.

3 John and Jerry are my cousins, and _____ of them like to eat fish.

4 We can offer a comfortable home to a young person of _____ gender.

5 We asked both Bob and Mary, but _____ one could offer a satisfactory explanation.

6-8 選出一個最適合填入空格中的答案。

6 Both of them got the flu; _____ was at work today.

① neither   ② either   ③ both   ④ any

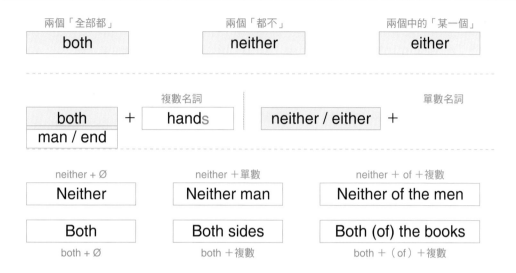

1. Both films were very good. / Both of the films were very good. 這兩部電影都很棒。
2. She invited both of us to the party. 她邀請我們倆去參加派對。
3. Neither road goes to the station. 兩條路都不是通往車站。
4. Neither of my parents likes my boyfriend. 我父母沒有一個喜歡我的男朋友。
5. Can either of your parents speak French? 你父母中有一位會說法文嗎？
6. A: Would you like the metal or plastic one?

   B: Either will do.

   A: 你要金屬的，還是塑膠的呢？

   B: 任何一個都可以。

---

7 There are three ways to get to the summit. You can go _____ way.

① either   ② both   ③ any   ④ neither

8 Oxford is not far from Stratford, so you can easily visit _____ in a day.

① either   ② neither   ③ both   ④ all

9 下列句中哪一句和其他三句意思不同？

① I don't know either of the boys.

② I know neither of the boys.

③ I don't know both of the boys.

④ I don't know the two boys.

代名詞

117

42 Other的類似形式

A ⎡ I'm going to have **another** piece of cake. 我正要吃另一塊蛋糕。

B
⎡ I have two pencils. I'll keep one, and you can have **the other (one)**.
我有兩枝鉛筆。我要留一枝,另一枝可以給你。

I have four pencils. I'll keep one, and you can have
the others / the **other ones**. 我有四枝鉛筆。我要留一枝,其他的都可以給你。

C ⎡ Some of these methods will work, but **others** will not.
這些方法中的一些可行,其他的就不可行了。

A other 基本上是「其他的」的意思。other 有 another、the other(s)、others 等類似形式。
another 可以看作是「an + other」,常搭配使用**單數動詞**,後面接**單數名詞**;是「許多個中的某一個」的意思。例句中,another piece of cake 是「另一片蛋糕」的意思,暗示已經吃了至少一片蛋糕。another piece of cake 也可以換成只用「another」,或「another one」和「another piece」也可以。

B the other 是「兩個中剩下的那一個」的意思,the others 是「許多個中剩下的全部」的意思。以例句來說,共有兩枝鉛筆「two pencils」,除了一枝「one」以外,剩下的就只有一枝,就用「the other」。鉛筆有四枝「four pencils」,除了一支「one」以外,剩下的有好幾枝,就用「the others」。這個 the others 也可以換成 the other ones 或 the other pencils。

C others 或者是「other +複數名詞」,是「許多個中的某一些」的意思,常和 some 搭配使用。some 是指「某一部分」,others 是指除了 some 以外的「剩下中的某一些」的意思。例句「Some of these . . . others will not」是「這些方法裡面,有一些有用,有一些沒用」的意思。others 可以換成 other ones 或 other methods。

概念習題

1-4 選出一個最適合填入空格中的答案。

1 Each of the twins wanted to know what _____ was doing.

① another ② the other ③ the others ④ others

2 Some TV shows are good, and _____ are not very funny.

① another ② the other ③ the others ④ others

3 There're three colors in the US flag. One is white, _____ are red and blue.

① another ② the other ③ the others ④ others

4 He finished his sausage and asked for _____ one.

① another ② the other ③ the others ④ others

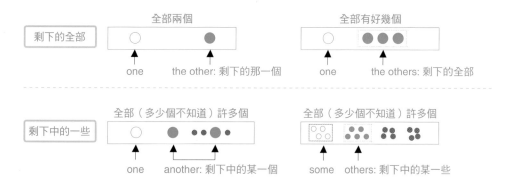

1. Our family grows apples. Here, please take one. Have another. We have a lot!
   我們家種蘋果。來，請拿一個，再拿一個。我們有很多！

2. I had a blue hat, but I seem to have lost it. I guess I'd better buy another one.
   我有一頂藍色的帽子，但我好像把它弄丟了。我想我最好再買一個。

3. Rebecca has two sisters. One is in college and the other is in high school.
   瑞貝卡有兩個姐姐。一個唸大學，另一個唸高中。

4. One man was arrested, but the other one got away.
   有一個人被逮捕，另一個逃跑了。

5. She's much brighter than all the other children in her class.
   她比班上其他的孩子要出色得多。

6. Why do some people go grey much earlier than others?
   為什麼有些人的頭髮比其他人的還早變白？

5-12 空格中填入 other 及其類似形其中之一，以符合句意。

5 There are two slices of cake left. I'm going to have one. Would you like _____?

6 We're going to have _____ baby.

7 There must be _____ ways of solving the problem.

8 We can fit _____ person in my car.

9 Ed doesn't like college. Some classes are too easy, but _____ are too difficult.

10 I've found one earring — do you know where _____ one is?

11 Switzerland borders on several countries. One is Germany. _____ is Italy.

12 I chose this coat in the end because _____ were all too expensive.

1-13 選出一個最適合填入空格中的答案。

1 Between _____, I think he is telling a lie.
① I and you ② you and I
③ you and me ④ you and myself

2 The ears of a rabbit are much longer than _____ of a dog.
① they ② them ③ that ④ those

3 On summer holidays, some people go to the seaside, and _____ to the mountains.
① another ② other
③ others ④ the other

4 _____ of our employees have a great deal of experience.
① A little ② Much ③ Those ④ Many

5 The school finally completed constructing the two buildings: one will be used as the student center, _____ as the guest house.
① other ② the other
③ another ④ others

6 Even after your explanation, we still have _____ of questions.
① a little ② a few
③ all ④ a number

7 _____ technicians offered their own unique solutions.
① Every ② Each ③ Any ④ Other

8 When lava reaches the surface, _____ temperature is ten times that of boiling water.
① its ② it's ③ their ④ theirs

9 Not all rainwater falling from a cloud reaches the ground; _____ of it is lost through evaporation.
① some ② no ③ any ④ either

10 Rumors break hearts and ruin lives. People can't protect _____ against rumors.
① themselves ② theirs
③ him or her ④ ones

11 Many students believe that small classes offer much better educational opportunities than large _____.
① one ② them ③ it ④ ones

12 The guitarists Rod and Jack both started their careers as actors, but neither of them _____ a big success. Both of them _____ they are happier as musicians.
① was — says ② was — say
③ were — says ④ were — say

13 Rabbits and hares are very like each other. _____ long ears, big eyes, short tails, and they eat plants.
① Both have ② Both has
③ All have ④ Either have
⑤ Any has

14-17 閱讀下列文字，並回答問題。

14 請找出錯誤使用的字，並更正。

We depend greatly on fossil fuels because about 75% of the energy we use comes from it.

15 選出劃線部分文法錯誤者，有兩處，並更正。

People often ask me what bungee jumping really is. It's very easy. Usually, ① <u>you</u> jump from about sixty meters, and find ② <u>you</u> flying like a bird. I know it sounds dangerous, but in fact it isn't. All ③ <u>you</u> have to do is jump from a bridge onto a river with a rope round ④ <u>you</u> ankles. It's quite a safe sport.

16 選出括弧中最符合上下文者。

(Many, Many of) people today like to exercise. Some like to run or swim. (Another, Others, The others) dance or play ball. Why do people like to exercise? Because it makes us healthy. Also it makes us sleep better at night.

17 選出一個最適合填入空格中的答案。

Cartoon makers may use signs to explain thoughts. For example, a light bulb above the head means a bright idea. Cartoon makers can say _____ with a simple drawing and _____ words.
① much — a few
② much — a little
③ a little — very little
④ little — few
⑤ very little — a few

18-25 選出劃線部分文法錯誤者。

18 Physics ① <u>has challenged</u> people ② <u>to search</u> into ③ <u>their</u> ④ <u>mysteries</u>.

19 You should get ① <u>a receipt</u> for every ② <u>purchases</u> ③ <u>no matter</u> now small ④ <u>it may be</u>.

20 Two of ① <u>the scheduled lecturers</u> ② <u>will be able</u> to speak this week ③ <u>but</u> ④ <u>the another</u> cannot.

21 Because of ① <u>the mobility</u> of Americans today ② <u>it is difficult</u> ③ <u>for him</u> to put down ④ <u>real roots</u>.

22 None of the shops ① <u>was</u> open, and there was ② <u>no bus</u>, so she ③ <u>walked home</u>. She spoke ④ <u>little English</u> and had ⑤ <u>few friend</u> there.

23 ① <u>Dogs</u> usually possess ② <u>hearing</u> ability far superior to ③ <u>those of</u> ④ <u>their</u> owners.

24 ① <u>Unfortunately</u>, I was sitting ② <u>at the</u> table ③ <u>with smokers</u> on ④ <u>either sides</u> of me.

25 ① <u>Today</u> ② <u>most of parents</u> are worried about ③ <u>their</u> ④ <u>children's</u> leisure life.

CHAPTER 7

形容詞和副詞
Adjectives & Adverbs

43 形容詞的功能和語序

A
> She is a **healthy** baby. 她是個健康寶寶。
>
> The baby is **healthy**. 這個寶寶很健康。

B
> A girl was carrying two small black plastic bags.
>
> 女孩提著兩個小黑色塑膠袋。
>
> This is an ~~alive~~ lobster.〔錯誤用法〕
>
> This lobster is alive. 這隻龍蝦是活的。

A 形容詞的**功能**是用來「描述」名詞和代名詞的。a baby，是「一個嬰兒」的意思，而 a healthy baby，是「一個健康的嬰兒」的意思。形容詞 healthy 是用來描述和說明 baby 的。

形容詞有兩種方式來描述名詞：(1) 放在**名詞前**的限定用法，(2) 放在 **be** 動詞後的敘述用法。例句中，healthy baby 的 healthy 是**限定用法**；baby is healthy 的 healthy 是**敘述用法**。兩種用法的意思都是「寶寶是健康的」。

B 形容詞和名詞一起使用時，**基本的語序**是「形容詞＋名詞」。這時不同種類的形容詞若同時出現，它們之間也有一定的順序，它們的順序是：數字→大小→新舊→顏色→材料。例句的順序即 two「數字」small「大小」→ black「顏色」→ plastic「材料」。

形容詞中也有不能用限定用法，只能用**敘述用法**的。這些形容詞叫做「敘述形容詞」，它們不能放在名詞前面。alive 就是最具代表性的敘述形容詞；alive lobster 是錯誤的用法。

1-4 找出下列各句中的形容詞，並標示出來。

1 Cindy looks very tired. She needs a long vacation.

2 An extraordinary number of important events took place near him.

3 This interesting book includes a good chapter about modern music.

4 My favorite place is famous for tall buildings and expensive restaurants.

5-9 請找出下列句子的錯誤，並更正。

5 You have worn a black big pearl necklace.

6 He saw black two bears in the forest.

7 When she was a child small, Helen had a terrible disease.

圖表整理

形容詞		名詞
healthy		baby

限定用法

名詞	連接動詞	形容詞
baby	is	healthy

敘述用法

數字	大小	新舊	顏色	材料	
two	small	old	black	plastic	bags

be 動詞＋敘述形容詞

lobster | is | alive

敘述形容詞＋名詞

~~alive lobster~~ 〔錯誤用法〕

▲ 最具代表性的敘述形容詞舉例

asleep (睡著的)　alike (相像的)　afraid (害怕的)　alone (單獨的)　alive (活著的)　awake (醒著的)

1. These are new shoes. 這些是新鞋。
2. These shoes are new. 這些鞋是新的。
3. This is an empty house. 這是一間空房子。
4. The house looks empty. 這個房子看起來沒人住。
5. A: You look tired. B: Yes, I feel tired.
   A: 你看起來很累。B: 是的，我感到疲累。
6. This fish doesn't smell good. 這條魚不好聞。
7. There was a large brown wooden table in the kitchen. 廚房裡有張咖啡色大木桌。

8 There are two green old microscopes on the table.

9 The domestic dog is loyal, courageous and intelligence.

10-11 10 選出文法錯誤者。11 選出一個最適合填入空格中的答案。

10 Boys wear ① fashionable clothes to ② attract grils. In ③ a similar way, some birds have ④ brightened feathers.

11 In adolescence, a young person may experience _____ due to confusing social demands.
   ① some emotional stress　　　　② stress some emotion
   ③ some stress emotional　　　　④ emotional stress some

44 副詞的形式和功能

A
Tom is a **careful** driver.〔形容詞〕湯姆是一位小心的駕駛者。
Tom drives **carefully**.〔副詞〕湯姆開車很小心。

B
I couldn't go shopping **yesterday** so I'll have to go **today**.〔修飾動詞〕
我昨天不能去購物，所以我今天必須去。

The house had a **fairly** large garden.〔修飾形容詞〕
這個房子有個相當大的花園。

The traffic is moving **very** slowly this morning.〔修飾副詞〕
今天早上的交通有些擁擠。

It will **probably** take about a month.〔修飾句子〕
這大概要花大約一個月的時間。

The engines make **quite** a noise.〔修飾名詞〕這些引擎發出很大的噪音。

A 副詞有很多種，其中最具代表性的副詞，就是「情狀副詞」。**情狀副詞**的形式大部分都是「形容詞＋ly」，它的功能是修飾**動詞**。
例句的「careful」是形容詞，修飾名詞 driver；「carefully」是副詞，修飾動詞 drives。careful 和 carefully 除了形式上有 -ly 的差異外；功能上，一個修飾名詞，一個修飾動詞，完全不同。

B 「副詞」基本上用來修飾**動詞**。不過因為副詞有許多種，所以除了動詞以外，也有修飾其他詞類的。
方式副詞大致上都修飾動詞。地方副詞、時間副詞，基本上也是修飾動詞，不過也有修飾句子的。A 項中的情狀副詞 carefully 修飾動詞 drives；B 項中的時間副詞 yesterday 和 today 也是修飾動詞 go。
fairly 和 very 是強化副詞，它們用來修飾形容詞「large」和副詞「slowly」。probably 修飾句子。quite 修飾名詞 a noise，只是，修飾名詞的副詞不多。

1-9 選出括弧中最符合上下文者。

1 The car was travelling at a very (slow, slowly) speed.

2 The car was travelling very (slow, slowly).

3 He's (real, really) angry with me for upsetting Sophie.

4 Classical music was playing (soft, softly) in the background.

5 It's nothing serious — (just, fairly) a small cut.

6 She had a (good, well) vacation.

7 Josephine is bright, cheerful, and (live, lively).

8 Microwave cooking is described as the first (absolute, absolutely) new method.

9 He can't (possible, possibly) have drunk all that on his own.

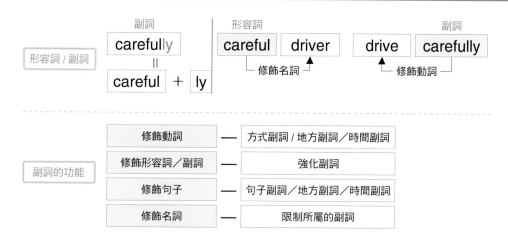

強化副詞	very, fairly, quite, so, pretty, much, too, really, absolutely
修飾句子的副詞	probably, possibly, really, certainly, obviously
修飾名詞的副詞	even, only, quite, also, just

1. The children seemed happy. 這些孩子似乎很開心。
2. The children played happily. 這些孩子玩得很開心。
3. He played the beautiful piano. He played the piano beautifully.
   他彈這架漂亮的鋼琴。他很會彈鋼琴。
4. A march is a highly rhythmic piece of music. 進行曲是節奏比較強的音樂。
5. You speak very good English. / You speak English very well. 你英文說得很流利。

10-12 選出一個最適合填入空格中的答案。

10 It is difficult to understand a foreign language if it is spoken _____.

① soon   ② fastly   ③ hurry   ④ quickly

11 They waited in a _____ manner outside the church.

① graceful and orderly   ② gracefully and orderly

③ gracefully and order   ④ graceful and order

12 The goalkeeper of the handball team played _____ in the Beijing Olympic Games.

① very excellent   ② much excellent

③ excellently good   ④ so excellently

45 副詞的位置

A　I opened the door **slowly**. 〔放在受詞之後〕我緩慢地開門。

B　Mary spoke **very well at the hall last night**. 〔方式＋地方＋時間〕
　　瑪莉昨晚在（大）會堂演說得非常好。

C　She **always** goes to work by car. 〔頻率副詞＋一般動詞〕她總是開車上班。
　　She is **always** late. 〔be 動詞＋頻率副詞〕她總是遲到。

英文中幾乎沒有什麼詞類會像**副詞**這樣，位置那麼多變。因為主詞和動詞是句子的核心要素，所以主詞和動詞的位置大致都是固定的，而副詞是句子中的選擇性要素，所以它的位置非常不定。隨著強調的強度、隨著副詞的長度、隨著句子的律動，它的位置都不同。再加上副詞的種類很多，所對應的位置就更多了。基本規則如下：

A　第一，大部分的副詞都位在動詞之後。動詞後面若有受詞，它就要接在受詞之後。例句中的 slowly 是副詞，the door 是受詞，所以放在 the door 之後。

B　第二，一個句子裡如果同時具有數個不同種類的副詞時，排列順序為：情狀副詞→地方副詞→時間副詞。例句中，very well 是「情狀副詞」，at the hall 是「地方副詞」，last night 是「時間副詞」。

C　第三，頻率副詞和 not 的位置一樣，也就是在 be 動詞之後，一般動詞之前；即「be 動詞／助動詞＋頻率副詞」、「頻率副詞＋一般動詞」。**always** 是最具代表性的頻率副詞，go 是一般動詞，is 是 be 動詞。

概念習題

1-5 將括弧內的字，依句意重組。

1 Anna worked (at school, hard, yesterday).

2 Christmas (often, is, mild) in this country.

3 The manager walked (out of the room, happily, at the end of the conference).

4 I (almost, forgotten, have) whether she said August or September.

5 Andreas played (at the concert, the violin, last week, beautifully).

6-9 重組句子。

6 last night / I / left / in the restaurant / my cell phone

7 at the meeting / last Friday / spoke / very loudly / Jess

▲ 最具代表性的頻率副詞

always (總是)	usually (通常)	often (經常)	sometimes (有時)
seldom (很少)	never (從不)	almost (幾乎)	quite (相當)
hardly (幾乎不)	scarcely (幾乎沒有)	really (確實)	little (一點)

1. They were discussing the problem reasonably. 他們正理性地討論這個問題。
2. The boy couldn't remember the accident clearly.
   這個男孩無法清楚地記起這場車禍。
3. I have to finish the work by tomorrow. 我明天前要完成這項工作。
4. Brian and Anne arrived safely last Tuesday. 布萊恩和安上週二安全抵達。
5. Kevin came here yesterday. 凱文昨天來這裡。
6. Luis often plays badminton. 路易斯常常打羽毛球。
7. My parents have always lived in Chicago. 我父母一直都住在芝加哥。

8 they / in the town / build / are going to / next year / a new school
9 in the park / the children / every Saturday / football / usually / play / merrily

10-11 選出一個最適合填入空格中的答案。

10 The lady was waiting _____.
   ① outside patiently the door   ② patiently outside the door
   ③ outside the door patiently   ④ the door patiently outside

11 Carnivorous plants _____ insects to obtain nitrogen.
   ① are generally trapped   ② trap generally
   ③ generally are trapped   ④ generally trap

46 Very/Too/Enough 和 Much

A

I arrived at the airport **very** late. 我很晚才到機場。

I arrived at the airport **too** late. 我太晚到機場了。

I arrived at the airport early **enough**. 我夠早到機場了。

Did you bring **enough** money? 你是否帶了足夠的錢？

B

Tony hasn't changed **much** in the last ten years. 〔否定句〕
過去十年裡，湯尼沒有太多的變化。

Mary likes him so **much**. 〔肯定句〕瑪莉很喜歡他。

The flower is **much** more beautiful. 〔修飾比較級〕這朵花更漂亮。

A very 是最具代表性的「強化副詞」，用來修飾**形容詞**和**副詞**，它的功能是更「強調、強化」句意。例句中 very late 的「very」就是用來強調 late，是「非常晚」的意思。
too 也是修飾形容詞和副詞的**強化副詞**，是「過度、太」的意思，含有**否定**的含義。very late 是「雖然很晚但還是搭上了飛機」，而 too late 則是「因為太晚了所以沒搭上飛機」的意思。
enough 是「足夠」的意思，它除了可以修飾**形容詞**和**副詞**外，也可以修飾**名詞**；它和 too 相反，經常為**肯定**的含義。very 和 too 都是放在形容詞和副詞之前修飾它們；而 enough 則是放在形容詞之後。不過 enough 在修飾名詞時，則是放在名詞前來修飾它。例句中，因為 early 是副詞，所以 enough 放在它後面；money 是名詞，所以 enough 放在它前面。

B much 是**不定代名詞**，不過它也時常當作**副詞**使用。當作「副詞」時，它可以修飾動詞、比較級、副詞片語、分詞、敘述形容詞等。修飾**動詞**時，句子主要是**否定句**或**疑問句**；句子若為肯定句時，much 單獨使用的情形幾乎沒有，多是以 very much、so much、too much 等形式出現。

1-6 選出括弧中最符合上下文者。

1 The suitcase is (very, too) heavy, but David can lift it.

2 The suitcase is (very, too) heavy. Brian can't lift it.

3 You have put (too, enough) salt in the soup. It doesn't need any more.

4 You have put (too, enough) much salt in the soup. I can't eat it.

5 I can't explain the problem. It's (very, too, enough) difficult.

6 We aren't working quickly (very, too, enough). We'd better hurry.

7-10 將括弧中提示的字加上 very、too、enough 其中之一，填入空格中。

7 They missed their plane because they didn't leave home _____ _____. (early)

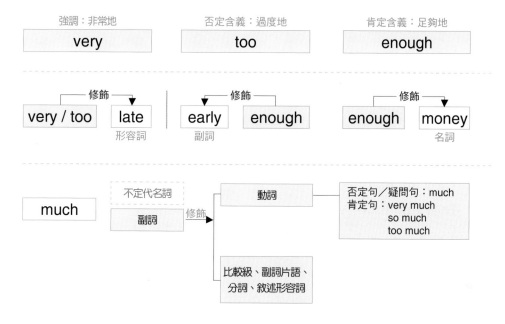

1. I can't reach the shelf — it's too high. 我碰不到那個架子，它太高了。
2. The shelf is very high, but I can reach it. 這個架子很高，但我可以碰到它。
3. The box is too heavy for me to lift. 這個箱子對我而言太重了，我沒辦法搬移它。
4. The box is very heavy. (But I can lift it.) 這個箱子太重了 (但是我可以搬移它)。
5. You can go to school when you're old enough. 你年紀夠大時，就可以去上學了。
6. I was getting too old for romantic relationships. 我很老了，不適合談戀愛。
7. The water is warm enough for me. 這個水溫對我來說夠暖了。
8. The water is too hot for me. 這水對我來說太燙了。
9. There aren't enough chairs for everyone in the room.
   這房間裡的椅子不夠給每個人坐。

8 They missed their plane because they left home _____ _____. (late)
9 They left home _____ _____, but they didn't miss their plane. (late)
10 This restaurant is _____ _____ for me. Let's leave. (crowded)

11-12 選出一個最適合填入空格中的答案。

11 I can't hear you! There's _____ noise!
　① too　　　　② enough　　　③ very much　　④ too much

12 The rooms are all _____ to take a third bed.
　① enough large　② too large　　③ very large　　④ large enough

形容詞和副詞

47 So/Such 和 Quite

A
The boy was **so** foolish.〔修飾形容詞／副詞〕這個男孩太愚笨了。
The boy was **such** a fool.〔修飾名詞〕這個男孩是如此愚笨的人。

B
She is **so** beautiful a girl. 她是個美麗的女孩。
She is **such** a beautiful girl. 她是個如此美麗的女孩。

C
They are ~~so beautiful girls~~.〔錯誤用法〕
They are **such** beautiful girls. 她們是如此美麗的女孩。

D
The food in the cafeteria is usually **quite** good.〔修飾形容詞／副詞〕
這家自助餐的餐點通常都相當不錯。
The cafeteria usually serves **quite** a good food.〔修飾名詞〕
這家自助餐通常提供相當不錯的餐點。

A so 和 such 是「如此的」的意思，是有強化意味的**副詞**。兩者的差異是，such 基本上修飾「名詞」；而 so 修飾「形容詞、副詞」。例句中 a fool 是名詞，foolish 是形容詞。

B 於「so ＋形容詞」之後再加名詞，變成「so ＋形容詞＋名詞」的形式也可以。「such ＋名詞」再加形容詞修飾，變成「such ＋形容詞＋名詞」的形式也可以。這時，這兩句的差別就只在不定冠詞 a 的位置上了，so 是「so ＋ beautiful ＋ **a** ＋ girl」這順序；such 是「such ＋ **a** ＋ beautiful ＋ girl」這順序。

C so 和 such 之後的名詞，如果是**複數名詞**或**不可數名詞**，就不能加「不定冠詞 a」。這時，so 的形式和 such 的形式完全一樣，都是 so/such beautiful girls 了。但因容易造成混淆，所以規定不用 so；也就是說，如果名詞沒有不定冠詞 a，就不能用 so。so 只能用在名詞有 a 修飾的時候。

D quite 是形容詞也是**副詞**，用來修飾名詞和動詞。修飾名詞時，要注意不定冠詞 a 的位置。

概念習題

1-6 空格中填入 such、so 其中之一，以符合句意。

1 The plan had been _____ neat.

2 It had been _____ a neat plan.

3 Various parts of the body require _____ different surgical skills.

4 I've never seen _____ beautiful a child.

5 There were _____ many people on the train.

6 The rejection of _____ initiatives shows that voters are unconcerned about them.

7-8 將括弧內的字，依句意重組。

7 Yesterday was (a, nice, such, day), wasn't it?

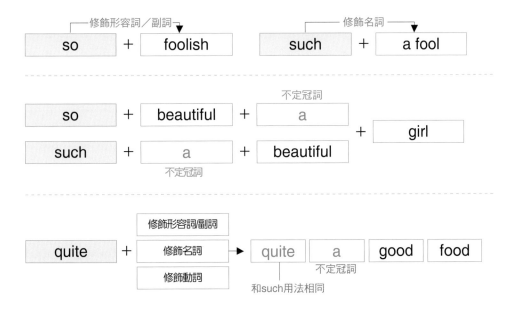

1. It is such an interesting story. / The story is so interesting.
   這是個有趣的故事。／這個故事是如此的有趣。

2. He works so slowly. / He's such a slow worker.
   他工作速度很慢。／他是動作如此慢的工作者。

3. We both have such busy schedules. 我們都有如此繁忙的行程表。

4. Why did you buy so much food? (so many/much 許多) 你為什麼買這麼多食物？

5. Why did you buy such a lot of food? (a lot of = such) 你為什麼買這麼多食物？

6. Ann's at college, and she's doing quite well. 安就讀大學，而且她功課很好。

7. That's quite a different matter. 那是相當不同的事件。

---

8 There was (of, traffic, quite, a lot) today.

9-11 選出一個最適合填入空格中的答案。

9 Dr. Kim had _____ interesting and original plans that they want to work with him.

① such   ② so   ③ very   ④ quite

10 A: My father is very strict. B: I think he is _____.

① quite strict a father   ② a quite strict father

③ a father quite strict   ④ quite a strict father

11 The extent of the disaster was _____ that the local authorities could not cope with.

① such a great   ② such great   ③ so a great   ④ so great

48 Hard/Hardly 和 Already/Yet 和 Still

A Ann is a **hard** worker. / Ann works **hard**. 安是個努力工作的人。／安工作努力。
We **hardly** know each other. 我們幾乎不了解對方。

B I have **already** got the tickets. 〔肯定句〕我已經買到票了。
Have you **got the tickets yet**? 〔疑問句〕你買到票了嗎？
I haven't **got the tickets yet**. 〔否定句〕我還沒買到票。

C The coffee is **still** hot. 〔肯定句〕這咖啡仍然很燙。
You **still** haven't got the tickets. 〔否定句〕你仍沒買到票。

A 「hard」本身可被當作形容詞用，也可當作副詞用；「努力的、努力地、困難的、困難地」等含義。例句中 a hard worker 的 hard 是形容詞，works hard 的 hard 是副詞。
「hardly」雖是在 hard 後附加 ly，不過它是另一個副詞，和 hard 一點關係也沒有。它是「幾乎不 . . .」的意思，和 not 很類似，在句中的位置也和 not 一樣。hardly know 和 don't know 的意思一樣。

B 「already」用在肯定句中，「yet」用在否定句和疑問句中。already 是「已經」的意思，表示「某事比預期的更早發生了」。yet 是「尚未」的意思，表示「正在期待某事，或某事仍在繼續中」。already 和 yet 在句子中的位置，和頻率副詞的位置一樣，不過 already 和 yet 還可以放在句尾。
例句的「have already got」是已經買到了的意思，暗示了買到的行為比預期的要早。「Have you got . . . yet?」是詢問票買到了沒，而「haven't got . . . yet」是還沒買到票；這兩句都暗示現在仍還在關心購票問題。

C still 幾乎都是用在肯定句中，表示「仍然、還是」的意思。still 表示某種狀況到目前為止仍在繼續，不過其中還含有「竟然、但是」的意味。本來是熱的咖啡，經過了一兩個小時後，應該已經涼了，但事實和預測不同，竟然還是熱的，這時就用 still hot 來表示。
still 若放在否定句中，具有強烈否定的含義。例句中的「still haven't got . . .」是應該早就買到的，但現在竟然還沒買到的意思。still 的位置也很特殊，大致上它都是緊接在主詞之後。

1-9 選出括弧中最符合上下文者。

1 I'm not surprised he failed his exam — he didn't exactly try very (hard, hardly).

2 She (hard, hardly) ate anything because she was not hungry.

3 We missed the school bus, which made us (late, lately) for the class.

4 Have you been doing anything interesting (late, lately)?

5 Luckily I found a phone booth quite (near, nearly).

6 I've (near, nearly) finished that book you lent me.

7 Look, it's (already, yet, still) snowing. How much longer can it go on?

8 I'm not hungry. I've (already, yet, still) eaten dinner.

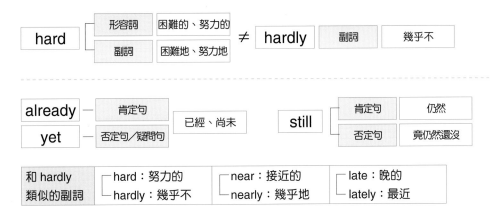

1. The day of his interview was drawing near. 他面試的日子就快到了。
2. I nearly always go home for lunch. (nearly = almost) 我幾乎都回家吃午餐。
3. I got up late this morning. 我今天早上晚起。
4. Have you seen Tom lately? (lately=recently) 你最近見過湯姆嗎？
5. I've already seen the report. 我已經看過報告了。
6. Have you finished the work yet? 你完成工作了嗎？
7. Jesse isn't home yet. He's still at work. 傑西還沒回家，他仍在工作。
8. Jason is eighteen, and he still can't swim. 傑森目前十八歲，但他還不會游泳。

9 I (already, yet, still) haven't finished painting the spare room.

10-12 選出一個最適合填入空格中的答案。

10 The automobile is very reliable and _____ ever needs repairs or maintenance.

① quite   ② nearly   ③ hardly   ④ lately

11 Although she hasn't really got the time, Emma _____ offered to help.

① yet   ② already   ③ near   ④ still

12 My manager said it was all right to turn in the report _____.

① near   ② nearly   ③ late   ④ lately

1-10 選出一個最適合填入空格中的答案。

1 I found a _____ in my bathtub this morning.
① big bug black   ② big black bug
③ bug big black   ④ bug black big

2 Scientists are _____ trying to map the human genome.
① current   ② currently
③ currency   ④ currentness

3 Despite his broken legs, John can walk _____ to get around.
① good enough   ② fine enough
③ well enough   ④ enough fast

4 _____ can hardly be found elsewhere in Europe.
① A so good market
② So good a market
③ A market so good
④ So a good market

5 We discussed this matter at a _____ early morning briefing.
① late   ② lately
③ recent   ④ recently

6 Yet two years later, the bill _____ has not been passed.
① still   ② always
③ already   ④ never

7 Because the refrigerator was disconnected, the meat smelled _____.
① bad   ② badly
③ badness   ④ very badly

8 _____ 50% of the eligible students chose not to enroll in the program.
① Closely   ② Nearly
③ Close   ④ Near

9 The Government was accused of placing _____ emphasis on artificial targets.
① enough   ② too much
③ very   ④ much too

10 The wild blue phlox grows in spring in _____ from Canada to the Gulf coast.
① woods moist   ② moist woods
③ wooden moist   ④ woods moisture

11-15 閱讀下列文字，並回答問題。

11 請找出使用錯誤的字，並更正。

Information is most important in our modern life. We can easy get information through the Internet. It is the network that connects so many computers all over the world. There are now about 200 million users around the world.

12 選出括弧中最符合上下文者。

The Messiah was a great success in London. All the nobility was present, even the royalty. During the "Hallelujah Chorus," the King was (too, so, such, enough) excited that he rose to his feet. So did the whole audience.

13 請找出文法錯誤的字，並更正。

In today's society, it is easier to do more at night. Stores stay open 24 hours a day. Companies want their employees to work lately. Television stations broadcast all day and all night.

14 請在空格中填入適當的字。

Near the lake, there were many people who made a lot of noise. Some people played loud music and danced. The place was so _____ that we couldn't rest.

15 選出劃線部分文法錯誤者。

In ① <u>previous</u> centuries, some people used coffee only as medicine. Other people believed that coffee caused religious visions. For this reason, the first coffeehouse opened in Mecca, an ② <u>important</u> religious city in Saudi Arabia. The coffeehouses were the clubs for ③ <u>socially</u>, political, and philosophical discussions. These clubs spread to Europe. Coffee is now the most ④ <u>popular</u> drink in the world. Coffee merchants trade ⑤ <u>nearly</u> 7 billion pounds of coffee in markets and stores each year. Americans drink 400 million cups of coffee a day.

16-26 選出劃線部分文法錯誤者。

16 Factory workers ① <u>may</u> suffer from ② <u>temporary</u> or ③ <u>permanently</u> loss of ④ <u>hearing</u>.

17 In order for us to be ① <u>successful</u> ② <u>in the field</u>, ③ <u>our</u> prices must be ④ <u>competitively</u>.

18 With the ① <u>help</u> of Woodrow Wilson, ② <u>the people</u> became ③ <u>orderly</u> and ④ <u>democratically</u>.

19 Learning to use a language ① <u>free</u> and ② <u>full</u> is a ③ <u>lengthy</u> and ④ <u>effortful</u> process.

20 The art ① <u>pleasing</u> ② <u>can't hardly</u> ③ <u>be reduced</u> to rules; your ④ <u>own good sense</u> will teach you more of it.

21 ① <u>When</u> I saw the smoke, I ② <u>called</u> the fire department but they ③ <u>haven't arrived</u> ④ <u>already</u>.

22 This ① <u>new program</u> ② <u>automatical</u> searches ③ <u>for the lowest</u> flight fare ④ <u>available</u>.

23 He ① <u>had never received</u> ② <u>any cash</u> from Saddam supporters and ③ <u>had</u> enjoyed his ④ <u>alone</u> trip to Iraq.

24 The two languages are ① <u>such</u> similar that ② <u>they</u> are ③ <u>mutually</u> ④ <u>intelligible</u>.

25 ① <u>Some</u> water is ② <u>enough safe</u> to drink, ③ <u>but</u> all surface water must be ④ <u>treated</u>.

26 ① <u>Certain</u> therapies encourage ② <u>patients</u> ③ <u>to act</u> in a ④ <u>way healthy</u>.

CHAPTER 8

介系詞
Prepositions

49 介系詞和介系詞片語

A — The glass is **on** the table. 這個杯子在桌上。

B — The people **on the train** were singing. 火車上的人在唱歌。
The children were playing **on the ground**. 小朋友在地上玩。
The golf club belongs **to** Paddy. 高爾夫球俱樂部是屬於佩蒂的。

A on、in、with 等被稱作「介系詞」，介系詞的數量比起其他詞類少很多。**介系詞**是「前置、放在前面」的意思，所以一定要以「介系詞＋受詞」的形式出現。「介系詞＋受詞」也被稱為**介系詞片語**。例句中 on the table 中的 on 是介系詞，the table 是它的受詞，而整個 on the table 是介系詞片語。

B 介系詞在句子中到底扮演什麼功能呢？
一是**形容詞**的功能，二是**副詞**的功能，三是和**動詞搭配使用**等三種功能。例句一的「on the train」是介系詞片語，用來修飾 the people，為「形容詞」功能；例句二「on the ground」也是介系詞片語，用來修飾動詞 were playing，為「副詞」功能；例句三「to Paddy」的 to，和動詞 belong 一起使用，變成 belong to 這個慣用語。在 Chapter 2 動詞和句型中學到的「不及物動詞＋介系詞」，就是這第三種功能。
在一個句子中，介系詞不能單獨存在，它必須結合受詞，並將它們視為一個整體，即介系詞片語。在介系詞片語中，最重要的是介系詞；但在句子中，介系詞片語必須視為一個整體來發揮功能。

概念習題

1 請找出下段文字中的介系詞，並標示出來。

I have just moved to a house in Bridge Street. Yesterday a beggar knocked at my door. He asked me for a meal and a glass of beer. In return for this, the beggar stood on his head and sang songs. I gave him a meal. He ate the food and drank the beer. Then he put a piece of cheese in his pocket and went away.

2 請找出下段文字中的介系詞，並標示出來，並說明它在句中的功能。

The Greenwood Boys are a group of popular singers. At present, they are visiting all parts of the country. They will be arriving here tomorrow. They will be coming by train and most of the young people in the town will be meeting them at the station. Tomorrow evening they will be singing at the Workers' Club. The Greenwood Boys will be staying for five days. During this time, they will give five performances. As usual, the police will have a difficult time.

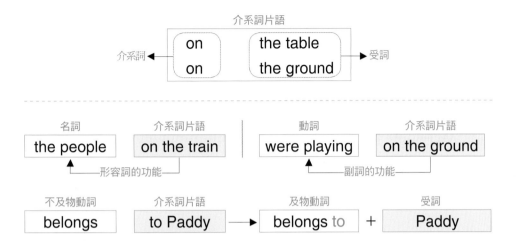

1. We bought a table of polished oak. 〔形容詞〕我們買了一個光滑的橡木桌。
2. Sarah and her husband have the same opinions about many things.
   莎拉和他先生在許多事上都持相同意見。
3. The mother sat the baby on the chair. 〔副詞〕那位母親把寶寶安置在椅子上。
4. Shirley and Sam likes to walk after dinner. 雪莉和山姆喜歡晚飯後去散步。
5. I usually agree with my parents. 〔和動詞搭配〕我通常同意我父母的看法。
6. He spent his time listening to the radio. 他花一些時間聽收音機。
7. Unlike most people in the office, I don't come to work by car. 〔綜合〕
   不像辦公室大部分的人,我不開車上班。

3-4 選出一個最適合填入空格中的答案。

3 I ran _____ to answer the door.

① downstairs   ② the downstairs   ③ to downstairs   ④ to the downstairs

4 _____ cows and horses, human beings are not able to digest cellulose.

① Unlikely   ② The   ③ Many   ④ Unlike

50 In/On/At

A

Emma is **in** the phone booth. 〔空間〕艾瑪正在電話亭裡。

Your keys are **on** the table. 〔面／線〕你的鑰匙在桌上。

I'll meet you **at** the station. 〔點〕我和你約在車站見面。

B

We bought the flat **in** 2009. 〔比一天長的時間〕我們在 2009 年買了這層公寓。

The wedding is **on** Friday. 〔一天〕婚禮於週五舉行。

The concert starts **at** six thirty. 〔比一天短的時間〕這場音樂會於 6:30 開始。

A　in、on、at 基本上是表示「場所」的概念。in 是「在……裡面」的意思，表示**地域、空間**的概念；on 是「在 ... 上面」的意思，表示**線、面**的概念；at 是「在……地點」的意思，表示**點**的概念。例句一「the phone booth」是空間的概念，所以用 in；例句二「the table」是面的概念，所以用 on；例句三「the station」是點的概念，所以用 at。因此可歸納為 in 用在最大的場所；at 用在最小的場所；on 則在這兩者中間。

B　in、on、at 也能表示「時間」的概念。in 用在「比一天長的時間」；on 用在「剛好一天的時間」；at 用在「比一天短的時間」。例句一 1994 是年，比一天長，所以用 in；例句二 Friday 是星期五，剛好一天，所以用 on；例句三 six thirty 是六點三十分，比一天短，所以用 at。不過，這個原則偶有例外，請注意。

🖋 概念習題

1-11 (1-8) 空格中填入 in、on、at、Ø 其中之一，以符合句意。
(9-11) 選出括弧中最符合上下文者。

1 Emma was born _____ 2008.

2 I got up _____ 7:30 this morning.

3 I bought that book _____ Saturday afternoon.

4 I'm leaving _____ next Friday.

5 My family often goes to the beach _____ the summer.

6 The clock _____ the wall showed one minute to twelve.

7 My brother is _____ the bus stop.

8 Mary's sitting _____ the table in the corner.

地域 / 空間	線 / 面	點
in the phone booth	**on** the table	**at** the station

比一天長的時間	剛好一天的時間	比一天短的時間
in 1994	**on** Friday	**at** six thirty

▲ in 的相反詞是 out of；on 的相反詞是 off；at 的相反詞是 away from

> An apple rolled out of the bag. 一顆蘋果從袋子裡滾出來。
> Our hotel is just off the main street. 我們的旅館剛好遠離主要街道。
> Life is so much quieter away from the city. 遠離城市的生活是如此幽靜。

1. Do you like swimming in the sea? 你喜歡在海中游泳嗎？
2. I'll put this picture on the wall. 我將把這幅畫掛在牆上。
3. There is someone at the door. 有個人在門口。
4. Turn left at the traffic lights. 在紅綠燈左轉。
5. We go to Florida every summer. 〔in every summer 是錯誤用法〕
   我們每年夏天都去佛羅里達。

　* every, last, next, this, tomorrow, yesterday 這些字前面的介系詞 in、on、at 要省略。

in + 2010 / September / the winter / the summer term 2010
在 2010 年 / 九月 / 冬天 / 2010 年夏季學期。

on + Wednesday / Monday morning / April 15 / that day
在星期三 / 星期一早上 / 四月十五日 / 那天。

at + three o'clock / lunchtime / the moment / night
在三點鐘 / 午餐時間 / 那一刻 / 晚上。

9 The sign says, "Keep (in, out, off) the grass."

10 Arnold stopped the engine and got (off, out, away) the bus.

11 Stay (in, away from, out of) the fire.

12-14 選出一個最適合填入空格中的答案。

12 We had dinner _____ a restaurant _____ Attleborough.
① in — at ② at — in ③ on — in ④ at — at

13 Emma was born _____ July 4, 2008.
① in ② at ③ on ④ Ø

14 The show will be broadcast _____ morning.
① in every ② in ③ on ④ every

介系詞

143

51 Over/Under、Above/Below、Up/Down

A He put the newspaper **over** his face. 他把報紙蓋在臉上。

The coin was **under** the sofa. 這枚硬幣在沙發下。

B The plane is **above** the clouds. 那架飛機在雲層上。

The sun went **below** the horizon. 太陽運行到地平線之下。

C He climbed **up** the ladder. 他爬上梯子。

We ran **down** the hill. 我們跑下山坡。

---

over、above、up 全部都是「上面」的意思。under、below、down 全部都是「下面」的意思。這些介系詞在意思上有很明顯的差異。

A over 是「覆蓋在……上面」的意思；under 剛好和 over 相反，是「被覆蓋在什麼下面」的意思。例句一，報紙 newspaper 的面積比臉 face 的面積大，報紙覆蓋在臉上，所以用 over。例句二，錢幣 coin 在沙發的下面，被覆蓋在沙發下面，所以用 under。

B above 是「位在……的上方」的意思；相反的，below 是「位在……的下方」的意思。例句一「plane above cloud」，所以可以知道飛機在雲的上方；例句二「sun below horizon」，所以可以知道太陽在地平線的下方。

C up 是「向上運動」的意思；相反的，down 是「向下運動」的意思。over / under 和 above / below 只表示位置，沒有運動的含義在其中；但 up / down 就含有運動的含義在其中了。例句一是「朝著梯子的上方爬」的意思；例句二是「朝著山的下方跑去」的意思。

概念習題

1-4 空格中填入 over、above、up 其中之一，以符合句意。

1 The clock is _____ the exit sign.

2 Paul jumped _____ the fence into the garden.

3 He was running _____ the road, shouting.

4 She held the umbrella _____ both of us.

5-7 空格中填入 under、below、down 其中之一，以符合句意。

5 The little boy hid _____ the bed.

6 Kate fell _____ some stairs and broke her wrist.

7 Night temperatures can drop _____ 15 degrees Celsius.

圖表整理

1. The plane flew over the mountains. 飛機飛越一座座的山。
2. The dog is under the desk. 這隻狗在書桌下。
3. The moon rose above the hill. 月亮升到山坡上。
4. There is a waterfall below the bridge. 這座橋下有瀑布。
5. She went up the stairs. Then she came down again. 她走上樓梯，然後又走下來。
6. The monkey climbed up the tree. 這隻猴子爬上樹。
7. He slid down the hill. 他滑下山坡。

8-11 選出一個最適合填入空格中的答案。

8 Tears were streaming _____ my face.

   ① under   ② below   ③ down   ④ up

9 Temperatures rarely rise _____ zero in winter.

   ① above   ② down   ③ up   ④ below

10 I put my hands _____ my eyes because I couldn't bear to watch.

   ① above   ② over   ③ down   ④ up

11 She buried her head _____ the covers, pretending to be asleep.

   ① down   ② below   ③ over   ④ under

52 Across/Along/Through/Around/Among/Between/Opposite/Next to

A

The dog swam **across** the river. 這隻狗游過這條河。

We walked **along** the road. 我們沿著這條路走。

The old highway goes **through** the city. 舊高速公路貫通這城市。

The new highway goes **around** the city. 新高速公路圍繞著這城市。

I saw a few familiar faces **among** the crowd. 我看到人群裡有熟悉的面孔。

The town lies **between** Rome and Florence.
這城鎮座落在羅馬和佛羅倫斯之間。

We're in the building **opposite** the government offices.
我們在政府辦公室對面的大樓裡。

The police station is **next to** the cinema. 警察局在電影院隔壁。

A **across** the river:「從河的這一岸，直線橫越過河，到對岸」的意思。

along the road:「沿著路的某一側」的意思。

through the city:「從城市的一處，穿過城市內，到另一處」的意思。

around the city:「繞城市的外圍一圈」的意思。

among the crowd:「在群眾之中」的意思。among 是「在三個以上的個體之中」的意思。

between Rome and Florence:「在羅馬和佛羅倫斯這兩個明確的個體之間」的意思。

opposite the government offices:「位在政府辦公室的對面」的意思。

next to the cinema:「在電影院的隔壁」的意思。意指「兩者在同一條線上並排」。

1-7 空格中填入 across、along、through、around 其中之一，以符合句意。

1 The cars are going _____ the tunnel.

2 My family sat _____ the table.

3 A small bridge goes _____ the river.

4 People are not allowed to go _____ the railway line.

5 Mrs. White turned _____ and wrote the title on the blackboard.

6 A bird flew into the room _____ a window.

7 We were driving _____ the road looking for a gas station.

8-13 空格中填入 among、between、opposite、next to 其中之一，以符合句意。

8 Jackson City is _____ Memphis and New Orleans.

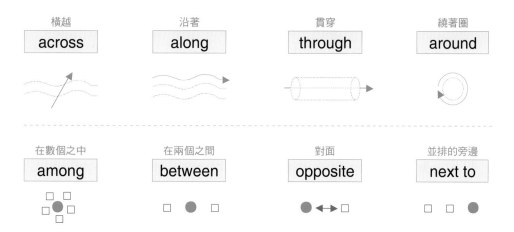

1. Trees grew along the river bank. 樹木沿著河岸生長。
2. They built a bridge across the river. 他們建立了一座橫跨這條河的橋。
3. Water flows through this pipe. 水流經這條管子。
4. The bus stop is just around the corner. 公車站牌就在街角。
5. The decision has caused a lot of anger among women.
   這個決定已引起女人間的怒火。
6. There is a narrow path between the two houses. 這兩棟房子之間有條窄巷。
7. The window is opposite the door. 這扇窗在門對面。
8. The post office is next to the cinema. 那間郵局在電影院旁。
9. Can I sit next to you? 我可以坐在你旁邊嗎？

---

9 We walked _____ the chestnut woods on the mountain slopes.

10 Tom and Jack sat _____ each other. They were playing chess.

11 She sat down _____ him on the sofa.

12 There's a cinema _____ my office. We can see it from my window.

13 The general opinion _____ police officers was that the law should be tightened.

14 選出一個最適合填入空格中的答案。

Are there any public holidays _____ Christmas and Easter?

① between　　② across　　③ around　　④ among

53 During/For/Since

A She worked as a lifeguard **during** the summer. 她在這個夏天從事救生員工作。

She worked as a lifeguard **for** three months. 她當過三個月的救生員。

B She has worked as a lifeguard **for** three months.
她當救生員已有三個月了。

She has worked as a lifeguard **since** May. 她從五月開始從事救生員工作。

A 介系詞 during 和 for 都是表示期間的字,不過在意思和用法上有些不同。

第一,**during** 用來回答「何時」(when),表示「事情發生的時候,是在什麼期間」;而 for 用來回答「有多久」(how long),表示「事情發生的時候,持續了多久」。也就是說,**during** 指在什麼時候發生的,for 指發生時持續了多久。during 翻譯成「在……期間」;for 翻譯成「……多久了」。

第二,during 之後要接「名詞」;for 之後要接「表示一段時間的詞組」。例句一,during 後面的 the summer 是名詞;例句二,for 之後的 three months 是表示一段時間的詞組。

例句一 'during the summer'「在暑假的時候」擔任這項工作,回答「在什麼時候擔任這項工作」這個問題;

例句二,'for three months 擔任這項工作「有三個月那麼久」,回答「擔任這項工作有多久」這個問題。

B 介系詞 for 和 since 之間的差別如下:

for 是「……多久了」的意思,後面接「表示一段時間的詞組」;**since** 是「自……以來(持續到現在)」的意思,後面一定要接「過去的一個時間點」。例句一,three months 是「表示一段時間的詞組」;for three months 是「持續了三個月的時間」的意思。例句二,May 則是「過去的一個時間點」;since May 是「自五月以來(到現在)」的意思。

 概念習題

1-2 選出括弧中最符合上下文者。

1 A: I've been waiting (for, since) forty minutes. B: I've been waiting (for, since) 6 o'clock.

2 A: It snowed (for, during) the morning. B: It snowed (for, during) three hours.

3-8 空格中填入 during、for、since 其中之一,以符合句意。

3 My parents were in New Jersey _____ two weeks.

4 Ampol has lived in Japan _____ 2008.

5 A lot of trees were blown down _____ the storm.

6 Despite his achievements, Jerry has felt bad _____ a long time as an outsider.

7 Rachel had a breakdown a few years ago, and _____ then she has been very shy.

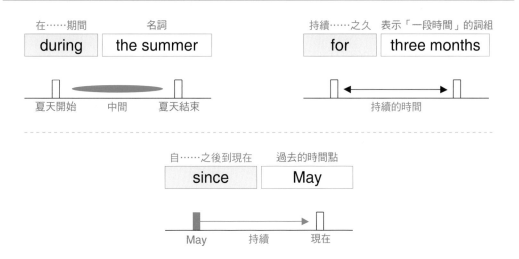

1. It must have rained during the night. 夜間一定下過雨。
2. We managed to stay awake during the whole meeting.
   我們設法讓自己在整個會議中保持清醒。
3. She's out of the office for three days. 她離開辦公室已經三天。
4. It rained for three days without stopping. 雨已經下了三天都沒停過。
5. Mark has been playing since two o'clock. 馬克從兩點玩到現在。
6. There have been many changes since the war. 戰爭之後，有了很大的改變。

8 The three new students got acquainted _____ the coffee break.

9-11 選出一個最適合填入空格中的答案。

9 _____ the flood, the Red Cross set up temporary shelters for the homeless.
　① During　　　② For　　　③ Since　　　④ While

10 The math skills of the students have risen steadily _____ more than a decade.
　① during　　　② for　　　③ since　　　④ while

11 The Al Qaeda leader has gone missing _____ the siege of Tora Bora.
　① during　　　② for　　　③ since　　　④ while

介系詞

54 Until/By 和 After/In

A
> I'll wait **until** five o'clock. 我將等到五點鐘。
>
> I'll have to leave **by** five o'clock. 我必須在五點前離開。

B
> The meeting will take place **after** the ceremony.
> 會議將在典禮結束後舉行。
>
> We're meeting **in** two weeks. 我們兩週後碰面。

A 介系詞 until 和 by 的中文翻譯都是「到……時候」。因為意思相近，所以很容易混淆，但這兩者有明顯不同的概念。**until** 是「直到……時候」的意思，表示「持續到那個時間點」；**by** 是「到……時候以前」的意思，表示「以那個時間點為基準，會在那之前發生」。

例句一，「wait until five o'clock」是「等到五點」的意思，表示等的行為持續到五點；例句二，「leave by five o'clock」是「五點前就要離開」的意思，表示離開的行為在五點以前就會發生。

另外，介系詞 until 會和表示持續一段時間的動詞 wait 一起使用，表示「在一段時間持續地等」；所以我們說「wait until . . .」。介系詞 by 則和表示瞬間發生的動詞 leave 一起使用，leave 表示「在某一個時間點瞬間離開」；所以我們說 leave by...。

B 介系詞 after 和 in 的中文翻譯都是「在……之後」。這兩者意思相近，但是概念不同。**after** 基本上是表示「A 在 B 之後」的「順序」；**in** 表示「在一段時間之後」的「期間」。例句一，「meeting . . . after the ceremony」是「會議在典禮之後」的意思，在於比較 meeting（發生在後）和 ceremony（發生在前）的順序。相反的，「in two weeks」是「兩週後」的意思，在表示單純的未來。因此介系詞 after 之後，要接可以互相比較的「名詞」，其後的 ceremony 就是名詞；介系詞 in 之後，則要接表示「一段時間的詞組」，其後的 two weeks 就是一段時間的詞組。

 概念習題

1-6 空格中填入 until、by 其中之一，以符合句意。

1 Mary will live in Korea _____ 2013.

2 Mary will have to leave Korea _____ 2013.

3 Mary had promised to be back to Korea _____ 2013.

4 The consumers have waited _____ Christmas holiday.

5 Jack has to pay the money back _____ the end of this month.

6 I hope to finish the painting _____ next Friday.

7-13 選出括弧中最符合上下文者。

7 You'll need to hand your project in (until, by) the end of the week.

8 Jason will be away (until, by) Tuesday.

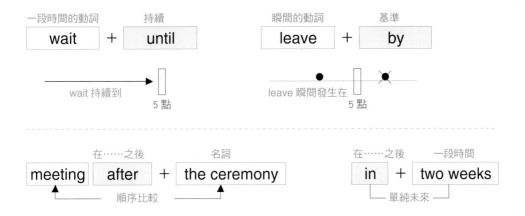

1. I slept till ten o'clock.〔sleep: 一段時間〕我睡到十點。
2. I have to finish this report by Thursday.〔finish: 瞬間〕週四前我要完成這份報告。
3. We went for a walk after dinner. 晚餐後我們去散步。
4. Lunch will be ready in five minutes. 午餐將在五分鐘後準備好。
5. Before eating the apple, I washed it carefully.〔before ↔ after〕
   吃蘋果前，我很仔細地清洗它。
6. Within 24 hours the deal was completed.〔within ↔ in〕
   這項交易在 24 小時內完成了。

9 The population of England will reach 70 million (until, by) 2030.

10 I'm just setting off, so I should be with you (after, in) half an hour.

11 John's grandparents often take a nap (after, in) lunch.

12 He said he would be back (before, within) two hours.

13 Most students feel a little nervous (before, within) an examination.

14-15 選出一個最適合填入空格中的答案。

14 I hope to get to your house _____ 7:00 at the latest.
   ① by   ② for   ③ until   ④ in

15 I'm moving into my new apartment next week. I'm staying with a friend _____ then.
   ① by   ② within   ③ until   ④ since

介系詞

151

55 其他的介系詞

(A)

He eats **like** a pig. 〔類似〕他像隻豬一樣地狼吞虎嚥地吃東西。

A flat stone was used **as** a table. 〔相同〕一塊平滑的石頭被用來當桌子。

(B)

She hung her coat **on** a hook. 〔接觸〕她把大衣吊在鉤子上。

Someone had taken the mirror **off** the wall. 〔分離〕
有人把牆上的鏡子拿走了。

(C)

A few days later Mary would be leaving **for** Chicago. 〔方向〕
瑪麗過些天會離開，去芝加哥。

The government is sending a spaceship **to** Mars. 〔目的地〕
政府發射一艘太空船到火星。

(D)

She arrived **by** taxi. 〔手段〕她搭計程車來的。

They had to send me home **in** a taxi/**on** a bus. 〔交通手段〕
他們必須搭計程車／公車送我回家。

(E)

They're holding an international conference **on** global warming.
〔例行公事的關於〕他們針對全球暖化議題召開國際會議。

Bob lied **about** his age. 〔一般的關於〕鮑伯謊報他的年齡。

(F)

He ruled **over** a large kingdom. 〔支配〕他統治一個大王國。

The meeting was adjourned **over** the holidays. 〔一段時間〕
會議因為假期而被迫暫停。

 概念習題

1-4 選出括弧中最符合上下文者。

1 (As, Like, For) a parent, I felt that more should be done to protect our children.

2 Look! The train (to, at, for) Manchester is approaching.

3 A good teacher has an easy authority (by, on, over) a class.

4 I couldn't see (for, as, off) the tears in my eye.

5-6 選出和提示句中劃線部分的介系詞含義相同的句子。

5 He continued to lie <u>on</u> his back and looked at clouds.

① He declined to give any information on the Presidential election.

② Most buses run on diesel.

③ Can you stand on your head?

G [We were surprised **at** the news. 〔驚訝於〕這個新聞讓我們很驚訝。
    [The talks aim **at** a compromise. 〔目標〕這次的會談在於謀求和解。

H [The movie is based **on** the book. 〔根據〕那部電影是根據這本書拍成的。

I [She took an English course **for** foreign students. 〔目的、意圖〕
    她為外國學生上了這門英文課。
    [He did ten years in prison **for** murder. 〔理由〕他因為謀殺罪而入獄十年。

A like / as：**like** 是「像……」的意思，表示「類似」。**as** 是「正如……」的意思，表示「相同」。例句中，he 和 pig 不是同一個東西；a flat stone 和 a table 則是同一個東西。

B on / off：**on** 是「靠著的」，表示「有接觸」。**off** 是「離開的」，表示「分離」。

C for / to：**for** 是「朝向哪裡」，表示「方向」。**to** 是「到達哪裡」，表示「目的地」。

D by / in(on)：**by** 是「藉由……」，表示「手段」。**in** 和 **on** 是「藉由……交通工具」，表「交通手段」時使用。**in** 用於 car/taxi 等較小的交通工具；**on** 用於 bus/train/plane 等較大的交通工具。by 之後不能接冠詞。

E on / about：兩者都是「關於……」的意思，而 **on** 還特別含有「例行公事」的意思。

F over：**over** 有「支配、優越」的意思；也有表示從頭到尾的整個「一段時間」的意思。

G at：**at** 是「因……」的意思，表示「受到刺激、原因」；還有「對準……」的意思，表示「目標」。

H on：**on** 是「根據……」的意思，表示「依存、根據」。

I for：**for** 是「為了……」的意思，表示「目的、意圖」。還有「因為……」的意思，表示「理由」。

---

6 They waved <u>at</u> us as we drove away.
  ① The matter was discussed at a meeting of the finance committee.
  ② Why does no one ever laugh at my jokes?
  ③ After aiming carefully at the bird, Tom missed it.

7-9 選出一個最適合填入空格中的答案。

7 Nick usually goes to school _____ his bike, but sometimes he goes _____ bus.
  ① on — on   ② in — by   ③ by — on   ④ on — by

8 Scotland is famous _____ its spectacular countryside.
  ① for   ② as   ③ at   ④ on

9 I was trying to scrape the mud _____ my boots.
  ① on   ② off   ③ at   ④ over

介系詞

153

56 是不是介系詞？

A
There's no one here **but** me. 這裡只有我，沒有別人。
There's no one here ~~but I~~. 〔錯誤用法〕

B
Like most people, I'd like to have enough money not to work.

就像大部分的人，我想要有足夠的錢而不用工作。

~~Alike most people~~, I'd like to have enough money not to work. 〔錯誤用法〕

C
They went out **in spite of** the rain. 儘管下雨，他們還是出門了。

A ··· 「but」常被拿來當作**連接詞**，不過它也可以當作**介系詞**來使用。當介系詞時，是「除了 . . . 以外」的意思，和 **except** 的意思一樣。以例句來解釋，因為介系詞後要接**受詞**，所以 but 後面應該接 me（受格），而非接 I（主格）。

B ··· alike 和 like 很像，但兩者的詞類完全不同。**like** 是「介系詞」；**alike** 是只能用來描述事物的「形容詞」。因此，要特別注意像 alike 這類「看起來像介系詞，卻不是介系詞」的字。

C ··· **in spite of** 整個當作一個介系詞來使用，是「儘管……還是」的意思。介系詞並不都是單一個字，也有像這樣由數個字組成的介系詞片語。

概念習題

1-4 選出一個最適合填入空格中的答案。

1 I don't think this jacket is _____.
① worthy the price ② worthy buying it
③ worth the price ④ worth of buying

2 _____ his artistic accomplishments, Morse is well-known for his work, the Morse Code.
① In addition to ② Instead ③ Beside ④ That is

3 People in some societies have differed _____ whether you may marry more than one time.
① concerned ② concerns ③ concerning ④ concern

看起來不像介系詞的介系詞		
but (但是)	besides (此外)	regarding / concerning (關於)
worth (值得)	toward/towards (朝向)	

看起來像介系詞，但不是介系詞的字			
alike (看起來像)	out (外面)	back (回去)	away (離開)

由數個字組成的介系詞片語		
according to (根據)	along with (和……在一起)	as to (至於)
away from (離開)	because of (由於)	due to (由於)
far from (完全不)	instead of (替代)	out of (從……離開)
owing to (由於)	prior to (在……以前)	regardless of (不管)
thanks to (向……道謝)	by means of (用)	in addition to (除……之外)
in charge of (負責)	in case of (萬一)	in front of (在……前面)
in place of (代替)	in regard to (關於)	in search of (尋找)
in view of (考慮到)	in spite of (不管)	in terms of (就……而論)
on account of (因為)	on behalf of (代表)	

4 Most news reporting was heavily _____ the government.

① bias   ② biased   ③ towards biased   ④ biased towards

5-8 選出劃線部分文法錯誤者。

5 No one but ① he knew exactly ② which questions ③ were going to ④ be asked ⑤ on this test.

6 ① Alike ② most of us, I find myself swamped ③ with news and information.

7 ① Despite of the increase in air ② fares, most people still ③ prefer to travel ④ by plane.

8 He ① did not get the telegram ② in time ③ because of it was delivered ④ late.

1-11 選出一個最適合填入空格中的答案。

1 A: When did they finally let him in?

B: _____.

① Since three hours ago

② For three hours

③ Three hours ago

④ In three hours

2 _____ other big cats, leopards are expert climbers.

① Most unlike   ② The most unlike

③ Alike most   ④ Unlike most

3 Please pay careful attention to the instructor _____ class.

① for   ② during   ③ at   ④ on

4 The South Korean President, Roh Moo Hyun, arrives _____ Beijing _____ Monday _____ talks with his Chinese counterpart, Hu Jintao.

① in — in — to   ② in — on — to

③ on — in — for   ④ on — in — to

⑤ in — on — for

5 The building work will be finished _____ next Friday.

① to   ② until   ③ by   ④ when

6 She has been absent from the office _____ a week.

① for   ② in   ③ since   ④ during

7 Her flight is scheduled to arrive early _____ morning.

① in   ② at   ③ this   ④ on

8 The whole island is nice and pleasant, and there are many sports facilities and beautiful scenes all _____ the island.

① across   ② by

③ next to   ④ opposite

9 The relationship _____ law and order is even more paradoxical.

① between   ② has been

③ has   ④ into

10 Of course, no one likes to think, "I am below average." And of course, each person is _____ average in some way. We want to set high goals for ourselves.

① above   ② over

③ below   ④ behind

11 She has gained a reputation _____ a daring, intrepid journalist.

① like   ② as   ③ about   ④ for

12-16 閱讀下列文字，並回答問題。

12 選出一組最適合填入空格中的介系詞。

Even flowers can work for us. Not only they look pretty but also one kind of flowers is used to tell how much smog is in the air _____ Tokyo. Its name is Winter Queen Gamma 3, which is a kind of begonia. When left out _____ six days in smog, it gets white spots _____ its leaves.

① over — since — in
② above — for — in
③ over — during — in
④ above — since — on
⑤ over — for — on

13 選出括弧中最符合上下文者。

Aztec children were taught at home (until, by) about 15 years of age. All children, however, were expected to attend school (for, during) some time when they were (among, between) 16 and 20 years old.

14 選出劃線部分文法錯誤者。

Baby goats jump ① around playfully and are generally annoying, ② so the connection ③ between baby goats and young humans ④ seem to make sense.

15 重組括弧內的字，使成為「我們的旅程越過原野、穿過森林」的意思。

(through, and, our trip, the woods, the field, across) warms them up like athletes stretching before a game.

16 選出一組最適合填入空格中的介系詞。

What is the Internet? It is a kind of worldwide communication system. _____ the Internet, you can get any information you need. It's _____ the biggest library in the world in your home.
① Through — as   ② Thorough — as
③ Through — like   ④ Thorough — like

17-23 選出劃線部分文法錯誤者。

17 People ① have studied writing for ② more than two thousand years. ③ Alike fingerprints, handwriting can be ④ used to identify someone.

18 ① In May 17, 1967, Alex Haley ② went to Juffure, ③ where he ④ met a griot.

19 He ① has learned Chinese ② since 5 years, but he ③ still can't speak it ④ well.

20 ① After three days, I ② will pick up my airline ticket. I'll ③ fly to New York six days ④ later.

21 Between 1906 ① to 1917, Emma Goldman devoted ② most of her efforts ③ to ④ writing and lecturing.

22 ① About 60 percent of the space ② on the ③ pages of newspapers is saved ④ over advertising.

23 Blood ① in vessels just under the ② nasal lining ③ it gives off its heat ④ to warm the air.

CHAPTER 9

子句和連接詞
Clauses & Conjunctions

57 子句／句子／連接詞

A ┌ the flower was very beautiful〔子句〕花很美麗。
  └ The flower was very beautiful.〔句子〕這朵花很美麗。

B ─ Luis had a big meal **because** he was hungry. 路易斯因為很餓，所以大吃一頓。

C ┌ Jim broke a flower vase **and** Tom lost our tickets.〔對等子句〕
  │ 吉姆打破花瓶，湯姆弄丟我們的票。
  │
  │ It isn't important **that** Tom lost our tickets.〔名詞子句〕
  │ 湯姆弄丟我們的票沒關係。
  │
  │ We couldn't go to the concert **because** Tom lost our tickets.〔副詞子句〕
  └ 因為湯姆弄丟了票，所以我們不能去音樂會。

A 「子句」（clause）是附屬在句子中的一個小句子的意思。說它是小句子，是因為它是一個完整的句子，也就是說，它也具備主詞、動詞、受詞／補語、修飾詞這樣的句子結構。要辨別是不是子句，最重要的就是判定有沒有動詞，如果有動詞就是子句，如果沒有動詞就不是子句。例句一，「the flower was very beautiful」是具「第二類句型」結構的子句。
　　「句子」（sentence）是子句再向上發展一個階段的最高單位。將子句最前面的單字字首改成**大寫**，然後在最後面加上**句號**（或**問號**或**驚嘆號**），就變成句子了。「The flower was very beautiful.」就是句子。

B 句子裡面可以含有一、二個子句，甚至有兩個以上的子句。當有兩個或兩個以上的子句時，這時就需要有一個媒介來連接它們，這個媒介就是「連接詞」。連接詞基本上是連接子句和子句，連接詞後面一定要接子句。例句中的連接詞 because，就是連接兩個子句。

C 子句的種類有好幾種，子句的種類是由它前面的**連接詞**來決定。因此，「學習子句的種類和它的功能」＝「學習連接詞的種類和它的功能」。例句的「Tom lost our tickets」這個子句，前面接 and 就變成**對等子句**；前面接 that 就變成**名詞子句**；前面接 because 就變成**副詞子句**。

 概念習題

1-3 選出一個最適合填入空格中的答案。

1 Although they call me old-fashioned, _____ handwritten letters.

　① but I like　　② I like　　③ I liking　　④ like

2 People _____ their money into savings accounts because they want a fixed rate.

　① putting　　② being put　　③ be put　　④ put

3 I am writing this letter _____ the long delays and the bad service from your staff.

　① since　　② if　　③ because of　　④ that

4-7 下列各句若有連接詞，請找出，並標示出來。

4 If you could solve the problem, would you let me know?

子句：和句子有相同結構　　　　　句子：子句→〔句首大寫＋句號〕

| the flower was very beautiful | The flower was very beautiful. |

Luis had a big meal | because | he was hungry. 子句＋連接詞＋子句

Tom lost our tickets (子句)

＋

連接詞

各式子句

and Tom lost our tickets　對等子句

that Tom lost our tickets　名詞子句

because Tom lost our tickets　副詞子句

1. having dinner at a restaurant　在餐廳吃晚餐
2. all the mess in the kitchen　廚房的凌亂

　　　　　　　　　　　　　　　　　非「子句」

3. she will pick up her son at 3:30　她將在 3:30 去接兒子
4. we had dinner at a restaurant　我們在餐廳吃晚餐
5. he hoped to study medicine　他希望可以學醫

　　　　　　　　　　　　　　　　　「子句」

6. He hoped to study medicine.　他希望可以學醫。
7. He'll scold me if he finds out.　如果被他發現了，他會罵我一頓。
8. If he finds out, he'll scold me.　如果被他發現了，他會罵我一頓。

　　　　　　　　　　　　　　　　　「句子」

---

5 Human activity wipes out more than a thousand animal species every year.

6 Rachel is a good tennis player but she's never played badminton.

7 From the time of Socrates to our own modern age, the human race has thought of the fundamental questions of life.

8-10 下列句子若有錯誤，請找出並更正。

8 Even he has a number of relatives, he never visits them.

9 Instead of they buy stocks, people with money can buy bonds.

10 The Swiss people work hard and their country being clean and prosperous.

子句和連接詞

58 對等連接詞 And/But/Or

A

We saw an elephant **and** a giraffe. 我們看到一隻象和一隻長頸鹿。

I got dressed **and** had my breakfast. 我換好衣服，並且吃完早餐了。

The sky is clear, **and** the sun is shining. 天空很藍，太陽很耀眼。

B

Apples **and** pears **are** fruit. 蘋果和梨子都是水果。

The boy is imaginative **but** idle. 這男孩很有想像力，但卻無所事事。

Is the wedding on Friday **or** on Saturday? 婚禮在星期五還是星期六？

A 決定子句種類的連接詞，大致可以分成「對等連接詞」、「名詞子句連接詞」、「副詞子句連接詞」三類。將句子裡的兩個子句，對等地連接起來的連接詞，稱作「對等連接詞」；以對等連接詞連接起來的子句，稱作「對等子句」。and、but、or 是最具代表性的**對等連接詞**。

「對等連接詞」的重要特點是：第一，不是只連接子句和子句，它也可以連接名詞和名詞、動詞和動詞、形容詞和形容詞，以及片語和片語等同詞類連接。以例句的連接詞 and 來說明：an elephant 和 a giraffe 是兩個名詞；got dressed 和 had my breakfast 是兩個動詞；the sky is clear 和 the sun is shining 是兩個子句。第二，對等連接詞所連接的兩個內容，是沒有重屬關係或上下關係的，兩者完全是「對等價值」的。所謂的對等價值，就是指兩者有「對等的形式」和「對等的功能」的意思。以 an elephant 和 a giraffe 為例，它們都是名詞，也就是說它們有「對等的形式」；它們都是受詞，也就是說它們有「對等的功能」。但是如果為 an elephant and brave，這樣的連接就是錯誤的。

B and 是列舉彼此相似的東西，表「追加」的意思時使用；but 是列舉彼此相反的東西，表「對立」的意思時使用；or 是列舉彼此不同的東西，表「選擇」的意思時使用。例句中，用 and 連接 apples 和 pears 這兩個歸為同一類的詞；用 but 連接 imaginative 和 idle 這兩個相反含義的詞；用 or 連接 on Friday 和 on Saturday 這兩個不同時間的詞。

 概念習題

1-4 下列各句有以對等連接詞連接兩部分，請標示出來。

1 Many pupils have extra classes in the evenings or on weekends.

2 I jumped into the river and swam to the other side.

3 At night we used to go out with our friends or stay at home listening to music.

4 Industrial designers are trained to create an attractive but functional form.

5-6 選出一個最適合填入空格中的答案。

5 The boy's arm was broken, _____ the bone did not protrude through the skin.

　① and　　　② but　　　③ or　　　④ so

名詞	an elephant	對等連接詞	名詞	a giraffe
動詞	got dressed	and / but / or	動詞	had my breakfast
子句	The sky is clear.		子句	The sun is shining.

對等地連接

apples **and** pears	imaginative **but** idle	on Friday **or** on Saturday
追加	對立	選擇
蘋果 + 梨	有想像力的 + 無所事事的	在星期五 ≠ 在星期六
相似內容	相反內容	其他內容

▲ or 和 and，也有以 either A or B 和 both A and B 等形式表現：

> You can have either sandwiches or apples. 你可以吃三明治或蘋果。
> Both men and women have complained about the advertisement.
> 男人和女人都抱怨那則廣告。

1. The river is wide **and** deep. 這條河又寬又深。
2. I have washed **and** dried dishes. 我已經清洗和擦乾盤子了。
3. He is good at painting with watercolors **or** with oil paints. 他擅長水彩畫或油畫。
4. Would you like some fruit juice **or** a cup of coffee? 你想喝點果汁或一杯咖啡嗎？
5. That book is good **but** expensive. 那是本好書，但是價格昂貴。

6 We can either eat now _____ after the show — it's up to you.

① and　　　　　② but　　　　　③ or　　　　　④ nor

7-12 空格中填入 and、but、or 其中之一，以符合句意。

7 A: Would you like some milk _____ cocoa? B: Yes, please.

8 A: Would you like some milk _____ cocoa? B: Cocoa, please.

9 I wanted to call you, _____ I didn't have your number.

10 Would you like to play tennis _____ golf tomorrow?

11 I usually drive to work, _____ I took the bus this morning.

12 In chemistry, it is easy to overlook a vital factor _____ draw the wrong conclusions.

59 That 子句

A ─ People say **that** walking may keep ourselves healthy.
大家都說走路可以維持健康。

B ─ I know (**that**) the earth is turning. 我知道地球在轉動。

That the earth is turning **is true.** 地球在轉動是事實。

The reason is (**that**) the earth is turning. 理由是地球在轉動。

We have evidence **that** the earth is turning. 我們有證據說明地球在轉動。

C ─ I'm sure ~~of~~ **that** the humans evolved from animals. 〔錯誤用法〕

A that 可以當作「連接詞引導子句」。「that +子句」，就稱做「that 子句」。「that 子句」被用來當作句子的一部分時，就稱作「從屬子句」。
   that 子句的「形式」是「that +完全子句」。例句「that walking may save our lives」是 that 子句，這個子句由連接詞 that 和完全子句「walking may save our lives」組成的。

B that 子句的「功能」是名詞的功能，時常在句子中被當成主詞或受詞，也可當作補語或同位語。例句一，that 子句被當作 know 的受詞；例句二，that 子句被當作主詞；例句三，that 子句被當作 is 的補語；例句四，that 子句被當作 evidence 的同位語。當 that 子句當受詞或補語時，連接詞「that 可以省略」；that 子句當做主詞或同位語時，連接詞「that 不可以省略」。

C that 子句雖有名詞的功能，但是不能當作介系詞的受詞，所以例句中的 of 要刪去才對。

概念習題

1-2 選出一個最適合填入空格中的答案。

1 Scientists have speculated that _____ at least one quadrillion living ants on the earth.
   ① is there   ② when there   ③ their existing   ④ there are

2 That people have a moral duty to help others _____ obvious to me.
   ① seems   ② seem   ③ seeming   ④ to seem

3 選出文法錯誤的句子。
   ① Did you know that she drove a freight wagon for many years?
   ② The trouble is that this carpet gets dirty very easily.
   ③ That John would do such a thing is hard to believe.
   ④ You can't always depend on that the trains arrive on time.

▲ that **子句當作主詞時，經常會用虛主詞** it **來代替：**

That the earth is turning | is true.

It | is true | that the earth is turning.

1. I think (that) Mr. and Mrs. Jones are coming to the party.
   我想瓊斯先生和太太就快來到宴會上了。

2. We assume (that) prices will continue to rise. 我們以為價格將會持續上漲。

3. One reason is that the intelligent person is less wasteful of materials.
   其中一個原因是聰明的人比較不會浪費東西。

4. His concern was (that) people would know his mistake.
   他擔心大家會知道他的錯誤。

5. The athlete fought openly over the demands that he practice more.
   這位運動員公然反抗過度訓練的要求。

4-9 找出 that **子句，並說明它在句中的功能**

4 Is it true she has gone back to teaching?

5 British doctors at last understood that rickets was caused by a vitamin deficiency.

6 The only trouble is the boys are too impatient.

7 Do you have evidence that stress is partially responsible for disease?

8 It seems strange to me that people in cities live in densely populated areas but don't know their neighbors.

9 One reason that the intelligent worker is more valuable than the unintelligent one is that the intelligent person is less wasteful of materials.

子句和連接詞

60 疑問詞子句

A
What **was Tom** doing?〔疑問句〕湯姆在做什麼？

Please tell me what **Tom was** doing.〔疑問詞子句〕請告訴我湯姆在做什麼？

B
I wonder **when** it will rain. 我在想什麼時候會下雨。

I'm interested in **whether** you can help me.
我想知道你是否能幫我的忙。

Why Jane went to Canada <u>is</u> a secret. 為什麼珍去加拿大是個秘密？

The question is **who** did it. 問題是誰做的。

C
She said **that** Peter signed the contract. 她說彼得簽了合約。

She asked **who** signed the contract. 她詢問是誰簽了合約。

A 名詞子句除了 that 子句以外，還有「疑問詞子句」。疑問詞子句必須將「疑問句語序」改成「直述句的語序」。也就是說，疑問句當作一個獨立的句子使用時，它就是疑問句；但當它換成直述句的語序，並被當作句子中的一部分來使用的話，它就變成疑問詞子句了。例句一 What was Tom doing? 是疑問句；例句二，what Tom was doing 則是疑問詞子句。

B 疑問詞子句的「功能」是名詞的功能。所以它可以用來當作**及物動詞的受詞**（如：when it will rain）、**介系詞的受詞**（如：whether you can help me）、**主詞**（如：Why Jane went to Canada）、**補語**（如：who did it）使用。

C 「that 子句」和「疑問詞子句」，兩者有相似處，但它們的「形式」和「含義」卻有很大的差異，一定要區分清楚。第一，在形式方面，that 子句是「除了連接詞 that 以外，剩下的就是完全子句」；而疑問詞子句是「包含疑問詞整個，算是一個完全子句」。例句一「that Peter signed the contract」，除 that 外，Peter signed the contract 是一個完全子句；例句二「who signed the contract」，要包含 who 才是一個完全子句。第二，在含義方面，that 子句是「是 ... 的」的直述句。疑問詞子句是「是 ... 的嗎？」的疑問句；疑問詞子句被當作「間接疑問句」用，只有形式不同而已，表現的內容幾乎和疑問句完全一樣。另外，請注意，that 子句不能和 ask、wonder、don't know 等字一起使用。

 概念習題

1-4 選出一個最適合填入空格中的答案。

1 The officer showed me _____ get to the bank.

① how can I　　② I can how　　③ I how can　　④ how I can

2 One of the participants in a conversation wonders _____ the other said.

① that　　② who　　③ what　　④ whether

3 I accidently discovered _____ the adult gorilla is a friendly animal.

① what　　② that　　③ who　　④ which

4 Do you know _____ ice cream Alice likes the best?

① which　　② that　　③ who　　④ why

疑問句語序

What was Tom doing? (疑問句)

↓

what Tom was doing (疑問詞子句)

直述句語序

疑問詞子句的功能 ─┬─ 及物動詞的受詞
                 ├─ 介系詞的受詞
                 ├─ 主詞
                 └─ 補語

that 子句	that	Peter signed the contract
疑問詞子句		who signed the contract

完全子句

that 子句 → 直述句
疑問詞子句 → 疑問句

1. I wonder what made him do it. 我在想是什麼讓他做那件事。
2. John inquired whether he could see her. 約翰詢問是否可以見到她。
3. They asked me why I was so late. 他們問我為什麼遲到。
4. I don't know how far it is to the post office. 我不知道這裡距離郵局有多遠。
5. What time Fred called doesn't matter. 佛瑞德什麼時候打來並不重要。
6. The answer seems to depend on whom you ask. 答案似乎是根據你問誰而定。
7. Ask Tom which hotel he stayed at. 去問湯姆他住哪一間旅館。

5-6 選出括弧中最符合上下文者。

5 (Why, What, Who) the man did something so terrible will never be known.

6 (That, What) will be carried in the next Space Shuttle has not yet been announced.

7-10 下列句子若有錯誤，請找出並更正。

7 We don't know that he returned to his quarters.

8 No one knows how long will they stay healthy, but the results are encouraging.

9 Scientists fully understand how teacher feedback affects students.

10 Success depends on that the media distributes information and recipes well.

61 副詞子句的形式和功能

A
> Mary moved quietly **because** she didn't want to wake them.
> 瑪麗悄悄地移動,因為她不想吵醒他們。
>
> **Although** Bill likes the plant, it was very heavy to carry.
> 儘管比爾喜歡這株植物,但是它太重了。

B
> We'll call off the hiking **when** it rains.〔副詞子句〕如果下雨,我們將取消健行。
> I don't know **when** it will rain.〔名詞子句〕我不知道什麼時候會下雨。

A⋯ 副詞子句的「形式」是「副詞子句連接詞+完全子句」。例句中的 because 和 although 是引導副詞子句的連接詞,它們後面的「she didn't want to wake them」和「Bill likes the plant」都是完全子句。
副詞子句的「功能」和副詞一樣,用來修飾**動詞**或**子句**。副詞子句的「位置」,在主要子句之前或主要子句之後。如果它在主要子句之後,就用來修飾動詞;如果它在主要子句之前,就用來修飾主要子句。例句一,「because . . . them」用來修飾動詞 moved;例句二,「although . . . plant」,用來修飾主要子句「it . . . carry」。

B⋯ 「副詞子句」和「名詞子句」在句子中,它們的功能是不同的。「名詞子句」在句子中都是當做主詞、受詞、補語等,扮演這類核心的功能。相反的,「副詞子句」當作修飾語,扮演選擇性的功能。換句話說,如果句子中的**名詞子句**被刪掉,那剩下的句子絕對是**不完全子句**;相反的,如果句子中的**副詞子句**被刪掉,那剩下的句子仍然是**完全子句**。
如果要判斷句子是名詞子句還是副詞子句,直接考慮上述的特點,就可以了。例句同樣都是 when 子句,「when it rains」是副詞子句;「when it will rain」則是名詞子句。如果省略了「when it rains」,剩下的「We'll call off the hiking」,仍是完全子句;如果省略了「when it will rain」,剩下的「I don't know」,是沒有受詞的不完全子句。

 概念習題

1 說明下列的 if 子句是副詞子句,還是名詞子句。
① I would like to know if Joe will go to the party tomorrow.
② A smile can give an impression of friendliness but should not be forced if it does not come naturally.

2-5 在提示句中選出合適的句子填入空格中,字首並改成大寫。

a. although they no longer love each other	b. that my keys are missing
c. because it causes the plant to freeze	d. that seat belts save lives

2 _____ has been proven in many studies.

3 _____, the couple have decided to stay together for their children.

副詞子句連接詞		完全子句
because	+	she didn't want to wake them
although		William likes the plant

副詞子句

動詞	主要子句後的副詞子句	主要子句前的副詞子句	主要子句
moved	because she … them	although Bill … plant	, it was … carry

修飾動詞　　　　　　　　　　　修飾子句

完全子句	副詞子句
We'll … hiking	when it rains

不完全子句	名詞子句
I don't know	when it … rain

1. We will stay home if it rains tomorrow. 如果明天下雨，我們將待在家。
2. If it rains tomorrow, we will stay home. 如果明天下雨，我們將待在家。
3. We'll all take a walk in the park after Mom finishes washing dishes.
   等媽媽洗完碗後，我們要去公園散步。
4. They went to a restaurant because it was Mary's birthday.
   因為瑪麗生日，所以他們去餐廳吃飯。
5. Although the night air was hot, they slept soundly.
   儘管晚上很悶熱，但是他們仍酣然入夢。
6. The boys walked until they reached Ethiopia.
   那個男孩一直走路，直到抵達衣索比亞。

4 I have noticed _____.

5 Frost is very harmful to vegetation _____.

6-8 選出一個最適合填入空格中的答案。

6 _____ students learn the basics, advanced development becomes easier.
   ① That　　　② Even　　　③ Diligent　　　④ When

7 When the customers washed the dishware with hot water, the wax _____.
   ① melting　　　② to melt　　　③ melted　　　④ melt

8 Rachel dropped a carton of eggs _____ she was coming out of the store.
   ① as　　　② that　　　③ during　　　④ what

62 副詞子句連接詞

A We left **after** the speeches ended. 演講結束，我們就離開了。

B I'll pay you double **if** you get the work finished soon.
如果你很快地完成工作，我將付你雙倍薪水。

C **Although** I was thirsty, I didn't drink. 雖然我口渴，但是我沒有喝東西。

D Stephen has been such a success **because** he never gives up.
史帝芬是如此的成功，因為他從不放棄。

E It was **so** dark **that** I couldn't see anything.
這裡很暗，我無法看到任何東西。

E I'll give him a map **so that** he can find the way.
我將給他一張地圖，讓他可以找到路。

G Do in Rome **as** the Romans do. 入境隨俗。

「副詞子句」的核心是引導副詞子句的連接詞，隨著連接詞「種類」的不同，整個副詞子句的含義都會不同。

A **after**：表示時間，是最具代表性的「時間連接詞」，而且最常被使用。

B **if**：表示條件，「如果……」的意思，為最具代表性的「條件連接詞」。

C **although**：表示和主要子句對立的關係，「雖然……但是」的意思，為最具代表性的「讓步連接詞」。

D **because**：「因為……」的意思，是最具代表性的「原因連接詞」。

E **so ... that**：「太……，所以……」的意思，是最具代表性的「結果連接詞」。

F **so that**：「如此一來，就可以……」的意思，是最具代表性的「目的連接詞」。so that 之後常會有「助動詞」。

G **as**：「像……」的意思，是最具代表性的「方式連接詞」。

 概念習題

1-7 選出括弧中最符合上下文者。

1 (Because, Even though) Sue got good grades, she received a scholarship.

2 (Because, Even though) Ann got good grades, she didn't receive a scholarship.

3 My brother is going to be so disappointed (if, unless) he gets the job.

4 My brother is going to be so delighted (if, unless) he gets the job.

5 I'll send some flowers today (so that, as, until) they get there on Mary's birthday.

6 Just (as, so) the French love their wine, so the English love their beer.

7 Paul likes ships and the sea so much (as, that) he has decided to become a sailor.

A. 時間連接詞	after the speeches ended
B. 條件連接詞	If you get the work finished soon
C. 讓步連接詞	Although I was thirsty
D. 原因連接詞	because he never gives up
E. 結果連接詞	so . . . that I couldn't see anything
F. 目的連接詞	so that he can find the way
G. 方式連接詞	as the Romans do

副詞子句連接詞

時間連接詞	when (當), after (之後), before (之前), until (直到), while (當), as (當⋯⋯時), since (自從), as soon as (和⋯⋯一樣快), once (一次)		
條件連接詞	if (如果), unless (除非)	讓步連接詞	although, (even) though (儘管)
原因連接詞	because/as/since (因為)	結果連接詞	so (如此), so/such...that (如此⋯⋯以至於)
方式連接詞	as (例如)	目的連接詞	so that, in order that (為了)

1. When I see Catherine, I'll invite her to the party.
   當我看到凱薩琳時,我要邀請她來宴會。
2. As it grew darker, it became colder. 愈晚愈冷。
3. We'll leave tomorrow unless it rains. 除非下雨,不然我們明天離開。
   * 表示「時間和條件的副詞子句」中,不能用「未來式」。
4. Although Eric was sad, he smiled. 雖然艾瑞克很傷心,但他仍然面帶微笑。
5. Since I haven't much money, I can't buy the car. 因為我沒錢,所以不能買車。
6. He needed some advice, so he wrote to the consultant.
   他需要一些建議,所以他寫信給顧問。
7. We'll leave early so (that) we won't arrive late. 我們要早點離開,才不會太晚抵達。
8. Mary bakes cakes as her mother did. 瑪麗和她媽媽一樣烤了蛋糕。

8 選出文法正確的句子。
① If the policeman will interview me about the accident, I'll tell the truth.
② We met a lot of nice people during we were taking our vacation.
③ I don't know as Susan has ever been in Portugal.
④ George ate lunch as soon as he finished his homework.

9-10 選出一個最適合填入空格中的答案。

9 _____ fish can hear, they have neither external ears nor eardrums.
① As   ② Although   ③ If   ④ When

10 The dinner conversation was _____ boring that Joe fell asleep in his dessert dish.
① so   ② very   ③ too   ④ much

子句和連接詞

171

1-11 選出一個最適合填入空格中的答案。

1 A virus is harmful because _____ reproduces by killing the host cell.
① it　② it is　③ why it　④ can

2 Dinosaurs did not exist _____ the early years of life on Earth.
① when　② while　③ during　④ if

3 In the alpine tundra, the summer sunshine is intense, _____ prevalent.
① winds to be
② winds are
③ and winds are
④ that winds are

4 _____ some mammals came to live in the sea is not known.
① Although
② How
③ Most
④ That

5 _____ is caused by a virus was not known until 1911.
① Measles
② That measles
③ As measles
④ Since measles

6 _____ I understand what you're trying to say, I don't agree with you in many ways.
① However
② When
③ As
④ Although

7 The testing item was _____ difficult that a lot of applicants could not solve it.
① so　② as　③ very　④ too

8 Endive can be used _____ as a salad green or as a cooking vegetable.
① such
② either
③ both
④ neither

9 All teaching materials here are free _____ they are otherwise indicated.
① unless
② that
③ however
④ although

10 Mary didn't remember her appointment with the doctor _____ arrived home.
① but she
② until she
③ she had
④ that she

11 I really wonder _____.
① that Jane failed the driving test
② who Jane failed the driving test
③ how did Jane fail the driving test
④ why Jane failed the driving test

12-15 閱讀下列文字，並回答問題。

12 選出劃線部分為文法正確者。
① Because rapidly growing economies in the developing world and continued growth among the industrialized nations, global energy use is climbing.
② Researchers found that young children understanding their mother's stress very quickly and become more stressed themselves.
③ Sometimes there are situations when it is better not to tell the truth. Often, it depends on that you want to save someone's feelings.

④ One of the workers in my company smokes in the office. The company has a rule against this, <u>but</u> he doesn't pay attention to the rule.

13 找出劃線部分的文法錯誤，並且更正。

I spoke in Korean to a young man who looked like a Korean. To my surprise, he answered in fluent English. He was from Vietnam. I wondered <u>why did he look</u> so much like a Korean.

14 選出括弧中最符合上下文者。

The best way to overcome writer's block is to just write something. For example, (if, unless) you can't think of a good opening, write another section of your story. Beginning to write anything tends to activate the writing part of your brain (so that, consequently) you can keep going. Eventually, you'll think of exactly (as, what) you need to say.

*writer's block: 指寫文章的時候，一開始時常會有寫不順的情形。

15 選出一個最適合填入空格中的答案。

Once, on a math test, the first page was full of instructions. Because the test time was not very long, I just went ahead _____ started to work. I spent almost all my time on Problem 5, so I couldn't finish the test. I didn't realize my mistake _____ my test was returned. In the instructions, in large letters, the teacher had said that Problem 5 was only for the students in the advanced class.

① therefore — until
② and — after
③ and — until
④ therefore — when

16-22 選出劃線部分文法錯誤者。

16 The researcher, ① <u>with</u> ② <u>her</u> assistants, ③ <u>having made</u> some important ④ <u>discoveries</u>.

17 Some educators ① <u>say that</u> children can learn ② <u>important</u> social skills ③ <u>during</u> they are doing something they ④ <u>enjoy</u>.

18 ① <u>Most VNR</u> ② <u>material looks</u> ③ <u>too realistic</u> that ④ <u>it's</u> hard for you to tell the difference.

19 I remember ① <u>when did Peter ask me</u> ② <u>if</u> I would marry him. I ③ <u>told</u> him ④ <u>that I would</u>.

20 The work is ① <u>too complicated</u>. You can hardly ② <u>finish it</u> in ③ <u>that</u> ④ <u>would</u> be a simple way.

21 Michelle ① <u>ordered a dress</u> ② <u>from the</u> catalog but ③ <u>so it arrived</u>, it was the ④ <u>wrong size</u>.

22 ① <u>That we</u> ② <u>start</u> in the morning, we ③ <u>feel</u> we must do ④ <u>hundreds of</u> tasks that day.

CHAPTER 10

關係子句
Relative Clauses

63 關係子句的形式、功能和關係詞

A

A cook is a person **who** cooks professionally.
廚師就是專業烹煮料理的人。

The article **which** I read on the train was very interesting.
這篇我在火車上閱讀的文章很有趣。

B

A cook is a person. **He** cooks professionally. 〔兩個句子〕
廚師是一個人。他烹煮料理很專業。

A cook is a person **who** cooks professionally. 〔一個句子〕
廚師就是專業烹煮料理的人。

A‧‧ 關係子句的「形式」，是「關係詞＋子句」。「關係詞＋子句」和在 Chapter 9（子句和連接詞）學過的疑問詞子句一樣，它們本身就是個完全子句。例句一，who 和 which 是關係詞，而「who cooks professionally」和「which I read on the train」是關係子句。

關係子句扮演了修飾名詞的「形容詞」的功能，因此關係子句又被稱為「形容詞子句」。接受關係子句修飾的名詞，稱作「先行詞」。例句中的「a person」和「the article」是先行詞，它們後面的關係子句，就是用來修飾這個先行詞（名詞）的。

B‧‧ 關係子句中的關係詞，具有什麼功能呢？「關係詞」，引導關係子句，並連接前面的名詞，具有「連接」的功能。

例句中的人稱代名詞 He，在句子中是主詞的功能，但它不具有連接兩個句子的連接功能。相反的，關係代名詞 who 有主詞的功能，還有連接的功能，所以它可以把兩個句子連接成一個。

 概念習題

1-4 找出下列各句中的關係詞子句，並整個標示出來。

1 The pianist who played at the concert last night is internationally famous.
2 Addy said that intelligence is something which is made up of different aspects.
3 Jobs that we think to be important will attract our attention and interest.
4 In my life, there were many times when I felt bored with what I was doing.

5-8 將提示的關係詞子句，放到句子的正確位置中。

5 The cakes were delicious. (which Melanie baked)
6 I wrote a letter to the woman. (whom I met at the meeting)
7 The couple have twelve grandchildren. (who have moved to our neighborhood)

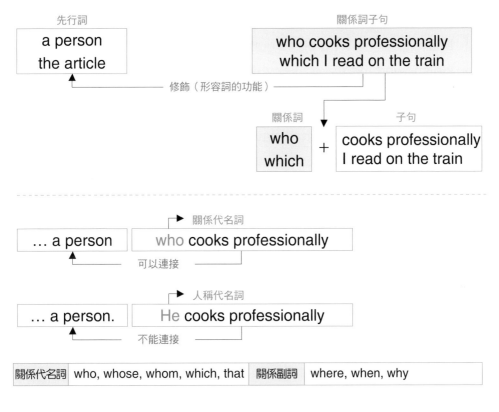

| 關係代名詞 | who, whose, whom, which, that | 關係副詞 | where, when, why |

1. Many people who receive spam mail are often upset.
   許多人收到垃圾信件都會覺得很討厭。
2. The man whom I met at the party was very imperious.
   那個我在舞會遇到的人，非常傲慢。
3. I know a woman whose daughter is a soldier. 我認識一位婦女，女兒是軍人。
4. The stream which flows between the valleys is deep and wide.
   那條流經兩個村莊之間的河流又深又寬。
5. This is the school where she taught English. 這是她任教英文的學校。

8 A typewriter is a machine. (which is used to print letters)

9-11 選出一個最適合填入空格中的答案。

9 People _____ about their personalities can be more successful.

① he knows　　② they know　　③ who know　　④ she knows

10 He lives in the old vila, and _____ is very uncomfortable.

① it　　② they　　③ which　　④ who

11 Bark is the rough surface _____ the trunk and branches of a tree.

① covers　　② it covers　　③ which covering　　④ that covers

64 關係代名詞的種類 who/which/that

A
I have a friend **who** plays guitar. 我有個會彈吉他的朋友。

He showed me the rocks **which** he had collected.
他拿他收集的石頭給我看。

B
I have a friend **who/that** plays guitar. 我有個會彈吉他的朋友。

He showed me the rocks **which/that** he had collected.
他拿他收集的石頭給我看。

Joanne is the **most** intelligent person **that** I know.
喬安是我認識的朋友中最聰明的。

關係子句是由「關係詞」和「子句」所組成。子句的位置上,可依句意放入各式各樣的子句;但在關係詞的位置上,卻只有幾個關係詞依一定的規則,才能放入。因此,學習關係子句時,**關係詞就是學習關鍵**。首先,先了解關係代名詞:

A 引導關係了句的**關係代名詞**有「who」和「which」兩種,要選擇用哪一種,完全由「先行詞」來決定。先行詞如果是人,就用 who;先行詞如果是**事物**,就用 which。例句中,「a friend」是人,所以用 who;「the rocks」是事物,所以用 which。

B 關係代名詞除 who 和 which 以外,還有一個「that」。這個 that 可以代替 who,也可以代替 which,不過如果先行詞中有 all、any、everything 等不定代名詞,或有最高級或 only 等限定詞,通常都會用 that 來取代 who 和 which。

1-4 選出括弧中最符合上下文者。

1 The phone (who, which) is on your desk isn't working right now.

2 The woman (who, which) was on the same bus helped me.

3 Louis knows the woman (that, which) is meeting us at the airport.

4 She is the greatest nurse (that, who) has ever lived.

5-8 將提示的兩個句子,改成關係子句。

5 Steam is a gas. It forms when water boils.
→ Steam _____.

6 The little boy ate candies the whole way. He sat next to me on the train.
→ The little boy _____.

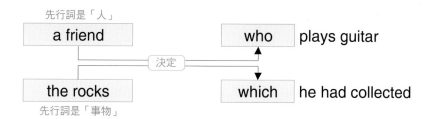

that = who	a friend who/that plays guitar
that = which	the rocks which/that he had collected
that > which	the most intelligent person that I know (不能用which)

1. The old castle which we visited was really interesting.
   我們參觀過的那座古堡很有趣。
2. The reporter interviewed the woman who owns the hotel.
   那位記者訪問了那間旅館的女主人。
3. The man whom I wanted to see had gone to Europe.
   那個我想見的人，已經去歐洲了。
4. The medicine that I took made me sleepy. 我吃的那些藥，讓我想睡覺。
5. All that is needed is a continuous supply of fuel oil. 我們很需要持續供給燃料油。
6. This is the most delicious food that I've ever eaten. 這是我吃過最美味的食物了。

7 The bomb caused a lot of damage. It went off near my neighborhood.
→ The bomb _____.

8 Any advice would be greatly appreciated. You can give me any advice.
→ Any advice _____.

9-10 選出一個最適合填入空格中的答案。

9 The old lady _____ gave me directions was very friendly.
　　① she　　　　② which　　　　③ who　　　　④ to

10 The water buffalo is the only kind of buffalo _____ has ever been tamed.
　　① who　　　　② which　　　　③ whom　　　　④ that

關係子句

179

65 關係代名詞的主格和受格 Who/Whom

A
Bill Gates is the man **who** has founded Microsoft.
比爾蓋茲創建了微軟。

Bill Gates is the man **whom** we met last night.
比爾蓋茲是我們昨晚遇見的人。

B
This is the house **which/that** has a beautiful backyard.
這是一間有著美麗後花園的房子。

This is the house **which/that** my brother bought last week.
這間房子是我哥哥上週買下的。

「關係代名詞」也是一種代名詞,所以和「人稱代名詞」一樣,它也有**主格、受格**和**所有格**。當關係代名詞是所有格時,who、which、that 都要改成 whose。(參照右側圖表)

A 兩例句的先行詞都是 the man,但是關係代名詞卻不同,一個是 who(主格),一個是 whom(受格);所以由此可以看出,關係代名詞的「格」,不是由先行詞決定,而是由「關係詞子句本身」所決定。在關係子句裡面,關係代名詞如果是「主詞」,就用「主格」;如果是「受詞」,就用「受格」。例句一,關係子句「who has founded Microsoft」的 who 就是主詞;例句二,關係子句「whom we met last night」的 whom 則是受詞。

關係子句和疑問句、疑問詞子句一樣,包含關係代名詞後才是一個完全子句。因此若將關係代名詞的位置空出來,剩下的子句,就是一個不完全子句。在這個不完全子句中,如果需要主詞,空出來的位置就填入主格;如果需要受詞,就填入受格。

B which 和 that 當作主格(例句一)和當作受格(例句二),形式完全一樣。

 概念習題

1-3 將提示的兩個句子,以關係代名詞連接成一句。

1 That guy sometimes sleeps. He has an earring.
→ That guy _____.

2 Ricky is carrying out research on artistic talents. Children have them.
→ Ricky _____.

3 English has an alphabet. It consists of 26 letters.
→ English _____.

4-8 空格中填入 who、whom、which 其中之一,以符合句意。

4 Hong Kong is the capital _____ is noted for its busy harbor.

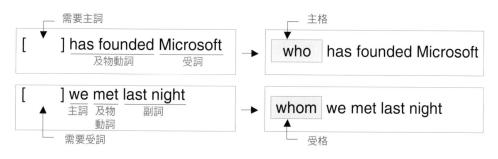

主格	受格	所有格
who	whom	
which	which	whose
that	that	

1. The woman who lives next door is very nice. 住在我隔壁的女子，人很好。
2. The man (whom) Harris saw at the party is Rachel's boss.
   那個海瑞絲在宴會看到的人是瑞秋的老板。
3. I received an e-mail which promises to make me rich.
   我收到一封承諾會讓我發大財的電子郵件。
4. Have you been to the restaurant that has just opened in town?
   你曾去過那間鎮上剛開幕的餐廳嗎？
5. I don't read all the e-mail (that) I receive.
   我並沒有閱讀我收到的所有電子郵件。

▲ 關係代名詞當做「受格」使用時，可以省略：

上面的例句中，當作受格的時候，whom/that 可以省略。

5 I met the movie star _____ I admire tremendously.

6 She is quick to reproach anyone _____ does not live up to her own high standards.

7 The suspect _____ the police were questioning has been released.

8 The girl is one of the few people _____ I think might be good at the job.

9-10 選出一個最適合填入空格中的答案。

9 We would like to know if you are one of those women _____ involved in politics.
   ① whom is   ② whom are   ③ who is   ④ who are

10 Joan could not eat the peaches her sister _____ from the store.
   ① to take   ② had taken   ③ took them   ④ who take

關係子句

181

66 關係代名詞的所有格：Whose

A

I have a friend **who** is a farmer. 我有個朋友是農夫。

[I have a friend. + **He** is a farmer.]

I have a friend **whose** father is a farmer. 我有個朋友的父親是農夫。

[I have a friend. + **His** father is a farmer.]

B

I have a friend whose father **is** a farmer. 我有個朋友的父親是農夫。

[His father is a farmer.]〔his father 是主詞〕

She is the woman whose car you **borrowed**. 她是借你車子的那個女人。

[You borrowed her car.]〔her car 是受詞〕

A 關係代名詞的「所有格」，無論是 who、which、that，所有格都是「whose」。A 項的例句，把 he 換成了 who；B 項的例句，把 his 換成了 whose。總而言之，在原來的句子裡是主格，換成關係子句後，在關係詞子句裡也是主格；在原來的句子裡是所有格，換成關係子句後，在關係子句裡一樣還是所有格。

B 「所有格關係代名詞」在關係子句中有什麼「功能」呢？「主格」和「受格」都是單獨使用，分別在關係子句中擔任主詞或受詞；但「所有格」卻一定要搭配名詞才行，這是所有格和主格、受格最大的不同點。而且要把「所有格＋名詞」視為一個整體，在關係子句中當作主詞或受詞。例句一，「whose father」是 is 的主詞；例句二，「whose car」是 borrowed 的受詞。

概念習題

1-3 將提示的兩個句子，以關係代名詞連接成一句。

1 He is an American architect. His works won $5,000 in the contest.
→ He _____.

2 This is the father. The actress has seduced his son.
→ This _____.

3 We must look up words. We do not know their meanings.
→ We _____.

4-6 空格中填入 who、whom、which、whose 其中之一，以符合句意。

4 The boy _____ nose my son broke was taken to the hospital.

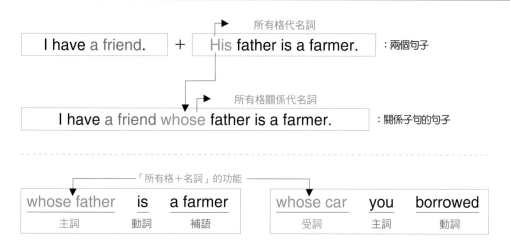

1. There is a rabbit whose ears were badly damaged.
   有一隻耳朵嚴重受傷的兔子。

2. It's the building whose windows were all broken.
   這是一棟全部玻璃都破了的大樓。

3. This is the man whose contract expires next year.
   這就是那個合約明年即將到期的人。

4. That is the girl whose bike I borrowed. 那是借我腳踏車的女孩。

5. Stevenson is an architect whose designs are excellent.
   史帝文生是個非常會設計的建築師。

   *上列例句中，whose ears / whose windows 的 whose 是 which 的所有格，其餘的是 who 的所有格。

---

5 Every year more infections resist every drug _____ doctors try.

6 My mother told me that she met a guy _____ personality is like mine.

7-9 選出一個最適合填入空格中的答案。

7 She is the woman _____ project was the most successful.
   ① her ② whom ③ and ④ whose

8 Mr. O'Nell is worried about other debts _____ his wife has been accumulating.
   ① whose ② who ③ which ④ whom

9 The man whose _____ robbed last night called the police.
   ① house ② house was ③ was ④ house he was

關係子句

67 介系詞＋關係代名詞

A [The house was very big.] + [I lived **in** the house.]

B [The house which I lived **in** was very big. 我住的房子很大。

C [The house **in** which I lived was very big. 我住的房子很大。

D [The house in that I lived was very big.〔錯誤用法〕
The house that I lived **in** was very big.〔正確用法〕我住的房子很大。

A/B 在「關係子句」中，關係代名詞也常被拿來當作「介系詞的受詞」。將 A 項的兩個句子結合，就成為表 B 項關係子句的句子。因為 the house 是介系詞 in 的受詞，所以關係代名詞 which 也是介系詞 in 的受詞。

C 當關係代名詞被拿來當作「介系詞的受詞」時，該介系詞時常會被移至關係代名詞之前。例句中的 in 就被移到它的受詞 which 的前面，變成了「in which I lived」。因此，如果關係代名詞前有介系詞，該介系詞就也要被包含在關係詞子句內，是關係子句的一員。這時要注意的是，因為介系詞後面的關係代名詞，已是介系詞的受詞，所以關係子句中，絕對不會再有其他的主詞或受詞出現。

D 請注意，關係代名詞 that 之前不能有**介系詞**。例句「in that I lived」，是「介系詞＋ that」，所以是錯誤的用法。不過如果介系詞和 that 分開，就可以用 that 了。

概念習題

1-3 將提示的兩個句子，以關係代名詞連接成一句。

1 This is the book. I obtained the information from the book.
→ This _____.

2 He gazed around the room. His entire family were assembled in the room.
→ He _____.

3 His artistic talents were wasted in the boring job. His father is very proud of them.
→ His artistic talents _____.

4-9 請找出下列關係子句的錯誤，並更正。

4 I like the people who I work with.

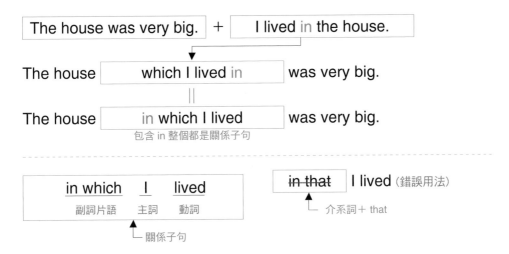

1. This is the boy with whom I went there. 這是和我一起來這裡的男孩。

2. The hotel had a good balcony from which we could look down on the city.
這個旅館有個很大的陽台，我們可以從那裡往下看到整個城市。

3. The small town in which I was born has changed into a large city.
我出生的小鎮，已經變成大城市了。

4. The people about whom the author wrote were factory workers.
這位作者寫的那些人物是工人。

5   These are principles in that we all believe.

6   The restaurant in which is always crowded is closed today.

7   A copy is not so valuable as the original from which the copy is made.

8   There are some things with which I have to speak to you.

9-10 選出一個最適合填入空格中的答案。

9   You should apply to the job _____ you are interested.
① in which   ② which   ③ for which   ④ in where

10   The autobiography is the book _____ the author describes his own experiences.
① which   ② which in   ③ in which   ④ at whom

68 關係副詞

A
This is the place **where** we first met. 這是我們初次見面的地方。
June is the month **when** I was born. 六月是我出生的月份。
This wasn't the reason **why** I left. 這不是我離開的原因。

B
This is the house **which** he lives **in**. 這是他居住的房子。
This is the house **where** he lives. 這是他居住的房子。

「關係副詞」的種類有 where、when、why 三種。基本上，它們的功能和關係代名詞完全一樣；也就是說，關係副詞也能引導關係子句來修飾先行詞，具備了「形容詞子句」的功能。

A 該用哪一個關係副詞，完全由前面的「先行詞」來決定。如果先行詞是「表示場所」的名詞，就用 where；如果先行詞是「表示時間」的名詞，就用 when；如果先行詞是「表示原因」，就用 why。例句中的「the place」表場所；「the month」表時間。

B 什麼時候用 which，什麼時候用 where 呢？舉例說明，B 項兩例句的先行詞都是 the house，但關係詞卻不同，一個用「which」；一個用「where」。因此可知，選擇用 which，還是 where，是由「關係子句」本身的「形式」來決定，而非先行詞。
which 一般都是當作關係子句中的**主詞**或**受詞**；where 則是當作關係子句中的**副詞**。因此，當關係詞的位置空出來的時候，如果該位置需要主詞或受詞，就填入 which；如果該位置需要副詞，就填入 where。

例句一，which 被當作是 in 的受詞；例句二，where 被當作是表示場所的副詞。
總結如下，相同的先行詞，由關係子句本身的形式來決定用 which，還是用 where；關係子句內需要名詞就用 which，關係子句內需要副詞就用 where。

概念習題

1-2 將提示的兩個句子，以關係副詞連接成一句。

1 I recently went back to the village. I was brought up there.
   → I _____.

2 Do you still remember the day? We first saw the Grand Canyon then.
   → Do you _____.

3-8 選出括弧中最符合上下文者。

3 That is the town (which, where) you lived until you were twelve years old.

4 That is the town (which, where) you lived in until you were twelve years old.

5 February is the month (which, when) has only 28 days.

1. My room is a place where I can relax. 我的房間是我可以放鬆的地方。
2. This is the year when the company should increase profits.
   這是公司必須提高獲利的一年。
3. The reason why I'm phoning you is to remind you of the party.
   我打電話給你，是要提醒你宴會的事。
4. That is the room where the meeting was held. 那是舉行會議的房間。
5. That is the room in which the meeting was held. 那是舉行會議的房間。
   *where=in which

6 That is the month (which, when) Monsoons arrive.

7 The reason (where, when, why) Peter came was that he wanted to see Rachel.

8 An individual can speak the language of the country (which, where) he is living.

9-11 選出一個最適合填入空格中的答案。

9 I would like to lie on the beach _____ there is plenty of sunshine.
   ① where   ② which   ③ when   ④ why

10 The hotel at _____ our family stayed wasn't very comfortable.
   ① where   ② that   ③ which   ④ whose

11 She lives in a home _____ people use computers a lot.
   ① when   ② which   ③ in where   ④ where

關係子句

187

69 關係子句轉換

A The bike was not for sale. My son wanted to buy **the bike**.
那台腳踏車不出售。我兒子想買那台腳踏車。

B The bike **which** my son wanted to buy was not for sale.
〔用關係詞子句結合〕我兒子想買的那台腳踏車沒有出售。

C [**which** my son wanted to buy]〔關係詞子句分離〕

D my son wanted to buy **the bike** [**which**]〔關係詞子句語序整理〕

使用「關係子句」時，最需要注意的是：確認有沒有使用「正確的關係詞」。為了要做到這點，首先要將關係子句圈出來看，然後再確認關係子句中的關係詞，是否使用正確。

A/B 首先，先看看獨立的兩個句子，換成關係子句時，有什麼特點。先將例句中獨立的句子「My son wanted to buy the bike.」和換成關係子句的「which my son wanted to buy」這兩個句子比較，就能發現如下的特點：第一，名詞 the bike 換成了關係詞 which；第二，把這個 which 移到關係子句的最前面。所以可以知道，一個句子中，有一個名詞被換成了關係詞，它的位置就要改變。

C/D 確認關係子句中的關係詞使用是否正確時，只要把關係詞還原到它原來在關係詞子句中的位置，然後審視句子的正確即可。首先，先將關係子句從整個句子中分離出來，接著，將其中的關係詞還原到它原來的位置。C 項中的「which my son wanted to buy」，就是被分離出來的關係詞子句，D 項中的「my son wanted to buy the bike」，則是將 which 換成原來的名詞（同先行詞），然後還原到原來的位置。如果這還原的句子是正確的，那關係詞就是用對了；如果這還原的句子是錯誤的，那關係詞就是用錯了。

　　總結上述說明，關係子句一定要包含了關係詞之後，才是一個完全子句。換句話說，關係詞也必須扮演一個名詞的角色，這樣組成的關係子句才是完全子句。

  概念習題

1-3 如提示般，找出下列句子的關係子句。

> I don't read e-mails that I receive from strange people.
> → I receive e-mails from strange people

1 I have a friend who buys almost all the things online.

　　→ _____

2 Pakistan is one of the countries the U.S. government describes as terrorists.

　　→ _____

3 The standards on which the metric system is based are slightly inaccurate.

　　→ _____

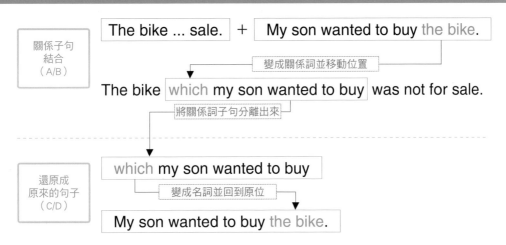

4-7 （4-6）選出一個最適合填入空格中的答案。（7）找出錯誤的地方。

4 People couldn't entirely achieve fire safety in houses _____ most fire deaths occur.

① where ② which ③ in where ④ whose

5 Wind power is an ancient energy source _____ we may return in the near future.

① on which ② to which ③ which ④ at where

6 The teacher _____ has not yet arrived.

① who I wrote to you ② I wrote to you about

③ I wrote to you about her ④ whom I wrote to you about her

7 I would like ① to write about several ② challenges which I ③ have faced them since I ④ came to this university.

70 名詞關係子句：What

A
The shop didn't have the thing **that** I wanted. 那間店沒有我想要的東西。

The shop didn't have **what** I wanted. 那間店沒有我想要的東西。

B
The shop didn't have **what** I wanted. 那間店沒有我想要的東西。

I wanted to know **what** happened to Mike.
我想知道麥克發生了什麼事。

A 關係詞中，what 和 who、which、that 的層次完全不同。what 的特點是它裡面包含了**先行詞**。這兩個例句的意思完全一樣，所以可以看出「先行詞（the thing）＋ that ＝ what」。what 裡面包含了 the thing。

因此，what 子句的「功能」也和其他關係子句不同，它時常是被當作「名詞」來使用。例句一，「that I wanted」是用來修飾前面的 the thing，具有「形容詞」的功能；例句二，「what I wanted」則是前面的動詞 have 的受詞，具有「名詞」的功能。要翻譯 what 子句時，前面被省略的先行詞也要翻譯出來，即「……的東西（名詞）」。

B what 子句的「形式」也和其他關係子句一樣。只要將「the thing that I wanted」中的 the thing 刪除，剩下的「that I wanted」，就跟「what I wanted」形式一樣了。that 是 wanted 的受詞，what 也是 wanted 的受詞。也就是說，what 是關係子句中的一個名詞，關係詞子句有它才是完全子句。

what 具有主詞和受詞的功能。例句一「what I wanted」中的 what 是 wanted 的受詞；例句二「what happened to Mike」中的 what，則是 happened 的主詞。

概念習題

1-8 空格中填入 that、which、what 其中之一，以符合句意。

1 I tried to understand _____ the foreigner was saying, but I couldn't.

2 I tried to understand the words _____ the foreigner was saying, but I couldn't.

3 Susan gives her children everything _____ they want.

4 _____ you have to think about is your profit.

5 Nirvana is the word _____ Hindus use to describe a sense of inner peace.

6 Water and petroleum are two liquids _____ occur in large quantities in nature.

7 An individual is presumed to be like _____ our society expects him to be.

8 From these beans, Europeans experienced their first taste of _____ seemed a very exotic beverage.

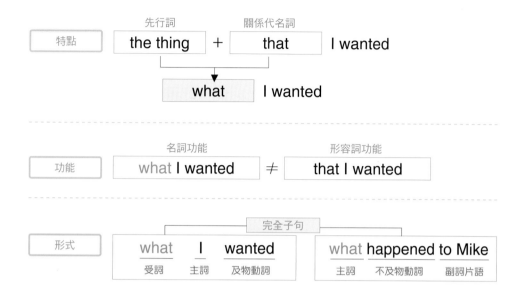

1. You must not believe all that you see. 不要盡信所見之事。
2. You must not believe what you see. 你不要相信你所看見的。
3. What Thomas is looking for is a job in advertising. 湯瑪士正在找廣告業的工作。
4. ~~That/Which~~ Thomas is looking for is a job in advertising.〔錯誤用法〕
5. I managed to get all the CDs that my son asked for. 我設法弄到我兒子要的 CD。
6. I managed to get all the ~~CDs what~~ my son asked for.〔錯誤用法〕
7. No one knows what will happen next. 沒有人知道接下來會發生什麼事。
8. No one knows ~~what it~~ will happen next.〔錯誤用法〕

9-11 選出一個最適合填入空格中的答案。

9 _____ is only a hot bowl of soup.

　① That you need 　　　　　　② What is needed

　③ That is needed 　　　　　　④ What you need it

10 This new style of painting needs our understanding of _____ painting should be.

　① that 　　　② any 　　　③ the 　　　④ what

11 The left hand does not know _____ .

　① what is the right hand doing 　　② what is doing the right hand something

　③ what the right hand is doing 　　④ what the right hand is doing something

71 特殊的先行詞

A ┌ **The man who** lives next door to Melanie **is rather strange.**
    └ 那位住在梅蘭妮隔壁的男子有點奇怪。

B ┌ **Jake, who** lives next door to Melanie, **is rather strange.**
    └ 住在梅蘭妮隔壁的傑克有點奇怪。

「先行詞」和「關係子句」之間有不加逗點的情形，也有加逗點的情形。**不加逗點時，關係子句稱作「限定子句」；加逗點時，關係子句稱作「非限定子句」。**

A 「限定子句」的功能是用來限定前面的先行詞。例句中，如果沒有關係子句，只用「man」，就只知道是某個男人，而不知道是特定的哪一個男人。但若有「which . . . Melanie」這個關係子句加以限定，就可以很清楚知道是「住在梅蘭妮隔壁的那個男子」了，這是因為關係子句將先行詞的含義加以限定的緣故。具有這種功能的關係子句，就被稱為「限定子句」。限定子句對先行詞提供了「必要的訊息」。

B 「非限定子句」用在不需對前面的先行詞加以限定的時候。例句中，因為先行詞「Jake」是人名，所以後面即使沒有關係子句，也可以具體地知道 Jake 是誰，就表示「先行詞本身已經有明確的限定」的意思。像這樣先行詞的含義本身已經有明確的限定，那關係子句就不限定先行詞，只具有「補允、說明」先行詞的功用，所以具有這樣功能的關係子句，就稱為「非限定子句」；對先行詞提供「補充的訊息」。因此關係子句的前面有無逗點，完全由先行詞的種類而定；大致來說，先行詞是「人名」、「國名」、「地名」等專有名詞時，關係子句前就要加逗點。

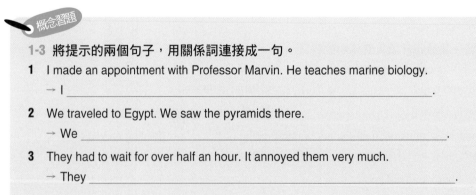

概念習題

1-3 將提示的兩個句子，用關係詞連接成一句。

1 I made an appointment with Professor Marvin. He teaches marine biology.
→ I _____ .

2 We traveled to Egypt. We saw the pyramids there.
→ We _____ .

3 They had to wait for over half an hour. It annoyed them very much.
→ They _____ .

一般名詞　　　沒有逗點　　　　　　　　限定子句

| The man | | who lives next door to Melanie |

專有名詞　　　逗點　　　　　　　　　非限定子句

| Jake | , | who lives next door to Melanie, |

連結　　　　　限定先行詞，一定需要的部分

The man　｜ who lives next door to Melanie

Jake　｜ , ｜ who lives next door to Melanie ,

獨立　　　追加說明先行詞，補充的部分

▲ 逗點後面（非限定子句）的關係代名詞不能用 that，要用 which，而且也不能省略。

Harry passed his driving test, ~~that~~ surprised everybody.〔錯誤用法〕
Harry passed his driving test, which surprised everybody.〔先行詞是前面子句全部〕
亨利通過駕照考試，讓每個人都好驚訝。

1. Professor Johnson, whom I admire, teaches chemistry.
   我所欽佩的強生教授教化學。
2. I'm flying to Chicago, where my family lives.
   我正飛往我家人的居住地——芝加哥。
3. I went to the movie with Sally, whom you met before.
   我和那位你見過的莎莉一起去看電影。
4. They are moving to Manchester, which is in the north-west.
   他們即將搬到西北部的曼徹斯特。

4 選出文法正確的句子。
   ① Adrian went to work at CERN which is a physics laboratory in Geneva.
   ② She showed me around the town, which was very kind of her.
   ③ I like the woman, that is kind to everybody.
   ④ I have three sisters, and all of whom are married.

5-6 選出一個最適合填入空格中的答案。

5 Alice has just come back from New Zealand _____ our family went last week.
   ① which　　　② where　　　③ , which　　　④ , where

6 The award was won by Michael Wood _____ highly respects.
   ① whom the coach　② who　　　③ , whom the coach　④ , the coach

關係子句

193

1-9 選出一個最適合填入空格中的答案。

1 Most folk songs are ballads _____ simple words and tell simple stories.
① have
② as have
③ they have
④ which have

2 A battery is a device _____ electricity by chemical means.
① it produces
② which it produces
③ produces
④ that produces

3 John went to see a friend _____ father is the president of his college.
① her
② who
③ what
④ whose

4 Do you recommend _____ you stayed during summer vacation?
① the hotel
② where
③ the hotel which
④ the hotel where

5 Effective remedies have been developed but doctors don't know exactly _____.
① what the cause is
② which the cause is
③ what is the cause
④ which is the cause

6 A desert is a region _____ an average of ten inches of rain falls in a year.
① which is
② in which
③ which has
④ in which is

7 Thieves _____ paintings from Notford art gallery have been arrested in Paris.
① stole
② who stealing
③ have stolen
④ who stole

8 People can get all the calcium their bodies require from the food they _____.
① eat
② eat them
③ eat it
④ to eat

9 Brad told me about his new job, _____ very much.
① that he's enjoying
② he's enjoying
③ which he's enjoying
④ he's enjoying it

10-16 閱讀下列文字，並回答問題。

10 請依照提示的字首字母，填入符合句意的關係詞。

There are also many tourists w_____ do not speak French; therefore, we need to train employees w_____ speak English and other languages at the train information desks. If we do this, I'm sure more visitors will come to Euro-Disney in comfort and safety.

11 選出一個最適合填入空格中的答案。

Ellen Dean, a 15-year-old Australian girl, was sitting next to a small river. She was relaxing with her feet in the water. Suddenly, a crocodile _____ was 2.9 meters long came out of the water and bit her legs. Fortunately, she was able to hold on to the branch of a tree. Her father saw _____ happened and jumped into the water with a knife. Finally, he killed the crocodile and saved her life.

① that — which　　② who — that
③ what — what　　④ which — who
⑤ that — what

12 請依句意，在空格中填入 be 動詞的正確形式。

The reason why people start talking about the weather or current events _____ that they are harmless and common to everyone.

13 請在下列文章中，找出被省略的兩個關係詞的位置，並標示出來。

An amazing new invention reduces the hours of television children watch every day. The technology is nicknamed "Square – Eyes." It is a tiny, computerized sensor that fits into children's shoes. It measures the number of steps the child takes during the day and sends this information to the family computer.

14 請找出文法錯誤的字，並且更正。

Two other communication devices that have come into common usage is the answering machine and its cousin, voice mail.

15 重組括弧內的字，以符合句意。

On the moving day, Sumi lost her hamster, Hamtori, but she couldn't find him anywhere. The family drove to their new house. Sumi looked around it. "Sumi," Mother called. "Look (your boots, what, of, found, one, I, in)." Hamtori was in the boot!

16 選出括弧中最符合上下文者。

Grades are based on how well you express your ideas in papers and how well you do on exams. Yet reading is the primary means (which, by which, what) you acquire your ideas and gather information.

17-22 選出劃線部分文法錯誤者。

17 Children ① whom parents ② are alcoholics are likely ③ to become alcoholics ④ themselves.

18 All of the facts ① what ② I have told you ③ are true and ④ can be found in this book.

19 Mr. Gilmore is one of those men who ① appears to be ② friendly; however, it is very hard ③ to deal with ④ him.

20 ① Reading for learning is ② something you will have to ③ do it ④ all your life.

21 The ① tiny wire-rims he ② worn only when he couldn't tolerate ③ his contact lens ④ were perched in front of very red eyes.

22 There ① is little possibility ② that crude oil prices will fall ③ below the present level, ④ where is already low.

CHAPTER 11

動名詞
Gerunds

72 動名詞的形式和特點

A
He wrote a short paragraph correctly.〔句子〕他正確地寫出一段文字。
→ ① **that** he wrote a short paragraph correctly〔that 子句〕
→ ② **because** he wrote a short paragraph correctly〔副詞子句〕
→ ③ (his) **writing** a short paragraph correctly〔動名詞片語〕

B
The student began **writing a short paragraph correctly**.
那個學生開始正確地寫出一段文字。

A 句子當作句子裡的一部分時，就要做變化形，可以同例句一、二，在句子前加連接詞；也可以同例句三，句子自己本身做變化。例句三以「原型動詞＋ing」為變化形的片語，就稱作「動名詞片語」。

一般所說的「動名詞」形式為「原型動詞＋ing」，即例句三的「writing」。而 writing 在句中只是「writing . . . correctly」的一部分，英文文法書對此兩者是有加以區分的，「writing」被稱作「動名詞」，而「writing . . . correctly」被稱作「動名詞片語」。另外，在句子中被視為一個整體的是動名詞片語，而非動名詞。如同「關係詞＋子句」變成「關係子句」一樣，在句中被視為一個整體；還有「動名詞＋片語」變成「動名詞片語」，在句中也是被視為一個整體。

事實上，一個句子裡單獨使用「原型動詞＋ing」的情形很少，幾乎都是「動名詞＋片語」的形式，所以提到「動名詞」，就是指「動名詞片語」；本書因此統一用「動名詞」來解說。

B 整個「動名詞」視為一個整體，當作句子中的一部分。「writing . . . correctly」整個被視為一個動名詞，當作「began」的受詞。

 概念習題

1-2 將提示的子句改成動名詞。
1 (a teenager) wants to pursue a singing career
2 (Sasha) spent all week preparing for the golf match

3-8 找出下列各句中的動名詞，並整個標示出來。
3 I like sleeping late in the morning.
4 I always put off going to the dentist until it's too late.
5 Postponing the proposed legislation is being considered by the committee.
6 Researchers studied the power of music by observing two groups of preschoolers.
7 Driving a car to New York in your situation will take five hours.

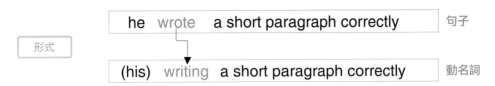

形式	he wrote a short paragraph correctly	句子
	(his) writing a short paragraph correctly	動名詞

▲ 完全子句 ➡ 動名詞的規則

he wrote a short paragraph correctly	⇒	(his) writing a short paragraph correctly

（1）主詞（he）省略。不能省略時，用所有格（his）。
（2）動詞（wrote）改成「原型動詞＋ing（writing）」。
（3）其他的字詞不變。

1. Drinking water is good for you. 喝水對你有益。
2. Tim enjoys doing housework. 提姆樂於做家事。
3. They avoided wasting time by taking a shortcut. 他們走捷徑，以避免浪費時間。
4. I'm thinking about going to Hawaii. 我正在考慮去夏威夷。

8 People cannot help feeling honored when they receive a nomination.

9-10 選出一個最適合填入空格中的答案。

9 In 1984, _____ a mammal from an adult cell was impossible.
① clone ② cloning ③ they cloned ④ the cloning

10 I was surprised at his extensive _____ of English grammar.
① know ② knew ③ knowing ④ knowledge

73 動名詞的功能

A

Taking five classes **is** too much work.〔主詞〕修五堂課太辛苦了。

I **enjoy** walking in the park.〔及物動詞的受詞〕我喜愛在公園裡散步。

Kate insisted **on** wearing a suit to the party.〔介系詞的受詞〕
凱特堅持穿套裝去參加派對。

His job **is** teaching English in a school.〔主詞補語〕
他的工作是在學校教英文。

B

I **enjoy** walking in the park. 我喜愛在公園裡散步。

I **refuse** ~~walking~~ in the park.〔錯誤用法〕

A──── 動名詞的「功能」是**名詞**。在句子中經常被當作主詞、及物動詞的受詞、介系詞的受詞、補語來使用。
雖然整個「動名詞」是很長的片語，卻只扮演了一個「名詞」的功能。
例句中的「Taking five classes / walking in the park / wearing a suit to the party / teaching English in a school」全部都是動名詞，它們分別被當作「主詞 / 及物動詞 enjoy 的受詞 / 介系詞 on 的受詞 / is 的補語」來使用。「動名詞」可以當作所有介系詞的受詞。

B──── 動名詞當作「及物動詞的受詞」使用時，只能被當作某些「特定動詞」的受詞。「enjoy」這個字可以用動名詞來當它的受詞，但是「refuse」卻不能用動名詞來當它的受詞。

概念習題

1-4 找出句中的動名詞，並說明它在句中的功能。

1 You should avoid giving any unnecessary information.

2 Nadia apologized for hurting her friend's feelings.

3 I was very tired after taking a long walk in the woods.

4 I turned round and left after opening the front door was prohibited by a guard.

5-7 選出一個最適合填入空格中的答案。

5 Ann is nervous about _____ home from work late at night.

  ① to walk   ② she walks   ③ walking   ④ walking to

6 _____ after children requires a lot of patience.

  ① Look   ② Looking   ③ People look   ④ Looked

	主詞	Taking five classes is too much work.
動名詞的功能 = 名詞的功能	及物動詞的受詞	I enjoy walking in the park.
	介系詞的受詞	Kate insisted on wearing a suit to the party.
	補語	His job is teaching English in a school.

▲ 可以用動名詞當受詞的及物動詞

admit (准許)	avoid (避免)	consider (考慮)	deny (否定)
enjoy (享受)	finish (完成)	give up (放棄)	mind (在意)
put off (拖延)	postpone (延遲)	stop (停止)	

1. Learning English is interesting. 學英文是有趣的。
2. Going to college is expensive. 唸大學的費用很貴。
3. They talked about getting a new car. 他們討論買新車的事。
4. I'm looking forward to going to the zoo. 我期待去動物園。
5. He didn't mind driving an old car. 他不在意開舊車。
6. Robert gave up playing football years ago. 羅伯特多年前就放棄踢足球了。
7. One of his bad habits is biting his nails. 他的壞習慣之一就是咬指甲。

7 By the time Jason arrived, they had already finished _____ the piano upstairs.
① moving to   ② moved   ③ to move   ④ moving

8-12 選出括弧中最符合上下文者。

8 Tracy, would you mind (mailing, to mail) this letter on your way to work?

9 Paula denied (eating, to eat, about eating) a whole box of sweets before dinner.

10 Liz believes (in helping, in help, helping, to help) others.

11 Max is afraid of (failing, failure) the driving test.

12 The accident was caused by the (failing, failure) of the reactor's cooling system.

74 深入了解動名詞

A
① Mary insisted on seeing her lawyer. 瑪麗堅持要見她的律師。

② Mary insisted on **our** staying for dinner with her.
瑪麗堅持要我們留下來和她一起吃晚餐。

B
She complains of **not** having time to exercise. 〔否定〕她抱怨沒時間運動。

C
I hate treating others like slaves. 我討厭像奴隸般對待別人。

I hate **being** treated like slaves. 〔被動〕我討厭被像奴隸般對待。

A 大致來說，如果動名詞所指涉的主詞和整個句子的主詞是一致的，通常會省略主詞；如果不能省略時，就要在動名詞前加「所有格」。例句一，動名詞「seeing her lawyer」，「seeing」前面的主詞就被省略了；那是因為 seeing 所指涉的主詞和整個句子的主詞一致，所以要省略；此例句的主詞是 Mary，中文意思是「瑪麗見她的律師」。例句二，動名詞「our staying for dinner with her」，是所有格加動名詞的情形；staying 所指涉的主詞是「we」，意思是「我們留下」。

B 動名詞前若加「not」，就變成動名詞的否定形式了。not 通常放在動名詞之前，not 也要被視為動名詞的一部分。例句「not having time to exercise」，可看作由「she does not have time to exercise」這個否定句轉變而來。

C 動名詞有「主動語態」和「被動語態」之分。動名詞以「原形動詞＋ing」為句首，就是主動語態；如果以「being ＋動詞過去分詞」為句首，就是被動語態。例句二的「being treated like slaves」是被動語態的動名詞，可視為將「I am treated like slaves」這個被動語態的句子，轉變成動名詞而來的。

 概念習題

1-4 將句子依照提示改成動名詞的形式。

> she threw a stone at them → Ann denied throwing a stone at them.

1 they do not help others → Rich people are accused of _____.
2 Mary goes to bed late → Mary's parents don't like _____.
3 they are corrected by the teacher → Students appreciate _____.
4 Tim didn't finish it in time → _____ made the boss angry.

5-8 選出括弧中最符合上下文者。

5 I walked on tiptoe and went out of the room without (noticing, being noticed).
6 The government officials are interested in (Jack's escaping, escaping) from prison.

1. I objected to her attending the meeting. 我反對她參加會議。
2. Bill's keeping his fish in the bathtub is quite unusual.
   比爾把魚養在浴缸裡，實在很怪。
3. If you go near a tiger, you risk being bitten. 如果你走近老虎，就有被咬的危險。
4. The cook was scolded for not putting enough salt in the soup.
   廚師因湯裡沒放足夠的鹽巴而被責罵。
5. I can't understand his not calling me. 我不能理解他為什麼不打電話給我。

7　(Planning, Being planned) your schedule carefully would be a help.

8　After (shooting, being shot) in the chest, her boyfriend was taken to hospital.

9-11　選出一個最適合填入空格中的答案。

9　Mike objected to _____ vitamins because he believed that they were useless.
　　① Ann taking　　② Ann's taking　　③ his took　　④ him taking

10　_____ a good sleep at night makes you look angry.
　　① Not getting　　② Not your getting　　③ Your not getting　　④ Getting not

11　The thief removed the treasure from the museum without _____.
　　① seeing　　② been seen　　③ being seen them　　④ being seen

動名詞

203

CHAPTER 11 單元綜合問題

1-11 選出一個最適合填入空格中的答案。

1 People everywhere enjoy _____.
① talking love   ② talking about love
③ to talk about love
④ in talking about love

2 _____ in the dark room is harmful to the eyes.
① Read   ② Reading
③ The reading   ④ You read

3 It goes without _____ that you'll be paid for all this extra time.
① says   ② to say
③ saying   ④ being saying

4 _____ able to speak the language is the greatest problem.
① Not being   ② Being not
③ Not is   ④ Is not

5 They didn't _____ the party till 10 p.m.
① finished preparing for
② finish to prepare
③ finish preparing for
④ finish to prepare for

6 Rose was angry about _____ to make coffee for everyone at the faculty meeting.
① asking   ② being asked
③ to be asked   ④ to ask

7 The airline is legally responsible for _____ its passengers.
① saving of   ② the saving
③ the safety   ④ the safety of

8 I can't imagine _____ how to solve the problem.
① your not knowing
② you not knowing
③ not your knowing
④ not you know

9 She _____ help thinking that she had seen him somewhere before.
① can not   ② could not
③ must not   ④ might not

10 The spouses of patients _____ the same conditions.
① was at a risk of developing
② were at a risk to development
③ were at a risk of developing
④ were at a risk of development

11 Each student is responsible for _____ the requirements for graduation.
① known   ② knowing
③ know   ④ knowledge

12-16 閱讀下列文字，並回答問題。

12 選出括弧中最符合上下文者。

He has been calling me George. My name is Jim. Most of the time I see him at the weight room at the health club, and he greets me with a big, "Hello, George!" I thought about (correcting, correction, correct) him, but he can't hear me because he has earphones on.

204

13 選出一個最適合填入空格中的答案。

Part-time jobs will help teens to choose their life-long jobs after graduation. Moreover, working with others _____ leadership, teamwork, and the ability to consider others.

① built   ② build
③ to build   ④ builds
⑤ building

14 選出劃線部分文法錯誤者。

The way of ① losing weight has nothing to do with jogging or ② starving yourself. You do not get fat because of ③ a lack of exercising and your body will adjust itself by ④ burning fewer calories when you try a low calorie diet. You can get slim by ⑤ eat the right foods at the right intervals each day.

15 空格中請填入 expose 的正確形式。

Many studies show that frequent _____ to intense noise pollution can damage a person's hearing temporarily or permanently.

16 選出一個最適合填入空格中的答案。

While Steve was employed with this office, he earned the respect and trust of his colleagues and supervisors. Moreover, Steve was one of our most successful salesmen. He was responsible for _____ sales to their highest point.

① rise   ② raise
③ rising   ④ raising

17-23 選出劃線部分文法錯誤者。

17 He is considering ① to purchase a new car ② because ③ the old one doesn't ④ drive well.

18 Through ① computers we can get ② information instantly just by ③ push ④ a few buttons.

19 When ① a ship ② goes down on their coast, they cannot help ③ regard it ④ as lawful plunder.

20 ① Not being able to ② hear it doesn't seem ③ as bad as not being ④ able to see.

21 They ① accuse ② athletes of being ③ ridiculously ④ overpaying.

22 After ① exhaustive researching his ② new work, the novelist grew ③ interested in ④ the Apollo moon mission.

23 Mr. Smith told Sue that ① her refusal ② to work ③ necessitated ④ her sending for her parent.

CHAPTER 12

不定詞
Infinitives

75 不定詞的形式和特點

A
He wrote a short paragraph correctly. 〔句子〕他正確地寫下一段文字。
→ ① (his) **writing** a short paragraph correctly〔動名詞〕
→ ② (for him) **to write** a short paragraph correctly〔不定詞〕

B
The student began **to write a short paragraph correctly**.
那個學生開始正確地寫下一段文字。

A 將句子改寫成例句一，就稱作「動名詞」；改寫成例句二，就稱作「不定詞」。如何形成不定詞的呢？只要將完全子句中的動詞，改成「to＋原型動詞」的形式即可。動名詞和不定詞唯一的不同，只是形式上，一個是「writing」，一個是「to write」。

由例句二可以知道，不定詞「to write . . . correctly」也是從完全子句「he wrote . . . correctly」改寫而來。

「不定詞」和動名詞一樣，要正確地以概念區分，也可以分成「不定詞」和「不定詞片語」。以例句來說，不定詞是指「to write」，而不定詞片語則是指「(for him) to write . . . correctly」。在句子中被視為一整體使用的，是不定詞片語，而非不定詞。這樣的定理，就像動名詞和動名詞片語的關係一樣。事實上，一個句子裡單獨使用「to＋原型動詞」的情形很少，幾乎都是「不定詞＋片語」的形成，所以「不定詞」就是指「不定詞片語」；本書統一以「不定詞」來解說。

B 「不定詞」也像動名詞一樣，被視為一個整體，當作句子中的一部分。例句中的「to write . . . correctly」整個被視為一個不定詞，當作「began」的受詞。

概念習題

1-2 將提示的子句分別改寫成動名詞和不定詞。

1 (they) did different things this weekend
動名詞：＿＿＿＿＿＿＿＿＿＿ 不定詞：＿＿＿＿＿＿＿＿＿＿

2 (he) discovered that light is made up of a composite of color
動名詞：＿＿＿＿＿＿＿＿＿＿ 不定詞：＿＿＿＿＿＿＿＿＿＿

3-7 找出下列句子中的不定詞，並標示出來。

3 To learn English well takes reading a lot in English.

4 I called some of my friends to invite them for dinner this weekend.

5 Customers will also be able to e-mail questions to the bank.

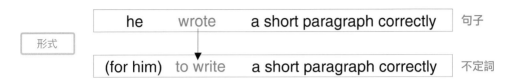

形式

| he | wrote | a short paragraph correctly | 句子 |
| (for him) | to write | a short paragraph correctly | 不定詞 |

▲ 完全子句 ➡ 不定詞的規則

he wrote a short paragraph correctly ➡ to write a short paragraph correctly

（1）主詞（he）省略。
（2）動詞（wrote）改寫成「to ＋原型動詞（write）」。
（3）其他的字詞不變。

1. I'm planning to fly to Chicago next week. 我正計劃下週飛往芝加哥。
2. I agreed to lend him some money. 我同意借他一些錢。
3. Barbara gets up early in the morning to study. 芭芭拉都會早起看書。
4. I've got lots of letters to write today. 我今天有很多封信要寫。

6　Mom expected me to stay up late every night this week and study for exams.

7　Their desire is to live a life that is free from the influence of civilized man.

8-9　選出一個最適合填入空格中的答案。

8　She'd like to _____ the techniques of ballet.
　　① improved　　② improving　　③ improvement　　④ improve

9　A good citizen thinks _____ the law is his own duty.
　　① that obey　　② to obey　　③ that obedience　　④ obedient

不定詞

76 深入了解不定詞

A
> I'm very eager to meet Maggie. 〔主詞〕我渴望見到瑪格。
>
> I'm very eager **for** Harold to meet **Maggie.** 我很希望哈洛德見到瑪格。

B
> It is important **not** to get too nervous in a job interview. 〔否定〕
> 工作面試很重要的就是不要太緊張。

C
> I don't want to be disturbed while studying. 〔被動〕
> 我讀書時不希望被打擾。

D
> She appears to **be** at the party alone. 她單獨出現在派對。
>
> = It appears she is at the party alone.
>
> She appears to **have left** the party alone. 〔完成〕她已獨自離開派對。
>
> = It appears she left the party alone.

A ···· 因為整個「不定詞」是由子句變化而來,所以基本上不定詞還是要有「主詞」。不定詞的主詞和整個句子的主詞一致,所以它可以省略;如果不能省略時,就在不定詞前加「for+受格」。例句一「to meet Maggie」的主詞,就是整個句子的主詞「I」;例句二,「for Harold to meet Maggie」的「Harold」是 meet 的主詞。

B ···· 不定詞前若加「not」,就是不定詞的否定句。not 要加在 to 的前面,而且 not 也算是不定詞的一部分。

C ···· 不定詞以「to be +過去分詞」為句首時,為被動語態不定詞。例句「to be disturbed」就是「I am disturbed」的意思。

D ···· 以例句來說,「to+原型動詞」的 to be 是「不定詞」;「to+完成式」的 to have left 是「完成不定詞」。因為不定詞中只有動詞原型,所以它本身是看不出時態;大致上來說,它的時態要和主要子句一致。如果不定詞的時態比主要子句的時態早發生,不定詞就用「完成式不定詞」。例句中的「to be」和「appears」是相同時態,to be 是「she is . . .」的意思;而「to have left」比「appears」還早發生,「to have left」是「she left . . .」的意思。

1-2 空格中填入適當的字,使兩句意思相同。

1 Young men have to spend their time wisely.

    = It's necessary _____ young men to spend their time wisely.

2 It seems that my grandmother was beautiful in her youth.

    = My grandmother seems to _____ beautiful in her youth.

3-7 選出括弧中最符合上下文者。

3 He seems (to be, to have been) rich now.

4 He seems (to have, to have had) bitter experiences while he was in the US.

5 Why did you decide (not to go, to not go, go to not) to the movies with them?

1. It isn't necessary for you to go to the conference. 你不需要出席這場會議。
2. She's arranged for her son to have tennis lessons. 她已為兒子安排網球課。
3. Alex promised not to be late. 艾力克斯承諾不遲到。
4. We've decided not to buy a new car. 我們已經決定不買新車了。
5. To love is more difficult than to be loved. 愛比被愛還難。
6. Tom is said to have moved to New York. 有人說湯姆已搬到紐約。
7. John's grandparents are said to have died a natural death.
   有人說約翰的祖父母已經去世了。

6 My brother worked hard (to not fire, not to fire, not to be fired).

7 The salesman was very glad (to receive, to have received) the order the day before.

8-10 選出一個最適合填入空格中的答案。

8 The accident seems to _____ at around 10 p.m. last night.
   ① happen   ② be happened   ③ have happened   ④ happened

9 I am worried about the appearance of the floor. I need _____ it.
   ① to wax   ② to be waxed   ③ waxing   ④ waxed

10 No one has better qualifications. Steve is sure to _____ for the position.
   ① choose   ② chosen   ③ have chosen   ④ be chosen

77 不定詞的名詞功能

A

Jimmy **refuses** to eat peas. 〔及物動詞的受詞〕吉米拒吃豌豆。

It is wrong to cheat during a test. 〔主詞〕在考試中作弊是不對的。

= To cheat during a test **is wrong**.

Your goal **is** to be able to speak English. 〔補語〕你的目標是能夠開口說英文。

Kate insisted **on** ~~to come with us~~. 〔錯誤用法〕凱特堅持和我們一起來。

A 不定詞具有「名詞」的功能。所以在句子中，常被拿來當作**及物動詞**的**受詞**和**主詞**，偶爾也被當作「補語」用。唯一和動名詞不同的是，不定詞不能拿來當作「介系詞的受詞」。例句一的「to eat peas」是及物動詞 refuse 的受詞；例句二「to cheat during a test」當作主詞；例句三的「to be able to speak English」是 is 的補語。介系詞 on 之後不能接**不定詞**，所以接「to come with us」是錯誤的。

B 不定詞當作及物動詞的受詞使用時，只能被當作某些「特定動詞」的受詞。「refuse」就是可以用不定詞當作受詞的特定動詞。

C 不定詞當「主詞」時，大致都會加「it」這個虛主詞來代替它。「To cheat during a test is wrong.」是可以成立的句子，但大多都是用「ɪt ɪs wrong to cheat during a test.」這個加了虛主詞的形式。

概念習題

1-4 找出下列句中的不定詞，並說明它在句中的功能。

1 I have decided not to accept the idea offered by a colleague.

2 To be an administrator is to have the worst job in the world.

3 A wife has an equal say with her husband in deciding whether to buy a camera.

4 It is a good idea not to waste money on a hotel.

5-9 找出下列句中的不定詞，並說明它在句中的功能。

5 We need (going, to go) to the shopping mall tomorrow.

6 Its goal will be (create, to create) a positive mood or feeling about the product.

7 What place would you like (visiting, to visit) the most?

8 You must not forget (when, which) to keep your mouth shut.

▲ 可以用不定詞當受詞的及物動詞

decide (決定)	expect (期待)	fail (失敗)	hope (希望)
manage (管理)	need (需要)	offer (提供)	plan (計畫)
refuse (拒絕)	want (想)	would like (想要)	

1. We expected to be happy. 我們希望能快樂。
2. I would like to visit the Grand Canyon. 我想去大峽谷玩。
3. It is important to get daily exercise. 每天運動很重要。
4. The wisest policy (for us) is not to interfere. 最明智的策略就是不干預。

   * 不定詞常和疑問詞搭配使用。這個「疑問詞＋不定詞」主要是當作受詞使用。

5. He learned how to sail a boat as a small boy.
   當他還是個男孩時，他就學划船了。

---

9 Charlie doesn't approve of (smoking, to smoke) in bed.

10-12 選出一個最適合填入空格中的答案。

10 It was easy _____ that the new scheme was a great improvement.
① see ② saw ③ to see ④ to seeing

11 A teenage boy whose parents stressed the importance of doing well in school may refuse _____.
① study ② to not study ③ studying ④ to study

12 To classify things _____ to arrange them in groups according to a plan.
① is ② be ③ are ④ to be

不定詞

213

78 不定詞的形容詞和副詞功能

A

I've got some letters **to write**. 〔受格關係〕我有一些信要寫。

Frank has no friends **to help him**. 〔主格關係〕法蘭克沒有朋友幫他。

Their chance **to go abroad** was lost. 〔同位語關係〕他們失去出國的機會。

B

Andy came here **(in order) to learn English**.
安迪來這裡 (為了) 學英文。

To find a good job, you have to study hard.
為了要找到好工作,你必須認真讀書。

A 不定詞具有「形容詞」的功能。「some letters / no friends / their chance」都是名詞,它們後面的不定詞「to write / to help him / to go abroad」分別用來修飾它們前面的名詞。不定詞一定要放在「名詞」後面來修飾它,這時不定詞就翻譯成「來……、要去……」之意,基本上都有「未來」的含義。

不定詞的形容詞功能方面,還有一個特點:是「完全子句」。「動名詞」和「不定詞」,還有後面要學的「分詞」,基本上都是完全子句。不過,當不定詞當作「形容詞」時,不定詞是「不完全子句」,它必須包含前面的名詞才是完全子句。例句一「some letters to write」中不定詞「to write」省略了主詞「I」,即使還原主詞成「I write」,仍是沒有受詞的不完全子句;必須將名詞「some letters」當作受詞,成為「I write some letters」才是完全子句。不定詞前面的名詞,成為不定詞的一部分後,主要是當作「受詞」、「主詞」或「同位語」。以例句來說,「some letters」成為 write 的受詞;「no friends」成為 help 的主詞;「chance」和「go abroad」是同位語。

B 不定詞還有修飾動詞或子句的「副詞」的功能。用「逗點」將不定詞獨立出來後,不定詞就可以修飾子句;「不加逗點」,就可以修飾動詞。不過修飾動詞或子句時,不定詞有「為了……、以便……」這個具「目的」的含義。例句一:如果在不定詞前加「in order」,目的的含義就更明顯了。例句一「to learn English」修飾動詞 came;例句二「to find a good job」修飾主要子句「you have to study hard」。

 概念習題

1-3 依提示,將括弧中的句子改成「名詞+不定詞」的形式,填入空格中。

> Would you like <u>something to read</u>? (you read something)

1 I have to go now. I've got _____. (I catch a train)

2 I can't do all this work alone. I need _____. (somebody helps me)

3 We need _____. (we put these things in a bag)

4-7 選出括弧中最符合上下文者。

4 Jack went abroad (for, to) a good education.

5 Jack went abroad (for, to) get a good education.

6 John stepped on the brake (to make, for making) a stop in time.

7 He needs some new clothes (to wear to the party, to wear it to the party).

圖表整理

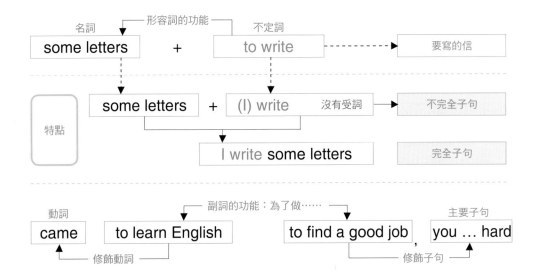

1. Ms. Drew has the ability to explain things clearly. 卓小姐可以清楚地解釋這些事。
2. This is the best time for Emily to study. 這是艾蜜莉讀書的最佳時機。
3. Let's go to the cafe (in order) to have coffee. 我們一起去咖啡店（為了）喝咖啡吧。
4. I turned on the radio to get information about weather.
   我打開收音機，收聽氣象資訊。
5. In order to make money, you need a paying job.
   為了要賺錢，你需要一份有給薪的工作。

8-9 找出句中的不定詞，並說明它在句中的功能。

8 To overcome the disease, governments are trying to eradicate the tsetse fly.

9 If teachers want to make mathematics interesting, they must give the student a challenge and an obstacle to overcome.

10-11 選出一個最適合填入空格中的答案。

10 _____ and promote good health, it is necessary to exercise regularly.

   ① Maintain　　② Maintaining　　③ To maintain　　④ For maintaining

11 The need _____ technique motivates ballerinas to exercise for hours daily.

   ① improve　　② to improve　　③ improves　　④ which improve

不定詞

215

79 動詞＋受詞＋不定詞

A

I expect to find it somewhere in my room.

我希望可以在房間裡的某個地方找到它。

I expect **you** to find it somewhere in your room.

我希望你可以在房間裡的某個地方找到它。

B

She doesn't allow anyone **to smoke** in the house.

她不允許任何人在房子裡抽菸。

She doesn't let anyone **smoke** in the house.

她不讓任何人在房子裡抽菸。

A 在含有不定詞的片語中，「動詞＋名詞（受詞）＋不定詞」這種句型的片語很重要。「expect you to find」就是一個明顯的例子，這是在「expect to find」中，加了受詞 you 所形成的句子。

例句中的「to find」接在「expect」這樣的特定動詞的後面，當作受詞；「you to find」也接在特定動詞「expect」之後，當作受詞。「expect」這個動詞讓「不定詞」和「受詞＋不定詞」這兩種情形都成立。「不定詞」和「受詞＋不定詞」這兩者的差異是**主詞**不同。「to find」的主詞，就是整個句子的主詞；而「you to find」的主詞是 you。

B 句型「動詞＋受詞＋不定詞」，又可再細分成「動詞＋受詞＋ to 原型動詞」和「動詞＋受詞＋原型動詞」兩種。allow anyone to smoke 是「動詞＋受詞＋ to 原型動詞」的形式；let anyone smoke 是「動詞＋受詞＋原型動詞」的形式。應該使用「to 原型動詞」，還是「原型動詞」，完全由前面的動詞來決定。例句一的一般動詞（allow）後面要用「to 原型動詞」；例句二的**使役動詞**（let）或**知覺動詞**後面，就要用「原型動詞」。

1-8 選出一個最適合填入空格中的答案。

1 Tyranny will not allow citizens (travel, to travel), open bank accounts, or get a job.

2 Having a car enables me (going, to go, go) places more easily.

3 Just seeing Woody Allen's face is enough to make me (laughing, to laugh, laugh).

4 I wouldn't advise (eating, to eat, eat) in that restaurant.

5 Sally got me (to applying, to apply, apply) for the job.

6 We are required (to wear, you to wear) our school uniforms over the clothes.

7 Susan saw the car (drove, to drive, drive) up outside the police station.

8 We hope that Mary will take us to the station.

= We (hope, want) Mary (to take, take) us to the station.

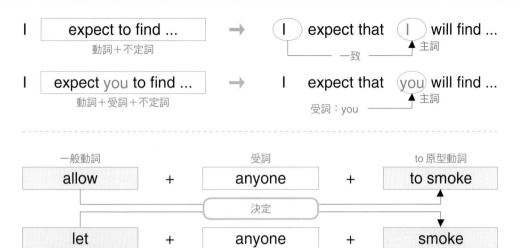

▲ 句型「動詞＋受詞＋不定詞」的動詞類型

一般動詞 (to 原型動詞)	advise (建議)　allow (允許)　ask (問)　cause (引起)　enable (使能夠) expect (期待)　encourage (鼓勵)　forbid (禁止)　force (迫使)　lead (引導) order (安排)　persuade/get (說服)　recommend (推薦)　remind (提醒) require (要求)　teach (教)　tell (告訴)　want (想要)　warn (警告)　help (幫助)
使役知覺動詞 原型動詞	have (有)　make (做)　let (讓)　help (幫助) see/watch/observe (看/注視/觀察)　hear (聽到)　feel (覺得)

1. I wouldn't advise anybody to stay in that hotel. 我不建議任何人住在那間旅館。
2. Reading short stories helped Al (to) learn more vocabulary.
   閱讀短篇故事幫助艾兒學到更多單字。
3. Film directors can have computers add different features into their scenes.
   電影導演可以用電腦在任何一個鏡頭裡加入不同的特效。

9-11 選出一個最適合填入空格中的答案。

9 I told my mother _____ for myself.

　① to let me to choose　　　　　② to let me choose

　③ let me to choose　　　　　　④ let me choose

10 Every man and woman _____ to enter the hall last year.

　① allowed　　② was allowed　　③ have allowed　　④ were allowed

11 請選出不能填入空格中者

　I _____ Tom carry her cases up the stairs.

　① helped　　　② observed　　　③ got　　　④ heard

不定詞

217

80 形容詞＋不定詞

A — I'm very **pleased** to see you. 我非常開心見到你。

B — Mary is **able** to cope with the work. 瑪麗有能力處理這項工作。

C — It is **difficult** to deal with the manager. 經理很難應付。
= The manager is **difficult** to deal with ∅.

D — You're really **kind** to help us. 你真好心幫我們的忙。
= It's really **kind** of you to help us.

A──「不定詞」可以搭配各式的形容詞。不定詞如果放在表示「高興、悲傷、生氣、驚訝」等「感情形容詞」之後，不定詞就用來表示該形容詞的原因，是「因……」的意思。例句中「to see you」就是「pleased」的原因。

B──例句中「be able to cope . . .」，看起來是在形容詞 able 之後，加上不定詞 to cope 的形式，但實際上，「be able to」是助動詞，後面接表示「能力、義務、可能性」的動詞 cope。

C──此例句是「虛主詞 it ＋不定詞 to deal . . . manager」的形式，像 difficult 這樣的特定形容詞經常用這樣的句型；簡單翻譯成「去做……是很困難的」的意思。
將不定詞的受詞「the manager」移到虛主詞「it」的位置，變成「The manager is . . . deal with.」的形式更常被使用。在轉換句子時要注意的是：（1）只有遇到像 difficult 這樣的特定形容詞，才能轉換。（2）即使不定詞 deal with 是及物動詞，它後面也不能接受詞（因為受詞已經移到主詞的位置了）。

D──像「kind」這樣的「品行形容詞」，後面如果接不定詞，該不定詞就是這形容詞的依據，是「竟……」的意思。例句的「It's kind of you . . . us.」將主詞 you 改成「of you」，然後移到「kind」的後面，you 的位置換成「it」；在這個句子中要特別注意的是，「of you」是不定詞「to help us」的主詞，不能用 for you。

 概念習題

1-2 空格中填入適當的字，使兩句意思相同。

1 It is hard to read his handwriting.
→ His handwriting _____.

2 She was careless to leave a camera on the bus.
→ It _____.

3-6 選出一個最適合填入空格中的答案。

3 (It, That, Mary) is impossible to solve the problem.

4 It was foolish (of him, for him) to buy the old-fashioned radio set.

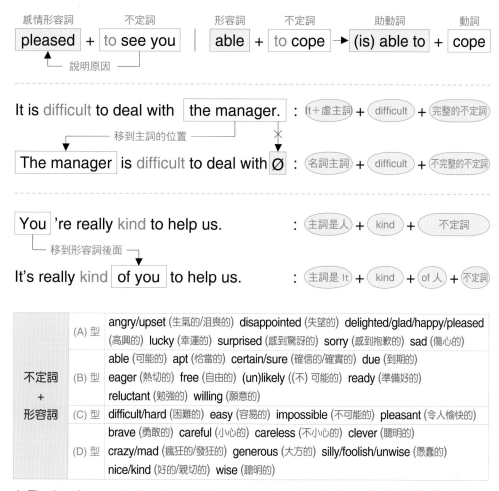

		angry/upset (生氣的/沮喪的) disappointed (失望的) delighted/glad/happy/pleased (高興的) lucky (幸運的) surprised (感到驚訝的) sorry (感到抱歉的) sad (傷心的)
不定詞 + 形容詞	(A) 型	angry/upset (生氣的/沮喪的) disappointed (失望的) delighted/glad/happy/pleased (高興的) lucky (幸運的) surprised (感到驚訝的) sorry (感到抱歉的) sad (傷心的)
	(B) 型	able (可能的) apt (恰當的) certain/sure (確信的/確實的) due (到期的) eager (熱切的) free (自由的) (un)likely ((不) 可能的) ready (準備好的) reluctant (勉強的) willing (願意的)
	(C) 型	difficult/hard (困難的) easy (容易的) impossible (不可能的) pleasant (令人愉快的)
	(D) 型	brave (勇敢的) careful (小心的) careless (不小心的) clever (聰明的) crazy/mad (瘋狂的/發瘋的) generous (大方的) silly/foolish/unwise (愚蠢的) nice/kind (好的/親切的) wise (聰明的)

1. The boy is easy to deceive. = It is easy to deceive the boy. 這男孩很容易哄騙。

2. It was foolish of you to spend so much. 你花了這麼多錢，真是傻瓜。

   = You're foolish to spend so much.

5 It wasn't necessary (of him, for him) to buy the old-fashioned radio set.

6 Mary's father was at first reluctant (to letting, let, to let) her go abroad alone.

7-9 選出一個最適合填入空格中的答案。

7 The girl is easy _____.

① to talk   ② to talk to   ③ to talk to him   ④ to be talked

8 It was very generous _____ to lend them your new car for their holiday.

① you   ② for you   ③ to you   ④ of you

9 Children who live in the country's rural areas are very _____ poor.

① likely to be   ② like to be   ③ likely of being   ④ likely to being

不定詞

1-11 選出一個最適合填入空格中的答案。

1 The headmaster would like to _____ Mr Smith's proposals to the school governors.
① recommend   ② recommending
③ recommendation④ recommended

2 It's impossible _____ him to support his family.
① with   ② on   ③ of   ④ for

3 _____ weight, you have to cut down on sugar and other sweet things.
① To lose   ② Losing
③ Loss of   ④ For losing

4 Ms. Kim _____ Johnny to take the test again.
① made   ② required
③ talked   ④ argued

5 A baby's first teeth _____ are generally the lower incisors.
① appearances   ② had appeared
③ to appear   ④ in appearing

6 In recent speeches, the officials pledged _____.
① not to let that happen
② to not let that to happen
③ not to let that to happen
④ to not let that happen

7 The tourist guide _____ a map if we went walking in the hills.
① advised to take us
② advised us take
③ advised us to take

8 It seems very difficult _____.
① to stop the child to cry
② holding the child's crying
③ restraining the child to cry
④ to keep the child from crying

9 There is no doubt that, in many countries, food has become much easier _____.
① to preparing   ② to have preparing
③ that prepares   ④ to prepare

10 I need something _____; any pen or pencil will do.
① to write with   ② to write with it
③ to write   ④ to write on

11 When Annie was inviting people to her party, Jason was annoyed to _____.
① forget
② have forgotten
③ be forgetting
④ have been forgotten

12-16 閱讀下列文字，並回答問題。

12 選出和提示句中不定詞相同用法的句子。

An author may write an introduction to describe how the book is organized and why it's organized that way.
① All you have to do is to put your small puppy in the purse.
② Lots of teens want to work after school hours although their parents don't like it.
③ It is not unusual for ballet dancers to wear out two pairs of toe shoes a day.

④ Perhaps the best way for young children to use computers is to use them only for a short time each day.
⑤ Boys lived at the school to receive their military training for wars.

13 請找出下列文法錯誤的字，並更正。

When we ask our friends for advice, we really want them agree with our actions. If they tell us we were wrong to behave as we had done, we react with surprise and refuse to accept what they say.

14 請選出意思是「觸碰式螢幕通常很容易讓使用者學會」的句子，填入空格。

One of the significant advantages of the touch screens is that it's very easy to use. The reason is that it's natural to point things with a finger. In addition, _____.

① the user is usually easy to learn touch screens
② touch screens are usually easy for the user to learn them
③ the user is usually easily learn touch screens
④ touch screens are usually easy for the user to learn

15 空格中請填入 study 的正確形式。

Many people try _____ a foreign language. They study it for a few weeks and stop. Some time later, they try it and stop again. This is not a good way. It is important _____ without stopping when you learn a foreign language.

16 空格中請填入 be 動詞的正確形式。

While flower giving is very popular these days, the most common reason to give flowers _____ to express romantic love.

17-23 選出劃線部分文法錯誤者。

17 ① Besides ② to be an outstanding student, he is ③ also ④ a leader in school government.

18 ① It was careless ② for you ③ to leave your tickets ④ behind in the taxi.

19 The ① library's periodicals will be ② temporarily ③ shut down ④ for renovating the facilities.

20 Large, ① complex societies ② have ③ a great deal of information that needs to ④ store.

21 The condition will ① be difficult to ② diagnose it children ③ who speak ④ these languages.

22 ① That may be difficult ② to believe I discovered a woman ③ living an active life ④ at the age of 139.

23 ① Anyone that is willing to ② spent the necessary time ③ will find this conference ④ to be a rewarding experience.

221

CHAPTER 13

分詞和分詞構句
Participles & Participle Structure

81 分詞的形式、功能和特點

A
a woman wears sunglasses（子句）→ Ø **wearing** sunglasses〔分詞〕
the people are invited to the party（子句）→ Ø **invited** to the party〔分詞〕

B
You should look for a woman **wearing** sunglasses.
你應該尋找一位戴太陽眼鏡的女子。

The people **invited** to the party can't come. 那些被邀請來派對的人不能來了。

C
You should look for a woman **who wears** sunglasses.
The people **who are invited** to the party can't come.

A. 「分詞」和動名詞、不定詞一樣，都是從子句變化而來。分詞也是從完全子句轉換而成，在轉換時因主動、被動的不同而分成「現在分詞」和「過去分詞」兩種。轉換的過程是：（1）將子句的主詞刪除。（2）子句如果是主動語態，動詞就換成現在分詞，其餘的字詞不變。（3）子句如果是被動語態，就將 be 動詞刪除，過去分詞為句首，其餘的字詞不變。例句一，「wearing sunglasses」是從主動語態轉換過來的現在分詞；例句二，「invited to the party」是從被動語態轉換過來的過去分詞。
正確來說，分詞分成「分詞」和「分詞片語」。「分詞」就是指「原型動詞＋ ing／原型動詞＋ ed」；「分詞片語」則是指包含分詞在內的整個子句。例句中，「wearing」和「invited」是分詞；「wearing sunglasses」和「invited to the party」是分詞片語。但實際上，這兩者並沒有分得那麼清楚，所以我們統一用「分詞」來解說。

B. 分詞具有修飾名詞的「形容詞」功能。例句一，分詞「wearing sunglasses」用來修飾名詞 a woman；例句二，分詞「invited to the party」用來修飾名詞 the people。因此，分詞又稱作「形容詞片語」。
談到分詞的特點，就像在前面提到的，分詞裡面是沒有「主詞」的，接受分詞修飾的「先行詞」，才是分詞的主詞。例句中，a woman 和 the people 是分詞修飾的名詞，同時也是分詞 wearing 和 invited 的主詞。

C. 分詞也可以被看成是「關係子句的一部分」。在關係子句中，如果關係代名詞當作主詞，就可以轉換成分詞。例句一，「the woman wearing sunglasses」和「the woman who wears sunglasses」意思完全一樣；例句二，「the people invited to the party」和「the people who are invited to the party」意思也完全一樣。

 概念習題

1-2 將下列句子依提示改寫成「名詞＋分詞」的形式。

A man stands at the door.	The author is known far and wide.
→ A man standing at the door	→ The author known far and wide

1 The car was repaired before Tuesday.

2 International human rights standards set the minimum age for marriage at 18.

3-5 找出下列句子中的分詞，並說明它在句中的功能。

3 The pig's new home was in the lower part of the barn smelling of hay.

4 The new city built with wide streets and beautiful houses was called Williamsburg.

5 Last week he submitted a report based on the idea that diet and environment were the real answers.

圖表整理

1. The boy reading the book is Steve. 正在讀這本書的男孩是史帝夫。
2. Do you know the path leading to the church? 你知道通往教堂的小路嗎？
3. I was awakened by a bell ringing. 我被門鈴聲吵醒。
4. All the cars manufactured in the factory are exported.
   這間工廠生產的車，全部都要出口。
5. The boy injured in the accident is my brother.
   在車禍受傷的那個男孩是我弟弟。

6-7 空格中填入適當的字，使兩句意思相同。（也可能填入兩個字以上）

6　The bridge built fifty years ago has proved safe.

　　= The bridge ＿＿＿＿＿＿＿＿＿＿ built fifty years ago has proved safe.

7　A woman who is living in Miami retired at the age of 39.

　　= A woman ＿＿＿＿＿＿＿＿＿＿ in Miami retired at the age of 39.

8　選出一個最適合填入空格中的答案。

　　This city was laid out in a design ＿＿＿＿＿ after that of Seattle.

　　① was patterning　②has patterned　　③ was patterned　　④ patterned

分詞和分詞構句

82 現在分詞和過去分詞

A People **using** the Web can shop from their homes.
使用網路的人們可在家購物。
[People **use** the Web: 主動]

B The book **published** last week is his first novel.
上週出版的這本書是他的第一本小說。
[The book **was published** last week: 被動]

「分詞」轉換的核心可以簡要分成兩點：第一，首先在很長的句子裡，找出哪個部分是轉換分詞的。第二，轉換的分詞，是現在分詞「原型動詞＋ **ing**」，還是過去分詞「原型動詞＋ **ed**」。以下將這兩點，再具體說明如下：

第一
在整個句子中，找出要轉換成分詞的部分，並將它和名詞一起圈出來。所以「People using the Web」和「The book published last week」被圈出來了。

第二
接著要判斷是要用哪一種分詞，所以要將分詞**還原**。兩例句就還原成「People (use) the Web」和「The book (publish) last week」了。

第三
判斷這個子句是**主動語態**，還是**被動語態**。因為例句一的 use 子句後有受詞，所以「People use the Web」是主動語態；例句二的 publish 子句後沒有受詞，所以「The book publish last week」是被動語態。

第四
如果是主動語態的句子，就用**現在分詞**；如果是被動語態的句子，就用**過去分詞**。因為例句一 use 是主動語態，所以換成「現在分詞 using」；例句二 publish 是被動語態，所以換成「過去分詞 published」。
因此，動詞要換成現在分詞，還是要換成過去分詞，最後判斷的依據是主動語態或被動語態。

 概念習題

1-4 找出下列句子中要換成分詞的動詞，並正確地換成分詞。

> Did you see the letter came this morning?
> Ans: came → coming

1 We live near the chemical company employs 2,000 people.
2 The window was broken in the storm has now been repaired.
3 A girl was sitting at a table was covered by a clean white cloth.
4 The controllers were assigned to the flight suspected that it had been hijacked.

5-8 下列句子若有錯誤，請找出並更正。
5 The man arresting by the police has been released this morning.
6 The students taken the examination waited for the results.

1. The people living next door come from Italy. 住在隔壁的鄰居來自義大利。
2. This is a book answering questions about the Web.
   這是一本回答關於網路問題的書。
3. The weapon used in the murder has now been found.
   在謀殺案中被使用的凶器已經找到。
4. There was a big red car parked outside the house. 有部紅色大車停在這棟房子外。

7 People experienced habitual loneliness have problems becoming close to others.

8 Between the US and Canada there is a famous bridge calling the Bridge of Peace.

9-11 選出一個最適合填入空格中的答案。

9 The amount of money _____ for a particular product is the price of that product.
  ① exchanging   ② exchanged   ③ to exchange   ④ is exchanged

10 I grew up in a culture _____ us literally a part of the nature.
  ① considers   ② considered   ③ which consider   ④ considering

11 Air law is defined as the law directly or indirectly _____ with civil aviation.
  ① is concerned   ② concerned   ③ concerning   ④ concerns

分詞和分詞構句

227

83 分詞和分詞形容詞

A
The number of **stolen** cars **has risen.** 汽車失竊率提高。

[The number of cars **stolen every year** has risen.]

I was woken early by the **singing** teddy bear. 我一早就被玩具音樂熊吵醒了。

[I was woken early by the teddy bear **singing loudly**.]

B
The test results **were pleasing.** 考試結果讓人雀躍不已。

The students **were pleased** (with the test results).
學生們雀躍不已 (對於考試結果)。

A 「分詞」大致的型態都是「原型動詞＋ ing/ed ＋其他字詞」，不過也只會有「原型動詞＋ ing/ed」的情況。如果是單一個詞，這時分詞就像形容詞一樣，必須放在「名詞」前面。以例句來說，在括弧中的「stolen every year」和「singing loudly」都是「分詞＋其他字詞」，放在名詞後面來修飾名詞；而例句一、二的「stolen」和「singing」都是單一個分詞，放在名詞前面來修飾名詞。

無論分詞是「原型動詞＋ ing/ed」（在名詞前面）類型，還是「原型動詞＋ ing/ed ＋其他字詞」（在名詞後面）類型，都還要再次分辨分詞是現在分詞（-ing），還是過去分詞（-ed）。如果名詞後面是現在分詞，那在名詞前面也要用現在分詞；如果在名詞後面是過去分詞，那在名詞前面也要用過去分詞。

B 在「原型動詞＋ ing/ed」形成的分詞中，如果該分詞固定被當作**形容詞**，就稱作「分詞形容詞」。分詞形容詞也有加 ing 和加 ed 兩種。

例句一，「the test result」用「pleasing」；而例句二「the students」則用「pleased」。原因是「the test result」和「please」的關係是主動的，「考試的結果讓學生高興」；而「the students」和「please」的關係是被動的，「學生們（因為考試的結果）而感到高興」。

被當作分詞形容詞的動詞，全都是以人為受詞，以及和情感有關的及物動詞。因此分詞形容詞，如果和人搭配使用，就用加 -ed 的形式；如果是和影響人的事物搭配使用，就用加 -ing 的形式。

概念習題

1-2 將粗體字動詞換成正確的分詞填入空格中。

1 The stories **amused** our daughter. → The stories were ＿＿＿＿＿＿.
→ Our daughter was ＿＿＿＿＿.

2 The opera **disappointed** the audience. → It was a ＿＿＿＿＿ opera.
→ We met a lot of ＿＿＿＿＿ audience.

3-4 選出一個最適合填入空格中的答案。

3 The book is full of information. It's very ＿＿＿＿.
① interest　　② interested　　③ interesting　　④ interests

▲ **主動和被動的分詞形容詞**

amusing / amused (好玩的) boring / bored (厭煩的) disappointing / disappointed (失望的)
depressing / depressed (沮喪的) exciting / excited (興奮的) frightening / frightened (吃驚的)
interesting / interested (有趣的) surprising / surprised (驚訝的) tiring / tired (疲憊的)

1. They need to drive under more controled condition.
   它們需要在更能操控的情形下運作。
2. It's one of the world's leading manufacturers of audio equipment.
   這是世界知名的音響設備製造商之一。
3. This is an interesting class. 這是有趣的一堂課。
4. This class is interesting. 這堂課很有趣。
5. We were bored on the way home. 在回家的路上，我們都感到很無聊。
6. The plane trip was boring. 這次的旅途很無趣。

4 Jack works on a ranch in the _____ interior.
① isolate   ② isolated   ③ isolation   ④ isolating

5-10 選出括弧中最符合上下文者。

5 I was (surprised, surprising) at the test results.

6 This wet weather is so (depressed, depressing).

7 The regional governor is able to expel (suspected, suspecting) trouble-makers.

8 We were (annoyed, annoying) because the bus was late.

9 *Ms.* magazine is one of the (led, leading) publications of the feminist movement.

10 Some houses in the village still don't have (run, running) water.

84 分詞構句的形式和功能

A

You should look for a woman **wearing sunglasses**.
你應該尋找一位戴太陽眼鏡的女子。

Asking his mother to forgive him, the boy burst into tears.
在請求母親原諒時，男孩號啕大哭。

B

Asking his mother to forgive him, the boy burst into tears.
在請求他母親原諒時，男孩號啕大哭。

As he asked his mother to forgive him, the boy burst into tears.

A 分詞主要用法是「名詞＋分詞」；不過也有沒有名詞，單獨一個分詞的情形，這種情形稱作「分詞構句」。例句一，「wearing sunglasses」放在名詞 a woman 之後，用來修飾名詞的分詞；例句二，「asking his mother . . . him」則是沒有名詞、單獨被使用的分詞構句。分詞構句可以放在主要子句之前，也可以放在主要子句之後。

B 分詞具有「形容詞」的功能；分詞構句卻具有「副詞子句」的功能。例句中，分詞構句「asking . . . him」，對主要子句「the boy . . . tears」而言，是扮演副詞子句的功能。
因為分詞構句具有副詞子句的功能，所以可以換成包含「連接詞」在內的副詞子句。這樣一來，就變成了「副詞子句連接詞＋主詞＋動詞＋其他字詞」的形式了。連接詞要選擇符合主要子句句意的連接詞，主詞和主要子句的主詞一致，動詞的時態也是和主要子句的時態一致。另外，為了符合主要子句的句意，分詞構句「asking . . . him」，換成副詞子句時，就是「as he asked . . . him」。

分詞構句轉換成副詞子句所使用的「連接詞」，大致是表示時間（when/after/as）、同時的狀況（while）、理由（because/since）、讓步（although）、假設（if）、延續（and then）等的連接詞。使用不同的連接詞，分詞構句也就有不同的含義。

1-3 空格中填入適當的字，使兩句意思相同。

1 After I finish my homework, I'm going to watch TV.
= _____ _____ _____, I'm going to watch TV.

2 Getting up at 4 a.m., Larry was very tired all day long.
= _____ _____ _____ up at 4 a.m., Larry was very tired all day long.

3 Gina had an accident while she drove to work this morning.
= Gina had an accident _____ _____ _____ this morning.

有名詞	分詞	
a woman	wearing sunglasses	分詞片語的形式 和 分詞的形式

沒有名詞	分詞片語
Ø	asking his mother to forgive him

分詞片語　　　　　　　　　　主要子句

Asking his mother to forgive him, | the boy burst into cry.

分詞片語的功能
＝
副詞子句

↓ 副詞子句：連接詞＋主詞＋動詞

As he asked his mother to forgive him

1. Seeing the dog coming towards her, she ran away.
   看見一隻狗朝她走來，她馬上跑開。
   = When she saw the dog coming towards her, she ran away.
2. Turning off the lights, I left the room. 關燈後，我便離開房間。
   = After I turned off the lights, I left the room.
3. Being unemployed, he hasn't got much money. 他因為失業，所以沒什麼錢。
   = Because he is unemployed, he hasn't got much money.
4. Being kept in the refrigerator, the fruit should remain fresh for weeks.
   把水果冰在冰箱，應該可以保鮮數個星期。
   = If it is kept in the refrigerator, the fruit should remain fresh for weeks.

4-5 選出一個最適合填入空格中的答案。

4 _____ the stars, the ancient Mayans developed a solar calendar.
① They studied　② As studied　③ Studying　④ They studying

5 Certain fish eggs contain a little oil, _____ them to float on the surface of the water.
① allowed　② it allowed　③ and allowing　④ allowing

6-7 選出劃線部分錯誤者。

6 The hospitals were ① flooded with people, ② complained of ③ headaches and stomach ④ pains.

7 ① Looking back, ② by we realized the cottage ③ had been covered ④ by the snow.

85 分詞構句的主詞和現在分詞、過去分詞、連接詞

A

Taking a trip across the country, **Julie** dropped her camera.〔正確用法〕

Taking a trip across the country, ~~Julie's camera~~ dropped.〔錯誤用法〕

遊歷那個國家時，茱麗弄丟了相機。

B

Asking his mother to forgive him, the boy burst into tears.

在請求他母親原諒時，男孩號啕大哭。

Taken in excessive amounts, vitamin can be harmful to you.

過度服用維他命對你有害。

C

While eating breakfast, Jane heard the door bell ring.

珍在吃早餐時，聽到門鈴響。

A ⋯⋯「分詞構句」的主詞要和「主要子句」的主詞一致。例句中，「Taking a trip across the country」是分詞構句，意思是「遊歷一個國家」；主要子句的主詞，就應該是遊歷的人。但是如果主要子句的主詞是事物「Julie's camera」，語意就不對了，所以是錯誤的。

B ⋯⋯分詞構句也分為「現在分詞（-ing）」和「過去分詞（-ed）」兩種。分詞構句區分的原理和分詞一樣。如果「主要子句的主詞＋分詞構句」為主動，就用「現在分詞（-ing）」；如果是被動，就用「過去分詞（-ed）」。例句一「the boy (ask) his mother to forgive him」，ask 應該是主動語態「asking」才正確；例句二「vitamin (take) in excessive amounts」，take 應該是被動語態「taken」才正確。

C ⋯⋯一般來說，「分詞構句」的前面，不加「連接詞」，不過有時為了使意思更加明確，也會加上副詞子句的連接詞。以例句來說，因為加上連接詞「while」，而使得意思更加地明確。

概念習題

1-3 選出一個最適合填入空格中的答案。

1 _____ the nervousness of the speaker, the director told a joke.

① Notes   ② Noted   ③ Noting   ④ When noted

2 Seriously burned in a terrible car accident, _____.

① Janet could not be protected from infection

② the doctor could not treat Janet well

③ her parents hoped for Janet's full recovery from the operation

④ an ambulance took Janet to the nearest hospital

3 Jane works as a journalist, _____ about the famous people.

① written   ② being written   ③ writes   ④ writing

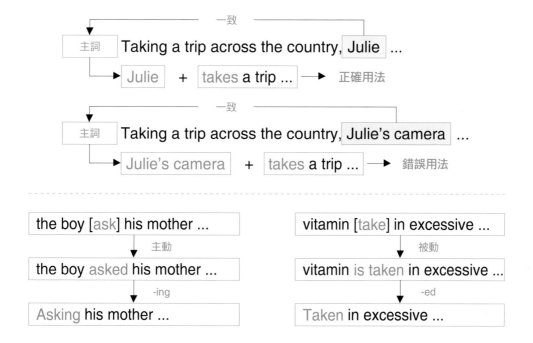

1. Arriving at the party, we saw lots of visitors sitting in the garden.
   抵達派對時，我們看到很多客人坐在花園裡。
2. Leaving the office room, the manager shut off all the lights.
   離開辦公室時，經理關掉所有電燈。
3. Trained as a gospel singer, Andrew Shredder expanded his singing style.
   被訓練為一位福音歌手，安卓‧史瑞德拓展了他的歌唱類型。
4. Since being imported into France, bananas have been very popular.
   自從香蕉被引進法國後，非常受到歡迎。

4-10 選出括弧中最符合上下文者。

4 (Taken, Taking) a wrong turn, we arrived half an hour late for the party.

5 (Waited, Waiting) for the bus, I met an old friend of mine.

6 After watching the boxing film, (the book was read by Barb, Barb read the book).

7 (Exhausted, Exhausting) after washing the windows, I fell into a deep sleep.

8 (Known, Knowing) mainly as a poet, Ray has written many successful novels.

9 Hearing the bad news, (Maria shed a few tears, her eyes were filled with tears).

10 (Compared, Comparing) with life in the country, life in the city is more complicated.

分詞和分詞構句

1-9 選出一個最適合填入空格中的答案。

1 Life must be very unpleasant for people _____ near busy airports.
① live
② lives
③ lived
④ living

2 Historically, the chief material _____ furniture has been wood, not stone.
① that they making
② which to make
③ making
④ for making

3 _____ by the lake, Karen noticed the fisherman on the dock.
① She jogged
② As she jogging
③ Jogged
④ Jogging

4 Justin saw a very _____ movie last Saturday. He was so _____ that his friends walked home with him.
① frightened — frightening
② frightened — frightened
③ frightening — frightened
④ frightening — frightening

5 One of the most mysterious places in the world is a small island _____ Easter Island.
① is called
② calling
③ called
④ is calling

6 One night I was sitting by the kitchen fire, _____ a letter from Joe.
① read
② I read
③ reading
④ and reading

7 Seaports made the import of raw materials and the export of _____ products easy.
① finish
② finishes
③ finished
④ finishing

8 _____ in a lucid style, the book describes the author's childhood experiences in Kentucky.
① Written
② Writing
③ Having written
④ To write

9 A man _____ to represent every minority group in the city was elected mayor.
① claims
② claimed
③ was claiming
④ claiming

10-15 閱讀下列文字，並回答問題。

10 下列文字中，有一個錯誤使用的單字，請找出並更正。

The aye-aye is a strange little creature lives in Madagascar. It has ears like those of a bat and a tail like that of a squirrel. It has amazingly long fingers and big eyes.

11 請在提示框中選出正確的字，填入空格中。

Humans are animals who are _____ and curious in new things. People get _____ easily when they don't have something _____.

interesting	interested
boring	bored

234

12 請在空格中填入 abandon 的正確形式。

Up ahead I knew there was a railway bridge and I thought we might be able to get across there. The path was wet and muddy. We could not see anyone, only _____ trucks and stores.

13 選出劃線部分文法錯誤者。

Halfway around the world, an American couple ① traveling by car in Australia was stopped by a policeman in Sydney for failing to signal before turning. ② Seeing that they were tourists, the officer gave them only a friendly warning. ③ Relieved, the American man responded with a smile and the thumbs–up sign. The policeman became very angry, and gave the driver an expensive ticket. Later, back in their hotel and ④ explained their experience, the tourists learned that in Australia the thumbs–up gesture is a very rude expression.

14 請在空格中填入動詞 use 的正確形式。

_____ their strong flippers, dolphins can go up to the shore and eat as many fish as they want.

15 選出括弧中最符合上下文者。

The brightly shining sun gives heat on this cold day. We brush the snow off the log carts, and start for the woods across an open field (covers, covered, covering) with a deep blanket of snow.

16-22 選出劃線部分文法錯誤者。

16 ① When we entering Tokyo proper, ② we drove right ③ through a tunnel that ④ opened into the Royal Gardens.

17 Mosques ① have the same design ② consists of an ③ open courtyard and ④ enclosed prayer halls.

18 DNA ① is the genetic material ② containing within ③ the nucleus of a person ④ cells.

19 ① The name Nebraska ② comes from the Oto ③ Indian word "nebrathka," ④ it means flat water.

20 ① Reading quickly, the book ② was soon finished and ③ returned to the library ④ without delay.

21 Both Kim and Lee ① lived in the same house ② nearly a year and ③ a half without a single word ④ spoke between them.

22 ① After a long negotiation with ② their employer, the workers decided to ③ call off their ④ intending strike.

CHAPTER 14

動名詞/不定詞/分詞
綜合分析

86 動名詞和不定詞（1）

A
> I **enjoy** walking in the park. 我樂於在公園裡散步。
> Jimmy **refuses** to eat peas. 吉米拒吃豌豆。

B
> I **remember** seeing the movie in 2009. 我記得在 2009 年看過這部電影了。
> Please **remember** to rent the movie. 請記得去租那部電影。
> I **tried** calling him but he wasn't at home. 我試著打給他，但是他不在家。
> I **tried** to open the window. 我試著打開窗戶。
> I couldn't **stop** laughing at her jokes. 她講的笑話讓我捧腹大笑，無法停止。
> I **stopped** to pick up a letter that I'd dropped. 我停下來，撿起我掉的信。

A 動名詞和不定詞，當作及物動詞的**受詞**時，只有某些特定的動詞，才能和它們一起使用。「及物動詞 enjoy」的受詞只能是**動名詞**；而「及物動詞 refuse」的受詞只能是**不定詞**。

B 有些動詞的受詞可以為「動名詞」或「不定詞」，不過這些動名詞或不定詞在意義上不相同。
「動詞 remember」後面接「動名詞」，表示**過去**；後面接「不定詞」，表示**未來**。例句中，seeing 是「過去看過」的意思；to rent 是「未來將要租」的意思。動詞「forget」和「remember」一樣，動名詞表示過去；不定詞表示未來。
動詞 try 後面接「動名詞」，表示「試著去做了某事」的意思；後面接「不定詞」，表示「想要試著去做某事」的意思。「動名詞」是動作已經完成的「過去」；「不定詞」是動作尚未完成的「未來」。例句中，calling 表示「曾叫過他的名字」；to open 表示「試著要去打開門」。
動詞 stop 後面接「動名詞」，表示「停住某動作」；後面接「不定詞」，表示「停下手邊正在做的事，要去做另一件事」。動名詞有「受詞」的功能；不定詞有「副詞子句」的功能。例句中，stop laughing 是「停止大笑」的意思；stop to pick up 是「停下手邊的工作，然後去撿」的意思。

概念習題

1-3 選出一個最適合填入空格中的答案。

1 He finally decided _____ his job and look for another one.
　① quit　　　② to quit　　　③ quitting　　　④ to quitting

2 Elizabeth stopped _____ last month to have a baby.
　① to working　② work　　　③ to work　　　④ working

3 Remember _____ an umbrella with you when you go out.
　① take　　　② to taking　　　③ to take　　　④ taking

1. Do you plan to use this kind of service? 你計畫要使用這種服務嗎？

2. Could you consider reducing the price to $50? 你可以考慮把價格降到 50 元嗎？

3. Archie forgot telling me that he changed his job.
   亞契忘了他告訴過我，他換工作的事。

4. Archie forgot to tell me that he changed his job. 亞契忘記要告訴我他換了工作。

5. You should try getting up earlier in the morning. 你應該試著早起。

6. He secretly tried to block her advancement in the Party.
   他暗自設法阻擋她前往派對。

7. The washing machine has stopped working. 這台洗衣機已經完全停止運作。

8. Would you stop to buy some stamps for me? 你可以停下來，去幫我買些郵票嗎？

---

4 選出下列句子中文法正確者。

① I'll never forget to visit Iguassu Falls for the first time.

② I used to watch TV and read all day. But now I enjoy to get exercise.

③ I can't help thinking she'd be better off without him.

④ The post office promised resuming first class mail delivery in March.

5-8 選出括弧中最符合上下文者。

5 You should avoid (eating, to eat) sweets and chocolate chip cookies.

6 I only just manage (finishing, to finish) the work on time.

7 However I tried (opening, to open) the window, it wouldn't budge an inch.

8 You cannot expect (liking, to like) all the people you will work with.

動名詞／不定詞／分詞 綜合分析

87 動名詞和不定詞（2）

A

My boss objected **to wasting** time in the office.〔to + V-ing〕
我老闆反對在辦公室裡浪費時間。

A small dog managed **to survive** the fire.〔to + 原型動詞〕
一隻小狗在火災中倖存下來。

B

My wife **is used to** eating raw fish.〔be used to + V-ing〕
我太太習慣吃生魚片。

My wife **used to** eat raw fish.〔used to + 原型動詞〕
我太太過去曾經習慣吃生魚片。

C

We're interested **in going** to a soccer game.〔形容詞＋介系詞＋ V-ing〕
我們對於去看足球比賽感興趣。

We were lucky **to visit** Disneyland.〔形容詞＋不定詞〕
我們很幸運地去迪士尼遊玩過。

A⋯⋯「介系詞的 to」和「不定詞的 to」，一樣是 to，卻很容易混淆。如果 to 是「介系詞」，後面就要接名詞或動名詞；如果 to 是「不定詞」，後面就要接**原型動詞**。例句一 object to 是「不及物動詞＋介系詞」，所以後面接「名詞」或「動名詞（即 wasting）」。相反的，例句二，動詞 manage 的受詞是「to 不定詞」，所以 to 之後要接「原型動詞（即 survive）」。

B⋯⋯要特別注意的是，句型「be used to + V-ing」和「used to ＋原型動詞」。**be used to** 是「有……的習慣、習慣……」的意思，是一個慣用語，to 是「介系詞」。**used to** 則是「過去習慣……」的意思，當作助動詞。因此，be used to 後面要接動名詞（或名詞）；而 used to 後面要接原型動詞。

C⋯⋯「形容詞」基本上可以和**不定詞**一起使用，不過不能和**動名詞**一起使用。若要接動名詞，動名詞前必須加上「介系詞」。也就是，可以用「形容詞＋不定詞」這個形式，或是用「形容詞＋介系詞＋動名詞」這個形式。例句一，interested 後面接「介系詞＋動名詞」；例句二，lucky 後面接「to 不定詞」。

概念習題

1-3 選出一個最適合填入空格中的答案。

1 The couple were looking forward _____ their grandchildren again.
　① to see　　② seeing　　③ to being seen　　④ to seeing

2 As a child, I _____ games outside until it got dark.
　① used to play　② am used to playing　③ use to play　④ used to playing

3 The company isn't capable _____ an order that large.
　① handling　　② to handle　　③ of handling　　④ to handling

介系詞 + to + 原型動詞	look forward to (盼望……) object to (反對……) dedicate to (奉獻給……) devote (oneself) to (將……奉獻給……) prefer A to B (選擇A，而不選擇B)
形容詞 + 介系詞 + 動名詞	be afraid of (害怕……) be capable of (有……能力的) be fond of (喜歡……) be good at (擅長……) be interested in (對……感興趣) be keen on (熱衷於……) be responsible for (對……負責) be sure of (確信……) be tired of (對……厭煩)

1. They looked forward to making kites. 他們期待製作風箏。
2. When we were sick, the doctor used to come to our house.
   以前當我們生病時，醫生都會來我們家看病。
3. My wife is used to taking exercise in the morning. 我太太習慣在早上做運動。
4. Mary is responsible for cleaning the classroom. 瑪麗負責打掃教室。
5. I was astonished to see people fighting on the program.
   我很訝異看到大家在節目上大打出手。

4-10 選出括弧中最符合上下文者。

4 My brother is fond (of pointing, to point) out my mistakes.

5 She has devoted all her energies to (care, caring) for homeless people.

6 The train is delayed. We are unlikely (on arriving, to arrive) on time.

7 Early people (used to think, are used to thinking) the sun went around the earth.

8 They failed to (finish, finishing) all the work in time.

9 Today a lot of children (used to play, are used to playing) computer games for hours instead of doing their schoolwork.

10 The employees objected to (be, being) asked to (work, working) long hours.

88 動名詞和分詞

A

Many people dislike **waiting in a long line.**〔動名詞〕
很多人都不喜歡在大排長龍中排隊等候。

There are many people **waiting in a long line.**〔分詞〕
有很多人正在大排長龍中等候。

B

Henry's job is **selling** computers.〔動名詞〕
亨利的工作是賣電腦。

Henry is **selling** computers.〔分詞〕
亨利正在賣電腦。

C

Leading the horses out of the stable **took two hours.**〔動名詞〕
引領馬群離開馬廄花了兩個小時。

Leading the horses out of the stable, Billy waved at us.〔分詞構句〕
比利對我們招手的時候，他正引領馬群離開馬廄。

Leading horses **fell down suddenly.**〔分詞〕
領路的馬群突然跌倒。

A 「動名詞」和「現在分詞」，兩者的形式一樣，但功能卻不同。在 dislike 之後的 waiting 是**受詞**，具有「名詞」的功能，因此它是**動名詞**。而 many people 之後的 waiting 是用來修飾名詞的「形容詞」，所以它是**現在分詞**。

B 「be + V-ing」大致來說，是表示動詞的進行式，不過也有可能是「be +動名詞」的情形。這完全根據主詞來判斷，如果「Henry's job」是主詞，「selling」就是動名詞，是「is」的補語；如果「Henry」是主詞，「is selling」就是動詞的進行式。

C 例句一，「Leading . . . stable」是 took 的主詞，所以「Leading . . . stable」是動名詞。例句二，「Leading . . . stable」這個句子和主要子句間有逗點隔開，彼此是分開的，所以整個是**分詞構句**。例句三，「leading horses」整個是主詞，其中 leading 是「分詞」，用來修飾名詞 horses。

 概念習題

1 下列各句中，哪一句和提示句中劃線部分用法相同。

Teaching English to children is what I really want to do.

① Libya is a leading producer of oil. It is located in North Africa.

② Mary is looking lovingly at the sleeping child in her arms.

③ When Ray was a boy, his favorite relaxation was listening to classical music.

④ He stood at the foot of a mountain abounding in cliffs near the sea.

2-3 選出劃線部分文法錯誤者。

2 The early settlers of Tennessee ① were ② artisans who were ③ skilled in ④ weaving rugs, designing quilts, and ⑤ carved wood.

主詞	動詞	補語：動名詞	主詞	動詞：進行式	受詞
Henry's job	is	selling computers.	Henry	is selling	computers.

主詞：動名詞	動詞
Leading the horses out of the stable	took ....

獨立的子句：分詞片語	主要子句
Leading the horses out of the stable,	Bill ...

分詞　名詞
Leading　horses
└─ 修飾 ─┘ ▲

1. They are taking advantage of student services. 他們正在找學生服務中心來幫忙。
2. Taking advantage of student services is very helpful.
   找學生服務中心是很有幫助的。
3. Letting children make their own decisions is best. 讓孩子自己做決定是最好的。
4. The couple have been letting their children make their own decisions.
   那對夫妻都讓孩子自己做決定。
5. Ron, look at those flying kites in the park! 朗恩，看那些在公園裡飄揚的風箏！
6. A lot of children are flying kites in the park. 許多孩子正在公園裡放風箏。
7. Children are excited about flying kites in the park.
   孩子們對於在公園裡放風箏感到很興奮。

3 ① Persuaded consumers ② to spend ③ more money is the ④ manufacturers' aim.

4 下列各句何者文法錯誤。
   ① Educating children well is everyone's focus.
   ② Plenty has been written about conquering Everest.
   ③ The only remaining question is whether we can raise the money.
   ④ The police have arrested a suspecting child killer.

動名詞／不定詞／分詞 綜合分析

89 不定詞和分詞

A

She got the computer **repaired** immediately. 〔-ed〕
她馬上就維修好電腦了。

She got the man **to repair** the computer immediately. 〔to 不定詞〕
她馬上就請這位男士幫她維修電腦。

You shouldn't let your family **interfere** with my plan. 〔原型動詞〕
你不該讓你的家人干涉我的計畫。

I could hear the rain **splashing** on the roof. 〔-ing〕
我可以聽見雨打在屋頂的聲音。

B

I saw him **cross** the river. 我看到他過河。

I saw him **crossing** the river. 我看到他正在過河。

A 英文句子中有「動詞＋名詞＋非限定子句」的形式。在非限定子句的位置上可以使用「動詞＋ ed（過去分詞）」、「to 不定詞」、「原型動詞」和「動詞＋ ing（現在分詞）」；在這個形式中，名詞和非限定子句的關係，經常是「主詞和動詞」的關係。
第一，使用「**過去分詞**」的情況是，前面的名詞和非限定子句是「被動」關係時；例句中的「computer」和「repair」就是被動關係。第二，使用**不定詞**（即例句中的 to repair）、**原型動詞**（即 interfere）和**現在分詞**（即 splashing）的情況是，前面的名詞和非限定子句是「主動」的關係時。第三，**現在分詞**（即 splashing），常放在表示知覺的動詞和其他幾個特定動詞之後，具有「正在進行」的含義。

B 像 see 這樣的「知覺動詞」，在名詞後接「原型動詞」或「原型動詞＋ ing」都可以。接原型動詞，表示整個動作完成了；接原型動詞＋ ing，表示動作未完成，還正在進行。例句一的「saw him cross . . .」，後面接「he crossed . . .」，表示看到他已經過河了，含有看到他過河的整個過程的意思。例句二的「saw him crossing . . .」，後面接「he was crossing . . .」，表示看到他正在過河的意思。

 概念習題

1-2 將括弧中提示字變換形式，然後填入空格中。

1 They should let old people _____ free on buses. (travel)
They should allow old people _____ free on buses. (travel)

2 You can get the computer _____ by Cathy. (fix)
You can get Cathy _____ the computer. (fix)

3-6 選出括弧中最符合上下文者。

3 Computerization should enable us (cut, to cut, cutting) production costs by half.

4 I wanted the letter (to type, typing, typed) double-spaced.

被動關係

特定動詞 I	+	名詞 the computer	+	-ed(分詞)：repaired
特定動詞 II	+	名詞 the man	+	不定詞：to repair
特定動詞 III	+	名詞 your family	+	原型動詞：interfere
特定動詞 IV	+	名詞 the rain	+	-ing(分詞)：splashing

主動關係

(I saw) him ｜cross｜ the river ➡ he ｜crossed｜ the river （完成）

(I saw) him ｜crossing｜ the river ➡ he ｜was crossing｜ the river （進行中）

▲ 特定動詞舉例

特定動詞 I	see (看到) hear (聽到) have/get (得到) want/like (想要/喜歡)
特定動詞 II、III	參照不定詞 Unit 79，p.127 的圖表
特定動詞 IV	see/watch/observe (看/注視/觀察) hear (聽到) feel (感覺到) smell (聞起來) find (找到)

1. Mom persuaded me to go for the job interview. 媽媽說服我去參加工作面試。
2. Mom made me go for the job interview. 是媽媽要我去參加工作面試的。
3. In the movie, we saw the baby growing smaller right before our eyes.
   在那部電影裡，我們看到那個寶寶在我們眼前漸漸變小。
4. Mary has just had the room decorated. 瑪麗才剛剛裝潢過房間。

5 Did you turn the stove off? I can smell something (burn, to burn, burning).

6 Mr. Smith had the client (submit, to submit, submitted) her questions in writing.

7-9 選出一個最適合填入空格中的答案。

7 In the film, George Lucas made their staff _____ complex battle scenes.
　① create　　② creates　　③ created　　④ to create

8 You'd better have your car _____ before going on a long journey.
　① service　　② was serviced　　③ serviced　　④ being serviced

9 I don't want Ricky _____ the conference.
　① hear　　② to hear　　③ heard　　④ hearing

動名詞／不定詞／分詞 綜合分析

1-10 選出一個最適合填入空格中的答案。

1 Brian is going to get the roof _____ as soon as possible.
① repair
② repairing
③ repaired
④ have repaired

2 The egg hit the man in the face. The audience couldn't stop _____.
① laughing
② to laugh
③ laughed
④ to laughing

3 We get so used to _____ people say, "I'm depressed" in this casual way.
① hear
② hearing
③ heard
④ of hearing

4 We tried _____ the fire out, but we were unsuccessful. We had to call the fire department.
① putting
② put
③ to putting
④ to put

5 My keys were in my pocket, but I don't remember _____ them there.
① being put
② putting
③ to put
④ to have put

6 Writing letters _____ a good exercise in English composition.
① is
② are
③ to be
④ in

7 During a job interview, you should show you're _____ the interviewer.
① enjoy talk to
② enjoying to talk
③ enjoying talking to
④ enjoyed talking to

8 The other day I heard him _____ ill of you and even calling you an idiot.
① speak
② to speak
③ speaking
④ spoken

9 Grand Master Han, who held a 9th degree black belt in Hapkido, dedicated his life _____ the martial art.
① spread
② spreading
③ to spread
④ to spreading

10 I am certainly looking forward to _____.
① watch the champion play
② watching the champion to play
③ watch the champion to play
④ watching the champion play

11-14 閱讀下列文字,並回答問題。

11 請在下列文字中找出使用錯誤的字,並更正。
Today we hiked deep into the rain forest. We saw beautiful, unusual birds and monkeys played in the trees. The guide showed us where to find strange plants and birds.

12 請在空格中填入 pick up 的正確形式。
In the United States, there are four main ways to travel: by bus, by car, by train and by plane. Going by bus is cheap. A bus usually stops _____ people in every city and town. But some buses stop only in the big cities.

13 選出劃線部分文法錯誤者。

Cartoons are drawings that tell stories or give messages. Most cartoons make people ① laughed. Some are serious. Many of them teach important lessons. They help people ② think. People who draw cartoons do clever things. They may make extra large heads and small bodies or huge hands and feet ③ to draw special attention to them.

14 選出劃線部分性質和其他三者不同者。

① Exercising in the morning can increase your energy for the day.
② People will find something interesting and then collect it. There are many people who get specialized knowledge about a certain area through collecting things.
③ The next step is to multiply the number of remaining fingers on the left hand by the number of those on the right.
④ According to wise men throughout the years, decreasing your desires is a sure way to happiness.

15-23 選出劃線部分文法錯誤者。

15 Laura ① had seen her father and her uncle ② died ③ of organ failure in ④ their mid 40s.

16 If you're ① planning ② to be near the post office, ③ could you stop ④ buying some stamps?

17 ① Giving unnecessary ② details sometimes cause ③ some ④ trouble.

18 Korean children are ① accustomed to have ② their parents ③ interfere with their ④ plans.

19 Research ① shows ② starting the day actively with morning exercise ③ is the key to ④ lose weight.

20 The ① learned woman is ② likely to hear herself ③ make fun of ④ on the public stage.

21 ① Offered movies ② during flights is one way airlines ③ make sure that passengers are ④ not bored.

22 Some methods ① to prevent soil erosion ② are ③ plowing parallel with the slopes of hills, ④ to plant trees on unproductive land, and ⑤ rotating crops.

23 John's wisdom teeth ① were troubling him, so he went to a dental surgeon ② to see ③ about having ④ them pull.

24 選出文法正確者。

① He tried to avoid to answer my questions.
② I have to leave now. I promised to not be late.
③ She doesn't allow smoking in the house.
④ I objected to have to rewrite the article.

CHAPTER 15

假設法
Subjunctives

90 直述法和假設法

A | If she **tries** harder next time, Mary **will** pass the exam. 〔直述法〕
如果瑪麗下次再用功些，就可以通過考試。

B | If she **tried** harder, Mary **would** pass the exam. 〔假設法〕
如果瑪麗當時再用功些，可能就可以通過考試。

「直述法」和「假設法」，大致區分如下：直述法，將事實原原本本地呈現出來的真實世界；而假設法，是表現推測、假設、想像的非真實世界。

A. **直述法**的句型，正如 A 項的例句，「if 子句（現在式動詞 tries）＋主要子句（現在式助動詞 will）」。**假設法**的句型，則如 B 項的例句，「if 子句（過去式動詞 tried）＋主要子句（過去式助動詞 would）」。但是，無論是直述法，還是假設法，if 子句中絕對不會出現**助動詞 will** 或 **would**。另外，在「假設法」中，即使是對未來的假設，也要用**過去式**。

B. 在含義上，直述法和假設法有什麼不同呢？「直述法」是對現實的假設；而「假設法」是完全脫離現實的純粹假設。

直述法「If she tries …」，是「如果瑪麗用功，就會通過考試」的意思，也就是，如果她用功，就會通過考試；如果不用功，就不會通過考試之意。直述法把焦點放在她考試通過或不通過，也就是 if 子句本身會造成的結果；相反的，假設法「If she tried . . .」，是「如果瑪麗當時用功，可能就會通過考試了」之意，焦點為事實上她並沒有用功，也就是和 if 子句相反的事實。

直述法的假設，它實現的可能為一半，即該假設實現的可能，連說話者本身也不確定。相反的，假設法表現的是，它實現的可能幾乎沒有，或非常非常的少之意。

概念習題

1-2 選出一個最適合填入空格中的答案。

1 If the sun _____ extinguished, all living things would die.
　① was　　　　　② is　　　　　③ will be　　　　　④ were

2 If the temperature of the earth rises, a lot of climate changes _____.
　① will occurred　② would occur　③ will occur　④ occurs

3-9 選出括弧中最符合上下文者。

3 If I (will go, go, went) to Miami next week, I will stay with my aunt and uncle.

4 If a girl rode on a bike in a thunderstorm, she (will, would) be dangerous.

5 If I (don't go, didn't go, went not) to see them, they would be hurt.

| 條件實現的可能性機率各一半之單純假設 | | |

假設法　現在
If she | tries | harder ..., Mary | will | pass ...

直述法
If she | tried | harder ..., Mary | would | pass ...
過去

已經知道不可能實現之現實假設

1. If we miss the bus, there will be another one.
如果我們錯過了這班公車，還有下一班。
2. If it doesn't rain, we'll be having a picnic. 如果沒下雨，我們就去野餐。
3. If I were you, I wouldn't buy that coat. 如果我是你，我不會買那件大衣。
4. If you stopped smoking, you'd probably feel healthier.
如果你戒菸，你可能會感到更健康。
5. If she didn't have to work, she could come with us.
如果她不用工作，她就可以和我們一起來。
① 主要子句的助動詞 will / would，也可以用 may / might、can / could、shall / should 取代。
② be 動詞用於假設法時，一律不能用 was，要用 were。

6　If you (travel, traveled) to the past, which time period (will, would) you visit?
7　If you (learn, learned) how to type, you'll be able to use a computer.
8　If I (win, won) a lot of money, I (will, would) buy a nice house and car.
9　If you need money, I (would, can, might) lend you some.

10-11 將括弧中提示的字改成正確的形式，然後填入空格中，以符合中文句意。
10　如果我有翅膀，我不用搭飛機就可以飛回家了。
　　If I _____ (have) wings, I _____ (will) not have to take an airplane to fly home.
11　如果潔琪今天需要幫忙，她就會打電話給我們。
　　If she _____ (need) help today, Jackie _____ (will) call us.

假設法

251

91 假設法：過去和過去完成

A
> If I **were** rich, I **would be** living in a big house.
> = I am not rich, so I am not living in a big house.
> 我要是有錢，我會住在大房子裡。

B
> If she **had tried** harder, Mary **would have passed** the exam.〔過去完成〕
> = As she didn't try harder, Mary didn't pass the exam.
> 如果瑪麗當時再努力點，就會通過考試。 —事實上並沒有努力。

A-B 假設法的「形式」，可分為「過去假設法」和「過去完成假設法」兩種。過去假設法的句型是「if 子句（過去式動詞 were）＋主要子句（過去式助動詞 would + be）」。過去完成假設法的句型是「if 子句（過去完成式動詞 had tried）＋主要子句（過去式助動詞 would ＋完成式動詞 have passed）」。

過去假設法和過去完成假設法的共同點為它們都是「事實和內容相反」。

如果是這樣，那過去假設法和過去完成假設法，有什麼不同呢？它們的「時態」不同。**過去假設法**，雖然形式和名稱是用「過去」兩個字，但是它的實際時態卻是**現在**或**未來**；**過去完成假設法**，它的實際時態就是**過去**。

假設法的時態為什麼和實際的時態不同呢？為的就是要區分「直述法」和「假設法」。因為假設法的含義和直述法的含義不同，所以用「時態」來表示它們的不同。現在的內容用「現在式」來表現，就是**直述法**；現在的內容用「過去式」來表現，就是**假設法**。如此一來，就可以從假設法的時態，來辨別是「假設法」，還是「直述法」了。

概念習題

1-2 選出一個最適合填入空格中的答案。

1 The climate _____ more extreme if the town were a long way from the sea.
　　① were　　　　② will be　　　　③ can be　　　　④ would be

2 I would have done better on the test if I _____ harder.
　　① study　　　　② studied　　　　③ had studied　　　　④ could study

3-9 選出括弧中最符合上下文者。

3 If you (wait, waited, had waited) for a few minutes, I'll come into town with you.

4 What (would happen, happened) to your family if you were to die in an accident?

5 If I (was not, were not, had not been) so busy, I would have visited you.

6 If I had seen the movie, I (could tell, could have told) you something about it.

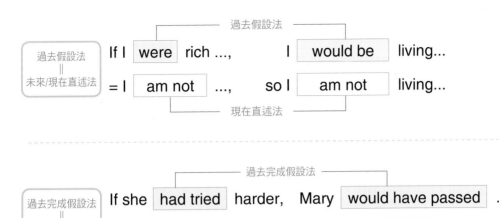

1. If he were a bit taller, he would be a policeman.
   如果他身高再更高些，就可以當警察了。

2. I wouldn't work for them if they paid me twice my current salary.
   如果他們付我兩倍目前薪資，我也不會為他們工作。

3. If you could make a clone of yourself, would you do it?
   如果你可以複製自己，你會這麼做嗎？
   *if 子句中可以使用助動詞 could。

4. If she hadn't called, I wouldn't have known. 如果她當時沒打來，我也不會知道。

5. If I had seen you, I would have said hello. 如果我當時看到你，我會向你打招呼。

7 If I (went, had gone) to the party last night, I would (see, have seen) Ann.

8 I would (wear, have worn) some warm clothes today, if I (were, had been) you.

9 In 1912, a large volcano erupted in Alaska. If it (erupted, had erupted) in downtown
   Los Angeles, it (will cause, would cause, would have caused) incredible damage.

10-11 空格中填入適當的字，使兩句意思相同。

10 The wind is blowing hard, so I won't take the boat out for a ride.

   = If the wind _____ not blowing hard, I _____ _____ the boat out for a ride.

11 A fallen tree blocked the road, so we didn't arrive on time.

   = If a fallen tree _____ not _____ the road, we _____ _____ _____ on time.

假設法

92 未來假設法／if 省略／混合假設法

A

If it **should** rain, can you bring in the wash from the garden?
如果會下雨，你可以把花園裡洗過的衣物拿進來嗎？

If it **were to** rain, the rope would snap.
如果下雨，繩子就會斷掉。

B

Had I known, I would have phoned you before.
我如果早知道，（我）就會打電話給你。

= If I **had** known, I would have phoned you before.

C

If I **had gone** to the party last night, I **would be** tired now.
如果我昨晚去參加派對，那我現在就會很疲憊。

- -

A 在 if 子句中，若再加入含實驗含義的「should」這個字，它的不確定性就又再增加了一點，而發生可能性就又再減少一點。不過因為這個 should 比較接近**直述法**，所以比起假設法，它的發生可能性會高一些。如果在 if 子句中，加入「were to」這兩個字，它的發生可能性就變成所有假設法中最低的了。現在就按發生可能性的高低整理如下：
（1）「if it rains」為**直述法**，表示一般的發生可能性。「可能會下雨，也可能不會下雨」；機率各一半。
（2）「if it should rain」的 **should**，因為在直述法中又添加了 should 這個字，所以發生可能性比直述法，再低一點。
（3）「if it rained」為**假設法**，表示可能性比 should 又再低一點，「雨大概不會下」的意思。
（4）「if it were to rain」的 **were to**，可能性最低，是「雨絕對不會下」之意。

B 假設法 if 子句中的 if 可以省略。如果省略了 if，後面的主詞和動詞就要「倒裝」。例句「Had I known」和「If I had known」這兩句的中文意思是相同的。

C 一般來說，「if 子句的時態」和「主要子句的時態」一致；「if 子句的假設法」和「主要子句的假設法」也一致。不過，如果 if 子句的時態和主要子句的時態不一致，那 if 子句的假設法和主要子句的假設法也就不一致了。if 子句的內容如果是**過去發生**，假設法就要用**過去完成式**；主要子句的內容如果是**現在發生**，假設法就要用**過去式**。

 概念習題

1-7 選出括弧中最符合上下文者。

1 If you (should, should be, were to) fired, your pension benefits will not be cut off.

2 (If I have, Had I) known he was coming, I would have invited him to dinner.

3 If I had learned the phonetic system, I would (be, have been) a better reader today.

4 (Should, Would) anyone telephone while I'm out, please tell him I'll be back soon.

5 (Were it, Had it been) all true, your actions would still not be justified.

6 Had the workers accepted a wage cut, the firm (would not have, had not) shut down.

7 I'm hungry because I didn't eat anything this morning. If I (ate, had eaten) breakfast, I wouldn't (be, have been) hungry now.

1. If anyone should ask for me, I'll be in the manager's office.
   如果有人要找我，我會在經理辦公室。

2. If the technology were to become available, they would expand the business.
   如果技術許可，他們會擴張他們的事業版圖。

3. Had I taken a job last year, I might not have had time to study.
   若我去年得到這份工作，也許我會沒時間讀書。

   = If I had taken a job last year, I might not have had time to study.

4. Were she in charge, Alice would do things differently.
   若是愛麗絲負責，她會有不同的行事風格。

   = If she were in charge, Alice would do things differently.

5. If he had started early in the morning, he would be here now.
   如果他當時早點出發，他現在就會在這裡了。

8-10 選出一個最適合填入空格中的答案。

8 _____ Alice, I would have given her your message.

① If I saw   ② Have I seen   ③ If I should see   ④ Had I seen

9 Should a foreign student _____ help, he must see the foreign student advisor.

① needing   ② needed   ③ need   ④ needs

10 I'm broke, but I _____ plenty of money now if I _____ so much yesterday.

① would have — did not spend   ② would have — had not spent
③ would have had — did not spend   ④ would have had — had not spent

93 I wish/But for/As if

A

I **wish** (that) I lived in a big city. 〔過去假設法〕我希望住在大城市。

= In fact, I do not live in a big city. 事實上，我不住在大城市。

I **wish** (that) you had told me about the dance. 〔過去完成假設法〕

我希望你已經告訴我關於跳舞的事。

= In fact, you did not tell me about the dance.

事實上，你沒告訴我關於跳舞的事。

B

But for his pension, he would starve. 〔過去假設法〕沒有退休金，他會挨餓。

= If it were not for his pension, he would starve.

But for Gordon, we would have lost the match. 〔過去完成假設法〕

當時要是沒有高登，我們就會輸掉比賽。

= If it hadn't been for Gordon, we would have lost ....

C

Steve looks **as if** he is getting better. 〔假設法〕史帝夫看起來好一點了。

Tom treats me **as if** I were a stranger. 〔假設法〕湯姆對我就像陌生人般。

A⋯⋯「(I) wish」之後如果接 that 子句，that 子句就要用假設法的**過去式**或**過去完成式**。如果用「假設法的過去式」，就表示「對現在事實的感嘆（或相反）」；如果用「假設法的過去完成式」，就表示「對過去事實的感嘆（或相反）」。

B⋯⋯有時也會以「but for / without」所引導的**副詞片語**，來代替「假設法 if 子句」，為「要是沒有⋯⋯」之意。副詞片語「but for / without . . .」也可以換成 if 子句，但要注意，必須符合「時態」，要正確地轉換成過去假設法或過去完成假設法其中之一。

C⋯⋯「as if」是「就像⋯⋯、正如⋯⋯」的意思，為表示「方式」的副詞子句。as if 之後用「直述法」或「假設法」都可以。用直述法是表示「實際上真有可能那樣」的意思；假設法是表示「實際上是和現實相反」的意思。例句一，「he is getting . . .」是直述法，是「實際上他恢復了」的意思；例句二，「I were . . .」是假設法，是「實際上我不是陌生人」的意思。

 概念習題

1-3 空格中填入適當的字，使兩句意思相同。

1 My children don't like the school they go to.

= I wish my children _____ the school they go to.

2 I didn't study anthropology while I was at university.

= I wish I _____.

3 Without water, all living things would die soon.

= If _____, all living things would die soon.

4-8 選出括弧中最符合上下文者。

4 Chang wishes he (were, had been) back in China now.

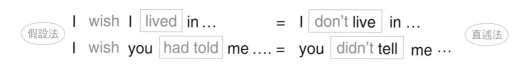

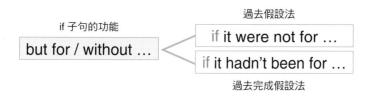

1. If only I were **not so nervous.** = I wish I were **not so nervous.** 我希望我沒那麼緊張。

2. If only I hadn't taken **the drug.** 真希望當時我沒吃藥。

   * if only = I wish

3. I wish I could have been **at the wedding.** 我希望當時我可以在婚禮現場。

   * I wish 後的 that 子句中也可以用 could。

4. But for **the sun, we** would die. 沒有太陽，我們會死亡。

5. I couldn't have done **the task** without **you.**
   如果當時沒有你，我不可能完成這項任務。

6. John looked as if **he** hadn't slept **very much.** 約翰看來似乎沒睡夠。

7. The stuffed dog barked as if **it** were **a real one.** 那玩具狗的吠叫聲像真的狗一樣。

5 I wish I (knew, had known) that Carol was in the hospital.

6 Take an umbrella. It looks as if it (is, were) going to rain.

7 The baby laughs as if he (understands, understood) what his mother says.

8 (I'd have, I had) crashed the car but for your warning.

9-10 選出一個最適合填入空格中的答案。

9 The champagne made me feel dizzy. I felt as if the room _____ around.

   ① spinning   ② were spinning   ③ will spin   ④ spins

10 I wish Susan _____ to my party last night.

   ① came   ② comes   ③ could have come   ④ could come

94 命令假設法－現在假設法

A

They demanded (that) the director **resign** immediately.

They demanded (that) the director ~~resigns~~ immediately.

They demanded (that) the director **should resign** immediately.

They told the director **to resign** immediately.

他們要求導演馬上辭職。

B

The company were faced with **the demand** that the director resign.

那間公司面臨請導演辭職的要求。

It is **appropriate** that the director resign. 導演辭職是恰當的。

「假設法」，大致可以分成使用「過去式的假設法」，和使用「原型的假設法」兩種。**過去式的假設法**，主要是用「if 子句假設法」來表現；**原型假設法**，主要是用「命令假設法」來表現。命令假設法又稱作「現在假設法」，主要表示命令、提議、要求等含義。

A　命令假設法的「形式」是「特定的動詞＋使用原型動詞的 that 子句」。特定的動詞就是具有要求、勸告、提議、決議、計畫、意圖等含義的動詞。如果是這樣的動詞，它後面的 that 子句就不能用直述法的時態，要用**原型動詞**。以例句一來說，主詞是 the director，為第三人稱單數，但動詞不用加 s 的「resigns」，要用原型動詞「resign」。若為英式用法，則可在原型動詞前加 should，用「should ＋原型動詞」。
命令假設法的「含義」，總結來說，是間接命令的意思。that 子句裡的「（should）＋原型動詞」是假設用法，表示「推定」，而非「斷定」；所以是「如果是……，就好了」之意，而非「是……」之意。這個含義再搭配前面出現的動詞，就形成了**間接命令**。此例句三和例句四「told the director to resign」意思相似。

B　這樣的 that 子句，並不一定只能放在**動詞**之後，它也可以放在**形容詞**或**名詞**之後。因為假設法的含義非常重要，只要 that 子句前的字具有 requisite（必須）的含義，不管它的詞類是什麼，就一定要用間接命令。例句一的「the demand」是名詞；例句二的「appropriate」是形容詞。

 概念習題

1-2 空格中填入適當的字，使兩句意思相同。

1 Mary insisted on John's having dinner with her.

= Mary insisted that John _____ dinner with her.

2 The doctor recommended me to take a long rest.

= The doctor recommended that I _____ _____ a long rest.

3-7 選出括弧中最符合上下文者。

3 Bill thinks he is a little heavy. Linda suggests that he (try, tries) jogging.

4 They complained that a neighbor (should play, played, plays) a radio too loudly.

5 They demand the travel company (not raise, doesn't raise, raises) its expenses.

有「必須」含義的字　　　　用「should +原型動詞」的 that 子句

demand　　+　　that the director (should) resign

間接命令的含義

told the director to resign　：　告訴對方「辭職會比較好」

▲ 採用「間接命令」的字詞

特定動詞	insist (堅持)　suggest (建議)　demand (需要)　recommend (推薦)　require (需要)　request (要求)　advise (勸告)
名詞	demand/requirement (需要)　order (次序)　decision (決定)
形容詞	essential (基本的)　necessary (必要的)　imperative (極重要的)　appropriate (恰當的)

1. I insist that the Council (should) reconsider its decisions.
   我堅持要議會（應該）重新考慮這個決定。
2. The doctor recommended (that) I (should) take more exercise.
   這位醫生建議我（應該）要多做運動。
3. His requirement is that the school (should) remain closed.
   他的要求是學校（應該）維持關閉。
4. It is essential that this mission (should) not fail. 重要的是這個任務（不許）失敗。

6 It's essential that something (is, to be, be) done about the problem.

7 It's a legal requirement that a foreigner (has, have, had) an insurance for his car.

8-9 選出一個最適合填入空格中的答案。

8 The government has insisted that a health warning _____ on cigarette packs.
① is printed　　　② be printed　　　③ has printed　　　④ should print

9 It seemed somehow appropriate that the meeting _____ held on that day.
① not be　　　② should not　　　③ were not　　　④ not

假設法

1-12 選出一個最適合填入空格中的答案。

1 Would you be willing to pay for this item, if it _____ less expensive?
① be   ② is
③ had been   ④ were

2 I _____ you double if you get the task finished by Thursday.
① would pay   ② would have paid
③ will have paid   ④ will pay

3 Justice requires that each person _____ the rights and freedoms of every other person.
① respects   ② should respect
③ be respected   ④ must respect

4 If it had _____ your help, I should have failed.
① not been   ② been not for
③ not been for   ④ not

5 I wasn't tired last night. If I _____ tired, I _____ home earlier.
① had — would have gone
② had been — would go
③ were — would go
④ had been — would have gone

6 I bet she wishes _____ in the whole affair then.
① she never got involved
② she'd never gotten involved
③ she'd never involved
④ she's never involved

7 If Korea had built more homes for poor people in the past, the housing problems now in some parts of this country _____ so serious.
① would not be
② will not have been
③ would not have been
④ will not be

8 Gary told me about the accident as if he _____ it himself.
① had seen   ② would see
③ has seen   ④ would have seen

9 _____ not to accept the above major changes, please cancel your booking.
① If you will decide
② Would you decide
③ Should you decide
④ If you decided

10 Many parents requested that Harry Potter _____ from bookshelves.
① banished   ② be banished
③ is banished   ④ to be banished

11 If you could have bought a record, what _____?
① will you buy
② would you buy
③ would you have bought
④ would you bought

12 _____, I'm sure he would have eaten it.
① If he were hungry
② Unless he had been hungry
③ However hungry he had been
④ Had he been hungry

13 選出一個不能填入空格中的答案。

_____ these interruptions, the meeting would have finished earlier.
① But for   ② Without
③ If it were not for
④ Had it not been for

14-17 閱讀下列文字，並回答問題。

14 選出劃線部分文法錯誤者。

For example, if he said, "Wow! That's it! ① Turn around and let me ② see the back. That color really ③ suits you! Those earrings match your dress perfectly, and you look ④ wonderful," most women ⑤ will be very happy.

15 選出一個最適合填入空格中的答案。

Unfortunately, I didn't have my address book with me when I was on vacation. If I _____ your address, I _____ you a postcard.
① had — have sent
② had had — had sent
③ had had — would send
④ had had — would have sent
⑤ had — would send

16 請找出文法錯誤的單字，並更正。

Instead of their planned honeymoon, Michele suggested that they spent a week helping poor people in Guatemala, so that's what they did.

17 選出劃線部分文法錯誤者。

An ancient Arabian traveler accidentally invented cheese, and for four thousand years people ① have continued making cheese. Milk spoiled quickly, but ② by making cheese, people ③ could preserve the milk's nutrition for long periods of time. Over two thousand varieties of cheese ④ are produced around the world. If you tasted a different kind each week, ⑤ it would have taken almost forty years to sample all the varieties.

18-23 選出劃線部分文法錯誤者。

18 There ① is a ② vital rule. If we ③ obeyed that rule, we shall never ④ get into trouble.

19 Many ① species ② might not survive at all, if it ③ were not for hunters ④ trying to kill them in the past.

20 She ① might enjoyed the workshop if she ② had prepared ③ more diligently ④ during the semester.

21 It ① is necessary that everyone ② realizes that reading ③ is ④ not only a mental process.

22 I ① wish you ② have not ③ changed the financial system without ④ checking with the chief manager of your division.

23 ① Had it not ② for the baby-sitter, they could not ③ go to the rock concert ④ tonight.

261

CHAPTER 16

比較級

Comparison

95 比較級

A [Clara is clever**er than** Sally. 柯拉瑞比莎莉聰明。

Health is **more** important **than** money. 健康比金錢重要。

B [clever ➡ clever**er**

important ➡ **more** important

good(well) ➡ **better**

A 針對兩個對象物，依據一定的標準作比較的句子，稱之為「比較級」。兩個相互比較的對象物，稱作「比較對象」；一定的標準，稱作「比較要素」。

例句中，因為 Clara 和 Sally；以及 health 和 money 彼此互相比較，所以全都是比較對象。Clara 和 Sally 依據 clever 的基準比較，health 和 money 依據 important 的基準比較。因為 clever 和 important 形成了一定的基準，所以它們兩者是比較要素。

比較級句子形式的核心是：在比較要素上加「-er 或 more」，並且在它後面再加上「than」這個字。

例句中，cleverer than 是在比較要素 clever 之後加「-er than」；more important than 是在比較要素 important 之後加「more than」。

B 因為只有「形容詞」和「副詞」才能變成比較要素，所以 -er 或 more 只能附加在形容詞或副詞上。如果形容詞或副詞是「單音節」的單字，它後面就加 **er**；如果是「多音節」的單字，就在它前面加 **more**。因為 clever 是單音節，所以在後面加 er，變成 cleverer；而 important 是多音節，所以在它前面加 more，變成 more important。good/well 的比較級都是 better，像這樣的不規則變化的字，必須額外記起來。

概念習題

1-8 請寫出下列各字的比較級。

1. small	→ _____	2. large	→ _____
3. big	→ _____	4. responsible	→ _____
5. bad	→ _____	6. little	→ _____
7. many	→ _____	8. pleased	→ _____

9-14 將括弧內提示的字改成比較級填入空格中，使句子成為比較級的句子。

9 Your handwriting is _____ mine. (good)

10 It's _____ today _____ yesterday. (hot)

11 Los Angeles has a _____ climate _____ Boston. (healthy)

圖表整理

Clara is clever er than Sally. Health is more important than money.

比較級形式的核心

	不加 er，而是加 more 的情況
① 三個音節以上的單字	more beautiful　more elegant　more famous
② 字尾是 -ed/-ing 的形容詞	more surprised　more annoyed　more boring
③ 字尾是 -ly 的副詞	more easily　more clearly

不規則變化（原型➡比較級➡最高級）
good/well → better → best　many/much → more → most　ill/bad → worse → worst little → less → least　far → farther → farthest

1. The top of the mountain is taller than the clouds. 這座山的山頂比那些雲層還高。
2. I think electronics is more difficult than mathematics. 我認為電子學比數學困難。

---

12 It's _____ to go by train _____ to go by bus. (comfortable)

13 We have _____ rain in the eastern part _____ in the western part. (much)

14 The wolf was _____ of us _____ we were of it. (scared)

15-16 選出劃線部分錯誤者。

15 Mary ① is getting ② heavy than she ③ wants to be; her clothing is ④ too tight ⑤ for her.

16 The company ① is found to hire a ② high percentage from ③ one group of ④ applicants than ⑤ another.

96 深入了解比較級

A
The population of Japan is much larger than **that** of Gamany.
The population of Japan is much larger than ~~Gamany~~.〔錯誤用法〕
日本人口比德國人口還多很多。

B
Henry is richer than Arthur (**is**). 亨利比亞瑟富有。
Jack works harder than his brother (**does**). 傑克比他哥哥還認真工作。

C
Sally is **less** clever than Clara. 莎拉沒有柯拉瑞聰明。
Money is **less** important than good health. 金錢沒有身體健康來的重要。

D
The faster you drive, the sooner we'll get there.
= As you drive fast, so we'll get there soon.
你開得愈快，我們就愈快到那裡。

A── 因為比較對象是互相比較的，所以**比較對象**一定要「可以彼此比較」，或「相同範疇」的單字才可以。例句中，「日本的人口（the population of Japan）」必須和「德國的人口（the population of Garmany）」比較，不能和「德國（Garmany）」比較。這時 than 後面若名詞（the population）重複出現，就要用代名詞 that 來代替。

B── 比較級 than 後面的「動詞」時常被**省略**，不過也有不能省略的時候。觀察 than 前面的動詞，如果前面的動詞是助動詞或 be 動詞，那麼 than 之後就也用助動詞或 be 動詞；如果前面的動詞是一般動詞，那麼 than 之後就用助動詞 do/does。

C── 比較級中表示「比……更……」之意的，稱作「優等比較級」；表示「比……較不……」之意的，稱作「劣等比較級」。優等比較級要加 -er 或 more；劣等比較級，則不論字長或短，一律在形容詞前加「less」。

D── 比較級中也有「the 比較級 … , the 比較級 …」這種句型的句子，翻譯成「愈……，就愈……」。the 之後的比較級，本來是原子句中的補語或副詞。例句中的 faster 是修飾 drive 的副詞；sooner 是修飾 get 的副詞。如果 the 比較級裡有 be 動詞，也可以省略。

 概念習題

1-2 空格中填入適當的字，使兩句意思相同。

1 ＿＿＿＿ ＿＿＿＿ you go up, ＿＿＿＿ ＿＿＿＿ the air becomes.
= As you go up high, so the air becomes rare.

2 This restaurant is nicer than the Pizza Hut.
= The Pizza Hut is ＿＿＿＿ ＿＿＿＿ than this restaurant.

3-8 選出括弧中最符合上下文者。

3 Isabell's composition is worse than (you, yours, you're).

4 (Much, The more) the customer complained, the more unpleasant the manager was.

5 Speech has become (better, less, Ø) important in our culture than writing.

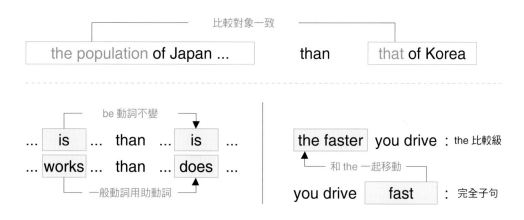

1. The salary of a teacher is lower than that of a lawyer. 教師的薪資比律師的低。

2. Your car is bigger than mine. 你的車比我的大。

3. He is taller than I am. He is taller than me. 他比我高。

　　*than 後面如果有動詞，就要接主格 I；如果沒有動詞，則可接受格 me，也可接主格 I。

4. This shopping mall is less busy than that one.
　　這個購物中心沒有那個購物中心人潮多。

5. Julia spends more on clothes than Melanie does.
　　茱麗亞花在購買衣服的錢比梅蘭妮花得多。

6. Trevor has more books than I do/have. 特瑞福的書比我的還多。

　　* 如果動詞是 have，than 後面接 have 或 do 都可以。

7. The colder the weather (is), the higher my heating bills are.
　　天氣愈冷，我的暖器費就愈高。

---

6 Mary's husband is two years older than (her, she) is.

7 Harriet's scored a lot more points than James (has, is, does).

8 Land values in the pinelands rose faster than (that, those) outside the pinelands.

9-10 選出一個最適合填入空格中的答案。

9 The salary of a modern athlete is much greater than _____.

　① a worker　　　② that a worker　　　③ that of a worker　　　④ salary a worker

10 The more you use e-mail and cellphones at work, _____ you may feel.

　① more the distracted　　　　　② the more distracted
　③ most distracting　　　　　　　④ more the distracting

97 原級

A — Clara is **as** clever **as** Sally. 柯拉瑞和莎莉一樣聰明。

B — Clara is **not as/so** clever **as** Sally. 柯拉瑞不像莎莉那樣聰明。
= Clara is less clever than Sally. 柯拉瑞沒有莎莉聰明。

C — Jim's car is **three times** as expensive as mine.
Jim's car is **three times** more expensive than mine.
吉姆的車比我的車貴三倍。

A... 原級的句型是「as . . . as」,是一種表示比較對象「同等」的比較形式。原級也有比較對象和比較要素,基本的原理和比較級都一樣。不同的是,比較級要用「-er/more than」,而原級用「as . . . as」。Clara 和 Sally 是比較對象,clever 是比較要素。

B... 如果原級是否定的,它的句型則是「not as . . . as」或「not so . . . as」,意思是「不像……那麼……」,和劣等比較有相同的含義。「Clara 不像 Sally 那樣聰明」和「Clara 沒有 Sally 不聰明」的意思一樣。

C... 表示「幾倍」的「倍數表現」,它的句型是「倍數詞＋原級」。倍數詞就是:twice(兩倍)、three times(三倍)、four times(四倍)等,和 half(一半)、a third(三分之一)、three fourth(四分之三)等。三倍以上也可以用比較級,但兩倍以下就不能用比較級了。

概念習題

1-2 空格中填入適當的字,使兩句意思相同。

1 This fabric feels smooth. Silk feels smooth.
→ This fabric feels _____ _____ _____ silk.

2 Jane speaks on the phone frequently. Her sister speaks frequently on the phone.
→ Jane speaks on the phone _____ _____ _____ her sister.

3-5 選出一個最適合填入空格中的答案。

3 The history of war is _____ as the history of man.
① too old ② so old ③ more old ④ as old

1. The film was as funny as his last one. 這部電影和他的上一部電影一樣有趣。
2. We'd better examine it as carefully as we can. 我們最好盡我們所能地仔細檢查它。
3. The garage of Mary's house is as big as that of John's.
   瑪麗家的車庫和約翰家的一樣大。
4. Today is not as/so cold as yesterday. 今天不像昨天那麼冷。
5. Mike is twice as heavy as Kevin. 麥克比凱文的體重重兩倍。
6. I don't read as many books as you (do). 我讀的書沒有你（讀的）多。
7. I don't read as books as you (do).
   *as . . . as 之間如果只有名詞，而沒有形容詞或副詞，為錯誤用法。

---

4 The price of the luxurious car at the dealer is as high _____.
 ① than the sports car   ② as the sports car
 ③ than that of the sports car   ④ as that of the sports car

5 Some of the doctors are paid almost _____ as the nurses.
 ① twice much as   ② as twice much   ③ twice as much   ④ as much twice

6-9 下列句子若有錯誤，請找出並更正。

6 The new strategy is not very effective as the previous one.
7 The Japanese eat seven times as fish as Americans.
8 The bills of the ruling party are as bad as the opposition party.
9 Children experience twice as much deep sleep than adults are.

98 最高級

A

Paul is tall**er than** Sofia. 保羅比蘇菲亞高。

Paul is the tall**est** of the **three** children. 保羅是三個孩子中最高的。

B

The church is **the** old**est** building in the town.

這間教堂是這個鎮上最古老的建築。

It's **the most** expensive hotel in London. 這是倫敦最貴的旅館。

C

Rachel is the most intelligent student **in** the class.

瑞秋是班上最聰明的學生。

A blue whale is the largest **of** all the animals.

藍鯨是所有動物中體積最大的。

This is the worst food (**that**) I have ever eaten. 這是我吃過最難吃的東西。

A 「兩者」比較時用**比較級**,「三者以上」比較時用**最高級**。以例句說明,因為是 Paul 和 Sofia 兩個比較,所以用比較級。因為是 three children 比較,所以用最高級。

B 最高級的「形式」是在形容詞或副詞上再加 est 或 most。附加的原則和比較級加 er 或 more 的原則一樣。最高級一般來說,一定要加定冠詞「the」,翻譯成「……是最……的」。例句中的「the oldest」和「the most expensive」都是最高級。

C 最高級也是比較表現的一種,所以大致來說,一定也要有一個範圍,才能比較。舉例來說,「最聰明的學生」,到底是全世界最聰明的,還是全年級中最聰明的,範圍一定要清楚。因此在最高級後面,就一定要接顯示這個範圍的字詞了。最具代表之表示範圍的字詞為:表示**場所**的「in」(即 in the class)、表**同類別**的名詞「of」(即 of all the animals),還有關係子句(即 that I have ever eaten)。而且關係子句中,大概都會有 ever 這個字。

1-4 將括弧內提示的字變成最高級,若有必要可加冠詞,填入空格中。

1 Friday is _____ (busy) day of the week.

2 Sydney Opera House is one of _____ (famous) buildings in the world.

3 John's idea is by far _____ (good) option.

4 My _____ (bad) fear was that we would run out of food.

5-10 選出括弧中最符合上下文者。

5 This is the largest company (in, of, that) the country.

6 It's the shortest day (in, of, that) the year.

7 That museum is one of the (large, larger, largest) and best known natural history museums in the country.

最高級中表示範圍的字詞	in the class : in + 場所名詞
	of all the animals : largest (animal) of all the animals ▶省略 相同名詞
	(that) I've ever eaten : 關係子句後面常有 ever 這個字

1. This is the best room in the hotel. 這是這間旅館最好的房間。

2. The largest city in Canada is Toronto. 加拿大最大的城市是多倫多。

3. This question is the most difficult of all. 這個問題是所有問題中最困難的。

4. The quickest way is along this path. 最快的方式就是沿著這條小路走。

5. I bought the cheapest bike (that) I could find.
   我買了一部比價後最便宜的腳踏車。

6. The Amazon is one of the longest rivers in the world.
   亞馬遜河是世界上最長的河流之一。

   *one of the longest rivers 是「one of ＋最高級＋複數名詞」的形式，也是經常使用的形式。

8　The new officers paid (less, least) care to the main problems than the former ones.

9　Although both Stephen King and Tom Clancy write thrilling books, King is the (good, better, best) storyteller.

10　Alex is my (least, the most) favorite member of staff.

11-12 選出一個最適合填入空格中的答案。

11　This is one of _____ expensive restaurants in Boston.

　　① more　　　② the best　　　③ most　　　④ the most

12　Of all the written sources, diaries are undoubtedly _____ entertaining.

　　① more　　　② most　　　③ the more　　　④ the most

比較級

271

CHAPTER 16 單元綜合問題

1-10 選出一個最適合填入空格中的答案。

1 The vacation was not _____ wonderful as you think.
① so ② more
③ very ④ that

2 London has _____ population than any other city in the United Kingdom.
① a larger ② as large
③ the largest ④ a very large

3 Thailand has some of the _____ exotic seafood dishes in Asia.
① almost ② most
③ mostly ④ most of

4 Korean parents expect to have more control over their children than most American parents _____.
① do ② have
③ expect ④ does

5 Frost occurs on low grounds more _____ than adjacent hills.
① frequent ② frequently
③ frequenter ④ frequence

6 The stronger _____ magnetic field, the greater the voltage produced by a generator.
① are the ② is the
③ is equal to ④ the

7 Sound travels faster through water _____.
① as through air
② than faster though air
③ than through air
④ as it through air

8 Jenny's writing skills are _____.
① better than Jim
② more than Jim
③ better than Jim's
④ more better than Jim's

9 People living outside of Greencastle give the city higher marks _____ own citizens.
① than it give the ② than do its
③ than does their ④ do than their

10 Tennis is _____ soccer.
① not so popular as
② so popular as
③ less popular than
④ more popular than

11-14 閱讀下列文字，並回答問題。

11 請找出文法錯誤的單字，並更正。

Scientists have recently shown that man's vocal apparatus is in several respects simpler than the great apes.

12 選出一個最適合填入空格中的答案。

The match was really exciting from the start. Holland scored a goal after ten minutes, and they were playing really well. After half time, however, England played _____. Rooney, my favorite player, was excellent. After six minutes, he scored the first goal. Ten minutes later he scored another goal, and the score was 2-1! I think Rooney's the _____ player.

① better — better   ② better — best
③ best — better   ④ best — best

13 選出劃線部分文法錯誤者。

The first computers were built ① <u>more
than</u> sixty years ago. They were not like
computers we have today. They were
② <u>much larger</u>. Some would not fit in
one room. They cost lots of money and
had ③ <u>so more</u> problems as follows.

14 請在空格中，分別填入 efficient 和 safe
的正確形式。

After two-year research and testing, we
believe that this improved product will
be less expensive, _____ and
_____ than any other product.

15-23 選出劃線部分文法錯誤者。

15 A male lion has ① <u>a large</u> collar of hair
around the face. Females ② <u>do not
have</u>. Male lions are also ③ <u>much large</u>
than ④ <u>females</u>.

16 Perhaps ① <u>because of</u> this experience,
I'm not ② <u>very</u> worried ③ <u>about</u>
earthquakes as ④ <u>I</u> used to be.

17 The ① <u>more</u> we looked at the ②
<u>abstract</u> painting, ③ <u>more</u> ④ <u>we liked</u> it.

18 Online shoppers ① <u>are now taking</u>
② <u>much time</u> to click the "buy" button
than they ③ <u>were</u> two years ④ <u>ago</u>.

19 Built at the beginning of the century, the
Library of Congress keeps one of
① <u>the larger</u> and ② <u>finest</u> ③ <u>collections
of books</u> ④ <u>in</u> the world.

20 The new computer ① <u>that</u> ② <u>I bought</u>
yesterday is ③ <u>as twice</u> ④ <u>fast</u> as the
old one.

21 ① <u>The new</u> employees enjoyed ② <u>their</u>
first day at work, although everyone
agreed ③ <u>that</u> the lunch was ④ <u>the bad</u>
food they had ever eaten.

22 Although both ① <u>of them</u> ② <u>are trying</u>
③ <u>to get</u> the scholarship, he has the
④ <u>highest</u> grades.

23 The risks of laser surgery ① <u>are</u> lower
than ② <u>conventional surgery</u>, but ③ <u>a
great</u> deal ④ <u>depends on</u> the skills of
individual surgeons.

CHAPTER 17

倒裝/強調/省略/對等
Inversion / Emphasis / Ellipsis / Parallelism

99 倒裝的兩種形式

A
> The chapel **stood** on top of a small hill. 禮拜堂就在那座小山的山頂上。
>
> → On top of a small hill **stood** the chapel.
>
> (On top of a small hill it **stood**.)

B
> Mary **was** able to complete the report **only** in this way.
>
> → **Only** in this way **was** Mary able to complete the report.
> 瑪麗只能用這個方法完成報告。
>
> She **broke** the rules of the game **at no** time.
>
> → At **no** time **did** she **break** the rules of the game.
> 她決不打破遊戲規則。

句子都是依據一定的語序排列而成的。「一般語序」，指將句子的元素按照**位置**的概念，整理成「主詞＋動詞＋受詞／補語」的語序而組成句子。「特殊語序」，指將一般語序按照**含義**的概念再改造，而組成句子；特殊語序又稱作「倒裝」。

A 如果句子不以主詞為句首，而以**補語**或**副詞片語**為句首，它之後的「主詞＋動詞」就要換成「動詞＋主詞」，稱作「一般倒裝」。但如果主詞是**代名詞**，就不能倒裝。例句中的「on top of a small hill」是表示場所的副詞片語，若置於句首，就要倒裝為「stood the chapel（動詞＋主詞）」的語序。主詞若是代名詞 it，就不能倒裝。

B 如果句子以「**否定的補語或副詞片語**」為句首，它後面就會發生「倒裝」的情形。助動詞或 be 動詞倒裝和一般倒裝不同，它是無條件地一律都要倒裝，它的語序和「疑問句」一樣；動詞如果是主要動詞，它的位置就要換成「主要動詞＋主詞」的語序；動詞如果是一般動詞，就要加助動詞 do，變成「do ＋主詞＋原型動詞」的語序。例句中，「only in this way」和「at no time」都是否定的副詞片語，所以後面的倒裝為「was ＋ Mary」和「did ＋ she ＋ break」。

1-3 將題目中的粗體字部分移至句首改寫。

1 The window must be left open **at no time**.
   → _____.

2 The gigantic aircraft rolled **slowly out of its hangar**.
   → _____.

3 Mary felt entirely comfortable **only with her family**.
   → _____.

4-8 請找出下列句子的錯誤，並更正。

4 They didn't read the play. Neither they acted it.

1. **Here** comes the bus. 公車來了。
   = Here it comes.
2. The door opened and **in** came the woman. 門被打開，走進一個女子。
3. **Only twice** did I go to the opera while I was in Italy.
   我在義大利時，只去看了兩次歌劇。
4. **Not a word** has she spoken to me since then. 從那之後，她就沒再和我說過話。
5. **Hardly** had Mary arrived home when it began to rain.
   瑪麗一回到家，就開始下雨了。
6. **Little** did I realize that Paul and I would be married. 我沒料到我和保羅會結婚。

5   Back went he to the supermarket to get some more vegetable.
6   Hardly Paul had entered the water when we knew he couldn't swim.
7   Never before a British Prime Minister has refused to step down.
8   Not until the seventeenth century did the idea of atoms appeared again.

9-10　選出一個最適合填入空格中的答案。
9   Pat does not accept constructive criticism well, nor _____ to listen to it.
    ① he appears　　② appears he　　③ does he appears　　④ does he appear
10 Just when I had to walk home, along _____ and she gave me a lift.
    ① Alice came　　② came Alice　　③ did Alice came　　④ did Alice come

倒裝／強調／省略／對等

277

100 倒裝的活用

A

"Mary agrees to the plan." "So does Tom."
「瑪麗同意這項計畫。」「湯姆也同意。」

"Mary will not agree to the plan." "Neither will Tom."
「瑪麗不會同意這項計畫。」「湯姆也不會同意。」

B

Parents watch more television than do their children./... than their children do.
〔兩個都是正確用法〕父母看的電視比他們孩子還多。

The bread was excellent, as was the apple pie./ ... as the apple pie was.
〔兩個都是正確用法〕這麵包超好吃，蘋果派也是。

C

Had I known, I would have phoned you before.
= If I had known, I would have phoned you before.
我記得之前打過電話給你。

A 為了避免字詞的重複出現，「so/neither ＋動詞＋主詞」這樣的句子，也適用「倒裝」的形式。so/neither 出現在句首，它後面就要變成「動詞＋主詞」這樣的倒裝形式。在這樣的片語中要注意的是，句型和動詞。句型一定要用「so/neither ＋動詞＋主詞」這個順序；順序若改變，意思就完全不同了，要特別注意。so 是用在前面的句子（子句）是肯定句的時候；neither 是用在前面的句子（子句）是否定句的時候。
在「動詞」方面，如果前面的句子用的動詞是助動詞或 be 動詞，後面就跟著用助動詞或 be 動詞；如果前面的句子的動詞是一般動詞，後面的句子就用助動詞 do。
例句一「so does Tom」，因為前句的動詞是 agrees，是一般動詞，所以後句用助動詞 does；例句二「neither will Tom」，用 will，因為前句有 will 助動詞，所以後句不變。

B 在「比較級／原級」的句子中，也會出現助動詞和 be 動詞倒裝的情形。不過在這類句子中，倒裝並不是很常出現，只限於主詞不是人稱代名詞時，才會出現這種不規則變化；而且不倒裝也可以，也是正確的。
例句一，「do their children」，用 do，因為前句的 watch 是一般動詞；例句二，「was the apple pie」，用 was，因為前句是 be 動詞；而「as . . . pie」，也是原級的一種。

C 假設法的 if 子句中，若省略連接詞 if，它後面的主詞和完成式的 have 也要倒裝。（請參考假設法 Chapter 16）

概念習題

1-6 根據提示句，以 so 或 neither 為句首，完成回答句。

1 The corn is ripening. ＿＿＿＿＿＿＿＿＿＿ the oranges.

2 The corn isn't ripening. ＿＿＿＿＿＿＿＿＿＿ the rice.

3 You've spilled coffee on the table. ＿＿＿＿＿＿＿＿＿＿ you.

4 I'd like to go there one day. ＿＿＿＿＿＿＿＿＿＿ I.

5 I didn't know that Ann was in hospital. ＿＿＿＿＿＿＿＿＿＿ Mary.

6 I went to bed quite late last night. ＿＿＿＿＿＿＿＿＿＿ your brother.

7 選出文法正確的句子。

① Emma went to Cambridge University, as was her sister.

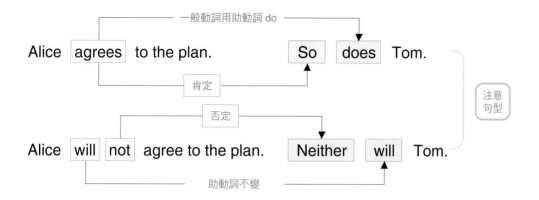

1. Alice can speak Chinese and so can I. 愛麗絲會說中文，我也會。
2. Alice can't speak Chinese and neither can I. 愛麗絲不會說中文，我也不會。
3. Paul went to the concert last night and so did Mary.
   保羅昨晚去聽音樂會，瑪麗也是。
4. A: I haven't got much work to do today.
   B: Neither have I.
   A: 我今天工作量不多。
   B: 我也是。
5. Chris works harder than do his friends. 克里斯比他的朋友們還努力工作。
6. She looks forward, as do her parents, to the completion of the building.
   她和她父母都期盼大樓的完工。
7. Were Dad here, he would know what to do.
   如果爸爸在這裡，他就會知道該怎麼做。

② If had Karen asked, I would have helped her.
③ Helen plays golf much better now than did she three years ago.
④ Should you changed your plans, please let me know.
⑤ I was opposed to building the golf links, as was everyone else in the village.

8-9 選出一個最適合填入空格中的答案。

8 Luke has cleaned the windows, and _____.

　① so has Tom　　② neither does Tom　　③ so does Tom　　④ so Tom does

9 Cave art developed in the Americas at an earlier time _____ on other continents.

　① as it did　　② than it did　　③ as did it　　④ than did it

101 It is . . . that 強調句

A

Ann bought the bike from Jack. 安向傑克買了一部腳踏車。

→ **It was** Ann **that/who** Ø bought the bike from Jack.

→ **It was** the bike **that** Ann bought Ø from Jack.

→ **It was** from Jack **that** Ann bought the bike Ø.

B

It **was** the bike that Ann bought Ø from Jack.

It **is** certain that Ann bought **the bike** from Jack.

安的確向傑克買了一部腳踏車。

A 在一句平鋪直述的句子中,若要特別強調某一部分,就要用「it is . . . that」這種「分隔句」。這種句子的形式是「It +強調的部分+ that +句子剩下的部分」。把想要強調的部分放在 it is 和 that 中間,剩下的部分全都寫在 that 後面即可。

例句「Ann bought the bike from the Jack」是一句平鋪直敘的句子。如果想要強調句子中的主詞 Ann,Ann 就要放在 it is 和 that 中間,除了 Ann 以外剩下的句子,寫在 that 後面,就是強調句了。要強調受詞 the bike,或要強調副詞片語 from the Jack 都是一樣的句型。不過,不能強調動詞 bought。

B 「it . . . that」強調句,和「it . . . that」虛主詞的句子,兩者要分清楚。

在「it . . . that」強調句中,「that 後面的子句」是**不完全子句**;而「it . . . that」虛主詞的句子,「that 後面的子句」是**完全子句**。因為「it . . . that」強調句,將原本平鋪直敘句中的某一項往前提出強調,所以 that 之後的子句,就一定是不完全子句;相反的,「it . . . that」虛主詞的句子,因為 that 子句用 it 先暫代,所以 that 子句本身仍然是完全子句。

在「it . . . that」強調句中,it 後面的「動詞」時常是 be 動詞,而且它的時態要和 that 之後的子句時態一致。was 和 bought 都是過去式,要彼此一致。相反的,it . . . that 虛主詞的句子,除了 be 動詞以外,也可能用其他的動詞,在時態上也沒有必要一定要一致。購買的時間是過去發生,所以用「bought」,而表示確實或表推測的時間是現在,所以用「is certain」。

1-3 用 it is . . . that 的強調句,來強調粗體字的部分。

1 **John** came running into the office with the boxes.

→ _____.

2 I was complaining about **the services**.

→ _____.

3 Karol sold her flat and moved in with her sister **in October**.

→ _____.

4 選出劃線部分文法錯誤者。

It ① is ② this house that he ③ has lived ④ since six years ⑤ ago.

強調的要素　　　　　　　剩下的部分

| Ann | bought the bike from the Jack. | | 強調句 |

不完全子句

| It was | Ann | that | bought the bike from the Jack. |

| That Ann bought the bike from the Jack | is certain. | | 虛主詞句 |

完全子句←that 子句

| It | is certain | that Ann bought the bike from the Jack. |

1. It is his dishonesty that you should criticize. 你應該批評他的不誠實。

2. It was late last night that a group of terrorists attacked an army post.
   昨天深夜，一群恐怖份子攻擊一個軍營。

3. It was the doctor that I was speaking to. 和我說話的是那位醫生。

4. It was surprising that Peter had an excellent exam result.
   彼得考試考得很好，真令人驚訝。

5-7 請找出下列句子的錯誤，並更正。

5 It was her who represented her country in the UN and later became an ambassador.

6 It were their parents who had encouraged them to continue their education.

7 It was because we were short of money that we decided to return.

8 找出句子結構和其他兩句不同者。

① It is well-known that a lot of battles were fought between Napoleon and his enemies.

② It is these very novels that Miss White reads as a pastime.

③ It seems obvious to me that her stories were aimed primarily at children.

102 省略的代表形式

A

Suzie can drive a car, and her brother **can**, too.

Suzie drives a car, and her brother **does**, too.
蘇西會開車，她弟弟也會。

B

Prices at present are reasonably stable, and will probably remain **so**.
目前的價格相當平穩，而且可能持續下去。

A: Is it going to rain? B: I hope **so**. / (I hope **not**.)
A：快下雨了嗎？B：我希望是。／（我希望不是。）

You asked me to leave, and **so** I did. 你要我離開，而我也離開了。

You asked him to leave, and **so** did I. 你要他離開，我也是（要他離開）。

在語言表現中，時常會適用兩個原則，那就是**經濟性**和**明確性**。所謂的「經濟性」，就是人們在說話時，會想要盡可能地縮減他的話語；而所謂的「明確性」，就是盡量縮減不必要的部分，而新的精簡的句子仍能符合原意；可以完全能滿足這兩項原則的就是「省略」。省略就是「縮減話語的方法」和「使用代語的方法」。

A 在句子中會用到省略的地方非常多。最具代表性的省略形式，就是**動詞後的省略**，而這時的動詞也要換成助動詞動詞，也就是說，如果前句的動詞是助動詞，後句的動詞仍為助動詞；如果前句的動詞是一般動詞，後句的動詞就要換成助動詞 do。例句中，因為 can 是助動詞，所以不變；因為 drives 是一般動詞，所以就換成助動詞 do。

B 使用 so 來當作代語，所謂的「so 的省略」，一共有三種形式。

第一 so 代替**形容詞**，當作「補語」來使用；或代替**子句**，當作「受詞」來使用的形式。例句中，「remain so」的 so，是代替前面的形容詞 stable，當作補語。

第二，用在特定的動詞之後，代替已經提過的整個句子。這時用法和意思與 so 完全相反的是 not，也就是說用 so 表示「是如此」，換成用 not 就表示「非如此」了。例句中，「hope so」的 so，是代替「it is going to rain」；「hope not」的 not 是代替「it is not going to rain」。

第三，使用「so ＋主詞＋助動詞」語語序的句子，句首放的 so 除表省略外，還含有「真的」之強調意味。因此，這和倒裝中學過的「so ＋助動詞＋主詞」意思不同。例句中，「so I did」是「我真的那樣做了」的意思；而「so did I」則是「我也那樣做了」。

 概念習題

1-5 粗體字是省略形式，參考句子前面部分，寫出省略了什麼。

1 She rarely sings, so I don't think she **will** tonight.

2 A: The children are late for class again. B: They always **are**.

3 A: I guess we should have booked a table in advance. B: Yes, we **should have**.

4 Bill hadn't been invited to the dinner, although his wife **had**.

5 Try not to leave anything behind as you **did** last time we went to Uncle Jim's.

6-9 參考句子前面部分，寫出粗體字是指什麼。

6 Jack hasn't found a job yet. He told me **so** yesterday.

7 A: Do you think you'll get a pay increase soon? B: I hope **so**.

Her brother	can drive a car.	→	Her brother	can.	其餘省略
Her brother	drive a car.	→	Her brother	does.	

助動詞→助動詞

一般動詞→助動詞 do

(You asked me to leave) So I did. → Yes, I did (left).

(You asked me to leave) So did I. → I did (asked), too

1. The club always has paid its way, and always will.
   這個俱樂部一直以來都經營得當，以後也是。

2. A: I didn't break the window. B: Nobody thinks that you did.
   A: 我沒有打破玻璃。B: 沒有人認為是你做的。

3. If he's a criminal, it's his parents who have made him so.
   他要是犯奸作科，那就是父母之過了。

4. Many people believe that the international situation will deteriorate. My father thinks so, but I believe not.
   許多人相信國際情勢將惡化。我父親也這麼想，但是我不認為。

5. A: It's starting to snow. B: So it is! A: 開始下雪了。B: 真的耶！

▲ 會用「I hope so/not」這形式的動詞

appear / seem (出現/似乎)　　expect / hope (期待/希望)
believe / guess / imagine / suppose / think (相信/猜想/想像/猜想/認為)

8　A: Can you lend me some money? B: I'm afraid **not**.

9　A: My eyes are slightly different colours. B: **So** they are.

10-11 選出一個最適合填入空格中的答案。

10　A: That's her brother — he looks like James Dean. B: _____.

　　① So does he　　② So he does　　③ But he did　　④ So is he

11　A: Alice studied hard for the exam at home last night.

　　B: _____. I saw him going to a cinema yesterday evening.

　　① But John did　　② But John didn't　　③ So was John　　④ But John wasn't

倒裝／強調／省略／對等

283

103 省略的活用

A

You can borrow my pen, if you **want**. 如果你要，我可以借你筆

A: Shall we go and visit Peter? B: I don't really **want to**.
A: 我們該去拜訪彼得嗎？B: 我不是很想去。

B

Alice enjoyed that trip as much **as** her mother did.
愛麗絲和她媽媽都很喜愛那次的旅行。

Mary can beat Julio more easily **than** Jo.
瑪麗比喬還容易打得過朱立歐。

C

A: Who is cooking dinner today? B: Joan **is**.
A: 今天誰會煮晚飯？B: 瓊恩會煮。

A: Does she like playing with dolls. B: Yes, she **does**.
A: 她喜歡玩娃娃嗎？B: 是的，她喜歡。

A ···「省略」發生在許多地方，並以多樣的形式出現，因此要歸納出它正確的原則，有些困難。因此，直接找出所有用到省略的句子，然後再來研究什麼被省略了，這應該是了解省略最好的方法了。
重複出現 to 不定詞時，不定詞就可以省略。不過省略不定詞有**兩種情形**，一種是從 to 開始省略；一種是留下 to，其餘的部分省略。如果不定詞被拿來當作 ask、know、wish、want 等的受詞時，就從 to 開始省略；但如果不是被拿來當作受詞，或即使被當作受詞，但卻是在否定句中，這時的 to 就要留下。例句中，「if you want」後省略了「to borrow my pen」，就是從 to 開始省略的情形。相反的，「I don't really want to」後省略了「go and visit Peter」，為否定句，所以以 to 被留下的情形。

B ···「比較級 than」和「原級 as」後，接「主詞」或接「主詞＋動詞」或接「受詞」，情形很多。這些情形，都是將後面的重複的語詞省略而形成的。例句中，「as her mother did」是由「as her mother enjoyed that trip」省略而來的；「than Jo」是由「than Mary can beat Jo」省略而來的。（參考比較級）

C ···「疑問句之回答句」，是最常出現省略的情形。如果主要動詞來詢問，就用主要動詞來回答；如果是用一般動詞來詢問，就用助動詞 do 來回答。例句一，「Joan is」是由「Joan is cooking dinner today」省略而來的；例句二，「she does」是由「she likes playing with dolls」省略而來的。

 概念習題

1-5 找出下列各句中省略的部分，並用 ˇ 標示出來。

1 There are more hungry people in the world today than there were in 1900.

2 I asked when she was leaving, and she said she didn't know.

3 His father was at Oxford when John Smith was.

4 A: You were supposed to buy some flour. B: Sorry, I forgot to.

5 A: Peter's never made a mistake before. B: Well, he has this time.

6-15 下列各句都是省略句。找出被省略的部分，並將它寫在省略的地方。

> If I am going too fast, please warn me (that I am going too fast.)

6 A: When shall we start playing the music? B: Whenever you would like.

重複出現不定詞的地方

比較級和原級之後

最具代表性之會省
略的地方

疑問句之回答句

1. Alex will collect us by 5 o'clock. He promised (to).
   艾力克斯將會在五點前來接我們，他承諾的。

2. We try, whenever we can, to leave a window open.
   我們試著不論何時都讓窗戶敞開著。

3. Somebody ought to help. Shall I ask John to?
   一定有人得幫忙，我可以尋求約翰的幫忙嗎？

4. She understands the problem better than he does. 她比他了解問題點。

5. Bob finished the exam at the same time as Rupert.
   鮑伯和魯伯特同一時間完成考試。

6. Don't ask me why, but the stone has been moved.
   不要問我為什麼，總之石頭已經被移開了。

7. A: Are you married? B: Yes, I am. / (No, I'm not.)
   A: 你結婚了嗎？B: 是的，我結婚。/(不，我還沒有。)

8. A: Will your parent be at the party?B: Yes, they will. / (No, they won't.)
   A: 你父母會來派對嗎？B: 是的，他們會。/(不，他們不來。)

7   I finished the exam when Shirley did.

8   If you need any of that firewood, I can give you plenty.

9   I had to admit that Simon's drawings were as good as my own.

10 A: Does Nigel usually walk to work? B: No, but his sister does.

11 Although Sarah is the oldest girl in the class, Emma is the tallest.

12 I won't disturb you again unless I have to.

13 Digital wristwatches are as cheap as digital alarm clocks.

14 When Tom resigns from the committee, I'm sure that a number of other people will.

15 A: Whom can Mary beat most easily? B: Rosa.

倒裝／強調／省略／對等

104 對等

A

Jason likes **going** to the races **and** **betting** on the horses. 〔正確用法〕

Jason likes **going** to the races **and** ~~to bet~~ on the horses. 〔錯誤用法〕

傑生喜歡去賽馬場賭馬。

B

My **sister** and her **husband** live in California. 我姊姊和他先生住在加州。

I told Tom **to cook** dinner this evening, **or** **(to) wash** the dishes.
我要湯姆今晚煮晚餐，或者 (去) 洗碗。

I didn't know **who** he is, **or** **where** he lives.
我不知道他是誰，或者他住在哪裡。

The plan was opposed not **by** Jane but **by** Peter.
那計畫是被彼得否決的，不是珍。

A 用對等連接詞「and/but/or」等，對等地連接兩個元素，稱作「對等」。對等地被連接的兩個元素，它們兩個的「結構」和「含義」必須一樣。尤其是在形式方面，更加嚴格，兩個元素一定要屬於相同的種類。例句一，由對等連接詞 and 來連接「going to the races」和「betting on the horses」，兩個都是動名詞，所以它們的形式相同，是正確的用法。例句二「going to the races」和「to bet on the horses」，一個是動名詞，一個是不定詞，它們的形式是不相同，所以是錯誤的用法。

B 用對等連接的兩個元素 A 和 B，它們的形式是非常多樣的。例句中的 sister 和 husband 它們是名詞；「to cook dinner this evening」和「(to) wash the dishes」是不定詞；「who he is」和「where he lives」是疑問詞子句；「by Jane」和「by Peter」是副詞片語。此外，還有動名詞、分詞、that 子句的對等。副詞片語對等的形式就有非常多種了。

 概念習題

1-4 下列各句中，什麼和什麼是對等連接，請說明。

1 George ate the fruit and drank the beer.

2 Most people will have read the book or seen the movie.

3 With Peter ill and the children at home, Jenny is finding life very difficult.

4 All the villagers rebuilt the houses damaged by the storm or washed away by the floods.

5-9 下列句子若有錯誤，請找出並更正。

5 I enjoy biting into a fresh orange and to taste the juicy sweetness.

6 I admire him for his patience, sincerity, and he is honest.

7 My son is usually interested in but a little frightened by lizards.

Jason likes [going] to the races and [betting] on the horses. 正確用法

相同形式

Jason likes [going] to the races and [to bet] on the horses. 錯誤用法

不同形式

名詞 — 不定詞 — 疑問詞子句 — 副詞片語 → 對等連接詞 ← 名詞 — 不定詞 — 疑問詞子句 — 副詞片語

1. Mom is washing and drying the pears. 媽媽正在清洗並擦乾梨子。
2. They are eating the food quickly and hungrily. 他們飢腸轆轆且狼吞虎嚥地吃東西。
3. Susan is ill, but will soon recover. 蘇珊生病了，但她將很快康復。
4. George is fond of working at night and getting up late in the morning.
   喬治喜歡在夜晚工作並晚起。
5. They were married in 2000, but divorced in 2010.
   他們在 2000 年結婚，2010 年離婚。
6. They sell manual and electric typewriters. 他們賣手動和電動打字機。
7. He spoke for the first motion but against the second motion.
   他贊成第一項動議，但反對第二項動議。

8 I told the children to sit down, be quiet and opening their reading books.

9 The guests were walking, talked, and drinking wine in the garden.

10-11 選出一個最適合填入空格中的答案。

10 Seismographs are used to locate oil, to determine ocean depth, and _____ and measure earthquakes.

    ① detect   ② detecting   ③ to detect   ④ are detected

11 In those days, they used to shoot the birds and _____ them on a single day.

    ① cook   ② cooks   ③ cooked   ④ cooking

倒裝／強調／省略／對等

1-10 選出一個最適合填入空格中的答案。

1 No longer _____ I know everything about Americans.
① I will think　　② will I think
③ think I will　　④ think will I

2 It was between 1830 and 1835 _____ the modern newspaper was born.
① where　　② that
③ which　　④ while

3 A mature frog _____ eight inches long and live seven years.
① grows　　② grow
③ may grow　　④ may be grown

4 The test administrator ordered us not to open our books until he told us

_____.
① to do so
② to open it
③ to do open books
④ to do them

5 Only after they are tanned _____ resistant to decomposition.
① can animal skins become
② can become animal skins
③ animal skins can become
④ that animal skins can become

6 A: My math skill has improved a lot in this class.
B: _____, too. All the students Mr. White teaches do well in mathematics.
① Mine have　　② Mine has
③ Mine is　　④ Mine are

7 Ellen Swallow Richards became the first woman to enter, graduate from, and _____ at the Massachusetts Institute of Technology.
① teach　　② a teacher
③ taught　　④ teaching

8 To answer quickly is more important than _____.
① accurate answer
② answering accurate
③ to answer accurately
④ your accurate answer

9 A: Have we missed the start of the film?
B: I'm afraid _____.
① that　　② it
③ so　　④ not

10 Here in this special diet drink _____ all the answers to your weight problems.
① are　　② is
③ does　　④ have

11-15 閱讀下列文字，並回答問題。

11 請找出文法錯誤的單字，並更正。

Today, people are not getting enough sleep. People take time from sleep to do other things. People work longer, go to meetings at night, eat supper late, watch television, or going out until late.

12 重組括弧內的字，使成為「年輕人不只不去國立公園的森林」之意。

(that, young people, just national forests, isn't, are avoiding, it). Kids these days aren't digging holes, building tree houses, catching frogs, or playing by the stream.

13 選出一個最適合填入空格中的答案。

In some cultures, advertisements usually describe the product and explain why it is better than others. But in other cultures, the message depends more on situations and feelings than it _____ on words.

① is   ② do
③ does   ④ are

14 選出和劃線部分意思最接近者。

A: This chemotherapy won't have any lasting effects on having kids, will it?
B: I'm afraid so.   *chemotherapy 化學療法

① The chemotherapy will have lasting effects on having kids.
② The chemotherapy will not have lasting effects on having kids.
③ I am scared of the chemotherapy.

15 劃線的 do 是「省略」用法，請找出文章中它省略的部分。

Just as humans <u>do</u>, animals communicate with body language and sometimes gestures. "Chimpanzees" in the wild communicate a wide variety of gestures and facial expressions. To express anger, for example, a chimp stands upright on two legs, waves her arms or throws branches.

16-21 選出劃線部分文法錯誤者。

16 The dance company ① <u>has</u> played ② <u>a role</u> in promoting global cultural exchanges and ③ <u>to introduce</u> unique arts from ④ <u>different countries</u>.

17 It was in a cave Magdalena ① <u>when</u> the ② <u>oldest</u> ③ <u>known</u> ears of cultivated corn were ④ <u>discovered</u>.

18 John, always successful, was ① <u>president of his high school class.</u> ② <u>So Peter was.</u> Both ③ <u>did become</u> ④ <u>great lawyers</u>.

19 Between my roommate ① <u>and me</u> ② <u>exist</u> ③ <u>an exceptionally close</u> relationship; ④ <u>neither of us has</u> any desire to request a change.

20 ① <u>An extended family</u> ② <u>consists</u> not only of parents and children ③ <u>but also</u> other relatives, such as grandparents and ④ <u>unmarried</u> aunts and uncles.

21 I saw the world ① <u>divided into</u> people who had ② <u>worked with</u> somebody and people who ③ <u>didn't</u>, and ④ <u>this</u> seemed really significant to me.

附錄：不規則動詞一覽表

原型	過去式	過去分詞	原型	過去式	過去分詞
is／am	was	been	lie	lay	lain
are	were	been	lose	lost	lost
beat	beat	beaten	make	made	made
become	became	become	mean	meant	meant
begin	began	begun	meet	met	met
bite	bit	bitten	mistake	mistook	mistaken
blow	blew	blown	overcome	overcame	overcome
break	broke	broken	pay	paid	paid
bring	brought	brought	ride	rode	ridden
build	built	built	ring	rang	rung
buy	bought	bought	rise	rose	risen
catch	caught	caught	run	ran	run
choose	chose	chosen	say	said	said
come	came	come	see	saw	seen
do	did	done	sell	sold	sold
draw	drew	drawn	send	sent	sent
drink	drank	drunk	sing	sang	sung
drive	drove	driven	sit	sat	sat
eat	ate	eaten	sleep	slept	slept
fall	fell	fallen	speak	spoke	spoke
feel	felt	felt	spend	spent	spent
fight	fought	fought	stand	stood	stood
find	found	found	swim	swam	swum
fly	flew	flown	take	took	taken
forget	forgot	forgotten	teach	taught	taught
forgive	forgave	forgiven	tell	told	told
freeze	froze	frozen	think	thought	thought
get	got	got/gotten	throw	threw	thrown
give	gave	given	wear	wore	worn
go	went	gone	win	won	won
grow	grew	grown	write	wrote	written
have／has	had	had	bet	bet	bet
hear	heard	heard	cost	cost	cost
hide	hid	hidden	cut	cut	cut
hold	held	hold	hit	hit	hit
keep	kept	kept	hurt	hurt	hurt
know	knew	known	let	let	let
lay	laid	laid	put	put	put
lead	led	led	quit	quit	quit
leave	left	left	read	read	read
lend	lent	lent	upset	upset	upset

ANSWERS

1

1.

	原型動詞	過去式	過去分詞
1	read	read	read
2	catch	caught	caught
3	leave	left	left
4	say	said	said
5	laugh	laughed	laughed
6	think	thought	thought
7	bring	brought	brought
8	go	went	gone
9	break	broke	broken
10	get	got	got / gotten
11	eat	ate	eaten
12	send	sent	sent
13	buy	bought	bought
14	lose	lost	lost
15	do	did	done
16	know	knew	known
17	cost	cost	cost
18	steal	stole	stolen
19	cut	cut	cut
20	take	took	taken
21	meet	met	met
22	give	gave	given
23	rise	rose	risen
24	hear	heard	heard

2. **are giving**

giving 是現在分詞，given 是過去分詞，不能當動詞用，所以要用 be 動詞「are giving」。

3. **hardened**

hard 是形容詞或副詞；hardness 是名詞，兩者都不能放在動詞的位置。

4. **differs**

difference 是名詞，所以不能放在動詞的位置。

5. **lose**

助動詞 will 後要接原型。lost 是 lose 的過去式；loss 是名詞。

6. **experience**

experiment 是表「實驗」的不及物動詞；experience 是表「經歷」的及物動詞。即使不考慮 a lot of difficulty 是受詞，從字面翻譯來看，experience 也比較恰當。

2

1. **does, likes**

主詞 he 是第三人稱單數。所以 do 和 like，分別要變成 does 和 likes。

2. **flies, has**

an eagle 和 it 都是第三人稱單數。所以 fly 和 have，分別要變成 flies 和 has。

3. **is, am, are**

my sister 是第三人稱單數，所以 be 動詞用 is；而 I 後面接的 be 動詞是 am。my sister and I 是複數，所以用 are。

4. ① **is**

因為「海王星距離太陽很遙遠」是一般事實，所以要用現在式。海王星 Neptune 是單數，所以用 is。

5. ⑤ **do not bite**

因為是表示一般事實，所以要用現在式。bite 是一般動詞，否定句就要加助動詞；因主詞是複數，所以不能用 does，要用 do。

6. was → **are**

主詞 factories 是複數；today 是現在式，所以 was 要改成 are。

7. Pablo're → **Pablo's / Pablo is**

因為 Pablo 是單數，所以不能用 are，要用 is。

8. goes → **went**

因為 when 子句中的 lived 是過去式，所以 goes 也要改成過去式 went。

9. worried → **worry**

因為「父母擔心子女」是一般事實，所以用現在式。

3

1. **Ø**

因為 collects 已表示是現在式的一般動詞，所以前面不能再出現 be 動詞。

2. **is**

collecting 前面要再加 is，構成現在進行式。

3. **does**

因為 work 是動詞現在式，所以要形成否定句就必須加助動詞 does。

4. **are dancing**

are dance 是錯誤用法。此句為現在進行式，所以動詞要加 ing。

5. ② rises

「太陽從東邊升起」是一般事實，所以要用現在式。

6. ⑤ are whispering

由「我聽不見他們說話」這句話可知，他們現在正在說話；所以用現在進行式。

7. is cooking

因為問「現在在哪裡？」，所以要用現在進行式回答。

8. always stays

因為有頻率副詞 always，所以不能用現在進行式，要用現在式。

9. is, wants

因為句意，所以即使有 right now 也不能用進行式。主詞是第三人稱單數，所以用動詞要用 wants。

10. is looking, look

如果 look 是「看」的意思，就可以用進行式；如果是「看起來」的意思，就不能用進行式。

11. talk, are talking

句意是「每天說」，所以要用現在式。如果有 right now，表示現在正在說，就用現在進行式。

4

1. ④ will contact

因為 in the near future 表示未來的時間，所以時態也要用未來式。

2. ④ am going to

從「已買了蔬菜」這點看來，可得知在說話的那個時間點之前，就決定要做沙拉了，所以用 be going to。

3. ④ call

雖然 next week 表示未來的時間，但 when 子句中不能用未來式，要用現在式。

4. will fly

因為 in three years 表示未來的時間，要用未來式。

5. rains

if 子句不能用未來式，要用現在式。

6. is going to

從「一點雲都沒有」這個事實，推測出將會是好天氣，所以是確實的推測。

7. see

因為是 when 子句，所以要用現在式。

8. am going to

從「已買了票」這點看來，可以知道在說話的那個時間點之前，就決定要去看了。

9. will have worked

when 子句用現在式，而主要子句要用未來式。

10. leave

因為 unless 也是表條件的子句，所以不能用未來式，要用現在式。

5

1. ② was washing

因為主要子句時態用 discovered 表示過去，所以 while 子句也用過去式。但是當 while 表示「在……期間正在進行某件事的時候」，強調「正在進行某件事」，則 while 子句就要用過去進行式。

2. ③ it will be snowing

when 子句用現在式，而主要子句要用未來式。這裡的 when 是表未來的某一時間點，強調「某一時間點」，所以主要子句要用未來進行式。

3. ② began

因為 1852 是過去的時間點，所以要用過去式。

4. quit

因為 six months ago 是過去的時間點，所以要用過去式。quit 為三態同形的動詞。

5. was cooking

因為手被燙到是過去時間點「正在做晚餐」的時候，所以 when 子句要用過去進行式。

6. will be having

因為表示未來某一時間點事情正在進行，所以用未來進行式。have 當「吃」的意思時，可以用進行式。

7. walks, took

因為前面句子中有 every morning，表示習慣，所以用現在式；後面的句子有 yesterday，所以用過去式。

8. go

used to 是強調過去的習慣，句型為「used to＋原型動詞」。

9. is raining

因為現在看到 Paul 正拿著雨傘，所以現在正在下雨。

10. was washing, dropped

從 last night 可看出是過去的時間點，因為有 while，所以用過去進行式。「掉落」是一瞬間的，所以用過去式。

11. go, will be standing

after 子句要用現在式。「我會站在門邊，以便讓你看見我」，這是在未來某一時間點會發生的，所以要用未來進行式。

6

1. 持續

因為有 for three years，表示一段時間，所以是持續狀態。

2. 完成

因現在剛看完，可知是現在之前的行為。表示完成。

3. 結果

將髒車洗了之後，結果就變乾淨了；所以表示結果。

4. ② has been

因為到目前為止，持續七天的時間都在古巴，所以用現在完成式。

5. ④ served

因為 1928 是過去的一個時間點，所以用過去式。

6. had

因為「現在已經好了」，表示現在已經不發燒，所以發燒就是局限在過去的事實。

7. has had

因為從半夜開始一直持續發燒到現在，所以要用現在完成式。

8. has not been

因為有 since，所以要用現在完成式。否定字 not 要放在 have 和過去分詞之間。

9. has brought

從「都長成大人」連接到「現在成功」，所以要用現在完成式。

10. for

「for＋一段時間」，a year 是表示一段期間，所以要用 for。

11. since

因為 has sent 是現在完成式，所以要用 since，以表示「自 1960 年代以來」。

7

1. ③ had died

因為兩週前，是以過去見面的時間點為基準來說的，所以兩週前是「更過去」，要用過去完成式。

2. ② have never met

因為現在不認識，而且到目前為止完全沒見過面，所以要用現在完成式。

3. ③ had seen

一起去的時間點是過去，而在這之前他已經看過兩次，所以要用過去完成式。

4. ② spoke

「在 1997 年」是一特定的過去時間點，要用過去式。

5. had gone

從「Jill 不在家」，可以知道她在這之前已經出去了，所以要用過去完成式。

6. went

因為全部都是在過去依序發生的事，所以要用過去式。當過去的好幾個行為一起發生時，即使這些行為有些時間差，但沒有一定要區分其先後的必要時，就全部都用過去式。

7. had seen

因為 looked 是過去式，所以見過他，是在這之前發生的，所以要用過去完成式。

8. have seen

因為 looks 是現在式，而見過他，是從過去某一時間持續到現在，所以用現在完成式。

9. broke

因為是昨天晚上發生的事，所以用過去式。

10. had stolen

因為到達、發現都是過去式，而被偷是在這此之前發生的，所以要用過去完成式來表現。

11. has stopped

「雨停了」可以用過去式 stopped 來表示，也可用現在完成式 has stopped 來表示。本題因為要連接「現在雨已經不下了」，所以用現在完成式 has stopped。

12. died

因為 ten years ago 是特定的一個過去的時間點，所以用過去式。

13. had already gone

already 是「已經」的意思，表示 Eric 回家，比到達舞會還要之前發生，所以要用過去完成式。

8

1. ② have taken

因為有 now，所以要用和「現在」有關的時態。現在完成式也可以和 now 搭配使用。

295

2. ③ will start

next week 指未來，所以用未來式。

3. ④ will have increased

「從現在到 2100 年將會發生什麼事」，時間從現在持續到未來，所以用未來完成式。

4. have known

「到現在為止，有 19 年的時間」，所以用現在完成式。

5. will have known

「到明年為止，有 20 年的時間」，所以用未來完成式。

6. have gone

因為是以「現在」為基準來問，所以用現在完成式來回答。

7. had gone

因為是以「過去」為基準，表示一種「結果」，所以用過去完成式。

8. will have gone

因為是發生在未來的一個時間點之前的事件，表示一種「結果」，所以用未來完成式。

9. will have cleared

by tomorrow evening 表示未來時間，在這個時間之前發生的事件，就用未來完成式。

10. will rise

指未來將會發生的事件，所以用未來式。

11. will have been

next Monday 是未來的一個時間點，for three years 是一段時間，因此用未來完成式。

Chapter 1 單元綜合問題

1. ④ consists of

consistent 和 consisting 不能當動詞用。因為主詞 alphabet 是第三人稱單數，所以動詞 consist 要加 s。

2. ② is

因為是一般事實，要用現在式。主詞 cause 是單數。

3. ① get home

when 子句要用現在式。

4. ③ has used

因為有 since，所以要用現在完成式。

5. ④ opened

「三年前的今天」是指過去，所以要用過去式。

6. ③ will have become

by the year 2018，即以未來時間點為基準，某些事情將結束，所以用未來完成式。

7. ④ had been suffering

「昨天晚上去世」是過去式；他從過去一直到昨天晚上持續受苦，所以用過去完成進行式。

8. ② are going to have

從「打掃房子」看出，要舉行舞會是早已決定好的，所以用 be going to。

9. ① have finished reading

when 子句中不能出現未來助動詞 will。所以只能選沒有 will 的 ① 了。

10. ④ had been married

by 之後有過去式 had，表示是以過去為基準，所以在過去之前發生的事，要用過去完成式。

11. bit, not bite

從 ran 和 fell 推測，整個是過去式，所以 bite 要用過去式 bit。第二個空格要填的動詞因為在助動詞 will 之後，所以一定要接原型動詞，而且從上下文看出要用否定句。

12. responded ， respond

因為整段內容是表示一般事實，所以要用現在式。

13. has invented

整段內容是現在式。而這裡談的是發明結束後，已經產生的一個產品，所以要用現在完成式。

14. was hurrying

when 子句不能用進行式，所以主要子句的 hurry 要用進行式。

15. ① always enjoy → have always enjoyed

for the past two years 表一段時間，要用現在完成式。

16. ④ established — have sent

因為第一個句子中有 1984 這個表過去的時間點，所以要用過去式。第二個句子中有 since then，所以要用現在完成式。

17. ③ having made → has made

句子裡面一定要有動詞。主詞 The professor 是第三人稱單數，所以要改成 has made。

18. ① Have → Did

when 子句的 were 表示過去，所以主要子句的時態也要用過去式。疑問句的形式是句首為助動詞 did。

19. ③ has been made → was made

ago 是表示過去的一個時間點，所以要用過去式。

20. ④ saw → had seen

realized 表示過去發生，所以「曾看過這個節目」是發生在這之前，所以要用過去完成式。

21. ① will eat → eat

因為是 when 子句，所以要用現在式代替未來式。

22. ② has fallen → fell

「現在變好了」用現在式，所以發生在前的生病，應該用過去式。

23. ③ is still believing → still believes

believe 如果表示想法，就不能用進行式。

24. ② have discovered → will have discovered

in the next few years 表示未來的時間，而「發現」是已經完成的事，所以要用未來完成式。

9

1. in

因為 occure 是不及物動詞，所以後面不能接受詞。

2. on

sit 是不及物動詞。

3. to

apologize 是不及物動詞。

4. to, Ø

come 是不及物動詞，meet 當「與……碰面」時，是及物動詞。也有「meet with」的用法，但句意不同，to meet with sb. = to have a meeting with sb.

5. on

lie 是不及物動詞。

6. to, for

walk 和 wait 都是不及物動詞。

7. Ø

research 一般都當作及物動詞。但若當作不及物動詞來用時，就要加介系詞 into。

8. Ø, about

book 可當 write 的受詞，故 write 是及物動詞；people 不能當 write 的受詞，故 write 是不及物動詞。

9. ② rose

因為空格後沒有名詞，所以空格要填不及物動詞。raise 是及物動詞，故此題選不及物動詞 rise。依句意用過去式最為恰當，所以答案是 rise 的過去式 rose。

10. ③ actively

因為 participate 是不及物動詞，所以後面要加 in。空格應該填入修飾動詞的副詞 actively。

11. ④ graduated from

graduate 是不及物動詞，後面要加 from。因為 last year 表示過去時間，所以要用過去式。

10

1. suddenly

如果 appear 是「出現」的意思，屬第一類句型中的不及物動詞，後接副詞。

2. joyless

如果 appear 是「看起來像……」的意思，則屬第二類句型中的不完全不及物動詞，後接形容詞。

3. easily

cut 是不及物動詞，後接副詞。

4. beautiful

如果 look 是「看起來是……」的意思，就是不完全不及物動詞，後接形容詞。

5. remains

doubt 是單數，所以 remains 是正確答案。

6. strange

如果 sound 是「聽起來是……」的意思，就是不完全不及物動詞，後接形容詞。

7. smoothly

work 是不及物動詞，後接副詞。

8. seems

主詞 difficulty 是單數，所以 seems 是正確答案。

9. uncomfortable

feel 可當作第三類句型的及物動詞，或第五類句型的不完全及物動詞來用；但這裡當作「覺得是……」的意思，為第二類句型不完全不及物動詞。因為主詞是人，補語就不能用抽象名詞，要用形容詞。

10. There, It's

there is/are 是「有……」的意思。第二個空格要填入一個代替 a red car 的 it。

11. ④ silent

keep 若有受詞，就可當第三類句型的及物動詞，或第五類句型的不完全及物動詞來用；但這裡因為沒有名詞和受詞，所以是「不完全不及物動詞」，空格要填入當補語的形容詞。

12. ③ were

主詞 many people 看是複數，時態從 last Saturday 看出是過去，所以 be 動詞為過去式。

11

1. ② arrived in

arrive 和 get 是不及物動詞。而 reach 是及物動詞，所以後面不能有介系詞。

2. ③ entered

enter 是及物動詞，所以後面不能有介系詞。

3. ② lay

lie 是不及物動詞，lay 是及物動詞。空格中要填不及物動詞，且從 raised 推斷為過去式，所以要用 lie 的過去式 lay。

4. ③ answered to → answered

answer 是及物動詞，所以要接受詞。① 的 talk 和 ② 的 disappear 都是不及物動詞。④ 的 think 常當作不及物動詞來用，後面如果接名詞，就要加 of 或 about。

5. F

marry 是及物動詞，所以後面不能接介系詞 with。

6. T

invite 是及物動詞，所以後面要接受詞。

7. F

如果 attend 是「參加」的意思，那就是及物動詞，後面不能加 to。

12

1. ③ remind

動詞 remind 不能當作授與動詞來用。remind＋人＋of＋事　提醒某人某事。

2. ② told

表「告訴」這個含意的動詞，屬授與動詞的只有 tell。talk＋to＋人＋about＋事＝mention＋事＋to＋人　告訴某人某事。

3. ③ for

要移動間接受詞的位置時，動詞 buy 要加介系詞 for。

4. ③

① to→for：make 要搭配介系詞 for。② 刪除 to：lend 是授與動詞，me 是間接受詞，所以要 to 刪除。④ created→made：create 不是授與動詞，要換成授與動詞 make 等才正確。⑤ for→to：動詞 offer 要搭配介系詞 to。

5. me → to me

動詞 explain 不是授與動詞。me 前面要加 to。

6. 刪去 to

show 是授與動詞，the officer 是間接受詞，所以介系詞 to 要刪除。

7. the doctor → to the doctor

describe 不是授與動詞，所以在 the doctor 前面要加 to。此句更好的表現方式是「describe my symptoms to the doctor」。

13

1.
① 第五類句型「不完全及物動詞」（最後我終於知道那本書很簡單。）
② 第三類句型「及物動詞」（最後我終於很容易地找到了那本書。）

2.
① 第四類句型「授與動詞」（她做了件新連身裙給女兒。）
① 第五類句型「不完全及物動詞」（她使她女兒成為一位醫師。）

3. ③ carefully

organize 是及物動詞，their day-to-day life 是受詞，所以空格要填副詞，用以修飾 organize。

4. ④ sleepy

make 是第五類句型的不完全及物動詞，people 是受詞，所以空格要填形容詞 sleepy，用來補充說明 people。

5. 正確句子

call 是不完全及物動詞，me 是受詞，a fat slob 是受詞補語。

6. 刪去 as

consider 是不完全及物動詞，myself 是受詞，a strong woman 是受詞補語。不需要 as，所以要刪除。

7. 正確句子

find 當作不完全及物動詞來用，him 是受詞，guilty 是形容詞，當作補語。

8. srongly → strong

make 是不完全及物動詞，the platform 是受詞，strong 是補語。在補語的位置不能放副詞。在受詞 the platform 和補語 strong 之間，如果 the platform is strong 的關係成立的話，就是不完全及物動詞。

9. 正確句子

leave 當作不完全及物動詞,具有讓受詞處於某種狀態的意思。poor 是形容詞,當作受詞補語來用。

14

1. of

2. to

3. in

4. with

5. out

6. off

7. as

8. up

9. ④ of

dispose 是不及物動詞,要有介系詞 of,後面才能接受詞。

10. ③ of

accuse 的受詞之後,還需要加 of。

11. ③ called it off

call off 是「及物動詞＋副詞」的形式;主詞 a strike 是第三人稱單數,所以代名詞用 it。如果受詞是代名詞,就要放在 call 和 off 之間。

12. ① with

replace 的受詞之後,還需要加 with 或 by。

Chapter 2 單元綜合問題

1. ④ sound different

sound 是「聽起來是……」的意思,當作不完全不及物動詞使用,補語的位置要用形容詞 different。

2. ③ with

cope with 是片語「處理……」的意思。

3. ④ there are

In New England 是表示地方的副詞,所以後面要接有主詞和動詞的完整句子。

4. ④ occurred to

come 和 happen 是不及物動詞,後面不能接受詞。bring 是及物動詞,所以刪去介系詞 to。occur to 是「不及物動詞＋介系詞」的形式,可接受詞 them。

5. ③ ask

ask of 是片語「要求……」的意思,在 of 後接間接受詞。此句也可寫成「My boss asked me a favor.」。

6. ④ attend

attend 是及物動詞,不需介系詞即可接受詞。

7. ① extinct

made 是不完全及物動詞,blacksmiths . . . cobblers 是受詞,所以空格要填受詞補語的形容詞。

8. ① pulled it out

pull out 是「及物動詞＋副詞」的形式;主詞 my tooth 是單數,所以代名詞要用 it。因為受詞是代名詞,所以受詞要放在動詞和副詞之間。

9. ① to your calling

object 是不及物動詞,所以需要介系詞 to。object to 是「反對……」的意思。

10. ④ teaches

可以接「名詞＋that 子句」的動詞,從選項中看來只有 teach;主詞為第三人稱單數,應寫為 teaches。

11. ④ explaining

從後面的介系詞 to 來判斷,explain 是正確答案。

12. ③

① to 要換成 for。② marry 是及物動詞,所以 with 要刪除。④ 應改為 wake him up 才正確。

13. ③

① complain 是不及物動詞,所以需要 of/about。② 主詞 languages 是複數,所以 is 要換成 are。④ explain 不是授與動詞,所以不能用「間接受詞＋直接受詞」的形式。必須把 his family 移到 the patient 後面,並改成 to his family 才正確。

14. ②

② approach 是及物動詞,後面的介系詞 to 要刪除。① lend 是授與動詞。③ lie 是不及物動詞。④ shorten 和 lengthen 都是不及物動詞。

15. ③

① talk 是不及物動詞,需要 about。② share 是及物動詞,所以要刪去 with。④ discuss 是及物動詞,所以要刪去 about。

16. ③ forget → remember

這是一段對 George 之死表示哀悼的文字。依照句意,意思是指「要記住並珍藏和他一起度過的幸福時光」,而非「要忘記並珍藏」。

17. hit, made, entered

hit 是及物動詞,所以不需要有 with。「弄出一個洞」

要用 make。enter 是及物動詞，所以不能有 into。

18. warmly → warm

keep 是不完全不及物動詞，後面要接形容詞。

19. have

因為前面有 over the years，所以用現在完成式，動詞為 have been。

20. to, to

explain 不是授與動詞。his students 不是間接受詞，所以前面要加 to。bring 是授與動詞，因為間接受詞 the class 移到了直接受詞的後面，所以前面要加 to。

21. difficult

find 當不完全及物動詞使用，it 是受詞，所以後面要接受詞補語 difficult。

22. ③ popularity → popular

became 是不完全不及物動詞，後面要接形容詞 popular。

23. ④ move away it → move it away

move away 是「及物動詞＋副詞」的形式，受詞是代名詞 it，所以要放在兩者中間才正確。

24. 刪去 ④ as

call 是不完全及物動詞，後面依序要接受詞和受詞補語；所以不需 as。

25. ② have → are

thirsty 是形容詞，前面應該是 be 動詞，而不能用及物動詞 have。

26. ③ to bring → to take

從句意上來看，不是「帶」她來醫院，而是「送」她去醫院的意思；所以動詞應改為 take。

27. 刪去① after

resemble 是及物動詞，不需加介系詞就可接受詞。

28. ② lay → lies

句意為西班牙「位於」東邊。lay 是「放」的意思；lie 才是「位於」的意思。

15

1. ④ ought to have

助動詞後面要用原型動詞。ought to 是助動詞，have 是原型動詞。passed 不是原型，所以不能用 had better 或 must。另外 may 後面加 to，也是錯誤用法。

2. ③ can not see

否定詞 not 要放在助動詞後。

3. Daniel will be working with his partner.

4. Johnny might not start his own business.

5. You must have said something to Jeff about me.

6. Julie should not have told him that she planned to remain single.

7. gone → go

may 是助動詞，所以後面要用原型動詞。

8. combating → combat

助動詞後面一定要用原型動詞。

9. to take → take

had better 是助動詞，所以要用原型動詞。

10. will calls → will call

will 是助動詞，所以後面要用原型動詞。

16

1. ④ would inherit

predict 是「預測」的意思，後面要接未來式。句中動詞 predicted 是過去式，所以助動詞也要用過去式 would 和 should。

2. ④ will insist

will 當作「重覆和習慣」的意思使用。① 的 insist 應改為 insists 才正確。③ 的 is going to 沒有「重覆和習慣」的意味。

3. ①

提示句表示「未來」。② 表示意志。③ 表示重覆和習慣。④ 表示預測。

4. ④

提示句表示「意志」。① 表示預測。② 表示未來。③ 表示重覆和習慣。

17

1. ④ Will

can 和 may 有「允諾」的意思，will 沒有允諾的意思。

2. ④ are able to

be able to 沒有「推測」的意思。

3. are, able to

can 當作「能力」的意思時，可以換成 be able to；not 要放在 be 動詞的後面。

4. are, allowed to

can 當作「允諾」的意思時，可以換成 be allowed to。

5. may be 較 can be 適合

perhaps 表示推測，所以要用 may 或 can。can 主要用於正式場合，所以在這裡用 may 比用 can 更適合。

6. ③

提示句表示可能性的推測。①表示能力。②表示允諾。

18

1. Phillip doesn't have to lock the door at the end of the day.

has/have to 具有助動詞的功能，但是不屬於助動詞，是一般動詞。要形成否定句的話，就要在前面加助動詞 do 或 does。

2. Must children stay in school until age sixteen?

must 是助動詞，所以要形成疑問句的話，主詞和 must 就要倒裝。

3. ① will have to

② 要用 has to。③ 要用 must。
④ will 和 must 都是助動詞，不能同時使用。

4. ① must not

句意指「做……是不行的」，所以要用 must not。

5. ② must

因為「心臟衰弱」，故推測有心臟病；這是強烈推測。

6. must not

從句意來看是「禁止」的意思，所以要選擇 must not。

7. doesn't have to

從句意來看，是「沒……的必要」的意思，所以選擇 doesn't have to。

8. had to

must 不能用於過去式的句子中，只能用於現在式或未來式的句子中；「must = have to」，所以把 have to 改為過去式 had to 即為正確答案。

9. can't

can't 有「不可能」的意思。

19

1. should, ought, had

是「should＋原型動詞」、「ought to＋原型動詞」、「had better＋原型動詞」。①、②、③ 意思相似。

2. ③ had better get

had better 是助動詞，所以後面要接原型動詞。

3. ③

提示句表示建議。①、②、④ 都是表示推測。

4. must

強烈地表示不可以，所以用 must。

5. had better not

had better 是助動詞，表示否定時，後面直接接 not。

6. ought not to

ought to 的否定要寫成 ought not to。

20

1. ④

① needs 要改成 need。② speak 要改成 to speak。
③ need do 要改成 needs to do。need 只有在否定句和疑問句中，才能當作助動詞；直述句中的 need，不能當作助動詞。

2. was used to → used to

「used to＋原型動詞」為「以前都會……」的意思；而「be used to＋Ving」則是「習慣……」的意思。

3. making → make

would rather 後面要接原型動詞。

4. ① used to trade

used to 為表示過去習慣的片語，後面接原型動詞。

5. ④ need not understand

① 要改為 need not understand 才正確。② 要改為 does not need to understand 才正確。③ 要改為 doesn't have to understand 才正確。

6. ④ rather not

would rather 是助動詞，所以 not 接在後面。

21

1. ③ Will I

will 在疑問句中，不能和第一人稱以及 we 搭配使用。

2. ③ Would you

will/would 表示「邀請」時，不能和第三人稱代名詞一起使用。

3. ② Would you like

「would like (to) .. ?」指「你想要……嗎？」

4. Could

對第二人稱提出鄭重要求時，不能用 May 或 Shall。

5. Shall

疑問句中的 Shall we 是「我們要不要一起去……？」的意思。

6. I'd like

I like 是「我喜歡」的意思。I would like 是「我現在想做某件事」或「想吃某東西」的意思。因為前面提到「肚子餓」，所以應該用 would like。I'd 是 I would 的縮寫。

7. likes

表示「喜歡」的意思時，就用 like。主詞為第三人稱單數，所以用 likes。

8. Shall

「Shall I . . . ？」是詢問對方「我可以做……嗎？」的意思，是詢問對方意見時經常會使用的句型。

22

1. may

maybe 表示推測，其推測程度和助動詞 may 和 can 相當。can 一般很少用在肯定句中，要用 may 才正確。

2. must

對應 certain 並表示推測的助動詞是 must。

3. ① must

從句意上來看，是強烈推測。

4. ④ will

表「重覆、習慣」要用 will。如果有酸滴在酸鹼試劑紙上，試劑紙顏色就會變紅，這屬於重覆。

5. can't

前面說他出去了，所以後面的推測是有確實根據的推測，有確實根據的推測要用 must 和 can't。

6. will

certainly 是「確實地」的意思。而 might 是最弱的推測，不能和 certainly 一起搭配使用。

7. ought

括弧的後面是「to＋原型」，所以要用 ought。

8. might

shall 沒有推測意思。

9. can

因為「專家失手」不是常發生的事，所以不能用 will。

10. might, may

從句意來看不是強烈推測，故用一般推測的字。

23

1. be

從前面的 is 可知是現在的時間，可見是對現在的推測，所以助動詞後要接原型動詞。

2. have been

從前面的 was 可知是過去的時間，可見是對過去的推測，所以助動詞後要接現在完成式 have＋動詞過去分詞。

3. have eaten

「現在冰箱沒有食物，因為過去被某人吃掉了」，對過去的推測，助動詞後要接現在完成式。

4. be

「因為某人已經全部吃完了，所以現在沒有剩下了」，對現在的推測，助動詞後要接原型動詞。

5. have left

後面有 last night 表示過去，所以「留下鑰匙」是推測過去，要在助動詞後接現在完成式。

6. have left

現在不在，表示之前已經離開了。

7. have let

因為有 last night，表示推測過去，所以要用現在完成式。

8. must

「早上起來暖器還是開著的，所以一定是昨天晚上忘記關了」，要用表示推測的助動詞 must。

9. needn't have washed

從「好像要下雨了」這句話可以看出，對「已經洗了衣服」這件事有後悔的意思；所以要用表示已經做了，卻後悔去做的 needn't。

10. might

前面有 not sure，所以不是確實的推測。should have＋動詞過去分詞是指「應該要做……」，不是推測。

11. didn't need to

因為前面有 no，所以表示沒有去拜託，沒有做就用 didn't need。

12. ③ must have rained

因為有 last night，表示對過去的推測，要用現在完成式。

13. ② should

從句意上來看，應該是「你應該要來的」的意思，所以要用表示應該的 should。

Chapter 3 單元綜合問題

1. ① can

雖然前面有 could 表示過去，但在引號中的內容為當下所引述，所以要用現在式，因此用 can。

2. ① May

因為是向對方請求，所以要用「May I...」的句型。

3. ① would

表示過去重覆的習慣時，要用 would。

4. ③ can't

從前面的 nonsense 判斷，後面一定是「不能相信」。

5. ② would

從句意來看，是表示「意志」，而且是過去式，所以用 would。

6. ① had to

從句意來看，空格應該表示「義務」，而且是過去式。因此不考慮不能用在過去式的 must 和現在完成式的 have had to。

7. ② would

從句意來解題。

8. ② he'd rather not

would rather 是助動詞。not 要放在 rather 後面。

9. ③ must have dropped

因為「弄丟了」，表示過去的遺失，所以對過去的推測要用「助動詞＋have＋動詞過去分詞」。

10. ① could not

因為天氣不佳，所以應該是不能享受假期。而且是對過去的推測，要用「助動詞＋have＋動詞過去分詞」。

11. ① didn't need to say

由 fortunately 推斷並沒有後悔的意思，所以是那個女子「不必說話」的意思，就用 didn't need。

12. ② have rewarded

previous meeting 是「之前的會議」的意思，所以知道是過去式；should 後面就要用現在完成式。

13. like→would like

like 是「喜歡」的意思。would like 是「現在想……」的意思。

14. needs to respond

a man 是單數，所以後面用 needs 的話，表示 need 是一般動詞，那麼 needs 後面就要用 to respond。如果後面用 need 的，表示 need 是助動詞，那麼 need 後面就要用原型動詞 respond。

15. ④ might have been

整句都是過去式，如果不是推測，而是斷定的話語，那就應該寫成「He or she was a parent...」。本句是對過去的推測，所以 was 要改成推測的助動詞 might，後面要用現在完成式 have been。

16. ② don't have to

依據句意來解題。

17. ② finish→to finish

因為 need 位在 will 後面，所以 need 是一般動詞，後面要接 to 不定詞。在肯定句中，need 不能當助動詞來用。

18. ② is able to→can

be able to 只有表示「能力」的含意，所以當 can 表推測含義時，be able to 就不能代替 can。

19. ③ submitting→submit

因為 submit 接在 must 後面，所以也要用原型。

20. ① should't help→shouldn't have helped

因為整個內容的時態是過去式，所以 should 後面應該要用「have＋動詞過去分詞」。

21. ① have→will have

雖然 if 子句中有現在式 is，但後面還有 tomorrow，所以整句應是未來式。if 子句是條件子句，所以要用現在式代替未來式，而主要子句則要有顯示未來式的助動詞 will 才對。

22. ② leaving→leave

因為 had better 是助動詞，所以後面要接原型。

23. ③ stealing→steal

would rather 後面如果有 than 的話，than 後面也要用原型。

24. ④ be smaller→have been smaller

因為是對過去的推測，所以後面要接「have＋動詞過去分詞」。

24

1. trees were planted

若受詞當主詞，整句就要變成被動語態。

2. Baseball, played

有 be 動詞 is 表示為被動語態，所以受詞要變成主詞。

3. The cheese, eaten by

因為有 was 表示為被動語態，所以受詞要變成主詞，主詞要搭配 by，一起放在句子最後面。

4. by bacteria and viruses

were caused 是被動語態，後面不能直接接名詞。

5. saw

因為後面有名詞 a huge elephant 當受詞，所以是主動語態。

6. were caught

後面不是名詞，而是「by＋名詞」，所以是被動語態。

7. received

後面有名詞 an award 當受詞，所以是主動語態。

8. ③ was taught by

如果用 ② 的 taught，形式正確，但句意不對。

9. ④ bought

如果用 ③ was bought by，形式正確，但句意錯誤。

25

I. In football, the ball is thrown by the quarterback.

2. The athlete was honored by sportswriters last year.

last year 是時間副詞，所以要放在「by＋名詞」之後。

3. The ball is being caught by the outfielder.

4. My homework has not been finished yet.

因為有 my，所以後面不需要加上 by me。主詞是單數，要用 has，not 放在 has 之後。

5. ③ has been postponed

①和④時態錯誤。②has been postponing 是主動語態的現在完成進行式。③是現在完成式的被動語態。

6. ② was being played

③和④是錯誤用法。①是過去進行式的主動語態。②因為後面沒有受詞，所以是過去進行式的被動語態。

7. should be spent

should been spent 是錯誤用法。

8. been

have paid 是主動語態的「已經付了」的意思。have been paid 是被動語態的「已經被付了」的意思；因

為後面有 by my boss，所以用被動語態。

9. have been

will have signed 是主動語態的「將已經簽了」的意思。will have been signed 是被動語態的「將已經被簽了」的意思；因後面有 by Bob，所以用被動語態。

26

I. were met

後面沒有受詞，且從 by our uncle 推斷，應該是被動語態，所以用 were met。

2. met

因後面有受詞 our uncle，所以是主動語態，用 met。

3. by their friends

were invited 是被動語態，不能接受詞，要接「by＋名詞」。

4. their friends

因為 invited 是主動語態，所以後面要接受詞。

5. has occurred

因為 occure 是不及物動詞，所以不能有被動語態。

6. is seen by

因為「頒獎典禮是被觀賞的」，所以要用被動語態。

7. was published

publish 是及物動詞，但後面卻沒有受詞，所以要用被動語態。

8. was originally played, is dominated

從句意來看，都用被動語態。

9. ③ was ruled

語態為被動語態。因為有 ago，所以時態用過去式。

10. ① happen

happen 是不及物動詞，所以不能有被動語態。主詞 events 是複數，所以 ③ 應改成 have happened。

II. ③ discussed

主詞是 the meeting，discuss 是及物動詞。the murder 是 discuss 的對象，所以是 discuss 的受詞；也就是說 the meeting 先被動地被召集（was called），然後再主動地討論（discussed）。

27

I. was told that George was ill

間接受詞 me 若當主詞，整句就要變成被動語態。

2. **has been offered the opportunity to study abroad**

間接受詞 Mike 若當主詞，整句就要變成被動語態。has offered 的被動語態是 has been offered。

3. **was mad President of the Royal Society**

Newton 是受詞。President of the Royal Society 是受詞補語，屬於第五類句型（不完全及物動詞）。

4. **was given**

give 是第四類句型的動詞（授與動詞），如果只看後面的 a flower，無法看出是要用主動還是被動；但因最後有 by her friend，就可以知道是被動語態了。

5. **gave**

後面有 to her friend，所以必定為主動語態。

6. **sent**

後面有間接受詞 her brother 和直接受詞 a telegram，所以用主動語態。

7. **evident**

consider 是第五類句型的動詞（不完全及物動詞），必須要有受詞補語；當句子變成被動語態，這個受詞補語也要保留下來，放在被動語態的過去分詞後面。

8. **didn't get punished**

從句意來看，要用被動語態。is not punished 要改成 was not punished 才是正確答案。因為 get 是一般動詞，否定句時，就要加助動詞 did。

9. ② **was called**

call 是第五類句型的動詞（不完全及物動詞），後面只有 Jim 這個名詞，表示受詞被移到前面當主詞了；而且後面還有 by，所以要用被動語態。call 和受詞、受詞補語之間，不能有 as 的。

10. ④ **was told**

當 tell 以 that 子句當作受詞時，一定要以「tell me that ＋子句」的形式來表現，所以中間一定要有間接受詞。間接受詞若當主詞，句子就變成被動語態，而形成「be told that＋子句」的形式。也就是說，that 子句前面沒有間接受詞時，tell 就要變成被動語態。

Chapter 4 單元綜合問題

1. ③ **can be stored**

因為是「資料是被儲存在電腦裡的」，所以要用被動語態。助動詞後要用原型動詞。

2. ② **is covered with**

不是南極大陸覆蓋，而是「被覆蓋」，所以是被動語態。被動語態不能直接接名詞，要用「by＋名詞」。

3. ④ **has disappeared**

disappear 是不及物動詞，所以不能用被動語態。② 和 ③ 是被動語態。

4. ④ **has been used**

因為是「鉛被用來當作材料」，所以要用被動語態。①、②、③ 全都是主動語態。

5. ① **was found**

find 是第五類句型的動詞，guilty 是形容詞當作受詞補語，沒有受詞，所以表示受詞當主詞，要用被動語態。時態上因為有 yeaterday，要用過去式。

6. ④ **been known**

know 是及物動詞，但後面卻沒有受詞，所以要用被動語態。沒有 ① 和 ③ 這樣的時態。

7. ③ **was told → told**

第一句沒有間接受詞，所以是被動語態。第二句有受詞 him，所以是主動語態。

8. ① **dream**

dream 是及物動詞，所以要用主動語態，後面可以接 that 子句當受詞。將 ④ 的 had 換成 have 才正確。

9. ④ **was covered → covered**

was covered 是被動語態，所以後面不能接名詞。① 誕生要用 be born。② wake up 要用被動語態。③ 用 that most of the children attended 這個關係詞子句來修飾 the school。was called 是被動語態，Telpochcalli 是受詞補語；即使換成被語動態，受詞補語也要留在後面。⑤ open 要用被動語態。

10. **pollute, are built, are destroyed, use**

the air and the seas 是受詞，所以 pollute 要用主動語態。主詞是 hotels，應該要用被動語態 are built。destroy 後沒有受詞，而且從和主詞 places 的關係看來，也要用被動語態 are destroyed。more water 是受詞，所以是主動語態，要用 use。

11. ⑤ **take → are taken**

take 是及物動詞，但後面卻沒有受詞，且從和主詞的關係看來，應該要用被動語態。①、②、③ 全都是後面有受詞的主動態。④ 是第五類句型的動詞 keep，沒有受詞，就要用被動語態。

12. ② **was brought → is processed**

bring 是及物動詞，但後面卻沒有受詞，所以要用被動語態。process（處理）後面也沒有受詞，以它和主詞 information 之間的關係看來，應該用被動語態。

13. **given**

對應空格這個動詞的主詞是 Flowers。flowers 和 give 的關係應該是被動的關係，而且 give 後面也沒有受

詞。被動語態 are presented . . . and are given . . . ；
而第二次重複出現的 are 可以省略，就變成了 are
presented . . . and given . . .。

14. ③ classify → be classified

classify 是「分類」這個意思的及物動詞。因為後面沒
有受詞，所以要用被動語態。

15. ② arrested and charged → was arrested and charged

arrest 是「逮捕」，charge 是「起訴」，都是及物動詞。
從和主詞的關係且後面沒有受詞來推斷，全部都要用
被動語態。

16. ② are generally eaten → generally eat

insects 是受詞，所以要用主動語態。

17. ① are commonly occurred → commonly occur

occure 是不及物動詞，所以不能用被動語態。

18. ① brought up → was brought up

bring up 是「養、養育」的意思，是及物動詞；後面
沒有受詞，所以要用被動語態。④ 的 lead 的受詞是
an ascetic life，所以用主動語態才正確。

19. ② is held → holds

後面的 about 395 men 是受詞，所以要用主動語態。
about 用在數字前面時，不是介系詞，是修飾數字的
副詞，是「大約」的意思。

20. ④ has been risen → has risen

rise 是不及物動詞，所以不能用被動語態。has been
risen 是現在完成式的被動語態。

21. ② regarded as → been regarded as

regard A as B 是「把 A 當作 B」的意思，regard 是及
物動詞。因為 regard 和 as 之間沒有受詞，所以要用
被動語態，has been regarded 才是正確解答。

28

1. Some people, cotton candy, a stick

Some people 是主詞，cotton candy 是及物動詞的受
詞，a stick 是介系詞受詞。

2. The successful flights, the early balloons, many people

The successful flights 是主詞，the early balloons 是
介系詞受詞，many people 是及物動詞受詞。

3. Develop → Development, grow → growth

develop 是動詞，「發展」的意思，不能當主詞；若要
當主詞，就要換成名詞 development。is 後面要接補

語，grow 是動詞，不能當補語，要把 grow 改成
growth，變成 gradual growth 才能當介系詞補語。

4. able → ability

had 是及物動詞，後面要接名詞當受詞，所以要將形
容詞 able 改成名詞 ability 才正確。

5. succeed → success

was 後面要接補語，succeed 是動詞，不能當補語。
另外，要將動詞 succeed 換成名詞 success，才能修
飾形容詞 grand。

6. perceive → perception

people's 是所有格，後面要接名詞，所以要將動詞
perceive 換成名詞 perception。

7. Mean → Meaning, pronounce → pronunciation

come 是動詞，前面要有名詞當主詞；所以要把動詞
mean 和 pronounce 都轉換成名詞。

8. different → difference

不定冠詞 a 後面要接名詞。

9. V

Ralph and his colleagues 是名詞，當主詞用。The
health . . . men 是名詞，當受詞用。study 是動詞。

10. N

句子的第一個字不能用動詞。studies 是主詞，所以
是名詞。

11. ② effects

定冠詞 The 後面要接名詞。affect 是動詞，effect 是
名詞。因為動詞是 are，所以主詞要用複數形 effects。

12. ③ terrorists

criminals 和要填入的字對比，而且由 of 連接句子。
criminals 是「罪犯」，是人物名詞，所以要填入的字
也應該是人物名詞；依照句意，應填入名詞 terrorists
（恐怖分子）的複數形。

29

1.

	名詞	U/C		名詞	U/C
1	advice	U	15	news	U
2	egg	C	16	hope	U, C
3	dollar	C	17	weather	U
4	apple	C	18	work	U
5	accident	C	19	toothpaste	U
6	cake	U, C	20	necklace	C
7	money	U	21	water	U
8	moon	U	22	job	C
9	jewelry	U	23	flower	C

10	island	C	24	ocean	C
11	traffic	U	25	information	U
12	music	U	26	mail	U
13	library	C	27	furniture	U
14	milk	U	28	envelope	C

2. two pieces of

bread 是不可數名詞，所以用 piece of 才可以計量。前面有 two，piece 就要用複數形 pieces。

3. vitamins, a vitamin pill

vitamin 是可數名詞，要用複數形；vitamin pill 是可數名詞。

4. an accident, water

accident 是可數名詞；water 是不可數名詞。

5. words

word 是「字」的意思，為可數名詞。vocabulary 是「字彙」，指所有的字，表示全體為不可數名詞。

6. a surprise

surprise 是可數名詞。

7. ④

① furniture 是不可數名詞，所以 A 要刪去；wood 也是不可數名詞，所以 a 也要刪去。② news 是不可數名詞，要把 them 改成 it。③ "a little" knowledge 是對的；thing 是可數名詞，thing 一定要用 a thing 或 things 兩者之一的形式出現。④ package 是「包裹」的意思，是可數名詞。

30

1.

	單數形	複數形		單數形	複數形
1	bag	bags	9	game	games
2	woman	women	10	child	children
3	mouse	mice	11	country	countries
4	day	days	12	person	persons/people
5	leaf	leaves	13	fox	foxes
6	library	libraries	14	tomato	tomatoes
7	church	churches	15	pen	pens
8	goose	geese	16	foot	feet

2. ③ such large

numbers 是複數名詞，前面不能加不定冠詞 a。

3. ④ information → cars

information 是不可數名詞。car 是可數名詞，此句應為複數形 cars。

4. tourist → tourists

tourist 是「觀光客」，是可數名詞。如果前面沒有不定冠詞 a，就要用複數形 tourists。

5. moneys → money

money 是不可數名詞，所以不能用複數形。

6. feets → feet

feet 就是 foot 的複數形，所以 feets 為錯誤用法。

7. way → ways

way 本身是可數名詞，前面的 dozens of 表示「數十個」，所以後面要用複數名詞。

8. has → have

species 單複數同形，因為這裡有 seven，所以 species 是複數形。主詞是複數，動詞 has 就要換成 have。

9. is → are

fish 單複數同形；more 表示更多，所以這裡的 fish 是複數形，be 動詞應為 are。

31

1. think

主詞為複數，所以動詞也要為複數。

2. was

three million dollars 雖然是複數，但視為一個整體，所以用單數動詞。

3. isn't

rabies 是「狂犬病」，疾病名稱的後面都接單數動詞。

4. some scissors

scissors 是複數形，也和複數動詞一起使用，前面不能加不定冠詞 a。

5. is

politics 為「政治學」之意，後面要接單數動詞。

6. have, them

trousers 是複數形，後面要接複數動詞。

7. A policeman

police 是集合名詞，指「全體警察」，所以要接複數動詞。如果要表示「一名警察」，就用 policeman。

8. black jeans

jeans 是複數形，後面接複數動詞，不能加不定冠詞 a。

9. are → is

表示距離的 forty miles 視為一個整體，後面要接單數動詞。

10. it is → they are

shoes 為複數形，要接複數動詞。因此，shoes 的代名詞為 they。

11. ① pair

② trousers 和 pants 意思相似，其前面加了不定詞 a，所以不正確。③、④ 都必須是複數形，所以不是正確答案。有複數概念，形式卻是單數的 ① pair 才是正確答案。

12. ③ worth it

fifty dollars 視為整體，所以代名詞為 it。

13. ③ Economics gives

economics 是「經濟學」的意思，為單數，後面接單數動詞。

32

1. student's

單數名詞的所有格，以加「's」這個形式來表示。

2. students'

規則變化的複數名詞所有格，在 s 後加「'」來表示。

3. woman'sv

單數名詞的所有格。

4. women's

不規則變化的複數名詞所有格，也是在名詞後面直接加「's」這個形式來表示。

5. ④ John's friends

John 的所有格是 John's。

6. ④ the boys' father

複數形 the boys 的所有格是 the boys'。

7. 正確句子

因為 Becky 和 Sylvia 是普通名詞，其所有格直接在名詞後加「's」即可。

8. thought thousands → thought of thousands

the taste and thought 和 thousands of women 都是名詞，如果它們之間要表示所有格關係，就要用介系詞 of 連結。

9. worker's → workers'

workers 的所有格為 workers'。

10. 正確句子

hairdresser 是「美容師」; hairdresser's 是「髮廊」。

11. cousins' → cousins

cousins'是「堂、表兄弟姐妹的」。從句意來看，是指堂表兄弟姐妹不在那裡，所以答案應為 cousins。

12. Asian's → Asians'

Asian 是「亞洲人」，為可數名詞。前面有 some，所以 Asian 應變成複數形 Asians；其所有格為 Asians'。

33

1. A

house 是可數名詞；單數用 a house，複數用 houses。

2. Ø

houses 是複數形，前面不可以有不定冠詞 a。

3. Ø

名詞表示一般的含義時，不可以有冠詞。

4. The

句意為「我們昨晚去的餐廳」，具有限定的意味，因此要加定冠詞 the。

5. some, a, an

oil 是不可數名詞，不能加不定冠詞。spare tire 和 old flashlight 是可數名詞，所以可以加不定冠詞。old 的字首為母音發音，所以要用 an。

6. Ø

weather 是不可數名詞，也沒有限定，所以不能加 the。

7. questions

question 是可數名詞。單數用 a question；複數用 questions。

8. The

因為限定「那家店賣的肉」，所以要加 the。

9. some, the

第一個 tomatoes 沒有限定，所以用 some。後面的 tomatoes 限定為「花園裡的」的，所以要加 the。

10. ② a —The

第一次出現的名詞用 a，該名詞重複出現時就用 the。

11. ④ the left side

因為限定為「在餐桌前爸爸的左邊」，所以要加 the。

12. ④ Flowers have

因為後面有 their，所以要用複數形。

Chapter 5 單元綜合問題

1. ② length

width 是 wide 的名詞；height 是 high 的名詞；long 的名詞是 length。這三個名詞都是 measured 的受詞。

2. ② nine inches

「9 吋」要寫成 nine inches。

3. ① cereal and milk

玉米片 cereal 和牛奶 milk 都是不可數名詞。

4. ④ women's

women's university 是女子大學之意。不規則複數名詞 women 的所有格為 women's。

5. ① Vegetables

vegetable 是可數名詞，不過在這裡表示「各種類的蔬菜」，因此用複數形。

6. ② significance

「介系詞 in＋名詞」當作受詞；social 是形容詞，用來修飾名詞，所以要填入名詞 significance。signify 是動詞，significant 是形容詞，significantly 是副詞。

7. ② mathematics teacher

mathematics teacher 為「數學老師」。因為前面有 a，所以判定為單數名詞。

8. ③ hand

「give . . . a hand」是片語，「幫忙」的意思。「give . . . a lift」是「讓……搭便車」的意思。

9. ② the democracy

democracy（民主）是不可數名詞，所以不能加不定冠詞 a。這裡限定是「他居住的社會的民主」，所以加定冠詞 the。

10. ④ job → a job

job 是可數名詞，要用 a job 或 jobs 兩種形式之一。① family，若意思為「家人」，就要接複數動詞。learner 是可數名詞。② evidence 是「證據」，為不可數名詞。③ research 是不可數名詞。

11. ④ things — impressions

thing 是可數名詞，若前面有 a number of，表示「許多」，要用複數形。impression 可以是可數名詞，也可以是不可數名詞；因為前面有 these，所以要用複數形。

12. ① library → libraries

one of 的後面要加複數名詞，「one of . . .」是「…… 其中之一」的意思。

13. doctors' → doctor's

依照句意，應為單數名詞所有格。

14. choice

缺少主詞，所以 choose 要改成名詞 choice。從動詞 makes 和 much 推斷，應為單數名詞。

15. ① extraordinary woman → an extraordinary woman

主詞 woman 是單數可數名詞，要加不定冠詞；但因前面有形容詞，所以不定冠詞要放在形容詞的前面。

16. ④ type → types

因為前面有 three，所以要用複數名詞。

17. ② games → game

因為前面有不定冠詞 a，所以要用單數名詞。soccer 表示一般含意，所以前面不用加冠詞。

18. ② are → is

news 是不可數名詞，所以後面代名詞為 it。television 不能加冠詞。

19. ② tooth → teeth

兔子有大門牙，門牙不只一顆，所以要用複數；而且主詞 rabbits 也為複數。

20. ③ sea creature → sea creatures

因為動詞是 are，所以主詞要是複數才對。而且 creature 是可數名詞。

21. ② child's → children's

children 的複數名詞所有格為 children's。

22. ④ starvations → starvation

starvation 是不可數名詞，因此不能用複數形。

23. ③ certain type → a certain type

type 是可數名詞；依照句意，應該為 a type 才正確。

24. ④ accurately → accuracy

with 是介系詞，所以後面要接名詞當受詞。accurately 是副詞，要換成名詞 accuracy 才正確。

34

1. They

Susan and her sister 是複數，所以要用 they。

2. it

the window 是單數，所以用 it。

3. She, it

Catherine 是女子名，所以用 she。a book 是事物，

所以用 it。

4. He, him
Peter Hamilton 是男子名，主格用 He，受格用 him。

5. me, you
是「老師對我們班的同學和我說話」的意思。對老師而言，學生們就是「你們」，所以用 you。

6. them
應填入 for 的受詞，所以要用受格 them。

7. ② them
應填入 call 的受詞，所以要用受格 them。

8. ③ it
應填入 spit 的受詞，所以要用受格 it。

9. ② them
應填入 work with 的受詞，所以要用受格 them。

35

I. Their
因為後面有 families 這名詞，所以要用所有格。

2. himself
主詞和受詞是同一人，所以受詞位置要用反身代名詞。主詞是 The statesman，反身代名詞為 himself。

3. her
人稱代名詞的受格。

4. yourself
因為是自己被切到，所以主詞和受詞是同一人。

5. Its → It's
its 是 it 的所有格；it's 是 it is 的縮寫。

6. 正確句子
his 可當所有格，也可當所有格代名詞。這裡指 his relatives，當所有格代名詞用，所以整句是正確的。

7. 正確句子
名詞或代名詞後面加反身代名詞，表示強調。myself 是用來強調 I 的。

8. Ours → Our
因為後面有名詞 successes 和 failures，所以要用所有格 our。

9. ④ himself
因為自己就是老闆，自己為自己做事。也就是說，主詞和受詞是同一人。

10. ③ ours
theirs 指 their scores，所以應該填入表 our scores 的所有格代名詞 ours。

11. ① its
因為後面有名詞 foreign policies，所以應該填入所有格；the government 是單數，所以所有格為 its。

36

I. this
因為有 here，所以要用 this。因為 form 是單數，所以不能用 these，要用 this。

2. that
experience 的代名詞是 that。因為 experience 是單數，所以不能用 those。

3. this
在電話中指稱對方時，不能用 that，要用 this。

4. those
因為 glasses 重複出現，所以省略 glasses。

5. those
要填入 achievements 的代名詞 those。

6. This is → These are
因為補語 cherry trees 是複數，所以主詞也要用複數。

7. that → this
因為前面有 here，所以應該用 this place。

8. those → that
news 是不可數名詞，不可用複數形的 these 或 those。

9. this → that
that 代替前面出現過的名詞 the number。

10. ④ These kinds
this 要接單數名詞；these 接複數名詞

11. ④ that
that 為 economic development 的代名詞。

12. ③ those
代替前面出現過的複數名詞 the ideas，要用 those。

37

I. house

2. hats

3. people

4. one

不是特定的 raincoat，指「一般雨衣中的某一件」，所以用 one。

5. one

指「許多書中的某一本」，非特指某一本，所以用 one。

6. it

因為是「我寄的電子郵件」，是特定的，所以要用 it。

7. one

「我喝一杯咖啡，你喝一杯咖啡」，並非一起喝一杯。

8. children was

one of 後面要接複數名詞，不過因為主詞是 one，所以動詞用 was。

9. ② have one made

因為去買一個書架，或訂做一個書架，都不是特定的，所以用 one。

10. ④ it

因為「我買的東西」，是特定的，所以用 it。that 是單數，ones 是複數，兩者不能一起用。

11. ③ color→colors

one of 後面要接複數名詞。

38

1. game

every 後面接單數名詞。

2. games

all 後面的名詞 game 是可數名詞，所以要用複數形。

3. Every

city 是可數名詞的單數形。every 後面接單數名詞。

4. Most

every 不能單獨出現，後面要接名詞。

5. Most

luggage 是不可數名詞，所以前面不可以用 every。

6. homework is

homework 是不可數名詞，所以要接單數動詞。

7. every

every day 是「每天」，all day 是「一整天」。從句意來看，應該是「每天」的意思才正確。

8. all

all day 是「一整天」。因為前面有 yesterday，所以應該不是 every day， all day 才正確。

9. ④

① 應該用 Most Koreans 或 Most of the Koreans。most 後面如果接 of，後面一定要加定冠詞 the。② 改成 every car 才正確。③ have 要換成 has，因為主詞 research 是不可數名詞。④ traffic lights「紅綠燈」是可數名詞。every 如果是「每……」的意思，後面就要接複數名詞。every ten yards 是「每十碼」的意思。

10. ③ Most of

因為後面有定冠詞 the，所以要用 most of。most the coal 和 the most of，都是錯誤用法。

11. ② Every

village 和 tribe 是可數名詞的單數，要用 every。

39

1. much

mail 是不可數名詞，所以前面不能加 many。

2. quite a

quite a few 和 many 是相同的意思。

3. very little

money 是不可數名詞，所以要用 little。

4. a little

因為後面提到要帶雨傘，所以可以確定會下雨。rain 是不可數名詞。

5. a few

problem 是可數名詞。

6. very few

lots of 是「很多」的意思，但後面有 but，所以後面要接相反含義的「幾乎沒有」。

7. ① little

句意是「他們不能給他許多訊息，所以他需要更多訊息」。如果後面不是 so，而是 but，就要填入 a little。

8. ③ a few

vending machines 是可數名詞的複數形，few/a few ＋可數名詞。

9. ④ many

splendour 是不可數名詞，前面不能加 many。

40

1. some

因為是肯定句，所以用 some。

2. any

因為有 not，所以是否定句，因此用 any。

3. no

句意是「被好好地照顧，所以沒有問題」。因為 problems 是否定的含義，所以前面要加 no。none 雖然也是否定含義，但因它是代名詞，所以不能放在名詞前面。

4. none

從 but 推斷，後面應該是否定含義。no 是形容詞，放在名詞前面；而 none 是代名詞，可以單獨使用。

5. something

因為是肯定句，所以用 something。

6. no

picture 是名詞，所以前面不能用 none，要用 no（形容詞）來修飾。

7. any

因為有 not，所以是否定句。help 是不可數名詞，所以不能加 a。

8. a

如果用 any，letter 就要改成 letters 才正確。

9. some

看起來是疑問句，實際上是直述句。以 Could you 或 Would you 為首的疑問句，很多時候都是表示恭敬謙遜的直述句。

10. Any

這裡的 any 不是指「多少量」，而是「任何」的意思。如果是這個意思，直述句就可以用 any，後面也可以接可數名詞的單數形。

11. ③ some

not all teachers left 不是「老師全部都沒離開」的意思，而是「不是全部的老師都離開了」的意思，為部分否定，所以要用 some 才正確。

12. ① a

因為是肯定句，所以要用 a 或 some。如果用 some，名詞要用複數 bears；而這裡為單數名詞，所以用 a。

13. ② none

no 是形容詞，後面要接名詞。none 是代名詞，可以單獨使用。

41

1. either

因為有 not，所以是否定句。book 是單數，所以不能用 both。

2. both

hands 是複數，所以用 both。

3. both

後面接動詞 like，而非 likes，所以用 both。

4. either

sex 是單數，所以不能用 both。如果用 neither，就含有否定的含義，不合文意。

5. neither

one 是單數，所以不能用 both。從 but 推斷，其後面應該是相反含義，應為否定句。

6. ① neither

因為兩個人都生病了，所以兩人都沒去上班。any 是三個以上才能用。

7. ③ any

因為前面有 three，所以表示兩者的 either、both、neither 都不正確。

8. ③ both

從句意來看，應該是「參觀兩個地方」，both 即為「兩者都……」的意思。如果用 either，是「兩者中挑一個參觀」的意思，所以用 either 不正確。

9. ①

②、③、④ 是「那兩個小孩我都不認識」的意思。① 是「那兩個小孩，我只認識其中一個」的意思。

42

1. ② the other

the twins 是「雙胞胎」。兩個人當中的另一個，要用 the other 來表示。

2. ④ others

和 some 對應的是 others。

3. ③ the others

三個顏色，除了一個顏色外，剩下兩個顏色。剩下兩個以上，是複數時，就用 the others 來表示。

4. ① another

「吃了一個，還想再吃一個」的意思。his sausage 是單數，要用 another。如果是複數 his sausages，就要用 some、others 等。

5. the other

因為是「兩者中的另一個」，所以用 the other。

6. another

「要有另一個孩子」的意思。因為是將再有一個 baby，不能斷定總共有幾個，但因 baby 是單數，所以 the other 或 others 都不正確，只能選 another。

7. other

「一定有其他的方法」的意思。因為 ways 是複數，所以要用形容詞 other。而 others 是代名詞，後面不能接名詞。

8. another

「車子還可以再載一個人」的意思。因為已經載了幾位，所以不能用 the other。

9. others

和 some 對應的是 others。

10. the other

耳環都是兩個的。找到了一個，剩下的就只有一個，所以用 the other。

11. Another

several 是「好幾個」。好幾個中的一個，而剩下的幾個中的一個，就用 another。

12. the others

指「剩下的全部」，所以用 the others。

Chapter 6 單元綜合問題

1. ③ you and me

between 是介系詞，後面要接受詞。

2. ④ those

the ears 是複數，所以它的代名詞要用 those。

3. ③ others

和 some 對應的是 others。

4. ④ Many

employees 是複數形，所以用 many。

5. ② the other

因為兩棟大樓，所以剩下的就只有一個，要用 the other。

6. ④ a number

questions 是複數形，所以不能用 a little。要改成 questions，才能用 a few，要改成 of the questions，才能用 all。a number of 就是 many 的意思。

7. ④ Other

technicians 是複數，所以不能用 every 和 each。any 也不能用在肯定句中。

8. ① its

要填入 lava 的所有格，所以用 its。

9. ① some

no 不能當名詞使用。any 用在否定句。either 只能搭配可數名詞使用；而 rainwater 是不可數名詞。

10. ① themselves

要填入 protect 的受詞，這個受詞和主詞是同一個。

11. ④ ones

從內容來看，應該填入 large classes，但因 classes 前面出現過了，所以這裡要用代名詞 ones。

12. ② was — say

neither 搭配單數動詞使用；both 搭配複數動詞使用。

13. ① Both have

因為提到 rabbits 和 hares 兩種動物，所以要用 both，並且接複數動詞。

14. it → them

it 是單數名詞的代名詞，而 fossil fuels 是複數，所以 it 要改成 them 才正確。

15. ② you → yourself, ④ you → your

②find 的主詞是 you，受詞也是 you。主詞和受詞如果是同一人，受詞就要用反身代名詞。④因為後面有名詞 ankles，所以要用所有格，you 要改成 your。

16. Many, Others

如果用 many of，後面接的名詞前就要加冠詞 the，變成 the people。能和 some 對應的就只有 others。

17. ① much — a few

a few 表示「許多」，後面接可數名詞。

18. ③ their → its

their 是 physics 的代名詞，而 physics 為單數名詞，所以 their 應該改成 its 才對。

19. ② purchases → purchase

every 後面都是接單數名詞。it 代替的就是 every purchase。

20. ④ the another → the others

the scheduled lectures 是「安排好的演講者」的意思。除其中兩位以外，剩下的全部應該是複數，所以要用 the others。the another 是錯誤用法。

21. ③ for him → for them

Americans 是複數，所以代名詞應改成 them。

22. ⑤ few friend → few friends

friend 是可數名詞，可加 few，friend 要改成複數形 friends。① none 可代替複數名詞，也可代替單數名詞。所以用 were 或 was 都可以。② 因為前面 be 動詞為單數 was，所以要用 bus。③ walk to home 是錯誤用法。④ English 是不可數名詞，所以要用 little。

23. ③ those → that

hearing ability 是單數，所以代名詞要改成 that。

24. ④ either sides → both sides 或 either side

either 後面要接單數名詞；both 後面可接複數名詞。

25. ② most of parents → most parents

most of parents 是錯誤用法。most parents 或 most of the parents 這兩種形式才為正確用法。

43

1. tired, long

2. extraordinary, important

3. interesting, good, modern

4. favorite, famous, tall, expensive

5. black big → big black

表示大小的形容詞，要放在顏色的形容詞前面。

6. black two → two black

表示數字的形容詞，要放在顏色的形容詞前面。

7. a child small → a small child

形容詞要放在名詞前面。

8. green old → old green

表示新舊的形容詞，要放在顏色的形容詞前面。

9. intelligence → intelligent

因為 is 後面的 loyal 和 courageous，都是形容詞，所以 intelligence 也要改成形容詞 intelligent。

10. ④ brightened → bright

因為要修飾名詞 feathers，所以要用形容詞 bright。

11. ① some emotional stress

因為 some 是代名詞，所以要放在最前面；名詞 stress 要放在最後面；形容詞 emotional 修飾名詞，所以放在名詞前面。

44

1. slow

因為 speed 是名詞，所以要用形容詞來修飾它。

2. slowly

副詞修飾動詞 was traveling。

3. really

副詞 really 修飾形容詞 angry。

4. softly

副詞 softly 修飾動詞 was playing。

5. just

just 是副詞，修飾 a small cut 全部。

6. good

good 是形容詞，well 是副詞。

7. lively

lively 雖然字尾有 -ly，但它不是副詞，而是形容詞，是「生氣勃勃的」的意思。

8. absolutely

absolute 可以和 new 一起來修飾名詞 method，要寫成「absolute and new」或「absolute, new」。

9. possibly

副詞用來修飾動詞。

10. ④ quickly

副詞修飾動詞。soon 是「很快地」的意思。fastly 是錯誤用法，要改成 fast 才正確。hurry 是動詞。

11. ① graceful and orderly

orderly 是由名詞 order 後加 ly 形成的，不是副詞，而是形容詞，是「秩序井然的」的意思。

12. ④ so excellently

副詞 excellently 修飾動詞 played；而 so 用來強調 excellently。

45

1. hard at school yesterday

順序依次為方式、地點、時間。

2. is often mild

頻率副詞 often，要放在 be 動詞之後。

3. happily out of the room at the end of the conference

順序為方式、地點、時間副詞。

4. have almost forgotten

程度副詞 almost，要放在完成式的 have 之後。

5. the violin beautifully at the concert last week

受詞 the violin 要放在最前面，後面的副詞順序為方式、地點、時間。

6. I left may cell phone in the restaurant last night.

在主詞、動詞、受詞後面，副詞順序為地方副詞、時間副詞。

7. Jess spoke very loudly at the meeting last Friday.

在主詞、動詞後面，副詞順序為方式、地點、時間。

8. They are going to build a new school in the town next year.

在主詞、助動詞、主要動詞後面，要接受詞。副詞順序為地方副詞、時間副詞。

9. The children usually play football merrily in the park every Saturday.

頻率副詞 usually 要放在一般動詞前面。副詞順序為方式、地點、時間副詞。

10. ② patiently outside the door

patiently 是方式副詞，outside the door 是地方副詞。順序為方式、地點。

11. ④ generally trap

因為後面有 insects 這受詞，所以要用主動態。①、③ 是被動語態。②、④ 是主動語態。頻率副詞 generally 要放在一般動詞 trap 的前面。

46

1. very

因為句意為「非常重，但能舉起來」，所以不能用否定含義的 too。

2. too

因為句意為「太重了，所以舉不起來」這個否定含義，所以用 too。

3. enough

句意為「鹽夠了，不需要了」，所以要放「足夠了的」enough 這個字。

4. too

因為句意為「放了太多鹽，太鹹不能吃」，所以要用 too 來表示「過多」的意思。

5. too

句意為「太難了，所以沒辦法解釋」，所以要用有否定含義的 too。

6. enough

enough 修飾 quickly；very 和 too 不能放在被修飾的字後面。

7. early enough

enough 要放在 early 後面。

8. too late

句意為「出門太晚，所以沒趕上飛機」。「太 ... ，以致不能」要用 too。

9. very late

句意為「出門很晚，還是趕上飛機了」。沒有否定含義，所以用 very late。

10. too crowded

句意為「餐廳太擁擠了，所以離開」，所以用有否定含義的 too。

11. ④ too much

句意為「太吵了，所以沒辦法聽見」，所以要用有否定含義的 too；但因 too 不能直接修飾名詞，所以加 much。

12. ④ large enough

enough 要放在 large 之後。雖然 very large 形式上正確，但後面不能接不定詞 to take。

47

1. so

so 修飾形容詞 neat。

2. such

such 修飾名詞。

3. such

such 修飾 different surgical skills。

4. so

so 也可以接名詞，用法為 so beautiful a child。

5. so

so 可以修飾 many 和 much。

6. such

initiatives 是名詞，「率先、肇端、創始」的意思，所以要用 such 來修飾它。

7. such a nice day

such＋不冠詞＋形容詞。

8. quite a lot of traffic

quite 修飾 a lot of。

9. ① such

interesting and original plans 是「形容詞＋名詞」，可以用副詞 such、very、quite 來修飾；又因為後面有 that 子句，所以三者中只能用 such。

10. ④ quite a strict father

quite 的用法和 such 完全一樣。

11. ④ so great

such 後面一定要有名詞，因為 great 是形容詞，所以①、② 都不正確。③ 形容詞前面不加冠詞 a。

48

1. hard

hard 是副詞，修飾動詞 try。

2. hardly

hardly 含有 not 的否定含義，在句中的位置也和 not 一樣。

3. late

句意為「上課遲到了」，所以用 late。lately 是「最近」。

4. lately

句意為「最近」的意思，而且為現在完成式，所以用 lately。

5. near

near 是在位置上表示「近的」之地方副詞。

6. nearly

nearly 是「幾乎」的意思，和 almost 的意思一樣，用來修飾動詞或 all、every、always 等。

7. still

yet 不能用在肯定句中。already 是「已經」的意思，和句中的 is snowing 意思不符。

8. already

yet 不能用在肯定句中。still 和句中的完成式 have eaten 意思不符。

9. still

still 若用在否定句中，要放在 not 前面。already 和 yet 不能放在 not 前面。

10. ③ hardly

hardly 和 ever 或 any 一起使用時，就是表示 never 或 no 的意思。從句意來看，在 and 後面要接否定含義的字，所以 hardly 最恰當。

11. ④ still

still 主要用在肯定句，指「仍然」，其中還含有「但是」

的意味。句中因為有「沒有時間」和「幫助」這對立的含義，所以用「但是」來連接是很自然的。

12. ③ late

turn in 是「繳交、提出」。從句意來看，空格應該要填入「晚地、遲地」這意思的字，所以 late 最恰當。

Chapter 7 單元綜合問題

1. ② big black bug

形容大小的形容詞，要放在顏色形容詞之前。

2. ② currently

副詞修飾動詞。

3. ③ well enough

副詞修飾動詞 walk。well 是副詞，enough 一定要放在後面修飾它，所以 well enough 才是正確的。

4. ② So good a market

要用「so＋形容詞＋不定冠詞 a＋名詞」這個順序。

5. ③ recent

lately 和 recently 是「在最近」的意思，要單獨使用，不能用來修飾形容詞或副詞。如果用 late，翻譯為「晚的簡報」，不符合句意；用 recent，翻譯為「最近的簡報」，才是正確答案。

6. ① still

still 用在否定句時，要放在 not 之前；而 always 要放在 not 之後。already 不能用在否定句中。never 和 not 兩者意義重複。

7. ① bad

smell 為不完全不及物動詞，所以後面要接形容詞。

8. ② Nearly

nearly 和 almost 都是副詞「大概」的意思，大多用來修飾數字。close 是形容詞「親密的」的意思，closely 是副詞「緊密地、親密地」的意思。

9. ② too much

emphasis 是名詞。③ very 不能修飾名詞。④ much too 是 too 的強調用法，和 too 一樣，不能修飾名詞。① enough 可以修飾名詞；但從句意來看，是「受到了批評」的意思，所以不能用肯定含義的 enough。② too much 是 much 的強調用法，可用來修飾名詞。

10. ② moist woods

moist 是形容詞，「潮濕的」的意思。順序為「形容詞＋名詞」，所以 ② 是正確答案。

11. easy → easily

can 和 get 之間是不能有形容詞。副詞修飾動詞。

12. so

excited 是形容詞，such 不能修飾形容詞；enough 要放在被修飾的形容詞後面；too 可以修飾 excited，但是因為後面有 that 子句，所以也不能用 too。

13. lately → late

句意為「工作到很晚」。lately 是「最近」的意思；late 才是「晚的、晚地」的意思，可以當形容詞，也可以當副詞，所以 work late 為正確答案。

14. noisy

noise 的形容詞是 noisy。

15. ③ socially → social

名詞 discussions 被 social、political、philosophical 三個形容詞修飾。② religious city 雖然是「形容詞＋名詞」的形式，不過實際是「宗教都市」這含意的複合名詞。④ 形容詞 popular 修飾名詞 drink，是正確的用法。⑤ nearly 和 almost 一樣都是副詞「大概」的意思，大多用來修飾數字。

16. ③ permanently → permanent

形容詞 permanent 修飾後面的名詞 loss。

17. ④ competitively → competitive

因為是 be 動詞的補語，所以要用形容詞 competitive 才正確。

18. ④ democratically → democratic

became 是不完全不及物動詞，所以後面要有形容詞當作補語。orderly 是名詞 order 加-ly，為形容詞。

19. ② full → fully

free 和 fully 是修飾動詞 use 的副詞，free 可當作形容詞，也可當作副詞，在這裡是副詞。而 full 是形容詞，要改成 fully 才是副詞。

20. ② can't hardly → can't 或 can hardly

因為 hardly 含有 not 的否定含義，所以在兩個否定字當中要刪除一個。

21. ④ already → yet

否定句要用 yet。

22. ② automatical → automatically

program 是名詞，也是主詞；searches 是動詞；副詞 automatically 修飾動詞。

23. ④ alone → lone

alone 是敘述形容詞，所以不能修飾名詞。

24. such → so

similar 是形容詞，不能用 such，要用 so 來修飾。

25. enough safe → safe enough

enough 要放在形容詞後面，修飾形容詞。

26. ④ way healthy → healthy way

way 是名詞，healthy 是形容詞；形容詞要放在名詞前面。

49

1.

I have just moved to a house in Bridge Street. Yesterday a beggar knocked at my door. He asked me for a meal and a glass of beer. In return for this, the beggar stood on his head and sang songs. I gave him a meal. He ate the food and drank the beer. Then he put a piece of cheese in his pocket and went away.

2.

of popular singers 是修飾 a group 的形容詞。at present 是表示「現在」的副詞。of the country 是修飾 all parts 的形容詞。by train 是修飾 coming 的副詞。of the young people 是修飾 most 的形容詞。at the station 是修飾 meeting 的副詞。at the Workers' Club 是修飾 singing 的副詞。for five days 是修飾 staying 的副詞。During this time 是修飾整個句子的副詞。As usual 是修飾整個句子的副詞。

3. ① downstairs

downstairs 是副詞，前面不能有冠詞或介系詞。

4. ④ Unlike

unlike 是介系詞，unlike cows and horses 是介系詞片語。介系詞片語若加逗點，就是副詞的功能。Unlikely 雖是副詞，但不符合此句用法。若用 the 或 many，the/many cows and horses 整句就是名詞，在句中當主詞、受詞或補語。因為 human being 之後是完整的句子，所以 human being 的前面不需要加名詞。

50

1. in
年度前面要用 in。

2. at
時間前面要用 at。

3. on
一般都用 in the afternoon，但是如果 afternoon 前面加了星期，那就要用 on Saturday afternoon。

4. Ø

若加了 next，就不能再加時間介系詞。

5. in

季節前要用 in。

6. on

因為是貼附在上面，所以要用 on。

7. at

在停車場，所以要用 at。

8. at

坐在椅子上用 on，但坐在餐桌或書桌前要用 at。

9. off

「遠離草地」的意思；「遠離」的片語是 keep off。

10. off

因為是從車上下來，所以要用 off。out 和 away 不是介系詞。

11. away from

從句意來看，是「遠離……」的意思。

12. ② at — in

restaurant 前面加的介系詞，可以是 in 也可以是 at。因為 Attleborough 是大場所，所以用 in。

13. ③ on

日期前面的介系詞用 on。

14. ④ every

一般都用 in the morning。但如果用 every morning，前面就不能再加介系詞了。

51

1. above

因為是在安全門標示的上方，所以要用 above。

2. over

「跳過籬笆」，可以看作是「在籬笆之上」。

3. up

持續 run 這個動作，要用 up。

4. over

雨傘「遮蓋」我們。

5. under

躲在床下，就是在床的「下方」。

6. down

因為是「向下跌落」的意思，所以要用 down。

7. below

溫度下降到……之下，要用 below。

8. ③ down

因為眼淚一定是向下流，所以不能用 up。

9. ① above

溫度上升到……之上，要用 above。

10. ② over

是用手「遮住」眼睛，所以要用 over。

11. ④ under

把臉埋到棉被下面，所以要用 under。

1. through

用 through 以表示「貫通」隧道之意。

2. around

因為是「繞著桌子坐」的意思，所以用 around。

3. across

「橋橫跨過河」的意思，所以用 across。

4. across

「橫越過鐵軌線」的意思，所以用 across。

5. around

turn around 是「轉身」之意。

6. through

「穿過窗戶」的意思，所以用 through。

7. along

「沿著」路走，所以用 along。

8. between

在兩者之間，所以用 between。

9. among

在樹林裡，即「在許多樹之間」，所以用 among。

10. opposite

opposite 表示相對。

11. next to

並排地「坐在旁邊」的意思。

12. opposite

馬路兩側對立的建築物，是「相對的」，用 opposite。

13. among

句意為「警察之間的普遍看法」，所以用 among。

14. ① between

因為是「兩者之間」，所以用 between。

53

1. for, since

表示「動作持續一段時間」就用 for；表示「動作持續一段時間的起點」時，用 since。

2. during, for

during 表示「在……期間」。表示「動作持續的一段時間」，用 for。

3. for

「for＋一段時間」。

4. since

自從 2008 年表示「一段時間的起點」。

5. during

during 表示「在暴風雨期間」。

6. for

for a long time 指「持續好長一段時間」，為慣用語。

7. since

8. during

during 表示「在短暫休息期間」。

9. ① During

during 表示「在水災期間」。

10. ② for

a decade 是「十年」的意思，表示「一段時間」。

11. ③ since

動詞是 has gone，時態為現在完成式，the siege of Tora Bora 可表示「一段時間的起點」，所以用 since。

54

1. until

live 為表示「持續」的動詞。

2. by

leave 為表示「瞬間」的動詞。

3. by

be back 為「回來」的意思，表示瞬間。

4. until

wait 為表示「期間」的動詞。

5. by

pay back 為表示「瞬間」的動詞。

6. by

finish 為表示「瞬間」的動詞。

7. by

hand in 為表示「瞬間」的動詞。

8. until

因為 be away 是「去了某處，不在的時候」之意，所以表示「一段時間」。

9. by

reach 為表示「瞬間」的動詞。

10. in

half an hour 為表示「一段時間」的片語，要用 in。

11. after

本句是比較「午餐時間」和「睡午覺」的順序。

12. within

two hours 表示「一段時間」。

13. before

本句是比較「考試」和「感覺緊張」的先後順序。

14. ① by

get to 為表示「瞬間」的動詞。

15. ③ until

stay 為表示期間的動詞。

55

1. As

主詞 I 和 parent 為同一人，所以用 as（身為……）。

2. for

「往曼徹斯特的火車」的意思，要用 for。

3. over

因為是支配「整個班級」的權威，所以要用 over。

4. for

表示「理由」，所以用 for。

5. ③

提示句是「背貼著地仰躺」，所以介系詞 on 是「接觸」的意思。① 的 on 是 about 的意思。② 的 on 是「根據」的意思。③ 是「倒立」，有「接觸」地面的意思。

6. ③

提示句中的 at 是「對準」的意思。① 的 at 表示地點。

② 的 at 表示刺激。③ 的 at 是對準之意。

7. ④ on — by

因為 bike 前面有 his , 所以要用 on。而 bus 前面沒有加冠詞，所以要用 by。

8. ① for

表示「理由」時，要用 for。be famous for 是慣用語。

9. ② off

因為是將靴子上的泥巴「刮除」，所以要用 off。

56

1. ③ worth the price

worth 是介系詞，worthy 是形容詞。worthy 後不能接受詞，worth 後要接受詞。④worth buying 才對。

2. ① In addition to

因為 Morse is well . . . 是完全子句，所以從空格到 accomplishments 必須是副詞。除了要填入的字，其他都是名詞，所以可以推斷空格要填入介系詞，整句才能是副詞。beside 雖然是介系詞，但意思是「在 . . . 旁邊」，表示地點，不能用在這裡。

3. ③ concerning

whether 之後是名詞子句，differ 是不及物動詞，後面不能接受詞，這裡應該要加介系詞。concerning 是介系詞，和 about 意思相同，其他的都不是介系詞。

4. ④ biased towards

① 的 bias 可當名詞或動詞使用。如果當名詞，後面的 the government 也是名詞；一個句子不能有兩個名詞，所以不正確。如果是動詞，前面有 was，be 動詞後面不能接原型動詞。② was biased 是被動語態，後面的 the government 是受詞，而被動語態後面不能接受詞，所以不正確。③ 介系詞 towards 後面接名詞，但 biased 不是名詞，所以不正確。④ was biased 是被動語態，towards 是介系詞，「介系詞＋名詞」是正確的。

5. ① he → him

but 是介系詞，所以後面要接受格 him。

6. ① Alike → Like

alike 是敘述形容詞，後面不能接名詞。most of us 是 like 的受詞，而 like most of us 整個是副詞的功能。

7. ① Despite of → Despite

despite 是介系詞，等於 in spite of；despite of 不是介系詞。

8. ③ because of → because

because 是連接詞，because of 是介系詞。it was

delivered late 不是名詞，所以不能當作 because of 的受詞，因此要改為 because 這樣的連接詞才正確。

Chapter 8 單元綜合問題

1. ③ Three hours ago

回答 when 的問題，用確實的時間「三小時前」回答即正確。①「從三小時前開始」的意思。②「持續了三小時」的意思。④「三小時後」的意思。

2. ④ Unlike most

unlike 是介系詞，most other big cats 是受詞，unlike . . . cats 整個是副詞的功能。

3. ② during

用 during class 表示「上課中」。

4. ⑤ in — on — for

北京是都市，所以用 in。Monday 是指某一天，所以用 on。表示「為了……」這目的時，要用「to 不定詞」，或「for＋名詞」，而 talks 是名詞，「會談」之意，所以前面加 for。

5. ③ by

finish 為表示「瞬間」的動詞，所以用 by。

6. ① for

「for＋一段時間」。

7. ③ this

一般都用 in the morning；但如果加 this、every，變成 this morning 或 every morning 時，前面就不能再加介系詞了。

8. ① across

across the island 是「遍及整個島」的意思。

9. ① between

「between A and B」是「在 A 和 B 之間」之意。「between law and order」整個當作形容詞，用來修飾前面的 the relationship。

10. ① above

從句意來看，應該要填入和 below 相反含意的字，所以 above 才是正確答案。

11. ② as

as 是「身為……」的意思。

12. ⑤ over — for — on

「整個東京」，所以要用 over Tokyo。「for＋一段時間 (six days)」。葉子上長白點，而白點是附在葉子上的，所以用 on。

13. until, for, between

were taught 是表示期間的動詞，所以要用 until。for ＋一段時間」。在 16 和 20 兩者之間，要用 between。

14. ④ seem → seems

seem 的主詞是 the connection，為單數名詞，所以 seem 加 s。

15. our trip across the field and through the woods

across 是「橫過、越過」; through 是「穿過、貫穿」。

16. ③ Through — like

through 是介系詞，thorough 是形容詞。形容詞後面不能有 the。網路不是圖書館，而是「網路扮演了像圖書館一樣功能」的意思，所以要用 like，不能用 as。

17. ③ Alike fingerprints → Like fingerprints

alike 是敘述形容詞，不能修飾名詞。要用 like，變成 like fingerprints 這個介系詞片語，整個當作副詞。

18. ① In → On

日期前面的介系詞要用 on。

19. ② since → for

「for＋一段時間」，在這裡是 5 years。

20. ① After three days → In three days

比較 A 和 B 的先後順序時才用 after；而 three days 是一段時間，所以不能和其他要素或順序比較。這裡用 in，表示「三天之後」。

21. ① to → and

因為 1906 和 1917 是兩個時間，所以要用 and 連接。

22. ④ over → for

從句意來看，是「為了廣告，空間被保留下來」，表目的要用 for。

23. ③ it gives → gives

Blood 是主詞，in vessels . . . lining 是介系詞片語，用來修飾主詞。因此 gives 應該就是本句的動詞，it 完全沒作用，所以將它刪去。

57

1. ② I like

因為用了連接詞 although，所以可以知道句子裡一定有兩個子句。因為從空格開始又是另一個子句，所以要用 I like 才對。

2. ④ put

因為從 because 開始，是「連接詞＋子句」，所以空格處要填入動詞，使這部份也變成一個子句。putting

或原型動詞 be 都不能用。

3. ③ because of

以空格為基準，前面是以動詞 am writing 引導的子句，而空格後沒有動詞，所以沒有子句。因此空格就不能放連接詞，要用 because of 介系詞。

4. If

if 是用來連接「you could solve . . .」和「would you let . . .」這兩個子句的。

5. 沒有

因為整個句子只有一個子句，所以不需要連接詞。

6. but

but 是用來連接「Rachel is . . .」和「she's never played . . . 」這兩個子句的。

7. Ø

要用連接詞的話，就要有兩個子句。有兩個子句，也就等於要有兩個動詞。而本句只有一個動詞「has thought of」，「From . . . age」是介系詞片語。

8. Even → Although

要連結 he has . . . 和 he never . . . 兩個子句，就需要有連接詞來連接，不過 even 是副詞不是連接詞，而從句意來看，需要的是 although 這意思的連接詞。

9. they buy → buying

instead of 是介系詞，後面不能接子句。若要接子句，就要變成連接詞，不過沒有和 instead of 意思一樣的連接詞，所以必須把後面的子句換成名詞或動名詞。

10. being → is

用連接詞 and 來連接兩個子句。所以不能用 being 來當作動詞，要換成 is。

58

1. in the evenings **or** at weekends

2. jumped into the river **and** swam to the other side

3. go out with our friends **or** stay at home listening to music

4. attractive **but** functional

5. ② but

因為兩個子句的內容是互相對立的，所以要用 but。

6. ③ or

either 通常和 or 連用。

7. and

從回答的句子推斷，可以知道是指 milk 和 cocoa 兩者，所以用 and 連接。

8. or

從回答的句子推斷，可以知道是指 milk 和 cocoa 兩者中選一，所以用 or 連接。

9. but

「想打電話，但沒辦法打」，所以要用 but。

10. or

兩者選一，表示選擇，所以用 or。

11. but

「平常開車上下班，但是今天搭公車」，所以用 but。

12. and

「⋯⋯和⋯⋯」，連接詞為 and。

59

1. ④ there are

因為空格前的 that 是連接詞，所以空格後應該是完全子句。依照句意，完全子句應該是「有⋯⋯」的意思，即「there＋be 動詞＋名詞片語」。主詞是複數，所以用 are。

2. ① seems

That ... others，是 that 子句的主詞。所以空格應該要填入動詞。

3. ④

that 子句放在介系詞 on 的後面是錯誤用法。that 子句不能當介系詞的受詞使用。

4. she has gone back to teaching →主詞

如果用 that 子句當主詞，可以用 it 來代替原來的 that 子句，並把 that 子句移到句尾，這時連接詞 that 可以省略。

5. that rickets was caused by a vitamin deficiency →及物動詞的受詞

that 子句位在及物動詞 understood 之後，當受詞。

6. the boys are too impatient →補語

that 子句當作補語時，that 可以省略。

7. that stress is partially responsible for disease →和名詞 evidence 是同位語

從整個句子的結構來看，you 是主詞，have 是動詞，evidence 是受詞。而且如果沒有 that 子句，仍是一個完全子句；因此 that 子句的功能，就是具體說明前面那個名詞，和名詞為同位語。

8. that people in cities . . . their neighbors →主詞

It 是虛主詞，that 子句是真正的主詞。

9. that the intelligent worker . . . the unintelligent one →和名詞 one reason 是同位語／that the intelligent person →補語

因為第一個 that 子句位在 one reason 之後，所以 that 子句一定是 one reason 的同位語。因為第二個 that 子句位在 is 之後，所以 that 子句是 is 的補語。

60

1. ④ how I can

show 是第四類句型的動詞，必須有兩個受詞；在這裡 me 是間接受詞，how 的疑問詞子句是直接受詞。因為疑問詞子句的句型是「疑問詞＋直述句」，所以 ④ 是正確答案。

2. ③ what

疑問詞子句中，因為 the other 是主詞，said 是動詞，所以需要 what 來當作 said 的受詞。

3. ② that

該用 that 子句，還是疑問詞子句，除了要由整個句子的結構來判斷之外，子句本身的形式也是判斷的重要標準。the adult gorilla 是主詞，is 是動詞，a friendly animal 是補語。句子本身沒有不足的部份，因此不能填入 what、who、which 等。應該要填入 that，形成 that 子句。

4. ① which

「which＋名詞」或「what＋名詞」，整個當作疑問詞。which ice cream 是「which＋名詞」的形式，在整個疑問詞子句中當作 likes 的受詞。Alice 是主詞，the best 是副詞。如果用 who 或 why，就不是直述句，所以不正確。

5. Why

從句首到 so terrible，都是疑問詞子句當主詞。因為 the man 是主詞，did 是動詞，something 是受詞，所以疑問詞應該要用副詞。

6. What

從句首到 Shuttle 是名詞子句當主詞。如果用 that 子句，沒有主詞，直接接 will 也不正確。所以要用 what，what 也當作 will 的主詞。

7. that → whether

that 子句不能當作 don't know 的受詞，因此要將 that 子句換成疑問詞子句，因為子句本身很完整，所以只要將疑問詞改為 whether 即正確。

8. will they → they will

how long 是疑問詞，they 是主詞，will stay 是動詞。

9. 正確句子

在以 how 為首的疑問詞子句中，teacher feedback 是主詞，affect 是動詞，students 是受詞，how 當副詞，所以這個句子是正確的。

10. that → whether

因為 that 子句不可當介系詞的受詞，所以 that 子句要換成疑問詞子句。而疑問詞子句整個並沒有不足的部份，所以只要在疑問詞的位置上填入 whether 即可。

61

1. ① 名詞子句　② 副詞子句

① 因為 if 子句位在 know 之後，所以是 know 的受詞，名詞子句可以當作受詞，副詞子句不能，所以可以推斷 if 子句是名詞子句。② 因為 should not be forced 是被語動態，所以後面不能有受詞，可以推斷 if 子句是副詞子句。

2. ⓓ That seat belts save lives

因為空格後是動詞 has been proven，所以空格要填入當作主詞的名詞子句。ⓑ 和 ⓓ 皆為名詞子句，但從句意判斷，ⓓ 較正確。

3. ⓐ Although they no longer love each other

逗點後的 the couple 之後是完全子句，所以空格要填入副詞子句。ⓐ 和 ⓒ 皆為副詞子句，但從句意判斷，ⓐ 較正確。

4. ⓑ that my keys are missing

空格是 have noticed 的受詞，所以應填入名詞子句。

5. ⓒ because it causes the plant to freeze

Frost . . . vegetation 是完全子句，所以空格要填入副詞子句。

6. ④ When

因為句子裡有兩個子句，所以應填入連接詞。如果用 that 就是名詞子句，當作主詞或受詞；但是這裡需要的是副詞子句，所以要填入 when，形成副詞子句。

7. ③ melted

When . . . hot water 是副詞子句，所以從 the wax 開始應該是主要子句，空格應填入動詞。又因為整個句子是過去時態，所以用過去式 melted。

8. ① as

空格應填入連接詞，以連接兩個子句。因為 during 是介系詞，所以不能用在這裡。that 和 what 是引導名詞子句，as 是引導副詞子句。因為 Rache . . . eggs

是完全子句，不需要其他的名詞子句，空格之後為副詞子句，所以用 as 最正確。

62

1. Because

表示「理由」，所以用 because。

2. Even though

依照句意，所以選擇 even though 才正確。

3. unless

unless 是「除非……」的意思。從和 disappointed 的關係看來，用 unless 最恰當。

4. if

從和 delighted 的關係看來，用 if 最正確。

5. so that

so that 是「……，以致……」，表示目的的連接詞。

6. as

so 如果當連接詞，就一定要有兩個子句。「just as . . . so」是慣用語，所以用 as。

7. that

和前面的 so 搭配使用，that 子句引導表示結果的副詞子句。

8. ④

① if 子句裡不能有 will，所以句子是錯誤的。在條件副詞子句中，不能有表示未來的助動詞 will。② during 是介系詞，不能引導子句；要將 during 換成 while 才正確。③ as 子句是副詞子句，不能當 know 的受詞，要將 as 換成 whether 才正確。

9. ② Although

從選項看來，都是引導副詞子句的連接詞。依照句意，所以 although 才正確。

10. ① so

boring 是形容詞，不能用 much，其他的 so、very、too 都可以修飾形容詞。不過因為要考慮和後面的 that 子句的關係，所以答案為 so；如此，後面的 that 子句就可以當作表示結果的副詞子句。

Chapter 9　單元綜合問題

1. ① it

because 是連接詞，所以後面要接子句。reproduces 是動詞，所以空格應該要填入主詞。

2. ③ during

空格後的 the early years of life on Earth 不是子句，而是個很長的名詞，所以空格不能填入連接詞，要填介系詞。選項中只有 during 是介系詞。

3. ③ and winds are

① winds to be prevalent 中，to be prevalent 用來修飾 winds，整個是一個名詞，但在整句中沒有作用。② 因為變成 winds are prevalent 子句，所以前面應該要有連接詞。④ that 也是連接詞，不過其引導的是名詞子句，就像 ① 一樣，在整句中沒有作用。③ 兩個子句用對等連接詞 and 連接，所以是正確答案。

4. ② How

從空格到 the sea，應該是名詞子句當作主詞，而且要和 is not known 連接。如果是用 how 的話，就變成疑問詞子句；如果是用 that 的話，就變成 that 子句。空格填入 that 或 how 形式上都正確，不過要依句意來選擇。要選擇 how，整個句意才通順。

5. ② That measles

that measles is caused by a virus 是名詞子句，是 was not known 的主詞。as 或 since 是副詞子句連接詞，要引導副詞子句，不能當主詞。這裡的 that 子句可當 was not known 的主詞，且 that 子句的事實現在已闡明，不過當時是不知道的，在邏輯上也沒有錯。

6. ④ Although

從空格到 to say 應是副詞子句。依照句意，although 最正確。

7. ① so

從後面 that 子句的關係推斷，應該要用 so。that 子句前若有 so，that 子句就是表示「結果」的副詞子句。

8. ② either

後面有 or，表示兩者其中之一，前面應該有 either。

9. ① unless

應填入連接詞，however 是副詞，所以不正確。that 引導名詞子句，也不正確。unless 和 although 是副詞子句連接詞，當補述；從句意判斷，unless 較正確。

10. ② until she

此題可依據句子的結構，來判斷用哪一個連接詞。由 not . . . until 是「直到……才……」。but she，不符句意。that she，變成名詞子句，不符形式。

11. ④ why Jane failed the driving test

wonder 後面不能用 that 子句當受詞，要用疑問詞子句當受詞。② who 沒有任何功能，因為 who 後面有主詞 Jane。③ did Jane fail 是疑問句，所以不正確。④ why Jane failed 直述句才正確。

12. ④

① because 是連接詞，後面要接子句。而 rapidly . . . developing world 是名詞，continued growth . . . nations 也是名詞，所以要將 because 換成 because of 這個介系詞，才能接名詞。② 是 Researchers found that 子句的結構，所以 understanding 要換成 understand 動詞的形式，才是子句。and 後面的 become 是和 understand 對比，所以 and 後面又再加一個子句。③ that 子句被當作介系詞 on 的受詞，所以是錯誤用法。要將 that 換成 whether。

13. why did he look → why he looked

疑問詞的子句不能用疑問句，要用直述句。

14. if, so that, what

unless 是「除非」的意思，是個有否定含義的連接詞；因此 unless 後不能有 not。consequently 不是連接詞，而是副詞，不能連接子句和子句。think of 後面要接名詞（或名詞子句）當作受詞。as 引導的子句是副詞子句，所以不能當作 think of 的受詞。

15. ③ and — until

therefore 是副詞，不是連接詞。not . . . until 是慣用片語。

16. ③ having made → has made

句子裡應該要有動詞，having made 是錯誤用法；要換成現在完成式 has made 才正確。

17. ③ during → while

during 是介系詞，不能引導子句。during 後的 they are doing 是子句。

18. ③ too realistic → so realistic

要將 too 換成 so，才能接後面的 that 子句。

19. ① when did Peter ask me → when Peter asked me

疑問詞的子句要用直述句。② 的 if 子句一般當作副詞子句，但也可當動詞的受詞，這裡當 ask 的受詞。

20. ③ that → what

in 是介系詞，that 子句不能當介系詞的受詞。若將 what 變成疑問詞子句，同時 what 又是 would 的主詞，就是完全子句了。

21. ③ so → when

「so it arrived, it was the wrong size」整個是 but 後的子句，而且這個子句用 so 這個連接詞來連接，表示結果，不過 so 不能放在第一句子句前，一定要放在第二句子句前才正確。把 so 換成 when，when it arrived 就變成了副詞子句，it was the wrong size 變成主要子句，這樣才是正確的。

22. ① That → Unless

that 子句是名詞子句，當作主詞或受詞。在這裡因為從 we feel 之後是完全子句，所以不需要主詞或受詞；因此要把 that 子句換成副詞子句，然後把 that 換成副詞子句的連接詞。而副詞子句連接詞有好多個，依照句意判斷，用 unless 最正確。

63

1. who played at the concert last night

the pianist 後面的 who . . . last night 是關係詞子句。

2. which is made up of different aspects

something 後面的 which . . . aspects 是關係詞子句。

3. that we think to be important

名詞 Jobs 後面的 that . . . important 是關係詞子句。

4. when I felt bored with what I was doing, what I was doing

many times 後面的 when 到最後都是關係詞子句，在其中又有 what I was doing 這個關係詞子句。

5. 修飾 cakes → The cakes which Melanie baked were delicious.

關係詞子句修飾名詞，句中的名詞只有 the cakes。

6. 修飾 woman → I wrote a letter to the woman whom I met at the meeting.

名詞有 a letter 和 a woman，從關係詞子句的內容判斷，應該是修飾 woman。

7. 修飾 couple → The couple who have moved to our neighborhood have twelve grandchildren.

從關係詞子句 who 的內容判斷，是修飾 the couple。

8. 修飾 machine → A typewriter is a machine which is used to print letters.

從關係詞子句的內容判斷，應該是修飾 machine。

9. ③ who know

從空格到 personalities 是一個子句，people can be . . . 又是一個子句。連接子句和子句要用關係詞，其他代名詞不能連接子句和子句。

10. ① it

兩個子句用連接詞 and 連接。因為主詞 the old vila 是單數，所以代名詞用 it。

11. ④ that covers

Bark is the rough surface 整個是完全子句，後面又連接另一個子句。這兩個子句要用關係代名詞連接。③的 covering 不能當動詞，所以不正確。

64

1. which

先行詞 phone 是事物，所以關係詞不能用 who。

2. who

先行詞是 woman，所以關係詞用 who。

3. that

先行詞是 woman，關係詞不能用 which；但可用 that。

4. that

先行詞 the greatest nurse 是最高級，最高級要用 that。

5. is a gas which (that) forms when water boils

從句意來看，不是修飾 steam，而是修飾 gas。

6. who sat next to me on the train ate candies the the whole way

He 指 little boy，所以要放在 little boy 後面。

7. which (that) went off near my neighborhood caused a lot of damage

It 指 the bomb，所以要放在 the bomb 後面。

8. which (that) you can give me would be greatly appreciated

將兩個 any advice 彼此連接起來。

9. ③ who

從空格開始到 directions，必須是關係詞子句才正確。因為先行詞是 lady，所以關係詞不能用 which，要用 who。用 to 形成不定詞，也可以用來修飾 lady，不過這樣 gave 就要改成原型動詞 give 才正確。

10. ④ that

因為先行詞中有 the only，所以要用 that。

65

1. who has an earring sometimes sleeps

he 指 that guy。

2. is carrying out research on artistic talents which children have

them 指 artistic talents，所以關係子句要接在 artistic talents 之後。

3. has an alphabet which (that) consists of 26 letters

it 指 alphabet，所以關係子句要接在 alphabet 之後。

4. which

先行詞 capital 是事物，所以關係詞不能用 who。

5. whom

先行詞是 movie star，也是關係詞子句中 admire 的受詞，所以要用 whom。

6. who

先行詞是 anyone，所以關係詞用 who。

7. whom

先行詞是嫌犯 suspect，也是關係子句中 questioning 的受詞，所以關係詞用 whom。

8. who

先行詞是 few people，是關係詞子句中 might be 的主詞。who might be ... job 整個是 I think 的受詞。

9. ④ who are

先行詞 those women 是複數。因為先行詞是複數，關係代名詞就是複數，動詞也要用複數動詞。

10. ② had taken

這是將 the peaches 和 her sister 之間的關係代名詞受格的 which 省略的句子。因此空格中要填入及物動詞，而且不能有及物動詞的受詞，因為被省略的關係代名詞，就是及物動詞的受詞。

66

1. is an American architect whose works won $5,000 in the contest

his 就是指前面的 an American architect，所以關係子句要接在 an American architect 之後。his 要換成 whose，並放在關係子句的最前面。

2. is the father whose son the actress has seduced

his 指 the father，所以關係子句要放在 the father 之後。his 要換成 whose，並和 son 一起放在關係子句的最前面。

3. must look up words whose meanings we do not know

their 指 words，所以關係子句要放在 words 之後。their meanings 要換成 whose meanings，然後放到關係子句的最前面。

4. whose

從空格開始到 broke 是關係子句，其中 my son 是主詞，broke 是及物動詞。所以前面應該變成 whose nose 的形式，當作 broke 的受詞。

5. which

先行詞 every drug 是事物。關係詞子句中，doctors 是主詞，try 是及物動詞，which 代表的 every drug 是受詞。

6. whose

在關係子句中 whose personality 是主詞，is 是動詞，like mine 是補語。

7. ④ whose

因為沒有連接詞，所以要用關係詞來連結。在關係子句中，whose project 是主詞，was 是動詞，the most successful 是補語。如果空格不填關係詞，也可以用 and her project was ... 這形式。

8. ③ which

從關係子句本身來看，his wife 是主詞，has been accumulating 是及物動詞，所以應該填入受格的關係代名詞。

9. ② house was

所有格 whose 後一定要接名詞，變成 whose house，是關係子句裡的主詞。像 ① 那樣後面直接接動詞 robbed，就不能沒有受詞。若改成被動語態 was robbed，沒有受詞就可以。如果選 ④，he 是主詞，was robbed 是動詞，而因是被動語態，所以後面不能接受詞 whose house。

67

1. is the book from which I obtained the information

兩句都有 the book，所以要換成關係詞。因為 book 是 from 的受詞，所以要和 from 一起，變成 from which 的形式移到關係詞子句的最前面。

2. gazed around the room in which his entire family were assembled

兩句都有 the room，所以要換成關係詞。因為 room 是 in 的受詞，所以要和 in 一起，變成 in which 的形式，移到關係詞子句的最前面。

3. of which his father is very proud were wasted in the boring job

them 是指 artistic talents，所以 them 要換成關係詞，而這關係詞又是 of 的受詞，所以 of 也要一起往前移。

4. who → whom

因為 who 是 with 的受詞，所以要換成受格 whom。

5. in that → in which

關係代名詞 that 不能放在介系詞之後，所以 that 要換成 which。

6. in which → which

如果用 in which，which 是 in 的受詞，就不能是 is 的主詞了。所以要將 in 刪除，which 變成 is 的主詞，這樣才是正確的句子。

7. 正確句子

把 from which 移到 made 後面，關係子句變成 the copy is made from which (the original)，是正確用法，所以本句無誤。

8. with which → which

因為 which 是 have 的受詞，所以 with 要刪除。這樣關係詞子句變成「I have which (something) to speak to you」(我有事要跟你說)，才是正確的用法。

9. ① in which

which 是 are interested in 的受詞，所以 in 要一起移到前面，變成 in which。

10. ③ in which

如果空格填入 which，which 就是關係子句裡的主詞或受詞。不過關係子句中的 the author 是主詞，describes 是動詞，his own experiences 是受詞，沒有 which 的位置；所以要用 in which，變成 in the book，這樣的副詞形式才正確。

68

1. recently went back to the village where I was brought up

there 指 village，所以 there 要改成 where，置於 village 後，引導關係子句。

2. still remember the day when we first saw the Grand Canyon?

then 指 the day，所以 then 要改成 when，置於 day 後，引導關係子句。

3. where

因為 lived 是不及物動詞，所以需要表示地點的副詞；where 有副詞的功能。

4. which

因為介系詞 in 需要受詞，所以要選擇有名詞功能的 which。

5. which

先行詞 month 是表示時間的名詞，但是在關係子句中需要 has 的主詞，所以要用 which。

6. when

在關係子句中 Monsoons 是主詞，arrive 是不及物動詞，所以需要副詞以形成正確的子句。

7. why

如果先行詞是 reason，關係詞就只能用 why。

8. where

在關係子句中 he 是主詞，is living 是不及物動詞，所以需要地方副詞 where。

9. ① where

因為關係子句是「there is＋名詞片語」是完全子句。所以空格需要副詞，不是名詞，又因為先行詞是 beach，所以表示地方的 where 最正確。

10. ③ which

因為空格在介系詞 at 之後，which 可以當受詞的關係代名詞，所以是正確答案。

11. ④ where

people 是主詞，use 是動詞，computers 是受詞，a lot 是副詞，所以要填入地方副詞 where。

69

1. a friend buys almost all the things online

關係代名詞 who 是關係子句的主詞。把 who 換成先行詞 a friend，然後當作是動詞 buys 的主詞即可。

2. the U.S. government describes the countries as terrorists

省略的關係代名詞 that 是 describes 的受詞。把 that 換成先行詞 the countries，放到 describes 之後即可。

3. the metric system is based on the standards

be based on 是慣用語，為「根據……」。把 on which 換成 on the standards，然後移到 based 之後即可。

4. ① where

關係詞子句裡 most fire deaths 是主詞，occur 是不及物動詞。所以應填入有「在家裡」這含義的副詞。

5. ② to which

return to A 是慣用語，為「把……還給 A」之意，所以應填入 to which。

6. ② I wrote to you about

關係子句的句意是「我寫給你的信中提到的那位老師」，所以是 I wrote to you about the teacher。這裡只有 the teacher 換成關係詞移到前面去，然後又被省略，所以就剩下 I wrote to you about。

7. ③ have faced them → have faced

關係代名詞 which，是關係子句中 faced 的受詞，所以 faced 後的 them 應該要刪去。

70

1. what

因為沒有先行詞，所以用 what。

2. that / which

因為先行詞是 the words，所以用 that 或 which。

3. that

先行詞是 everything。

4. What

因為沒有先行詞，所以用 what。

5. that / which

the words 是先行詞。

6. that / which

two liquids 是先行詞。

7. what

因為沒有先行詞，所以用 what。

8. what

因為沒有先行詞，所以用 what。

9. ② What is needed

因為沒有先行詞，所以不能用 that。④ 如果改為 what you need，what 是 need 的受詞，這樣就正確了。

10. ④ what

因為是 of 的受詞，所以需要名詞子句。因為沒有先行詞，所以不能用 that。any 或 the 都不能形成名詞。所以用 what，在 what painting should be 中，what 被當作是 be 動詞的補語。

11. ③ what the right hand is doing

the right hand 是主詞，is doing 是動詞，what 是受詞。關係子句除了關係詞會有例外，其他都是直述句。

71

1. made an appointment with Professor Marvin, who teaches marine biology

因為先行詞 Professor Marvin 是「人名」，所以關係詞之前一定要加逗點。

2. traveled to Egypt, where we saw the pyramids

因為先行詞 Egypt 是「專有名詞」，所以關係詞之前一定要加逗點。

3. had to wait for over half an hour, which annoyed them very much

which 的先行詞是「前面的整個子句」，這也是在關係

詞之前要加逗點的情形。

4. ②

② which 的先行詞是前面整個子句，所以 which 前加逗點是正確的。① CERN 是「歐洲核子研究委員會」，是專有名詞，所以 which 前要加逗點。③ that 可以代替 who，不過前面不能加逗點。④ 在沒有連接詞的情況下，用關係詞連接兩個子句。所以要將 and all of whom 改成 and all of them，或者刪除 and 變成 all of whom 皆可。

5. ④ , where

紐西蘭是國家名，是專有名詞，所以關係詞之前一定要加逗點。在關係子句裡，went 是不及物動詞，所以需要的是表示地方的副詞。

6. ③ , whom the coach

Michale Wood 是人名，所以關係詞之前一定要加逗點。關係詞子句的結構是 the coach 是主詞，respects 是及物動詞，所以關係詞是受詞，要用 whom。

Chapter 10 單元綜合問題

1. ④ which have

關係代名詞 which 是主詞，後面有 have 和 tell 兩個動詞。③ 如果用 they have，那關係代名詞就一定是當作受詞而被省略，不過因為 simple words 和 simple stories 也是受詞，那就沒有關係代名詞可以放置的位置，所以是不正確的。② 如果用 as have，have 就沒有主詞了，因為 as 是連接詞，所以也是錯誤的。

2. ④ that produces

關係代名詞 that 是主詞，produces 是及物動詞，electricity 是受詞。① 和 ② 是相同的形式，which 應該被當作受詞來用，而 electricity 也是受詞，所以是錯誤用法。

3. ④ whose

whose father 是主詞，is 是動詞，the president 到最後是補語。

4. ④ the hotel where

如果填 recommend 的受詞 the hotel，那空格之後就是關係子句，用來修飾 the hotel。但是因關係子句的 you 是主詞，stayed 是不及物動詞，所以需要的是表示地方的副詞。如果用 ② 的 where，where 之後的句子都變成 recommend 的受詞，變成「請推薦你暑假期間停留的地方」，不合邏輯，所以不正確。

5. ① what the cause is

因為沒有 know 的受詞，所以推斷沒有先行詞，因此不能用 which，要用 what。因為 the cause 是主詞，what 是 is 的補語，所以應該是 what the cause is。

6. ② in which

關係子句裡 an average of ten inches of rain 是主詞，falls 是不及物動詞，所以應該填入表示地方的 in which。從 rain falls 降雨量這名詞來看，③ 的 which has 好像也對，不過 rain fall 是不可數名詞，所以不能用複數形 rain falls。

7. ④ who stole

找出句後 have been arrested 的主詞，是解本題最好的方法。如果用 ① 的 stole，Thieves stole paintings from Notford art gallery 是完全子句，不過後面的 have been arrested 就沒有主詞了，所以是錯誤用法。如果選 ② 的 who stealing，關係子句裡沒有動詞，所以也是不正確的。

8. ① eat

their bodies require 是省略了 that 的關係子句，用來修飾先行詞 the calcium。they 以後也是關係子句，用來修飾 the food，省略的關係詞應該是 eat 的受詞，所以不能用 eat them 或 eat it。

9. ③ which he's enjoying

因為兩個子句沒有連接詞，所以要用關係子句來連接。因為有逗點，所以不能用 that。另外，逗點之後，任何關係詞都不能省略。

10. who, who

要用關係詞子句來連接，先行詞是 tourists 和 employees，所以要用關係詞 who。又因為空格後的 do not speak 和 speak 都是動詞，所以用主格 who 才是正確答案。

11. ⑤ that — what

因為 a crocodile 是先行詞，所以要用 which 或 that。第二個空格是 saw 的受詞，也就是說沒有先行詞，所以要用 what。

12. is

整句的主詞是 the reason，why . . . current events 是關係子句，用來修飾 the reason。主詞是第三人稱單數，而時態是現在式，所以 be 動詞要用 is。

13. ① television (that／which) children, ② steps (that／which) the child

關係代名詞的受格省略，先行詞和關係詞子句的主詞，就會並排在一起。也就是說，名詞和名詞直接接在一起。(square-eyes：指熱中看電視的人)

14. is → are

整句的主詞是 Two . . . devices，為複數，所以 be 動詞不能用 is，要用 are。that have . . . usage 是關係子句，用來修飾主詞。

15. what I found in one of your boots

一隻靴子是 one of your boots。因為整個是名詞子句，所以應是以 what 為首的關係子句才正確，然後用 I 當主詞，found 當動詞，其他的字放到 in 後面。

16. by which

the primary means 是先行詞，所以不能用 what。關係子句裡，you 是主詞，acquire 是及物動詞，your ideas 是受詞；gather 是及物動詞、information 是受詞，都不需要主詞或受詞，所以不能用 which。

17. ① whom parents → whose parents

parents 是主詞，are 是 be 動詞，alcoholics 是補語，所以沒有 whom 這樣的受詞可以放置的位置。改成 whose parents，整個當作主詞，才是正確用法。

18. ① what → that／which

因為先行詞是 the facts，所以要將 what 改成 that 或 which。

19. ① appears → appear

先行詞 those men 是複數。因為主詞是複數，所以動詞 appears 的 s 要刪除。

20. ③ do it → do

這個句子在 something 和 you 之間，省略了關係代名詞的受格 that。因為該關係代名詞應該是 do 的受詞，所以 it 要省略。

21. ② worn → wore

he 前面的關係代名詞 that 被省略了，從 (that) . . . his contact lens 是關係子句。在關係子句中，worn 應該是動詞，所以時態應該是過去式 wore，而非過去分詞 worn。④ 因為主詞 the tiny wire-rims 為複數，所以用 were 沒有錯誤。

22. ④ where → which

where 到句子最後是關係子句，其中 where 是副詞，不能當 is 的主詞，因此要將 where 換成 which 才正確。② that 不是關係詞，而是作同位語的連接詞。

72

1. wanting to pursue a singing career

將動詞 wants 改成原型 want，然後加 ing。

2. spending all week preparing for the golf match

將動詞 spent 改成原型 spend，然後加 ing。

3. sleeping lat in the morning

從 sleeping 開始到最後，整個都是動名詞。

4. going to the dentist

until it's too late 是最終的時間，所以不能包含在動名詞中。

5. Postponing the proposed legislation

因為 is being considered 是整個句子的動詞，所以不能包含在動名詞中。

6. observing two groups of preschoolers

從 observing . . . preschoolers 都是動名詞。

7. Driving a car to New York in you situation

will take 是整個句子的動詞，所以不包含在動名詞中。

8. feeling honored when they receive a nomination

從句意來看，從 when 到最後都要包含在動名詞中。

9. ② cloning

重點要找出 was 的主詞。動詞 clone 是「複製」的意思。如果用 ① 的 clone 和 ③ 的 they cloned，was impossible 就沒有主詞了。動名詞前面不能有冠詞，所以 the cloning 是錯誤用法。

10. ④ knowledge

介系詞 at 要接受詞，所以 his extensive . . . grammar 整個應該是名詞或動名詞。如果用動名詞 knowing，那後面的 of 就要刪去；因為在動名詞裡，know 是及物動詞，所以 English grammar 就應該是受詞。又，因為 extensive 是形容詞，不能修飾動名詞。④ extensive 可修飾 knowledge，也可和 of 連接。

73

1. giving any unnecessary information →動詞 avoid 的受詞

2. hurting her friend's feelings →介系詞 for 的受詞

3. taking a long walk in the woods →介系詞 after 的受詞

4. opening the front door →was 的主詞

after 後面有 was prohibited 這個動詞，所以 after 當作連接詞，連接詞後面的 opening the front door 是 was prohibited 的主詞。

5. ③ walking

about 是介系詞，後面不能有子句或不定詞。「走路回家」不能用 walk to home，要用 walk home。

6. ② Looking

把 looking after children 整個變成動名詞，當 requires 的主詞。look after 是片語，「照顧」之意。

7. ④ moving

當 finish 後面要接受詞時，不能用不定詞，要用動名詞。句意為「搬鋼琴」，所以要用及物動詞 move，及物動詞後面不能加 to。

8. mailing

動詞 mind 要用動名詞當作受詞。

9. eating

deny 是及物動詞，要用動名詞當受詞。不需要 about。

10. in helping

believe 不能直接用動名詞或不定詞當作受詞。不過 believe in 是和 believe 不同含義的慣用語，這時就可以用名詞或動名詞，當介系詞 in 的受詞。不能選 in help 的原因是，若將 help 當作名詞，後面又接代名詞 others，為錯誤用法。

11. failing

of 後面可接動名詞或名詞。如果選名詞 failure，後面有另一個名詞 the driving test，語意不通。failing the driving test 為動名詞，the driving test 是 fail 的受詞。

12. failure

因為前面有定冠詞 the，後面有介系詞 of，所以不能用動名詞的形式。

74

1. not helping others

動名詞的否定型，就是在 ing 前加 not。

2. her going to bed late

整句的主詞不是 Mary，而是 Mary's parents。動名詞的所有格是 her 才正確。

3. being corrected by the teacher

動名詞有被動含義，所以要換成被動語態的動名詞。

4. Tim's not finishing it in time

整個句子為動名詞當作主詞，所以動名詞中不能單獨出現 Tim，要把 Tim 換成 Tim's。not 要放在所有格 Tim's 的後面。

5. being noticed

因為 notice 是及物動詞，所以後面要有受詞；這裡沒有受詞，而且從句意推斷，不是「沒注意」，而是「沒被注意」，所以應該用被動語態才正確。

6. Jack's escaping

如果用 escaping，the government officials 就變成它的主詞，這樣句意不通。

7. Planning

因為 Being planned 是被動語態，所以後面不能有受詞。因為 your schedule 是名詞，要當受詞用。

8. being shot

若選 shooting，後面就要有受詞，但這裡並沒有受詞。

9. ② Ann's taking

object to 的 to 是介系詞,所以後面要有名詞或動名詞。如果動名詞的主詞是人,原則上要改成所有格。

10. ① Not getting

因為句子裡有 you,所以動名詞中不能再有所有格 your,否定的 not 要放在 ing 前面。

11. ④ being seen

從句意判斷,應該是「沒被看見」的意思,所以要用被動語態的動名詞才對。been seen 不是動名詞。

Chapter 11 單元綜合問題

1. ② talking about love

enjoy 後面要用動名詞當受詞。因為動名詞裡,talk 是不及物動詞,不能直接接受詞 love,要加 about。

2. ② Reading

Reading . . . room 都是動名詞,可作為 is 的主詞。動名詞前不能有冠詞。

3. ③ saying

因為 without 是介系詞,所以動名詞 saying 最合適。動名詞不能用進行式 being saying。而且 it goes without saying 是「不用説、更別説」的意思。

4. ① Not being

在動名詞中 not 要放在 ing 前面。即使是 be 動詞也一樣,not 要放在前面。

5. ③ finish preparing for

finish 要用動名詞當受詞,而 didn't 後要用原型動詞。

6. ② being asked

about 是介系詞,不能接不定詞,要接動名詞。從句意判斷,不是邀請,而是「被邀請」,所以要用被動語態 being asked。

7. ④ the safety of

在介系詞 for 後要接名詞或動名詞。如果接動名詞,就應該是 saving its passengers。如果用 safety,後面就要有 of,才能連接名詞。

8. ① your not knowing

imagine 後要用動名詞。所有格要放在 not 的前面。

9. ② could not

因為後面的 had seen 是過去完成式,所以要用過去式 could。現在式的 can 不能接過去完成式。

10. ③ were at a risk of developing

因為主詞 spouses 是複數,所以動詞要用 were。risk 後,要用 to 還是要用 of,要由後面的形式來決定,

因為後面的 the same condition 是名詞,所以要用動名詞 developing,就是 risk of developing。如果用 development,那 development 後面還要再加一個 of,才能連接後面的名詞。

11. ② knowing

介系詞 for 要接名詞或動名詞。因為從 the requirements 之後是名詞,所以要用 knowing,使整個變成動名詞。如果用名詞 knowledge,要加介系詞 of。

12. correcting

前面有介系詞 about,後面有受詞 him。所以要用動名詞形式 correcting him,才能當作 about 的受詞。

13. ④ builds

動名詞 working with others 當主詞。因為動名詞被視為單數,所以不能用 build,要用 builds。前面的 will help 不是表示未來式,是表示「習慣」之意的一種現在式。

14. ⑤ eat → eating

因為 by 是介系詞,所以後面接的動詞要加 ing。

15. exposure

frequent . . . pollution 是 can damage 的主詞,所以空格應該要填入動名詞 exposing 或名詞 exposure。如果用 exposing,後面就一定要接受詞,且前面的形容詞 frequent,也要變成副詞 frequently 才正確。形容詞 frequent 修飾 exposure,連接後面的介系詞 to,所以 exposure 是正確答案。

16. ④ raising

介系詞 for 要接動名詞 rising 或 raising。rise 是不及物動詞,不能接受詞 sales,所以要用及物動詞 raise。raising sales to their highest point 是 for 的受詞。

17. ① to purchase → purchasing

consider 要用動名詞當受詞,而非不定詞。

18. ③ push → pushing

by 是介系詞,後面的動詞要加 ing。

19. ③ regard → regarding

cannot help 後面要接動名詞。

20. ② hear it → hear

動名詞 Not being able to hear 當作主詞,doesn't seem 是動詞,所以要刪去 it。

21. ④ overpaying → overpaid

being overpaying 是主動語態,being overpaid 是被動語態。因為 overpay 後面沒有受詞,所以可以判定是被動語態。另外,動名詞也不能有進行式,所以 being overpaying 是錯誤用法。

22. ① exhaustive → exhaustively

research 是動詞，his new work 是受詞。exhaustive 是形容詞，不能修飾動詞 research，要改成副詞 exhaustively，才能修飾動詞。

23. ④ her → 刪去 her

her 是動名詞 sending 的主詞。但因為句子前面有人名 Sue，因此不須特別加上動名詞的主詞。

75

1.
動名詞：(their) doing different things this weekend
不定詞： (for them) to do different things this weekend

2.
動名詞： (his) discovering that light is made up of a composite of color
不定詞： (for him) to discover that light is made up of a composite of color

3. To learn English well

to learn English well，整個是不定詞。

4. to invite them for dinner this weekend

從 invite 到 weekend，內容告一段落。

5. to e-mail questions to the bank

e-mail 當作動詞用。

6. to stay up late every night this week and study for exams

不定詞為「to＋原型動詞」。

7. to live a life that is free from the influence of civilized man

不定詞裡也會有關係詞子句。that is free ... 是關係詞子句，修飾 a life。

8. ④ improve

不定詞為「to＋原型動詞」。

9. ② to obey

that 子句為 think 的受詞。該 that 子句裡，連接詞 that 被省略，不定詞 to obey the law 當主詞，is 是動詞。

76

1. for

young men 是 spend 的主詞。因為 spend 變成 to 的不定詞形式，主詞也要變成「for＋受格」的形式。

2. have been

祖母的美麗是過去的事，要用過去式。過去時態要變成不定詞時，要用完成式不定詞。was 的完成式是 have been。

3. to be

seems 的時態和 now 一致，句型為「to＋原型動詞」。

4. to have had

從 was 推斷，可以知道所說的痛苦經驗是過去的事，所以要用完成式不定詞 to have had。

5. not to go

不定詞要變成否定型時，not 要放在 to 之前。

6. not to be fired

fire 是及物動詞。因為後面沒有受詞，所以應該是被動語態，而且從句意判斷，用被動語態也比較恰當。

7. to have received

the day before 以過去為基準，指之前的某一天。比訂購的時間要更早之前發生，因此用完成式不定詞。

8. ③ have happened

seems 是現在式，事件發生的時間點是過去 last night，所以要用完成式不定詞。

9. ① to wax

need 後面要用不定詞。因為 it 是受詞，有受詞就是主動語態，不是被動語態。

10. ④ be chosen

to 後面要接動詞原型，變成不定詞。因為 Steve 被提出來移到前面，所以句子就要變成被動語態。③ 雖是完成式不定詞，表示過去時間，但句意指的是未來將會發生的事，所以不正確。

77

1. not to accept the idea offered by a colleague → 動詞 decided 的受詞

2. To be an administrator → 主詞／to have the worst job in the world → 補語

3. whether to buy a camera → 動名詞 deciding 的受詞

不定詞前面有疑問詞，所以疑問詞也是不定詞的一部分，這樣的不定詞經常當名詞用。

4. not to waste money on a hotel → 補語

not 也包含在不定詞裡面，it 是代替主詞的虛主詞。

5. to go

動詞 need 要用不定詞當受詞。

6. to create

因為是 be 動詞的補語，所以不能用動詞 create，要用不定詞 to create。

7. to visit

would like 之後要用不定詞。

8. when

不定詞前之要放什麼疑問詞，可以從不定詞裡需要什麼要素來做判斷。keep 是動詞，your mouth 是受詞，shut 是受詞補語，所以沒有需要 which 的地方；因此填入副詞 when 才正確。

9. smoking

介系詞 of 後不能接不定詞。

10. ③ to see

it 是虛主詞，所以後面一定要有真主詞。真主詞一般都是不定詞或 that 子句。不定詞 to see that the new scheme . . . 是真主詞。

11. ④ to study

refuse 要用不定詞做受詞。② 要改成 not to study。

12. ① is

句子沒有動詞，故空格應填入動詞。To classify things 是主詞，不定詞後面要接單數動詞，所以答案為 is。

78

1. a train to catch

受詞 train 是名詞，所以將 catch 改成不定詞即可。

2. somebody to help me

主詞 somebody 是名詞，所以將 helps me 改成不定詞即可。

3. a bag to put these things in

a bag 是名詞，所以將 put 之後的句子改成不定詞即可。請注意，介系詞 in 不要漏掉。

4. for

因為 a good education 是名詞，所以不能用不定詞。介系詞 for 表示目的，可表達出和不定詞相同的含義。

5. to

get 是動詞，所以後面不能接介系詞 for；因此要選 to，變成不定詞，表示「以便……」之意才正確。

6. to make

用不定詞來表示目的，是「以便……」的意思。選項中的介系詞 for，後接動名詞來表達不定詞的含義，這樣不正確。在英文裡，要用動詞表達目的時，一定要用不定詞，不能用「for＋動名詞」。

7. to wear to the party

不定詞修飾名詞 same new clothes，且被當作不定詞中 wear 的受詞。所以 wear 的受詞 it 要刪去。

8. To overcome the disease →當副詞用／to eradicate the tsetse fly →當受詞用（當作名詞用）

如果不定詞被逗點獨立出來，這個不定詞就具有表示目的的含義的副詞功能。位在及物動詞 try 之後的不定詞，當作 try 的受詞。

9. to make mathematics interesting →當 want 的受詞／to overcome →修飾前面的名詞

want 後的不定詞，是 want 的受詞。to overcome 是用來修飾前面的名詞。

10. ③ To maintain

maintain 和 promote 前加 to，讓此句 to maintain . . . health 成為不定詞。

11. ② to improve

整個句子的動詞應該是 motivates；名詞 the need 當主詞，所以要用不定詞當形容詞來修飾名詞。

79

1. to travel

allow 是動詞，名詞後面要接 to 不定詞。

2. to go

enable 也是動詞，名詞後面要接 to 不定詞。

3. laugh

因為 make 是使役動詞，所以名詞後不能接 to 不定詞或動名詞。

4. eating

advise 後面接名詞，然後再接不定詞。但如果沒有名詞，就不能接不定詞，要接動名詞。因為這裡的 advise 後沒有名詞，所以選 eating 才正確。

5. to apply

動詞 get 後面要接 to 不定詞。

6. to wear

require 後面接「名詞＋不定詞」。但這裡不能選 you to wear 為答案，因為 required 是被動語態。如果 require 要用被動語態，就不能接名詞，只能接 to 不定詞。

7. drive

因為 saw 是感官動詞，所以名詞後不能接過去式動詞或 to 不定詞。

8. want, to take

動詞 hope 可以直接接 to 不定詞，但不能接「名詞＋

to 不定詞」。want 可以接「名詞＋to 不定詞」。

9. ② to let me choose
動詞 tell 後面接名詞，然後再接 to 不定詞。因為 let 是使役動詞，所以名詞後要接「to 原型動詞」。

10. ② was allowed
動詞 allow 後面接名詞，然後再接 to 不定詞。如果沒有名詞，又接了 to 不定詞，就表示 allow 一定是被動語態。every 後面接單數名詞和單數動詞。如果用 and 連接兩個單數名詞，後面都要接單數動詞。

11 ③ got
因為 carry 是原型，所以空格應該是使役動詞、感官動詞或 help。因為 get 是一般動詞，所以要用 to carry。

80

1. is hard to read
形容詞 hard 後面若接不定詞，該不定詞的受詞，可以當全句的主詞。

2. was careless of her to leave a camera on the bus
性格形容詞修飾的主詞（人），可以換成「of＋受格」的形式，移到形容詞之後。she 變成 of her，放到 careless 後。

3. It
It 是虛主詞；真主詞 to solve the problem 本身是一個完全子句。如果動詞是 is impossible，那 Mary 就不會是主詞。從句意判定，Mary 是 solve the problem 的主詞，如果選 Mary，應該改成 for Mary to solve the problem。如果要用 That 當主詞，那不定詞就不能有受詞。不過因為不定詞 to solve the problem 是完全子句，所以不能選 that。

4. of him
foolish 是形容詞，所以後面要用 of him。這個 him 不是後面的 to buy 的主詞，而是 was foolish 的主詞。

5. for him
him 是 to buy 的主詞，for him to buy . . . radio set 整個是不定詞，為真主詞，被 it 虛主詞所代替。

6. to let
「be reluctant＋to 不定詞」，是「不願去……」之意的慣用語。reluctant 後面要接 to 不定詞。

7. ② to talk to
在形容詞 easy 後面有 to 不定詞時，不定詞的受詞可以當作主詞。因為主詞不是 it，而是名詞 the girl，可以知道這個 girl 是不定詞的受詞，因此不定詞後不能再有受詞。因為 talk 是不及物動詞，如果有受詞，那

就一定要用 talk to 的形式。

8. ④ of you
generous 是「慷慨的」之意，是品性形容詞；因此後面要接「of＋受格」。

9. ① likely to be
likely 是形容詞，後面接不定詞。② 的 like 是在 are 之後，所以 like 應該是介系詞，不能接不定詞。

Chapter 12 單元綜合問題

1. ① recommend
不定詞的形式是「to＋原型動詞」。

2. ④ for
不定詞的主詞要用「for＋受格」的形式。

3. ① To lose
當要表示目的含意，「為了要……、以便……」之意時，要用不定詞。這時用 for losing 不正確。

4. ② required
Johnny 是名詞，後面接了不定詞 to take。用這種形式的動詞，在選項中只有 require。

5. ③ to appear
teeth 是名詞，後面的 are 是動詞。空格應該是要填入修飾名詞 teeth 的修飾詞。不定詞也可以當作修飾名詞的形容詞用。

6. ① not to let that happen
不定詞是否定的時候，not 要放在 to 之前。let 是使役動詞，名詞後要接原型動詞。

7. ③ advised us to take
advise 後面的名詞之後，要接不定詞。

8. ④ to keep the child from crying
應填入虛主詞 it 替代的真主詞；因為前面有 difficult，所以不能用動名詞，要用不定詞。①、④ 中的 stop，不是「名詞＋不定詞」的形式，所以不考慮。「keep＋名詞＋from＋-ing」是「不讓……去做……」之意。

9. ④ to prepare
在 that 子句中，food 是主詞，動詞後有形容詞 easy。easy 後如果有不定詞，不定詞的受詞可以當作整句的主詞移到前面。因為名詞 food 是主詞，所以可以知道它是不定詞的受詞，被移到前面來了，這時不定詞後面就不能有受詞。所以正確答案是 to prepare。

10. ① to write with
因為筆是拿著才能寫字的，所以要加介系詞 with。

11. ④ have been forgotten

因為 Jason 不高興自己被忘記了，所以 forget 要用被動語態。雖然選項中沒有 be forgotten，不過有 have been forgotten 可以考慮；而且忘掉這件事比生氣還早發生，所以不定詞要用完成式不定詞。

12. ⑤

to describe「以便去……」，有表示目的的含義。從句意來看，才能正確地看出來。用法與此相同的 ⑤ 的 to receive，同樣有「以便去……」的含義。① 的 to put 是名詞的功能，是 is 的補語。② 的 to work，當作動詞 want 的受詞。③ 的 to wear out 是 it 的真主詞，是名詞的功能。④ 的 to use 是修飾名詞 way 的形容詞的功能。

13. want them agree with→want them **to** agree with

動詞 want 後面接受詞，受詞後不是接原型不定詞，而是要接 to 不定詞。to behave 放在形容詞 wrong 後，用來說明 wrong 的原因，所以是正確用法。to accept 當作動詞 refuse 的受詞，也是正確用法。

14. ④ touch screens are usually easy for the user to learn

be 動詞後的 easy 是重要關鍵。形容詞 easy 後若有不定詞，不定詞的受詞可以移到前面當全句的主語。因為 the user 是不定詞 to learn 的主語，所以不定詞 to learn 前面要用「for＋受格」的形式。

15. to study, to study

動詞 try，要用 to 不定詞或動名詞當受詞。第二個空格應該填入 it 的真主詞，且在 important 後要用不定詞，不能用動名詞。

16. is

主語是 the most common reason，to give flowers 當作形容詞，用來修飾名詞。在時態方面，因為前面出現了 is，所以是現在式。主語是單數，時態是現在式，所以 is 是正確答案。

17. ② to be → being

besides 是介系詞，不能接不定詞，要接動名詞。

18. ② for → of

careless 是品性形容詞，後面要用「of＋受格」形式。

19. ④ for renovating → to renovate

當要表示「以便……」這個目的含義時，如果有動詞，一定要用不定詞，不能用「for＋動名詞」這個形式。

20. ④ store → be stored

因為「資料被儲存」，所以要用被動語態 be stored。

21. ② diagnose it → diagnose

因為 diagnose 的受詞 the condition 移到前面去當主詞，所以 diagnose 後面的 it 要刪去。

22. ① That → It

因為是代替 to believe . . . 的虛主詞，所以要用 it。

23. ② spent → spend

be willing 後面應該用不定詞。因為不定詞的形式是「to＋動詞原型」，所以 spent 應該改成原型 spend。

81

1. The car repaired before Tuesday

2. International human rights standards setting the minimum age for marriage at 18

3. smelling of hay →修飾前面的名詞 the barn

分詞修飾前面的名詞，具有形容詞的功能。

4. built with wide streets and beautiful houses →修飾前面的名詞 the new city

5. based on the idea that diet and environment were the real answers →修飾名詞 a report

因為 idea 後的 that 子句，和 idea 是同位語，所以也屬於分詞的一部分。

6. which was

分詞可以換成關係子句。因為 built 是過去分詞，所以再加入「關係代名詞＋be 動詞」即可。

7. living

使用分詞時，不能用 being living 這樣的進行式形式；因為現在分詞-ing 已經有進行的含意了。把 a woman who lives in Miami . . . 換成分詞 a woman living in Miami . . . 即正確。

8. ④ patterned

選項中就只有過去分詞 patterned 可修飾 a design。

82

1. employs → employing

employ 要換成分詞，整個才是正確的句子。chemical company 和 employ 的關係是主動關係，且後面有受詞 2,000 people，因此要改為現在分詞 employing。

2. was broken → broken

was broken 要改成分詞，因為 the window 和 was broken 是被動關係，所以要改成過去分詞 broken。

3. was covered → covered

was covered 要改成分詞。因為 a table 和 was covered 是被動關係，所以要改為過去分詞 covered。

4. were assigned → assigned

were assigned 要改為分詞。因 the controllers 和 were assigned 是被動關係，所以要用過去分詞 assigned。

5. arresting → arrested

因為 arrest 後面沒有受詞，只有 by the police，所以名詞 the man 和 arrest 的關係是被動關係，因此應該改為過去分詞 arrested。

6. taken → taking

因為 take 後面有受詞 the examination，所以 take 應該用主動語態 taking。

7. experienced → experiencing

因為 habitual loneliness 是 experience 的受詞，所以 experience 是主動語態，改為分詞就是 experiencing。

8. calling → called

call 是第五類句型的動詞，若為主動語態，後面就要有受詞和受詞補語；若為被動語態，則只要有受詞補語即可。換句話說，如果 call 後面有兩個名詞，就是主動語態；如果只有一個受詞，就是被動語態。因為只有 the Bridge of Peace 一個受詞，所以是被動語態，call 應該改為過去分詞。

9. ② exchanged

因為 exchange 是「交換、換錢」的意思，所以和前面的名詞 money 的關係應該是被動的關係；所以 exchanged 是最恰當的答案。

10. ④ considering

consider 是第五類句型的動詞。有 us 和 a part of the nature 兩個名詞，所以可以判定是主動語態。也可以像 ③ 那樣用關係詞，不過時態要一致，要改成 which considered。

11. ② concerned

be concerned with 指「和……有關」。因為 concern 有被動含義，改為分詞時，要用過去分詞 concerned。

83

1. amusing, amused

the story 和 amuse 是主動關係，要用 amusing。our daughter 和 amuse 是被動關係，要用 amused。

2. disappointing, disappointed

opera 和 disappoint 是主動關係；audience 和 disappoint 是被動關係。

3. ③ interesting

it 指 the book。因為書是讓我們覺得有趣的事物，為主動關係，所以用 interesting。

4. ② isolated

interior 是「內部、內陸」；isolate 是「使孤立」，兩個合起來是「被孤立起來的內陸」的意思，所以要用被動語態 isolated。如果用 isolating interior，意思為「正在孤立的內陸」，並不合邏輯。

5. surprised

「我被驚嚇」之意，所以要用被動語態 surprised。

6. depressing

因為是天氣使我們憂鬱，對天氣而言為主動語態，所以用 depressing。

7. suspected

因為從問題製造者的立場來看，是被懷疑的，所以要用被動語態 suspected。

8. annoyed

不是我們正在煩惱，而是我們被弄得很煩，所以要用被動態 annoyed。

9. leading

leading 是「居於領先地位的」之意，雖然是分詞，但也是形容詞。

10. running

「流動之水」的意思，所以用主動語態 running。run 是不及物動詞。

84

1. Finishing my homework

有連接詞的子句要改成分詞構句時，要刪去連接詞，再刪去主詞，最後將動詞改為分詞。

2. Because he got

將分詞改成有連接詞的子句時，順序要相反。先加上合適的連接詞，然後是被省略的主詞，最後將分詞改成符合時態的動詞。因為 was 是過去，所以 getting 要改成 got。

3. driving to work

表示同時發生的 while 子句，也可以用分詞構句來表達。這時分詞構句大致都是在主要子句之後。

4. ③ Studying

若為有連接詞的子句，就應該是 As they studied。若為分詞構句，就是 Studying。

5. ④ allowing

① 和 ② 前面要有連接詞才正確。③ 因為有連接詞，所以不能用分詞構句。

6. ② complained → complaining

因為動詞 complain 前面沒有連接詞，所以要改成分詞構句。complain of 是「抱怨」，雖然是「不及物動詞＋介系詞」的型態，但具有及物動詞的功能。因為後面有受詞 headaches and stomach pains，所以是主動語態，換成分詞要改為 complaining。

7. ② by →刪去 by

因為前面有分詞構句 Looking back，所以後面不能接介系詞 by。Looking back 也可以改成 We looked back，不過這樣一來，we 就重複使用了；所以直接刪去 by 即為正確答案。

85

1. ③ Noting

因為此句沒有連接詞，所以空格應該填入分詞構句。因為 note 後面有名詞 the nervousness，所以主動語態的 noting 即為正確答案。

2. ① Janet could not be protected from infection

分詞構句的主詞要和主要子句的主詞一致。從句意判斷，分詞構句的主詞是應該為 Janet，所以 ① 是正確答案。

3. ④ writing

write 的主詞是 Jane（a journalist）。因為 Jane 寫關於名人的文章，所以是主動語態，要用 writing。

4. Taking

後面有受詞 a wrong turn，所以是主動語態 taking。

5. Waiting

因為 wait 是不及物動詞，所以不能用被動語態過去分詞 waited。

6. Barb read the book

分詞構句和主要子句的主詞必須一致。

7. Exhausted

exhausted 是被動之意，而 exhausting 是主動之意。從句意判定，是被動語態，所以答案為 exhausted。

8. Known

know 是及物動詞，因為後面沒有受詞，所以要用被動語態 known。

9. Maria shed a few tears

分詞構句和主要子句的主詞必須一致。

10. Compared

compare 是及物動詞，因為後面沒有受詞，所以是被動語態，要用 compared。

Chapter 13 單元綜合問題

1. ④ living

要填入修飾 people 的分詞，因為 live 是不及物動詞，所以不能用 lived。

2. ④ for making

如果選分詞 making，the chief material 就變成 make 的主詞，那麼意思就是「材料做傢俱」，這樣並不合邏輯。因此要加 for，以表示材料的用途是為了製作傢俱，for making furniture 才正確。① 的 that 是關係詞，子句沒有動詞，that 要改成 by which 才正確。② 是「疑問詞＋不定詞」的形式，當作名詞。

3. ④ Jogging

因為沒有連接詞，所以要用分詞構句；jog 是不及物動詞，所以要用主動語態的 jogging。

4. ③ frightening — frightened

電影讓 Justin 感覺害怕，所以用主動語態 frightening。

5. ③ called

空格應該要填入分詞。call 是第五類句型的動詞，而後面只有名詞 Easter Island，要用被動語態 called。

6. ③ reading

如果不用連接詞，就要用分詞；相反的，如果用連接詞 and，就不能用分詞。因為後面有受詞 a letter，所以要用主動語態 reading。

7. ③ finished

「完成品」英文是 finished products。

8. ① Written

主要子句的主詞是 the book，也是 write 的主詞。即使 write 後沒有受詞，book 和 write 仍是被動關係。③ having written 為完成式，是主動語態。④ 不定詞不能用主動語態，要用被動語態才正確。

9. ④ claiming

後面有動詞 was elected，所以空格不要填入分詞。claim 要用不定詞當受詞。因為不定詞 to represent，當作 claim 的受詞，所以 claim 要為主動語態。

10. lives → living

因為前面有 be 動詞 is，所以 lives 要改為分詞，修飾前面的 creature。因為 live 是不及物動詞，所以不能用被動語態 lived。

11. interested, bored, interesting

be interested in 是「對……感興趣」。第二個空格應該填入「無聊」之意的字詞，依照內容，主詞是 people，people 感覺無聊，所以要用被動語態 bored。第三個空格修飾 something，因為是它本身很有趣，所以要

用主動語態 interesting。

12. abandoned
依照句意，為被動語態，所以答案為 abandoned。

13. ④ explained → explaining
explain 當作分詞構句，因為後面有受詞 their experience，所以要用主動語態 explaining。① 分詞 traveling 修飾 an American couple；又因為 travel 是不及物動詞，所以用主動語態 traveling 是正確的。② seeing 是分詞構句，而且後面的 that 子句有受詞，所以用主動語態 seeing 也是正確的。③ 因為 relieve 是不及物動詞當作形容詞，為「安心的、令人鬆一口氣的」之意，所以要改成分詞 relieved。

14. Using
要用分詞構句。因為 use 是及物動詞，後面又有受詞 their flippers，所以是主動語態，應該要用 using。

15. covered
空格要填入分詞，以修飾 an open field，才是正確用法。cover 是及物動詞，後面沒有受詞，所以要用被動語態的 covered。

16. ① When we entering → When entering 或 Entering 或 When we entered
要改為有連接詞的子句或分詞構句。

17. ② consists of → consisting of
因為有 have 和 consists of 這兩個動詞，所以其中一個要改成分詞。如果把 have 改成 having，那麼 Mosques 就是主詞，consists of 是動詞，但因主詞是複數，所以動詞不能為 consists。因此，consists of 改成分詞，才是正確答案。

18. ② containing → contained
contain 是及物動詞。如果用 containing，就是主動態，後面就要有當作受詞的名詞；但因句中沒有受詞，所以要換成被動語態 contained。

19. ④ it means → and it means 或 meaning
如果句子裡有兩個子句，那句子裡就一定要有連接詞。如果不用連接詞，就要改成分詞構句或其他形式。這裡如果把 it means 換成 meaning，就是分詞構句，為正確用法。因為 meaning 的主詞就是前面的名詞 nebrathka，所以 meaning 前不須出現代名詞。

20. ① Reading → Read
分詞構句的主詞，就是主要子句的主詞 the book。the book 和 read 是被動關係，所以要用過去分詞 read。③ return 是及物動詞，finished 和 returned 兩者對比，同時對應前面的 was，所以兩者都是被動語態。

21. ④ spoke → spoken
without 是介系詞，後面不能接子句。若用 spoke，就變成子句，並不正確。如果把 spoke 改成分詞 spoken，後面接名詞 a single word ... 即為正確用法。word 和 speak 是被動關係，所以不能用 speaking。

22. ④ intending → intended
句意為「已經打算好罷工」；因此就罷工而言，是被人打算，所以要用被動語態 intended。

86

1. ② to quit
動詞 decide 後面，要用不定詞當它的受詞。

2. ④ working
從內容判定，是「把工作就那樣放下」的意思，所以 stop 後要接 ing。如果用 to work，是把原來做的工作停下來，去做另一件事的意思，這和本題句意不符。

3. ③ to take
「出門的時候要記得帶傘」是未來會發生的事；所以用不定詞。

4. ③
① 因為是「忘不掉第一次參觀瀑布的景象」之意，所以 forget 後應該接 visiting。② enjoy 後面要接動名詞，當它的受詞。④ promise 後面要接不定詞，當它的受詞。

5. eating
avoid 後面要接動名詞，當它的受詞。

6. to finish
manage 後面要接不定詞，當它的受詞。

7. to open
try 後面要接動名詞；但如果是「努力地試著要去……」之意，就要接不定詞了。從內容判斷，即為「努力地試著要去……」之意，所以答案為 try to open。

8. to like
expect 後面要接不定詞來當受詞。

87

1. ④ to seeing
look forward to＋Ving。

2. ① used to play
used to 為「過去習慣……」；be used to 表示一直以來的習慣。若將 am 改成 was，也是正確答案。

3. ③ of handing

be capable of 後面要接名詞或動名詞。

4. of pointing

be fond of 是慣用語,「喜歡……」之意。

5. caring

devote A to B 是慣用語,「把 A 奉獻給 B」之意。因為 to 是介系詞,所以後面要用動名詞。

6. to arrive

「be unlikely + to 不定詞」是「不像會……」的意思。「be likely + to 不定詞」是「像是會……」的意思。

7. used to think

若將 are used to thinking 改成 were used to thinking,也是正確答案。

8. finish

fail 後面要接不定詞。

9. are used to playing

前面有 today,所以不能用表示過去的 used to play。

10. being, work

因為 object to 的 to 是介系詞,所以後面要用 being。be asked 的後面要接不定詞。

88

1. ③ listening to

提示句的 Teaching English to children 當主詞,所以要用動名詞。③ 分詞 listening to classical music 是 was 的補語,為正確答案。① leading 用來修飾 producer 的分詞。② is looking 是 look 的現在進行式。④ abounding in 之後的句子,都是修飾 a mountain 的分詞。

2. ⑤ carved → carving

weaving rugs、desiging quilts、carving wood 對比,因此一致為動名詞。

3. ① Persuaded → Persuading

如果改為 persuading,整個就是動名詞,是句子的主詞;而動名詞是單數,所以 be 動詞 is 是正確的。

4. ④ suspecting → suspected

分詞 suspecting 用來修飾 child killer;句意為「被懷疑」,所以要用被動語態 suspected 才正確。① Educating 當作動名詞,為正確用法。② conquering 也是當作動名詞,為正確用法。③ remain 是不及物動詞,為分詞,用來修飾 question,為正確用法。

89

1. travel, to travel

從 people 和 travel 的關係,以及 travel 是不及物動詞來判定,應該是主動語態。因為 let 是使役動詞,所以要用原型 travel。第二句中因為 allow 是一般動詞,所以要用 to travel。

2. fixed, to fix

第一句中因為「電腦被修理」,the computer 和 fix 為被動關係;因此要用過去分詞 fixed。第二句中因為「Cathy 修理電腦」,Cathy 和 fix the computer 為主動關係。get 是一般動詞,所以要用 to fix。

3. to cut

enable 的名詞後面接 to 不定詞。

4. typed

因為 the letter 和 type 是被動關係,所以過去分詞 typed 才是正確答案。

5. burning

smell 是感官動詞,所以後面不能用 to burn;而且依照句意,含有進行的意味,所以 burning 是正確答案。

6. submit

the client 和 submit 是主動關係。had 是使役動詞,所以名詞後要接原型動詞。

7. ① create

their staff 和 create 是主動關係。因為 made 是使役動詞,所以後面接原型動詞。

8. ③ serviced

your car 和 service 是被動關係,所以要用過去分詞 serviced。

9. ② to hear

Ricky 和 hear the conference 是主動關係。want 是一般動詞,所以用 to hear。

Chapter 14 單元綜合問題

1. ③ repaired

the roof 和 repair 是被動關係。所以表示被動的過去分詞 repaired 為正確答案。

2. ① laughing

cannot 是「沒辦法……」的意思。

3. ② hearing

get used to Ving 是「習慣於……」之意。

4. ④ to put

如果 try 後面有 to 不定詞，就表示該內容尚未實現；如果 try 後是動名詞，就表示該內容已經實現。依照句意「火還沒滅」，所以滅火這件事尚未實現，因此用 to put。

5. ② putting

remember 後面若接不定詞，表示未來要去做的事；如果 remember 後面接動名詞，表示過去已做的事。因為說鑰匙已經在皮包裡，表示過去就放進去了，所以要用動名詞。

6. ① is

writing 是動名詞，動名詞要接單數動詞。

7. ③ enjoying talking to

① you're enjoy 是錯誤用法。④ you're enjoyed 是被動語態，但後面不能接受詞，所以是錯誤用法。② enjoy 的受詞必須為動名詞，所以用 to 不定詞是錯誤用法。

8. ③ speaking

從內容判斷，him 和 speak ill of you 是主動關係。因為 heard 是感官動詞，所以後面接原型動詞 speak 或進行式 speaking；但因這裡的 and 後面有 calling，所以要用 speaking。

9. ④ to spreading

dedicate A to B 是「把 A 獻給 B」；to 是介系詞。

10. ④ watching the champion play

因為 look forward to 的 to 是介系詞，所以後面要用動名詞。因為 watch 是感官動詞，所以 champion 後面不能接 to 不定詞。

11. played → playing

saw 是感官動詞，如果受詞後面用 played，就是被動語態。不過因為 birds and monkeys 和 play 是主動關係，所以要用 playing，不能用 played。

12. to pick up

stop picking up 是「停止載人」；stop to pick up 是「停下來去載人」。

13. ① laughed → laugh

因為 people 和 laugh 是主動關係，所以用原型動詞 laugh。

14. ③

③ 分詞 remaining 用來修飾 fingers。其餘 ①、②、④ 的 Exercising、collecting、decreasing 都當動名詞。

15. ② died → die

had seen 是感官動詞，her father and her uncle 是受詞，如果後面接 died，就表示為被動語態。但因 die

是不及物動詞，不能用被動語態。

16. ④ buying → to buy

從句意判斷，是「停下來，去買郵票」之意，所以應該要用 stop to buy 才正確。stop buying 是「停止買郵票」這個動作，和句意不符。

17. ① Giving → Given

如果把 Giving 改成 Given，這個分詞修飾後面的 details，details 成為主詞，後面的動詞為 cause，為正確用法。

18. ① accustomed to have → accustomed to having

因為 be accustomed 後面的 to 是介系詞，所以動詞要加 ing。interfere with 是「干涉」之意。

19. ④ lose → losing

the key to 的 to 是介系詞，所以後面的動詞要加 ing。show 後面的連接詞 that 省略了，後面的 starting... exercise 是動名詞，當 is 的主詞

20. ③ make fun of → made fun of

make fun of 是及物動詞，為「開……的玩笑」之意。

21. ① Offered → Offering

如果用 Offered，就變成分詞，用來修飾 movies；主詞 movies 為複數名詞，後面的 is 要改成 are 才正確。但因為 is 是固定的，所以就要將 offered 改成 Offering，即動名詞當主詞。

22. ④ to plant → planting

② are 後面的 plowing...hills、planting...land、rotating crops 都是動名詞，當 are 的補語。

23. ④ them pull → them pulled

having them pull 的 having 是使役動詞，them 是 wisdom teeth 的代名詞。因為是牙齒被拔，所以要換成被動語態的過去分詞 pulled。

24. ③

如果動詞 allow 後有名詞，後面就要用不定詞；如果沒有名詞，就要用動名詞。① avoid 要以動名詞當受詞，所以 to answer 要改成 answering。② 雖然 promise 的受詞是不定詞，不過不定詞為否定型時，not 要放在 to 前面，變成 not to be late。④ 因為 object to 的 to 是介系詞，所以動詞要加 ing。

90

1. ④ were

因為此句是純粹的假設，所以要用假設法。而且主要子句用 would，也是表示是假設法。使用假設法時，要用 were，不是 was。

2. ③ will occur

因為 if 子句的動詞是 rises，為現在式，所以是直述法；主要子句的助動詞要用 will 才正確。

3. go

if 子句中不能出現未來助動詞 will。主要子句用 will stay，可以知道是直述法；所以 if 子句也要用直述法的時態。

4. would

句子是純粹的假設狀況，所以要用假設法。另外 if 子句裡的 rode 是過去時態，也是假設法的推斷。

5. didn't go

主要子句有 would be，所以是假設法。

6. traveled, would

因為實際而言，過去並沒有去旅行，所以用假設法。

7. learn

主要子句用 will be，表示是直述法。

8. won, would

win 是中了彩券、樂透等狀況時使用，為一種假設，所以用假設法。

9. can

因為 if 子句中有 need，為現在式，也是直述法。因此，助動詞的現在型 can 是正確答案。

10. had, would

實際上並不會有翅膀，所以用假設法。

11. needs, will

為實際可能發生的內容，所以要用直述法。

91

1. ④ would be

因為 if 子句的時態是 were，所以是過去假設法。

2. ③ had studied

因為主要子句是 would have done，是過去完成假設法；所以 if 子句要用過去完成式。

3. wait

主要子句是 I'll come，所以是直述法。

4. would happen

if 子句用 were，所以是假設法。

5. had not been

主要子句是 would have visited，所以是過去完成假設法。

6. could have told

if 子句是 had seen，是假設法。主要子句不是只能用 will 這個助動詞而已，用其他的助動詞也可以。

7. had gone, have seen

從 last night 可看出實際的時間已過去，這裡對應的假設法就要用過去完成。

8. wear, were

today 表示現在；假設法要用過去假設法。

9. had erupted, would have caused

1912 年已過去，實際爆發是 Alaska，LA 的爆發只是假設而已，所以要用假設法。因為是對應過去的假設法，所以要用過去完成假設法。

10. were, would take

此句將表示現在的直述法，改成假設法，就用過去假設法。

11. had, blocked, would (could) have arrived

如果要將表示過去的直述法改成假設法，就要用過去完成假設法。

92

1. should be

因為 fired 不是原型，所以不能用 should 或 were to。

2. Had I

由 if I had known 轉換而來的。

3. be

雖然 if 子句的假設法是 had learned，是過去完成，不過主要子句中有 today 表示是現在的時間點，所以要用過去假設法。

4. Should

由 if anyone should telephone ... 轉換而來。if 子句裡可以用 should；除了某些例外，if 子句裡不會出現 would。

5. Were it

主要子句有 would not be，是過去假設法，所以 if 子句也要用過去式。

6. would not have

if 子句是過去完成假設法，主要子句一定要用助動詞的過去式。假設法的核心就是這個助動詞的過去式。

7. had eaten, be

意思是「如果早上有吃早餐，現在就不會肚子餓了」。因為早上是過去的時間點，所以要換成假設法，就要用過去完成；因為是現在的時間點，換成假設法時，

就要用過去式。

8. ④ Had I seen

主要子句有 would have given，是過去完成假設法。Had I seen 和 If I had seen 是相同的表現方式。

9. ③ need

助動詞 should 為首，後面一定要接原型動詞。因為主詞是 a foreign student，後面要接原型動詞 need。

10. ② would have — had not spent

因為主要子句中有 now，所以用過去假設法。因為 if 子句中有 yesterday，所以要用過去完成假設法。

93

1. liked

因為 wish 片語是表示和事實相反，所以不能再用提示句中的 not。如果提示句的時態是現在，wish 片語就要用過去假設法。如果提示句的時態是過去，wish 片語就要用過去完成假設法。因為 don't like 是現在式，所以要換成過去式的 liked。

2. had studied anthropology while I was at university

因為 didn't study 是過去式，所以 wish 片語要用過去完成式。

3. it were not for water

主要子句是過去假設法，所以 if 子句也要換成過去式。

4. were

因為後面有 now，表示實際的時間點是現在。現在時間要用假設法來表現時，就要用過去式。

5. had known

後面有 was，是過去時態。因為實際時間是過去，所以適用假設法的 wish 句，就要用過去完成式。

6. is

as if 後可接直述法，也可接假設法。「要帶雨傘，是因為實際上天氣看起來像要下雨的樣子」，所以 as if 後用直述法是正確的。

7. understood

因為實際上「孩子並沒有聽懂媽媽說的話」，所以用假設法。

8. I'd have

but for 取代 if 子句，所以前面的主要子句要用相對應的子句才正確，假設法的主要子句一定要有過去式的助動詞 would。I'd have 是 I would have 的縮寫型。

9. ② were spinning

此句為假設法。除了選過去式的 were spinning 外，其他選項都不正確。

10. ③ could have come

因為有 last night，所以可以知道是過去的時間，所以 wish 之後的句子要換成過去完成式；所以助動詞 can，只能用 could come 或 could have come 兩種形式。could come 是過去假設法；could have come 是過去完成假設法。

94

1. have

因為是要 John 和她一起吃午餐，所以 insist 後面 that 子句的動詞要用原型。

2. should take

recommend 後的 that 子句，要用「should ＋原型動詞」。

3. try

suggest 後面要接原型動詞。

4. played

complain 是不能用假設法的動詞，所以 that 子句要用自述法。

5. not raise

that 子句要加 not 時，not 要放在原型動詞前面。that 子句裡的 that 可以省略。

6. be

如果 essential 後面接 that 子句，that 子句的動詞就要為原型或加助動詞 should。

7. have

requirement 和 require 除詞性不同之外，它們的意思完全一樣。requirement 後面若接 that 子句，that 子句的動詞就要為原型或加助動詞 should。

8. ② be printed

從內容判斷，警告詞被印刷，所以要用被動語態。

9. ① not be

形容詞 appropriate 若接 that 子句，that 子句的動詞要用原型或加助動詞 should，not 要放在原型動詞前面。因為 held 是過去分詞，所以前面要有 be。

Chapter 15 單元綜合問題

1. ② is

前面的 would 不是假設法的 would，而是表示謙遜的 would。整個內容是說明現實的內容，要用直述法。

2. ④ will pay

因為內容是具體的，且 if 子句裡的時態是現在式，所以是直述法。will pay 表示簡單未來式即為正確答案。

3. ② should respect

require 後的 that 子句裡，要用 should 或原型動詞。因為 the rights . . . 整個句子是受詞，所以不能用被動語態，要用主動語態。

4. ③ not been for

表示「要不是……」之意。

5. ④ had been — would have gone

從前面的 I wasn't 可看出，是過去直述法。如果過去直述法要換成假設法，就要用過去完成假設法。

6. ② she'd never gotten involved

從 wish 後面的 then 可看出，是表示過去的時間點。因此空格中要填入過去完成假設法。另外，involve 要用被動語態 be involved in 或 get involved in 才正確。② 要將 get involved 的 get 換成過去完成式 had gotten；又將這個 had 和主詞縮寫，變成 she'd，所以是正確的。

7. ① would not be

雖然 if 子句中有 had built，是過去完成式，但因為主要子句中有 now，所以要用過去假設法。過去假設法是「過去式助動詞＋原型動詞」。

8. ① had seen

如果 as if 後面的內容是用直述法，空格就要填入 had seen。因為前面的動詞是 told，而看到是更早之前發生，所以要用過去完成式。即使 as if 後面的內容是假設法，空格也要填入 had seen。因為在假設法中只能填入過去式 saw 或過去完成式 had seen；這裡要用 had seen，是因為 had seen 在 told 之前。

9. ③ Should you decide

因為 if 子句裡不能用 will 和 would，所以即使省略 if，①、② 也不可能是正確答案。④ decided 是過去式，表示是假設法；但是主要子句是命令句，是直述法。should you decide 和 if you should decide 意思相同。

10. ② be banished

request 後面若接 that 子句，that 子句的動詞就要為原型或加助動詞 should。banish 是「放逐」之意的及物動詞，但因後面沒有受詞，所以要用被動語態；從句意推斷，也是被動語態才正確。

11. ③ would you have bought

if 子句裡也可以用助動詞 could。could buy 是過去假設法，could have bought 是過去完成假設法。因為一致性，所以主要子句中要填入 would have bought。

12. ④ Had he been hungry

因為主要子句是 would have eaten，所以 if 子句裡也要用過去完成式。

13. ③ If it were not for

使用 but for 或 without 時和時態無關。但是如果要換成 if，時態就要正確。因為主要子句是過去完成式，所以 if 子句也要用過去完成式。

14. ⑤ will → would

這段文字是由 if 子句和主要子句組合而成。引號裡的內容也是 if 子句中一部分，if 子句的動詞是過去式 said，所以是假設法。為了一致性，主要子句也要為假設法，因此 will 應該改成 would。

15. ④ had had — would have sent

事實用假設法表現時，因實際的時間是過去，所以假設法要用過去完成式。have 的過去完成是 had had。

16. spent → spend

suggest 後面的 that 子句的動詞要用原型或加助動詞 should。

17. ⑤ it would have taken → it would take

前面的 if 子句的時態是 tasted，是過去假設法，所以主要子句也要換成過去假設法 would take。

18. ③ obeyed → obey

主要子句用現在型助動詞 shall，所以是直述法。因此 obeyed 要改成現在型 obey 才正確。

19. ③ were not → had not been

即使主要子句的時態是假設法過去 might not survive，但 if 子句並不就是無條件地要用過去 were。因為 if 子句中有 in the past 這個表示過去的時間點，所以動詞要用過去完成式 had not been。

20. ① might enjoyed → might have enjoyed

基本上助動詞 might 後面不能用過去式或過去分詞 enjoyed。因為 during the semester 是表示過去的時間點，所以整個要用過去完成假設法。

21. ② realizes → realize

necessary 後面若有 that 子句，that 子句的動詞就要為原型或加助動詞 should。

22. ② have → had

在 wish 片語中，無條件地要用假設法。因為 have 是現在型，所以不是假設法。

23. ① Had it → Were it

綜合 tonight（現在時間）和 could not go（過去假設法），可以推斷是過去假設法。If it were not for . . . 可以換成 Were it not for . . . ，兩者意思完全一樣。

95

1. smaller

2. larger

   以 e 結尾的單字，不須重複加 e，只要加 r，即為比較級。

3. bigger

   比較級時，子音前是若為短母音，最後的子音就要重覆一次，再加 er。

4. more responsible

   responsible 是三個音節的單字，所以不能加 er，要加 more。

5. worse

   bad 是不規則變化的形容詞。

6. less

   little 也是不規則變化的形容詞。

7. more

   many 也是不規則變化的形容詞。

8. more pleased

   pleased 雖然是形容詞，不過它是由過去分詞變化而來的形容詞。過去分詞型或現在分詞型的形容詞，比較級都是加 more。

9. better than

   good 的比較級是 better，然後後面再加 than，以形成完整的比較級。

10. hotter, than

    hot 的比較級是 hotter，後面再加 than。

11. healthier, than

    healthy 的比較級是 healthier。

12. more comfortable, than

    comfortable 的比較級要在前面加 more。

13. more, than

    much 是不規則變化的形容詞。

14. more scared, than

    scared 是分詞型形容詞，所以前面加 more，形成比較級。

15. ② heavy → heavier

    因為有 than，所以是比較級。只有形容詞和副詞才有比較級，所以要把 heavy 改成 heavier。

16. ② high percentage → higher percentage

    因為 ⑤ 有 than，所以它前面一定是比較級形式的單字才正確；所以將 high 改成 higher。

96

1. The higher, the rarer

   「As..., as...」（當……，就會愈……）和「the 比較級...，the 比較級...」（愈……，就愈……）意思相近。

2. less nice

   因為比較對象互相對調，所以優等比較要變成劣等比較。在劣等比較的單字前，要無條件地加 less。

3. yours

   主詞是伊莎貝爾的 composition，所以比較對象也應該是 your composition。your composition 的所有格代名詞為 yours。

4. The more

   因為後面有 the more unpleasant，所以前面也要有「the＋比較級」。

5. less

   因為後面有 than，所以前面一定要用比較級。若為優等比較，就要用 more important；若為劣等比較，就用 less important。better 是 good 的比較級，本身就是比較級，所以不能當其他形容詞的比較級用。

6. she

   比較對象是 Mary's husband 和 she，他們都是當作主詞；而且受格 her 也不能當作 is 的主詞。

7. has

   than 後面的動詞和 than 前面的動詞要一致。Harriet's scored 是 Harriet has scored 的縮寫。has scored 是完成式，所以後面再次出現時，也只能用 has。

8. those

   比較對象是 land values，為複數名詞；所以後面重複出現時，要用複數 those，不能用單數 that。

9. ③ that of a worker

   這是比較運動選手的 salary 和勞工的 salary 的句子。因為 salary 是單數名詞，所以要用 that。

10. ② the more distracted

    前面有 the more，所以空格也要用「the＋比較級」。

97

1. as smooth as

   「as＋原級＋as」，smooth 為原級。

2. as frequently as

「as＋原級＋as」，frequently 為原級。

3. ④ as old

原級的正確用法是 as . . . as；so . . . as 是錯誤用法。

4. ④ as that of the sports car

因為是原級，所以空格要用 as 開始，比較對象也要一致。因為 the price 是單數，所以一定要用 that of。

5. ③ twice as much

倍數詞 twice，一定要放在「as＋原級＋as」的前面。

6. very → so 或者 as

因為後面接 as，所以要將 very 換成 as 或 so。否定句的時候，第一個 as 也可以換成 so。

7. as fish as → much fish as

as 和 as 中間，不能沒有形容詞或副詞。因為 fish 是名詞，所以前面要加形容詞。因為句意為「許多魚肉」，要用 many 或 much；魚肉是不可數名詞，要用 much。

8. the opposition party → those of the opposition party

比較對象是 the bills，因為 bills 是複數，所以後面要再出現一次時，用 those。

9. than adults are → as adults do

若將 than 換成 as，即為「as＋原級＋as」的形式。twice 是倍數詞的功能。另外，動詞也要一致，因為前面的 experience 是一般動詞，所以 are 應該要換成 do。

98

1. the busiest

2. the most famous

famous 前面要加 most。

3. the best

good 是不規則變化，它的最高級是 best。

4. worst

因為前面有所有格 my，所以不能加 the。

5. in

the country 表示地方。

6. of

day 和 year 是名詞，所以用 of 連接。

7. largest

和後面的 best 對比。one of 後面經常用最高級。

8. less

後面有 than，所以為比較級。less 是 little 的比較級。

9. better

對象是兩者比較時，要用比較級；三者以上比較時，要用最高級。

10. least

雖然 favorite 的最高級是 most favorite，不過在這裡不是正確答案。因為 the 和所有格不能對比出現。劣等比較時，比較級要用 less，最高級要用 least。

11. ④ the most

因句中沒有 than，所以非比較級，應為最高級，所以選擇 more 不正確。best 是 good 的最高級，又因後面接名詞 restaurants，所以要加定冠詞 the。

12. ② most

of all the written sources 是「在所有的紀錄中」之意，因此可以推斷紀錄有三個以上，為最高級。entertaining 是形容詞，最高級加 most，但不加定冠詞 the，因為後面沒有接名詞。

Chapter 16　單元綜合問題

1. ① so

基本句型是「as＋原級＋as」，但否定句時可用（not）as . . . as 或（not）so . . . as，兩者皆可。

2. ① a larger

後面有 than，表示為比較級，前面就要加 er 或 more。

3. ② most

exotic 是形容詞「異國的」。雖然 almost 可以修飾形容詞，但不能放在 the 之後。mostly 是「大概、大部分」的意思，在這裡不能修飾形容詞。exotic 的最高級是 most exotic，而非 most of exotic。

4. ① do

動詞不是比較對象時，than 前面和後面的動詞要一致。因為前面的動詞是一般動詞 expect，所以後面用 do。因為主詞 parents 是複數，所以用 do，而非 does。

5. ② frequently

應該用形容詞的比較級，還是用副詞的比較級時，不能單看比較級，而是要還原原來的句子，才能判斷。所有比較級的句子，將 than 之後的句子全都刪去不看，就變成原來的句子了。此句原來的句子應為 Frost occurs on low grounds . . . ，因此可以知道應該填入可以修飾 occurs 的副詞才正確。

6. ④ the

這是「the＋比較級」的問題。如果空格填入 is 和 are

等 be 動詞，主詞就是 the magnetic field，這是主詞和動詞倒裝的形式。但是在「the＋比較級」的句子中，除了慣用的表現方式外，一般是不倒裝的。④ 的主詞是 the magnetic field，後面的 is 被省略；因為在「the＋比較級」的句子中，be 動詞經常被省略。

7. ③ than through air

因為有 faster，所以要加 than。在 than 之後絕對不能再重複出現 er 或 more 了。

8. ③ better than Jim's

不是 Jenny 和 Jim 比較，而是 Jenny 的寫作技巧和 Jim 的寫作技巧比較。Jim's 就是「Jim 的」，也就是「Jim 的寫作技巧」之意。better 是 good 的比較級。more better 為兩個比較級連接在一起，這是錯誤用法。

9. ② than do its

因為是比較級，所以一定要有 than。① it 是指城市 Greencastle，但句意非指都市本身在打分數；而且 give 也要換成 do。own 只能用在所有格後面。③ 因為 than 後面有動詞 does，所以主詞一定是 their own citizens。不過因為 their 應該是指 Greencastle，所以應該改成 its。另外，應該為「居民們」為城市打分數，所以 does 要改成 do 才正確。④ 在比較級中，從句首一直到 than 之前的句子為完全子句。所以 than 前的 do 是全沒必要的。② 為正確答案。

10. ② so popular as

原級的用法是 as popular as；不是 so popular as。

11. the great apes → the great ape's

不是人的聲帶和猿比較，而是人的聲帶和猿的聲帶做比較。因為前面有 vocal apparatus，所以後面應該為 that of the great ape 或 the great ape's 才正確。

12. ② better — best

荷蘭和英國比較，所以用比較級 better。從句意判斷，第二個空格應該最高級，指「在許多選手中」。

13. ③ so more → so many

more 是 many 的比較級，後面 than 之後的句子省略，因此找不出比較對象，所以要把 more 還原成 many，變成 so many problems，這才是正確的用法。

14. more efficient, safer

從句意判斷，空格應該填入優等比較。efficient 的比較級要加 more；safe 的比較級加 er 即可。

15. ③ much large → much larger

有 than，所以前面的形容詞一定加 er 或 more。much 是修飾比較級 larger 最具代表性的副詞。

16. ② very → as

因為後面有 as，所以前面的 very 要換成 as，為句型

「as＋原級＋as」。如此即前面的 I'm（現在）和後面的 I used to be（過去）彼此比較。

17. ③ more → the more

因為前面的 the more 是「the＋比較級」，所以後面也要用 the more，為「the＋比較級」的形式對應。

18. ② much time → more time

因為後面有 than，所以前面一定要加 er 或 more。因為要加形容詞或副詞，所以 much 要換成 more。

19. ① the larger → the largest

如果用比較級 larger，和後面的 finest 不一致，所以要用最高級；而且也能和 in the world 呼應。

20. ③ as twice → twice as

倍數表現是「倍數詞＋as＋原級＋as」。因為 twice 是倍數詞，所以要放在 as 的前面。

21. ④ the bad → the worst

後面的 they had ever eaten 是省略了關係代名詞 that 的關係子句，其中的 ever，多放在最高級的後面，是最高級的強調用法。另外，從整個句子的內容判斷，也要用最高級的 the worst。

22. ④ highest → higher

前面有 both，可知比較對象有兩個，因此用比較級。

23. ② conventional surgery → those of conventional surgery

比較對象是雷射手術的危險和傳統手術的危險。the risks 是複數，所以不能用 that of，要用 those of。

99

1. At no time must the window be left open.

at no time 不是主詞，而且它裡面有否定詞，所以 at no time 若放在句首，後面的助動詞 must 就要倒裝，主詞 the window 和 must 交換位置即正確。

2. Slowly out of its hangar rolled the gigantic aircraft.

slowly out of its hangar 不是主詞，也沒有否定詞，所以為一般倒裝，將動詞 rolled 和主詞 the gigantic aircraft 交換位置即正確。

3. Only with her family did Mary feel entirely comfortable.

only with her family 是介系詞片語，不是主詞，且裡面有否定含義詞的 only，所以後面的動詞要倒裝；felt 是一般動詞，句型為「did＋主詞＋原型動詞」。

4. Neither hey acted it. → Neither did they act it.

因為 neither 是否定詞，所以動詞要倒裝。act 為一般

動詞，所以同上題句型，要加 did。

5. Back went he → Back he went

此句為一般倒裝，但有時不須倒裝。當主詞是代名詞時就不須倒裝；此句的 he 是代名詞，所以不用倒裝。

6. Hardly Paul had entered → Hardly had Paul entered

因為 had entered 是過去完成式，所以只要 had 和主詞 Paul 交換位置即可。

7. Never before a British Prime Minister has refused → Never before has a British Prime Minister refused

never before 像慣用語一樣，時常出現在現在完成式中。因為有否定詞 never，所以動詞要倒裝。has refused 是現在完成式，所以只要 has 和主詞 a British Prime Minister 交換位置即正確。

8. appeared → appear

not 是否定詞，the idea of atoms 是主詞，appear 是一般動詞，倒裝句型為「did＋主詞＋原型動詞」。

9. ④ does he appear

要倒裝。appear 是一般動詞，倒裝句型為「does＋he＋appear」。主詞是第三人稱單數 he，所以用 does。

10. ② came Alice

along 是副詞，又因不是否定詞，所以用一般倒裝。come along 如同慣用語，所以 along 移到前面時，就要倒裝；即主詞 Alice 和動詞 came 的位置交換。

100

1. So are

因為前面是肯定句，所以要用 so。前面的動詞是 be 動詞 is，所以空格中也要填入 be 動詞；因為主詞 the oranges 是複數，所以要用 are。

2. Neither is

前面是否定句，要用 neither。前面用 be 動詞，後面也要用 be 動詞，因 the rice 是單數，所以要填 is。

3. So have

因為前面是肯定句，所以要以 so 為首。前面的動詞是 have spilled，因為一致性，所以要也用 have。

4. So would

因為前面是肯定句，所以要以 so 為首。因為前面的動詞是 I'd like，I'd like 就是 I would like，助動詞是 would，所以空格也填入助動詞 would。

5. Neither did

前面是否定句，所以要以 neither 為首。know 是一般

動詞，所以要加 do；此句是過去式，do 要改成 did。

6. So did

因為前面是肯定句，所以要以 so 為首。went 是過去式動詞，所以為 did。

7. ⑤

① went 是一般動詞，所以 as was her sister 要改成 as did her sister。② 要改成 If Karen had asked 或 Had Karen asked。③ 雖然 than 後面也要倒裝，但主詞若為代名詞，就不須倒裝。因為 she 是代名詞，所以為 than she did。④ If 省略後，should 移到主詞前面，後面接原型動詞，所以 changed 要改成 change 才正確。⑤ 即使此句 as 不是「as＋原級＋as」的句型，但若 as 翻譯成「像……」，後面也可以出現倒裝。因為前面的動詞是 was，所以 as 後面也要為 was。

8. ① so has Tom

因為前面是肯定句，所以用 so。has cleaned 是現在完成式，後面也要用 has。

9. ② than it did

因為有比較級 earlier，所以後面要加 than。主詞 it 為代名詞，因此不須倒裝。

101

1. It was John that /who came running into the office with the boxes.

因為從 came 可以看出時態是過去式，所以 it 後面要用 was，然後再接要強調的字 John。如果強調的字詞是人，that 也可以換成 who。

2. It was the services that I was complaining about.

the services 是 about 的受詞，將它移到前面，about 仍留在原位；如果沒有這個 about，就是錯誤用法。

3. It was in October that Karol sold her flat and moved in with her sister.

像 in October 這樣的時間副詞，也可以作強調用。此外，地方副詞、方式副詞等也都可以當作強調用。

4. ② this house → in this house

it is that 是強調句的最大的特點，在整個句子中，如果將 it is that 刪去，剩下的句子必須是完整的句子才正確。this house 在此句無功能；所以要用 in this house 這個地方副詞，才能放在 has lived 後面。

5. her → she

It was who 是強調片語，因為在 who 後面是動詞 represented，所以要填入主詞；將受格 her 改成主格 she 即為正確答案。

6. It were → It was

強調的部分是複數 their parents；但因 be 動詞的主詞是 it，不是 their parents，所以要用 was。

7. 正確句子

強調的部分是副詞子句 because we were short of money。請注意，不是所有的副詞子句都可以當作強調之用，只有 because 子句可以強調。

8. ②

① 和 ③ 都是 It that 虛主詞和真主詞的句子，且 that 之後的句子完整。② it is that 的強調句，要加 reads 的受詞 these very novels，that 子句才完整。

102

1. will sing

助動詞 will 後面要接動詞。

2. are late for class

要知道省略了什麼，只了解句子正確的中文意義，即能解題了。但要注意，省略的部分不包括 again。

3. should have booked a table in advance

除了和前面重複的部分，剩下的句子全部不變。請注意，後面不能用「Yes, we should」，要用「Yes, we should have」。如果前面是 should book（should＋原型），後面才能用「Yes, we should」。但如果前面是 should have booked（should＋完成式），後面就要用「Yes, we should have」才正確。

4. had been invited to the dinner

從 although 推斷，應該是他太太被邀請之意。

5. (you) left something (anything) behind

省略一般動詞時要用動詞 do 來代替。anything 前面有 not，所以可以用 anything；但省略的部分不是否定句而是肯定句，所以要用 something 來代替 anything。

6. Jack hasn't found a job yet

也有 so 代替前面整個句子的情況。

7. I'll get a pay increase soon

只要了解句子的中文意義，就能解題了。

8. I cannot lend you any money

把前面的句子換成否定句即可。some 也要換成 any。

9. (they are) slightly different colours

so they are 為「真的是那樣」之意。

10. ② So he does

so does he 是「他也這樣做」的意思，這裡和句意不符。請注意，so 後面是主詞＋動詞的順序。

11. ② But John didn't

在 B 說的話中提到 John 要去看電影，所以不像 Alice 那樣在家看書；因此為否定。

103

1. There are more hungry people in the world today than there were √ in 1900.

省略 hungry people in the world。

2. I asked when she was leaving, and she said she didn't know √ .

省略 when she was leaving。

3. His father was at Oxford when John Smith was √ .

省略 at Oxford。

4. You were supposed to buy some flour. / Sorry, I forgot to √ .

省略 buy some flour。

5. Peter's never made a mistake before. / Well, he has √ this time.

省略 made a mistake。

6. (would like) to play the music

7. (Shirley) finished the exam

did 代替前面的一般動詞和後面的受詞。

8. (plenty) of that firewood

9. (my own) drawings

雖然「所有格＋own」後面接名詞，但如果該名詞前面已經提過，它就要被省略。

10. (his sister) walks to work

does 代替前面的一般動詞和後面的句子。

11. (the tallest) girl in the class

即使前面已經提過，但最高級後面的名詞仍不省略。

12. (I have to) disturb you

to 不定詞的內容若重複出現，to 保留，其後皆省略。

13. (digital alarm clocks) are

這是原級和比較級的省略。這時 are 後的 cheap 不能再出現。

14. (will) resign from the committee

因為是用助動詞，故從原型動詞開始復原句子即可。

15. Mary can beat most easily (Rosa)

這是回答疑問句的句子。將和疑問句重複的部分都省略之後，剩下的句子皆完整回答。

104

1. ate the fruit 和 drank the beer 對等

    這要看 and 的後面，才會知道和什麼對等。

2. read the book 和 seen the movie 對等

    兩個現在完成式對等，第二個現在完成式的 have 可以省略，只用過去分詞即可。or 後的 seen 寫成 have seen 也可以，不過最近都將 have 省略，只用 seen。

3. Peter ill 和 the children at home 對等

    with 是共用詞，指 With Peter ill and with the children at home。因為 with 重複，所以被省略了。

4. damaged by the storm 和 washed away by the floods 對等

    兩個分詞都修飾 the houses。

5. to taste → tasting

    and 接 to taste，前面也要有不定詞。前面是 biting；enjoy 的受詞為動名詞，所以 to taste 要改成 tasting。

6. he is honest → honesty

    for 後面的名詞對等。patience 和 sincerity 之間沒有連接詞 and，表示後面還有名詞要對等。

7. 正確句子

    interested in 和 a little frightened by 後面共同的對象都是 lizards。

8. opening → open

    這是 to sit down、(to) be quiet、(to) open 三個不定詞對等的句子。重複出現不定詞時，重複的 to 要省略，只用原型動詞即可。

9. talked → talking

    這是 were walking、(were) talking、(were) drinking 三個進行式對等的句子。were 只要出現一次，後面重複的都省略。

10. ③ to detect

    這是 to locate oil、to determine ocean depth、to detect and measure earthquakes 三個不定詞對等的句子。因為第二個不定詞 to determine 有 to，所以第三個不定詞也一定要有 to。第三個 to detect and measure 中，detect and measure 整個視為一整個不定詞，所以不能用 to detect and to measure。

11. ① cook

    used to 之後要用原型動詞 shoot 和 cook。

Chapter 17 單元綜合問題

1. ② will I think

no longer 非主詞，同時也是否定語，所以後面的助動詞要倒裝，將主詞 I 和 will 交換位置就可以了。

2. ② that

    it is that 是強調句。

3. ③ may grow

    因為後面有 and live，所以只能選 may grow。因為 frog 是單數，如果用 grows，那就要用 and lives。而因為 grow 是不及物動詞，所以也不能用被動語態。

4. ① to do so

    要代替前面的內容時，大多用 do so。但有時也會用 do it，但絕對不會用 do them。因為前面有 open，所以後面不須再重複出現 open。

5. ① can animal skins become

    only after they are tanned 是在 after 子句前加 only 的副詞子句。副詞子句放在句首，後面就要倒裝。即使不倒裝，因為前面加了 only 有否定的含意，所以後面的助動詞也要倒裝。把主詞 animal skins 和助動詞 can 的位置交換就是正確答案。

6. ② Mine has

    mine 是所有格代名詞，代替 my math skill，為單數，而且因為前面的動詞是 has improved，是現在完成式，所以省略主詞時，只保留 has。

7. ① teach

    為 to enter、graduate from、teach 三個不定詞對筆，所以 to 只要出現一次即可。

8. ③ to answer accurately

    因為比較對象是 to answer quickly 和 to answer accurately 這兩個，所以它們的形式要一致。

9. ③ so

    I'm afraid 要後接 so 或 not。如果接 so，表示「錯過了電影開始的部分」；如果接 not，就表示「不是那樣」。

10. ① are

    Here in this special diet drink 不是名詞，不能當主詞，所以後面要倒裝，空格要填入動詞，然後接主詞。all the answers . . . problems 整個是名詞，也就是主詞。如果空格填入 does 或 have，主詞後面就要有原型動詞或過去分詞；不過主詞後面什麼都沒有，所以不能選這兩個。因為主詞 answers 是複數，所以要用 are。here in 之後的句子是補語。

11. or going out → or go out

    對應主詞 People 的動詞是 work、go、eat 等，所以 going out 要改成 go out 才正確。

12. It isn't just national forests that young people are avoiding.

整個句子是 it is that 的強調句。it is 和 that 之間必須為強調的部分 just national forest。

13. ③ does

因為 depends 是一般動詞,所以要用 do 來代替。因為 it 是單數,所以 do 要改成 does。

14. ①

I'm afraid 是表示「恐怕」。第一句話提到,某化學療法的治療會對懷孕有影響,是不好的事。I'm afraid 後面用 so,表示很自然地會有那樣的結果之意。所以 I'm afraid so 是「擔心會有影響」的意思。

15. communicated with body language and sometimes gestures

do 的位置要放入 communicate . . . gestures 才正確。兩個完全相同的話不須重複出現,此句的主詞是動物,所以人的部分要省略刪去。

16. ③ to introduce → introduced

如果 and 後有不定詞,and 前面也要有不定詞才正確。因為這裡沒有 to 不定詞,所以 ③ 的 to introduce 要把 to 刪去。因為有動詞 has played,所以為了要和它對比,形式就要一致。兩個都有 has,所以只要填

入 introduced 即可。

17. ① when → that

整個句子是 it is that 的強調句。

18. ② So Peter was → So was Peter

從句意判斷,應該是「Peter 也是那樣」。要表示這個意思,句型應用「so +動詞+主詞」,而非「so +主詞+動詞」。So Peter was 指「Peter 真的是那樣」。

19. ② exist → exists

因為 between . . . me 不是名詞,所以不是主詞。exist 的主詞是後面的 an . . . relationship,為單數;因此 exist 後要加 s。

20. ③ but also other → but also of other

not only 和 but also 是對比句。因為 not only 後面有「of +名詞」,所以 but also 後也要有「of +名詞」。即使介系詞重複,也不能省略,這樣意思才明確完整。

21. ③ didn't → hadn't

③ 是代替 had worked 之後的句子。因 had worked 是過去完成式,所以要取代 did,要用 had。

家圖書館出版品預行編目資料

Grammar for Tests! 英文文法概念總整理 / 柳澤尚
著 ; 彭尊聖, 鄭玉瑋譯 -- [臺北市]：寂天文化,
2011.1　面 ;　公分

　　ISBN　978-986-184-831-0　(平裝)

　　　1. 英語　　2. 語法

　805.16　　　　　　　　　　　100000300

作者	柳澤尚
翻譯	彭尊聖／鄭玉瑋
編輯	鄭玉瑋
校對	林育華
主編	黃鈺云
製程管理	林欣穎
出版者	寂天文化事業股份有限公司
電話	02-2365-9739
傳真	02-2365-9835
網址	www.icosmos.com.tw
讀者服務	onlineservice@icosmos.com.tw
出版日期	2011 年 1 月初版一刷

郵撥帳號	1998620-0 寂天文化事業股份有限公司 劃撥金額600（含）元以上者，郵資免費。 訂購金額600元以下者，加收60元運費。 〔若有破損，請寄回更換，謝謝。〕